NO LESS THAN THE JOURNEY

Wesley Curnow, a young Cornish miner, arrives in the United States to seek an uncle who is working on the mines in Missouri. Taking passage on a boat from New York, bound for New Orleans, he meets up with a charismatic US marshal who is *en route* to the western territories to bring law to the area. After a gunfight with pirates on the Mississippi River and an encounter with an attractive half-Mexican croupier, Wes parts company with his companions only to find his uncle has been forced to move away. Wes faces a serious altercation with German miners, meets an old 'Mountainman' who teaches him proficiency with a revolver, and then faces a journey overland through inhospitable country. But can he survive the journey?

E. V. THOMPSON

NO LESS THAN THE JOURNEY

Complete and Unabridged

CHARNWOOD
Leicester

First published in Great Britain in 2008 by
Robert Hale Limited
London

First Charnwood Edition
published 2009
by arrangement with
Robert Hale Limited
London

British Library CIP Data

Thompson, E. V. (Ernest Victor), *1931 –*
   No less than the journey
   1. English- -United States- -Fiction.
   2. Miners- -Missouri- -Fiction.
   3. Adventure stories. 4. Large type books.
   I. Title
   823.9′14–dc22

   ISBN 978–1–84782–809–5

Published by
F. A. Thorpe (Publishing)
Anstey, Leicestershire

Set by Words & Graphics Ltd.
Anstey, Leicestershire
Printed and bound in Great Britain by
T. J. International Ltd., Padstow, Cornwall

This book is printed on acid-free paper

I believe a leaf of grass is no less than the journey-work of the stars.

Walt Whitman (1819 – 1891),
'Song of Myself'.

BOOK 1

1

'God Almighty, Mister, if you aimed a cow's teat the way you did that gun, you'd have a clean bucket come the end of milking time!'

Ignoring the raucous laughter from the men crowding about himself and the woefully inadequate sharpshooter, United States Marshal Aaron Berryman added, 'Tell me, lad, is that why you gave up farming and decided to try your hand at something else?'

The object of his derision, a raw-boned countryman of Scandinavian extraction, looked sheepish. 'No, Marshal. I gave up farming because unless you're finding gold there's no money to be made digging in the ground.'

'Not if you farm the way you shoot,' agreed Aaron, scornfully, 'All right, check the rifle's empty and leave it on the deck.'

Switching his attention to the amused spectators, he said, 'Now you've had your fun, which of you is going to show me how it should be done?'

All but one of the men about him managed to be looking elsewhere when Aaron's glance touched on them. The man who met his gaze was aged about twenty-five. Dark-eyed and black-haired, he was deceptively slim.

'You . . . what's your name?'

'Wesley — Wes Curnow.'

The young man's accent brought a momentary frown to the face of the US Marshal and he asked, 'Where you from, son?'

'From Cornwall — that's in England.'

Aaron nodded. 'I have heard of it. What are you doing on board?'

'I'm a miner. I'm leaving the ship at New Orleans to travel up the Mississippi. I've got the offer of work in Missouri.'

'Then you and me are going to be travelling together for a while. Can you shoot?'

Wes nodded. 'My pa was gamekeeper on a large estate and was as good a shot as anyone I've met. He taught me.'

Aaron gave Wes an enigmatic look. 'I know nothing about gamekeepers — but I know a hell of a lot about shooting. Pick up that gun and we'll see what you can do . . . '

* * *

It had been no more than thirty-six hours since Aaron Berryman had limped slowly up the gangway of the steamship *Northern Star* moored alongside a wharf in New York's dockland area, a small, leather trunk balanced upon one shoulder. Few of the passengers lining the guard rails gave him more than a cursory glance.

Had they done so, it was doubtful whether they would have been even mildly impressed. Slightly-built and of below average height, he looked even smaller because of a tendency to walk with bowed shoulders, apparently more interested in the placement of his feet than in anything, or anyone, ahead of him.

If a glance from his pale grey eyes had been intercepted, they would have noticed he had a slight squint.

But there had been many new arrivals on the ship that day and there was nothing about this man to provoke particular interest.

The ship had left Plymouth, England, thirteen days before, bringing immigrants to America to commence a new life in this vast and exciting country.

A number of the immigrants were Cornish miners, seeking an escape from the grinding poverty that had been their lot since a collapse in the price of tin and copper had put thousands of men out of work.

Most of the Cornishmen who crossed the Atlantic on the *Northern Star* left the ship at New York, heading for copper mines on the shores of Lake Michigan. Here they would join relatives and friends already settled in the New World.

Those who remained on board were making their way to other mining areas, Arizona; Missouri; the goldfields of California — and a few to the silver mines of Mexico.

When it left New York, the *Northern Star* would plough a slow and insignificant furrow through the waters off the east coast of America, disembarking immigrants and other passengers at ports along the way until it reached Tampico, in Mexico. Here, the last of the immigrant miners would go ashore and make their way to silver mines in the mountains. The cheap wooden bunks in which they had slept, puked and occasionally succeeded in uncomfortable copulation, would be ripped from the holds in order that Mexican cattle might be taken on board and accommodated in far less crowded conditions for their journey eastwards across the Atlantic Ocean to the markets of Europe.

A day-and-a-half out of New York, the Boatswain's mate of the *Northern Star* toured the ship, attracting the attention of the passengers by blowing a whistle. When he was satisfied they were listening, he announced that passengers disembarking at New Orleans with the intention of travelling to destinations on the Mississippi River should muster on the main deck.

Responding to the summons, Wes found himself in the company of some thirty fellow passengers all of whom were wondering why they had been chosen from the two hundred or so others taking passage on the *Northern Star*.

He had not long to find out. The captain appeared on the deck — accompanied by the man with a limp who Wes had seen come on board at New York.

Wasting no time, the captain said, 'I thank you for your time, gentlemen. You have been asked to assemble on a matter of considerable importance,' then, indicating the insignificant man standing beside him, he continued, 'but Marshal Berryman will be able to tell you about it with far more authority than I.'

Turning to his companion, he said, 'They're all yours, Marshal.'

'Thank you, Captain Tyrell, I'm grateful to you for your cooperation.'

As the captain of the ship made his way back to the bridge, Marshal Berryman's gaze passed from man to man standing on the deck before him, and no one in the group felt he had been overlooked.

'Gentlemen, I've called you together because of something that's likely to affect each and every one of us who'll be travelling up the Mississippi from New Orleans. As I'm sure you all know, although the river is probably the cheapest way of travelling to wherever it is you're going, it ain't necessarily the easiest. The Mississippi is a fickle river — and, believe me, I'm a Missourian and I know what I'm talking about. My father was a river-boat pilot and I'd travel with him whenever he'd let me. With time a man gets to know the river — and the river seems to know the men who love it.'

Pausing, his glance went around the group on the deck before he spoke again. 'Unfortunately, just lately travellers have had more than the river itself to cope with. The North and the South stopped fighting each other some years ago — thank God! — but there's a whole mess of men from both sides who enjoyed the violence and killing of war so much they're not yet ready to give it up. Some have found their way to the Mississippi and formed themselves into a pirate gang, terrorising passengers on river-boats like the one we'll be travelling on and stealing money and United States mail. My idea is that after a little bit of working out together, we'll all go upriver on the same boat and teach these river pirates a lesson they won't forget for as long as they live, which with any luck won't be for very much longer.'

His words brought an upsurge of sound from the men listening to him. Some were excited at the prospect of a confrontation with river pirates. Others, in the main the older men, were more apprehensive.

It was one of the latter who addressed a question to Aaron Berryman. 'This sounds like very serious business, Marshal. Am I right in assuming you intend taking command in any fight that takes place between us and these 'river pirates', as you call them?'

'That's what I have in mind, Mister. Do you have a better idea?'

'Yes, Marshal. With all due respect, I think I might have more experience in commanding men in situations such as this. I fought in the war as a Confederate captain and saw my fair share of action. No doubt you fought too and, seeing as how you're now a United States Marshal, I presume you fought for the army of the North. May I ask what rank you were, Sir?'

'There's no North or South now, Captain,' Aaron replied, firmly. 'The war is over. We're all Americans, just as we were before it began.'

'I'm happy enough to go along with that, Marshal, but we're talking of fighting and commanding men.' Almost triumphantly, he repeated his question, 'What rank did you hold,

Sir — and how much actual action did you see at first hand?'

'I saw enough to know what fighting is all about, Captain and, yes, I fought for the North. My first battle was at Bull Run, in July, 'sixty one. The last in Alabama, in April, eighteen sixty-five — and I didn't miss too many in between, despite this . . . '

He slapped the leg that was the cause of his limp, adding, 'When I left the army I was a brevet Brigadier General. Is there anything else you'd like to know?'

Abashed, the ex-Confederate captain said, 'No, Sir. You've more than proved your credentials as far as I'm concerned. I'll be proud to serve under you against these river pirates.'

'Thank you, Captain. I'll be happy to have someone with your experience fighting with me but I don't think I caught your name . . . '

'It's Harrison Schuster, General. Before the war my family had one of the greatest plantations in the whole of Kentucky. The land is still ours, but trouble's the only crop that's thrived there since the war.'

'You reaped what was sown by your folk over very many years,' Aaron retorted, 'but we all belong to a great new nation now and lawlessness is a threat to us all.'

Turning away from Schuster, Aaron appealed to the other men, 'Now, how many of you men have handled a gun before . . . ?'

2

✒

For the remainder of the voyage to New Orleans Marshal Aaron Berryman held shooting instruction twice a day for the men who would be going up the Mississippi river with him. It was immediately apparent to everyone that Wes was better than average when it came to handling a rifle, but Aaron was appalled to learn he had never fired a handgun.

On the second day of instruction, after practise with a Henry fifteen-shot repeating rifle came to an end, the marshal signalled for Wes to remain behind when the others dispersed.

When they were more-or-less alone, he reached beneath his coat and pulled out a handgun. Passing it to Wes, he said, 'Have you ever seen one of these before?'

Looking at the gun in his hand, Wes shook his head. 'No, but it's a beautifully made weapon.'

Aaron inclined his head in agreement. 'It's certainly that and familiarisation with it could one day make the difference between living and dying. That's a Colt revolver, boy. There are gunfighters in this country — good gunfighters — who favour other guns, but seven out of ten of 'em will be carrying some form of Colt. This one fires a forty-four calibre bullet, and that's big enough to stop anything smaller than a buffalo.

Besides, if you're close enough to be using a handgun against another man the size of the bullet it fires won't matter. It's the accuracy of the man using it which will decide the outcome. Right, now I'll show you what to do with it . . . '

For the remainder of the voyage, Marshal Berryman made Wes practise using the Colt revolver for at least two hours every day. By the time the *Northern Star* berthed in New Orleans, Wes was able to hit targets fixed to the ship's rail with at least three of the Colt's six bullets.

Despite this, Aaron was still not satisfied. As he told Wes, 'There are a great many mean men out there who can score six out of six, son. Until you can match 'em, shot-for-shot; put the bullets where they need to go, and get them off a fraction of a second faster than the other man, you'd do better to stay East of the Mississippi. But we'll keep practising. Perhaps you'll improve when you own a gun of your own.'

* * *

New Orleans was a vibrant and exciting sea port and the dock area particularly busy. Goods from almost every country in the world were brought in by freighter and sailing ship. In addition, produce was piled high on the dockside, carried downriver from the interior. Cotton plantations, devastated by years of war, were producing crops once more, giving employment to men and women who had once been slaves. Now, they were paid labourers — although few outsiders could have detected any difference.

11

The night-life of New Orleans was brash and memorable. Taverns and saloons vied with brothels and gambling-houses for custom, providing every possible diversion in a bid to attract custom.

Yet, even in this thriving town, the deep wounds caused by the late Civil War were still much in evidence — and when one particular incident flared up, Wes witnessed Aaron Berryman in action.

From conversations Wes had overheard on board the *Northern Star*, he realized that to plantation owners, the words 'freedom' and 'slaves' were mutually exclusive. War had cost them dearly, yet, in effect, it had done little to change the social structure of the Southern States.

This was particularly evident in the bars of New Orleans. Crowded with seamen, frontiersmen and townsfolk, there was not a freed slave to be seen. Furthermore, when men had drunk enough to burst forth in song, their ditties were more often than not those which had found favour with soldiers of the Confederate army.

Despite this, many of the women who worked in the saloons had a high proportion of African, Mexican or Native American blood coursing through their veins.

It was one of these saloon women who was responsible for reinforcing the importance Marshal Berryman had placed upon the handgun when giving weapon instruction on board the *Northern Star*.

Wes and Aaron had become friends during

their passage on the *Northern Star* and, to celebrate their first night ashore in New Orleans, Aaron took Wes on a tour of the riverside saloons.

In what would later in the day become one of the sea port's busiest establishments, they arrived at a fairly quiet time. As a result, the 'hostesses', employed on a commission basis by the saloon owner, descended upon the new arrivals. Fortunately, a crowd of mining men from upriver entered the saloon almost immediately and all but one of the girls abandoned the two men in the hope of more lucrative pickings.

The girl who remained squeezed herself onto the padded seat between Wes and Aaron and introduced herself as 'Lola'. Unlike many of the other girls in the room, Lola had no African blood in her veins, although she clearly had a Mexican background.

Looking from the United States marshal to Wes, she asked, 'You boys just arrived in New Orleans? Where you from — and where are you going?'

As Wes and Aaron exchanged glances, Lola added, 'Most men who arrive in New Orleans are moving on to somewhere else. Usually heading West, each chasing his own particular dream.'

'That's a mighty perceptive remark, Lola,' Aaron said, 'But you're right, we're heading upriver, maybe not chasing dreams, but looking for a chance to do what we're best at. Wes here is from England. He means to go mining in Missouri.'

13

Lola showed immediate interest. Turning to Wes, she said, eagerly, 'You are an English miner? So was my father. He came to Mexico from Cornwall to mine silver when he was still a young man.'

'I'm from Cornwall too,' Wes said, 'Where is your father now?'

It was as though his words extinguished a light. Lola's enthusiasm disappeared, 'He's dead. My mother too. There was a raid on the mine by the soldiers of Juaraz and they were both killed.' Bitterly, she added, 'I should have died too. Instead, they made me a whore.'

Almost casually, Aaron observed, 'Juaraz was supported by the United States government. Why come to New Orleans to earn a living in the country responsible for the death of your parents?'

Giving Aaron a direct look, Lola said, 'When I came to New Orleans, Louisiana was fighting against the United States. I was only fifteen then and knew far less than I do now.'

'In wartime we all grow up a whole lot quicker than we should,' Aaron observed, 'But the war's been over for quite a while now — yet you're still here.'

Moved by her story, Wes said, 'Surely you don't intend spending the rest of your life working here, in this saloon?'

Lola cast a glance around the saloon and it came to rest upon a woman who was probably twice her own age, but who looked even older, 'And end up like Mary? No, Señor, I intend getting out of here, and very soon.'

Looking around her once more, to ensure no one was eaves-dropping, she dropped her voice and said, 'You say you are heading upriver . . . what boat will you be travelling on?'

'We're booked on the *Missouri Belle*, leaving the day after tomorrow,' Wes said, before Aaron could reply, 'Have you heard of her? Do you know if she's a comfortable boat?'

Lola clapped her hands together gleefully, 'I hope so, I really do. I will be going upriver on the same boat. One of the men who owns her was in here a few days ago. He offered me work on board — as a croupier. I will be sailing with you!'

'I heard the *Missouri Belle* had a casino on board,' Aaron said, casually, 'That means there'll be a lot of money changing hands, no doubt.'

'I hope so,' Lola said, unaware of the meaningful glances exchanged between Aaron and Wes, 'I am working on commission. The more money that's spent at my table, the more I will earn.'

'You'll earn far more on board the *Missouri Belle* than in a New Orleans saloon — one way or another,' Aaron said, meaningfully.

'Yes . . . yes, I *will*.' Lola's chin rose aggressively, 'But I will be earning my living as a croupier. I will be the one to decide whether or not to earn extra money for myself.'

She looked nervously around the saloon before adding, 'While I work here I must do as I am told, but see very little of the money I earn.'

'I'm sure you'll do well on the *Missouri Belle*,' Aaron commented, 'There'll be all sorts on board. Talking of which do you know anything of

15

the man sitting over there, beneath the large mirror? He's giving the impression of having drunk enough to be trouble, but I'm not so sure it isn't an act.'

'I don't like him!' Lola said, emphatically. 'His name is Lansdale, Remus Lansdale. He is in here often. He claims his family lost their fortune to the North during the war and is very bitter that the South did not win.'

Aaron sighed, 'How are we ever going to build a great country when so many men are still fighting the war? Do you know if he carries a gun, Lola?'

The bar girl said quickly, 'Carrying a gun is not allowed in New Orleans.'

'That isn't what I asked. What do you know?'

Lola looked increasingly ill-at-ease, but she answered his question, 'One of the girls who goes upstairs with him claims that he carries a handgun in a specially made pocket in the lining of his coat.'

'Did he show it off to her?' Aaron asked.

'I doubt it,' Lola replied, 'She probably found it by going through his pockets when he was asleep. Ivy has a reputation among the girls for 'rolling' her men if they've had enough to drink. One day she'll meet with a client who hasn't drunk as much as she thinks and take the beating she deserves. Until that happens she'll carry on. She's not very bright.'

Aaron was still watching the man who was the subject of their conversation. Without looking at Lola, he said, quietly, 'Ivy may not be very bright, but her observation might well save a

16

man's life. I don't think Lansdale's as drunk as he'd like everyone to believe. He's watching the door as though he's waiting for someone. Does he have any particular friends — or enemies?'

'As far as I know he has no friends,' Lola replied, 'As for enemies . . . ' She shrugged, 'You might as well include anyone who doesn't speak with a Southern accent.'

'But there's no one in particular?' Aaron persisted, 'I've been watching him for some minutes. He's very much on edge, as though he's waiting for something or for *someone*.'

'What business is it of yours?' Lola demanded, suddenly curious, 'You're only passing through New Orleans. What happens here shouldn't concern you.'

Aware that Lola was brighter than the average saloon girl Aaron said, 'That's perfectly true, but I've fought in the war, seen a lot of men killed and met with a whole lot of killers. That man has something on his mind — and he's carrying a gun. If a gunfight was to start in here, lots of folk would likely be hurt — you, me and Wes among them.'

Lola was obviously frightened and, somewhat incredulously, Wes asked, 'You don't really think he's waiting to shoot someone, Aaron?'

'I don't know the man well enough to say for certain,' Aaron admitted, 'But he's made that drink in front of him last for a hell of a long time. I'll repeat my question, Lola. Is there anyone in particular he might be waiting for?'

After only a brief few moments of thought, Lola nodded, 'There's been a man in here a couple of times lately. He goes upstairs with Sadie — she's the tall, dark-skinned girl sitting at the far end of the bar. When a man's in bed with a girl he usually ends up talking for longer than he's doing anything else. This stranger boasted to Sadie that he's an ex-Union officer and has helped free more slaves, and thrown more landowners off their plantations than anyone else in the whole of the Union army. It's probably a lot of hot air, but it's possible Lansdale thinks he might have had something to do with his family losing their land. I believe Sadie's mother was a pampered slave-girl on Lansdale's family plantation and she and Lansdale talk a lot together . . . '

At that moment a tall dark-haired man with an immaculately trimmed beard entered the saloon and Lola said, excitedly, 'That's the ex-Union officer now.'

Pausing in the doorway, the new arrival looked about the room until he spotted Sadie. Smiling, he advanced towards her.

Suddenly nervous, the woman switched her glance to Lansdale, and nodded almost imperceptibly. From that moment events moved quickly.

Before the self-styled ex-Union army officer reached the bar, Lansdale reached inside his coat and his hand came out clutching a heavy revolver.

As the gun rose to point at the newcomer, Wes saw with a start that Aaron was also holding a revolver and the US Marshal called loudly, 'Hold it, Lansdale . . . hold it right there, or you're a dead man.'

The Southerner's body jerked as though he had already been shot, then he spun around to look at Aaron.

Wes expected him to size up the situation and lower the gun. Instead, Lansdale raised the revolver to point at the US Marshal!

'Don't be foolish, Lansdale.' Aaron warned the other man, but instead of lowering the revolver, Lansdale thumbed back the hammer, the sound loud in the silence that had fallen upon the saloon.

Before Lansdale could pull the trigger of his gun, Aaron fanned the hammer of his own gun with the heel of his left hand and fired — then fired again.

The impact of the first bullet threw Lansdale back in his seat. The second sent the Southerner and his chair crashing backwards to the floor.

There was a sudden, disbelieving pause in the saloon, then men were rushing to where Lansdale lay sprawled on his back on the saloon floor.

Someone shouted for a doctor to be called, but Aaron said, laconically, 'You're wasting your time. Send for an undertaker instead.'

Wes found the next minutes utterly confusing. Lansdale was lifted from the ground and laid upon three tables that were hastily placed together. Then a hush fell upon the saloon as a deputy sheriff entered from the street.

It took him only a few minutes to make sense of the dozen different stories that were given to him by witnesses of the shooting. When he was satisfied he had some semblance of the truth, he said to Aaron, 'You're the man who shot him?'

When Aaron nodded agreement, the deputy sheriff asked, 'Are you aware there's an ordinance against carrying guns in public in New Orleans.'

'I am.'

Looking mildly apologetic, the deputy sheriff said, 'Then you'll know I have no alternative but to arrest you and take you into custody.'

Wes was about to protest that Aaron was a United States Marshal, but Aaron caught his eye. His expression was sufficient to ensure Wes's silence.

Aaron stood up. Handing his revolver butt first to the deputy sheriff, he said, 'Then I guess you'd better do your duty, Deputy.'

There were a great many murmurings of dissent when Aaron was led outside by the deputy sheriff. It erupted into noisy outrage when the door closed behind the lawman and his prisoner.

Lola was being particularly vocal in her indignation when the man who had been Lansdale's intended victim came to the table where she sat with Wes.

Addressing Wes, he said, 'Are you a friend of the man who just saved my life, sir?'

Wes nodded, not certain yet whether or not he liked this man, 'I don't think he would dispute that. I certainly wouldn't.'

'Then I'm honoured to meet you, sir. My name is Ira Gottland and I owe my life to your

20

friend. I'd like to know his name so I can go to the New Orleans authorities and explain what happened. Hopefully it will be sufficient to obtain his release.'

Remembering Aaron's glance when the deputy sheriff had arrested him and aware that he did not want his identity known to too many people, Wes said, 'I've no doubt he'll be able to satisfy the New Orleans authorities that he acted to save your life, Mister Gottland. If he still hasn't been released by tomorrow morning I'll be happy to come with you to the sheriff's office and see if we can't arrange his release.'

'I'm grateful to you, sir . . . But you still haven't told me his name.'

Aware that Aaron's name would not remain a secret for long, Wes said, 'It's Aaron Berryman.'

It was immediately apparent that Ira Gottland recognized the name. 'Aaron Berryman? Not General Berryman of the Union army?'

'I believe that was his rank during the war,' Wes agreed, 'A *brigadier* general, but he doesn't use it now.'

'Jesus!' Gottland struggled to find words, ' . . . I was under his command in more than one battle and I'd have been happy to fight for whatever cause he supported, anywhere in the world — as would any other soldier who served with him. I'm going along to the sheriff's office right now. If they don't release him immediately I know damned well where I can find a hundred men right here in New Orleans who'll march to the gaol and take it apart if they don't release

21

General Berryman right away. You coming with me, Mister?'

It was Aaron himself who made it unnecessary for Wes to give Ira Gottland an answer. While Ira was threatening to raise an army to take on the New Orleans sheriff's office, Aaron walked through the door of the saloon.

As he took his place at the table where he had been seated before, Wes said, 'I didn't think they would be able to keep you for very long, Aaron — and it's just as well . . . '

Nodding in Ira's direction, he said, 'This is Ira Gottland. I believe he served under your command during the Civil War. He was about to organise an army of ex-Union soldiers to come and break you out of gaol.'

'We'd have done it too, General,' Ira said, earnestly, seemingly scarcely able to contain his feelings at being in the presence of a man he had declared to be a hero, 'I'm speaking for a whole lot of men when I say you were the best commanding officer in the whole of the Union army. Whenever we went into battle we all knew where to find you. You'd be right up front, where the fighting was fiercest.'

'I'm pleased to say there'll be no need to start a new Battle of New Orleans,' Aaron said, 'We met the sheriff at the end of the street. When he was told what had happened, he had me released.'

Wes realized that Aaron must have revealed to the sheriff that he was a United States marshal, but he remained silent.

Not so Ira, 'Hell, General, anyone who knew

you would have done the same, but they're pretty strict about carrying guns in New Orleans, you were lucky the sheriff decided to overlook that.'

'I told him I was just passing through and would be gone by this time tomorrow. He told me to come down to his office in the morning and make a statement, then he released me.'

Aaron lied without batting an eyelid and Gottland accepted his explanation without question, 'Well, General, now you're back I hope you'll let me buy you a drink. You do that and I'll be the proudest man in New Orleans tonight.'

'Since you put it that way, Ira, I'm happy to oblige you. I could murder a beer.'

When a flustered Ira had hurried away to the bar, Lola said to Aaron, 'Were you really a general in the Union army? In Mexico a general is almost as important as the president.'

'I think most Mexican generals have a shot at becoming president,' Aaron agreed, 'But I was only a *brigadier* general, I guess that's on a par with a Mexican vice president.'

After studying his face seriously for a few moments, Lola smiled, 'I think you are having a joke with me, Señor General, but it seems you are important enough for the sheriff to have you set free, even though you killed a man. I have not met with a man so important before.'

'You just keep your thoughts to yourself, Lola. It looks as though my drink is on the way. When it arrives, I'd be obliged if we talked about ex-Captain Gottland, and not about me. I'd like to learn a little of what he's been doing since he left the Union army — if he ever served in it.'

23

3

It was the early hours of the morning before Wes and Aaron made their way back to their hotel which was close to the river-boat terminal, but there was still a great deal of activity going on in the riverside area.

When Wes commented on this, Aaron replied, 'There's always something happening on the river, Wes, the Mississippi must be one of the most exciting rivers in the whole world. When you travel on it you can never really predict how long it is going to be before you arrive at your destination whether you're going up, or downriver. Sometimes there's so much water a pilot hardly knows whether he's still on the river, or steaming across plantation land. Other times it's so shallow he's likely to be stranded on a sandbank where a week before he'd have been steaming at full speed. The river's forever changing course, too. A town where a steamboat called in on its way downriver might be a mile distant by the time it heads back to St Louis. It's what makes a river pilot's life so interesting.'

'Wasn't Ira Gottland saying something about that, back in the saloon.'

'Gottland was saying a whole lot about a great many things,' Aaron said, tight-lipped.

Glancing at his companion, Wes said, 'You

24

don't like him, do you?'

'I don't know him well enough to say whether I like, or dislike him,' Aaron replied, tersely, 'I suppose you could say that's much the same.'

'Yet he served with you during the war,' Wes pointed out.

'So he says,' Aaron replied, 'but I'm damned if I can remember him — not by sight anyway, although I fancy I've heard the name mentioned.'

'It's hardly surprising you don't remember him,' Wes commented, 'There must have been hundreds of officers — thousands, even — who served under your command at one time or another. You can't be expected to remember them all.'

'That's where you're wrong,' Aaron said, 'I pride myself on never forgetting a single one of the good officers who served with me during the war — and not a few of the bad ones. Gottland's name rings a bell with me, but it's a warning bell, not a celebratory one.'

'Is that why you said nothing when he said he was going upriver on the same boat as us?'

'You've got it in one. I was impressed with Lola too. When he mentioned he was going upriver on the *Missouri Belle* she never batted an eyelid. It's a great pity she's a whore, she'd have made a good wife for an ambitious man.'

'Do you think Gottland is up to no good?' Wes asked.

'I wish I knew,' Aaron replied. 'When we meet up with the others who are travelling with us we must make it clear that we don't acknowledge each other on board the *Missouri Belle* until — and unless — I need to call for their help.'

★ ★ ★

The quay where the riverboat had its berth was the scene of great activity when Aaron and Wes boarded the stern-wheeled steamer. Bales of raw cotton, brought down the Mississippi river by boats during the night were heaped in piles as tall as a mansion, waiting to be shipped across the city to the docks, for transportation to the continents of the world.

Meanwhile, wagon-loads of trade goods were waiting at the riverside to be loaded on the *Missouri Belle* for carriage upriver to a rapidly advancing frontier.

It was a scene of activity that was both exciting and confusing.

The previous evening Aaron had called a meeting of the men from the *Northern Star* who would be travelling upriver with them on the Missouri Belle and told them of his suspicions of Ira.

Earlier, at Aaron's expense, each man had armed himself with a rifle or a handgun, together with an impressive amount of ammunition for both. As a result, Wes was now the proud possessor of a Winchester repeating rifle, purchased under Aaron's guidance, and a heavy Colt revolver, the latest addition to the company's range, loaned to him by the US Marshal.

Wes and Aaron were among the first

passengers to board the riverboat on which they would be sharing a cabin. Because of their earlier suspicions, they did not leave their cabin until the boat had passed the busy town of Baton Rouge on its long journey upriver, then they made their way to the saloon which, after dinner would be transformed into a gambling casino.

By this time the sun had set and although the riverboat had a powerful light mounted above the bow, Aaron told Wes the pilot was guided as much by his knowledge of the river and the feel of the boat as by what he was able to see of the capricious river.

The two men were just finishing their meal when Ira Gottland entered the saloon chatting to three other men. When Aaron stiffened perceptibly, Wes asked, 'What is it? Do you know the men with Gottland?'

'One of them,' Aaron replied, tight-lipped. 'He rode with an irregular Confederate group that boasted some of the worst thieves and murderers to be found on the frontier. If that's the company Gottland keeps then he's definitely up to no good.'

Resuming his meal, he said to Wes, 'Pretend you haven't seen them together and talk naturally about the boat . . . the weather . . . anything you like, but whatever you do don't let Gottland think you suspect anything.'

Wes did his best to do as Aaron asked and succeeded in resisting the almost overpowering urge to look up and see what Gottland and his friends were doing.

He was making an innocuous remark about

the vast size of the Mississippi River when a shadow fell across the table. Looking up he saw Ira Gottland beaming down at them. 'General . . . Wes! What a pleasant surprise, I had no idea we were to be travelling companions!'

'Well now,' said Aaron, matching the others geniality, 'I guess Wes and I are equally surprised. If you're eating, take a seat.'

When Ira said he was not having a meal, Aaron invited him to help himself to a whisky from the bottle that stood on the table, adding, 'You'll find it a sight better than the rot-gut they sell in the New Orleans saloons — but what are you doing on board . . . ?'

While Aaron was talking, Wes cast a surreptitious glance around the saloon. There was no sign of the men with whom Ira had entered the room.

Seating himself at the table and helping himself to a generous measure of their whisky, Ira said, 'I'm on my way upriver to stay with a friend who's bought land not far from Vicksburg. He's made a whole lot of money selling timber as fuel to riverboats. Now he wants to do something with the land he's cleared. I'm going up there to help . . . but how about you two, how far upriver are you travelling.'

He addressed the question to Wes, who allowed the US Marshal to answer for him, 'We're both travelling to Missouri, Wes to do what he was doing in England — mining. As for me, like yourself, I'm going to visit a friend in Jefferson City. Did you ever serve under General Pike?'

Ira shook his head, 'Can't say I did, but I've heard of him. I guess you two old war-horses will have a whole lot to talk about.'

'That's what old soldiers do best when the fighting's done, Ira. We talk about the way things *should* have been done. Winning battles with the advantage of hindsight. It's easier than fighting 'em on the spot.'

'Don't put yourself down, general,' said Ira, 'You did damn well when you were fighting them Rebs — and you'd do it just as well if you had to do it all again — you proved that, back in New Orleans. I'm living proof of that!'

'No, Ira, shooting that man in New Orleans only confirmed what I already knew. I'm not a fighting man any more. I've stopped carrying a gun now so I won't get myself mixed up in anything like that again. But how about you, are you travelling alone, or are there any more ex-Union men I'm likely to meet up with?'

'I'm on my own, General. Like you, I'm just relaxing and enjoying travelling upriver on one of the finest stern-wheelers on the Mississippi. I believe it's a mighty fine gambling boat too, once the eating's done.' Putting down his empty glass, he asked, 'Am I likely to see you here later?'

'Possibly,' Aaron replied, 'The girl we were talking to when we met you in the New Orleans saloon told us she'd be on the boat as a croupier. I might just come along to see how she's making out.'

★　★　★

29

Later that evening Wes and Aaron returned to the saloon which was now a busy and noisy casino. Lola was here and seemed pleased to see them — particularly Aaron.

It soon became apparent she was an inexperienced croupier and as a result many of the more serious riverboat gamblers chose to play at her table.

Wes knew nothing of the games being played. This, together with a need to conserve his money meant he took no part in what was going on.

It was clear that Aaron was familiar with all the games being played and he too chose to gamble at Lola's table, where he was a consistent winner.

At some time during the evening Ira put in an appearance, but he lacked Aaron's good luck. After being dealt a number of losing hands, he drifted away.

Wes remained in the casino until midnight, when he informed Aaron he was going back to their cabin.

'That's fine, Wes,' said the US Marshal, cheerily, 'I'll be back there before too long, but I'm riding a winning streak right now. I'll stay until my luck changes.'

Despite Aaron's words, when Wes woke the next morning and looked across the cabin to Aaron's bunk it was empty and had not been slept in. The US Marshal did not return to the cabin until Wes was dressed and shaved ready for breakfast.

'I didn't realize the casino would be operating all night,' Wes commented, drily.

'It wasn't,' the US Marshal replied matter-of-factly, 'The plug was pulled on it around four o'clock.'

When Wes responded with a raised eyebrow, Aaron said, 'I went back to Lola's cabin. We had things to chat about.'

'It's past eight o'clock now. It must have been more of a debate than a chat!'

Wes had been attracted to Lola from their first meeting and there was an element of resentment in his response.

Aaron shrugged, 'Call it what you like, Wes. Lola is a bright girl. She weighed up Ira and has singled out the men we saw with him earlier in the evening. She told me they've been asking a whole lot more questions than casual gambling passengers usually do.'

'What sort of questions?' Wes asked.

'They're particularly interested in the amount of money taken by the casino; where it's put for safekeeping when the casino closes down — and who holds the key to the safe.'

'Hardly the sort of questions a casual gambler is likely to ask,' Wes agreed, 'but if they intend getting their hands on the casino takings surely they'll leave it until the very last minute to rob the boat. Ira will be leaving the *Missouri Belle* in a couple of day's time.'

'True,' said Aaron, 'But if Ira and his friends have enough men to back 'em up they'll figure on taking all the cash that's being carried onboard. They won't leave behind a large amount sitting in the safe. The place where he's asked the captain to land him is a well-wooded

31

and sparsely populated stretch of the river. If he's planning to have friends come aboard there they'll reckon on overpowering the sort of opposition they're expecting and being able to take as long as they like to do what they want. I'm confident we'll give them a nasty surprise, Wes, but it could be a hard fight.'

Wes felt a surge of excitement — and fear — at Aaron's words, but the US Marshal had not finished talking, ' . . . We need to warn the others what to expect and when to be ready, but I don't want to be seen talking to anyone. Ira's not happy about having me on board and I don't want him suspecting anything. Try to talk to Harrison Schuster without being seen. Have him pass on to the others what we're expecting to happen. We should reach the place where Ira wants the boat to land him in a couple of days. I'll let Harrison know more nearer the time. Gottland and his gang will be expecting to take everyone on board by surprise but the first thing they'll want to do is secure the pilot-house, I intend that you and I will be there waiting for them.'

Looking speculatively at the Cornishman, Aaron said, 'There's just one thing we need to get clear, Wes.'

'What's that?'

'When Ira's men come bursting into the pilot-house you don't ask any questions. If I say so, you shoot — and you shoot to kill, is that understood?'

Wes nodded, but the gesture did not satisfy Aaron. 'If you're uncertain of being able to do it you're no good to me, Wes. We're dealing with killers. Men who won't hesitate to kill men, women or children to get what they want. If you have any doubts about being able to kill a man I don't want you in the pilot house with me. Even the slightest hesitation could result in both of us dying and many of those on board the *Missouri Belle* along with us. That includes Lola — unless they decide they'd like to take her with 'em, and that would be a whole lot worse for her.'

'I won't let you down, Aaron.'

After only a moment's hesitation, Aaron nodded, apparently satisfied. 'Good. Our lives and that of the pilot will depend on you, boy. Now, I'll tell you what I have planned for the others . . . '

4

For the next forty-eight hours life on board the *Missouri Belle* was little different to that of any other Mississippi river-boat. The passengers enjoyed good food and comfortable accommodation during the day and when night fell men adjourned to the casino. Here they gambled their money and flirted with the female croupiers who, with a display of sympathy that convinced all but the most cynical — or experienced — gambler, sweetened the losses made by most players.

Although there were a number of men who did not spend the night hours trying to make a fortune in the casino, their absence provoked no curiosity. Many passengers were working-men, travelling upriver on the stern-wheeler because it was the cheapest form of travel to wherever they were going.

Such men could not afford to risk their meagre capital on the spin of a roulette wheel. Their presence on board was disregarded by croupiers, gamblers — and by those who had boarded the *Missouri Belle* with more sinister pursuits in mind.

The latter would have been disconcerted had they been aware of the number of firearms in the possession of some of these 'working-men'.

Aaron had briefed the men in considerable detail before they boarded the stern-wheeler. Now they were all on the riverboat together he ignored them, leaving Wes to carry any instructions on his behalf, while he spent much of the evening and night in the casino.

When questioned about this by Wes, his excuse was that he was taking stock of the other gamblers, identifying those who were rich and likely to be targets for the river pirates. At the same time he hoped to pick out those who were also seeking out the richest men — but for very different reasons.

In the meantime, Aaron also made such progress with Lola that he now did not return to the cabin he shared with Wes until the breakfast bell had been sounded on board the *Missouri Belle*.

After his second absence, when he put in an appearance and changed his clothes in readiness for the new day, he said, 'Last night was very interesting, Wes.'

'I don't doubt it,' Wes replied, caustically, 'I'm sure Lola has a great many talents to offer a man.'

Looking sharply at Wes, Aaron said, 'It has nothing to do with Lola — at least, not directly. One of the men we saw with Ira was in the casino last night. He'd been drinking more than was good for a man with something on his mind. He tried to persuade Lola to let him come to her cabin when the casino closed. He wouldn't take no for an answer, so I stepped in and told him she had other plans. He told me to make the most of her while I could, because it wouldn't be long before she found out that a Southern private was more than a match in bed for a Yankee general. Now, neither you, nor any of the others on board have mentioned anything about my rank in the Union army, so it must have come from Ira. Such a boast would seem to confirm what we already believe is going to happen.'

Wes agreed. 'When is it we arrive at the place where Ira wants the *Missouri Belle* to put him ashore?'

'Soon after first light tomorrow,' Aaron replied, 'It's the ideal time as far as Ira and his friends are concerned. Most passengers will still be in their beds and the crew will be no more than half awake.'

His words gave Wes a moment of near-panic. The thought of fighting for his life against river pirates had never seemed quite real to him before. Now it was less than twenty-four hours away it had suddenly become very real indeed!

'I hope everyone is quite sure of what they have to do,' he said, anxiously.

'I've put my orders and anything else I feel should be known into writing, Wes. I want you to take it to Captain Schuster. He is to take care of Ira and those of his men who are on board with him. Tell him to pass on the details to the others before coming to this cabin to speak to me after dark tonight. Everyone will need to be up and fully awake before daylight and know exactly what's expected of them. Timing is important. I want to catch every one of those murdering

36

sons-of-bitches — dead or alive. Either way they'll no longer be a threat to decent folk.'

'How about me, Aaron?' Wes asked, 'What *exactly* do you want me to do?'

'You'll come with me to the pilot house to deal with whoever comes there to put a gun to the pilot's head — and we'll need to get there long before dawn breaks. One of Ira's men will come there for sure to make certain the pilot doesn't try to pull the boat back from the bank when he realizes what's going on. They'll also have another couple of men down on the boiler deck to keep the engineer in line, but we'll leave Schuster to deal with them. The main thing is not to scare off Ira's friends who'll be waiting onshore. We don't want to open fire until they're all at least halfway up the gang-plank.' Aaron spoke without the slightest hint of excitement or apprehension in his voice.

Wes wondered how he could remain so calm when discussing something that would result in the deaths of many men — the outcome of which was by no means certain. Then he remembered what Aaron had said to Schuster when they were all taking passage on the *Northern Star* from New York. He had mentioned his involvement in almost every major battle that had taken place in the recent Civil War. He would regard a gun battle involving probably no more than fifty men as little more than a skirmish.

'How will we spend today?' Wes asked him.

'Once you've spoken to Schuster you can spend it how you like,' Aaron replied. 'I intend sleeping for much of the day. I suggest you do the same. We'll be up long before dawn so that we're wide-awake when things start happening. Now, let's go and see what's on offer for breakfast. Right now I could eat half a horse . . . '

5

Wes took to his bunk for a couple of hours that afternoon but slept fitfully. He fared no better when he returned that night. Aaron's relaxed snores did nothing to help.

When he did eventually fall into a disturbed sleep it seemed to him he was shaken only minutes later by Aaron. The US Marshal did nothing to make him feel any less aggrieved when he said, 'I'm proud of you, boy. Anyone who can sleep that well before a battle is a man I want with me when the action begins.'

'What time is it?' Wes asked, not yet fully in possession of his senses.

'We have about an hour to dawn,' was Aaron's reply. 'Check your guns and we'll make our way to the pilot house. Pilot Stavros is working the night shift. He tells me he'll have a Colt tucked in his belt, just in case we can't cope.'

'Do you think we'll need to use our guns?' Wes asked anxiously, trying hard to keep a tremor from his voice.

'Perhaps not in the pilot house, but we'll certainly use 'em when Ira's friends try to come onboard. Does that worry you?'

'I'll manage.' Wes replied, hoping he sounded convincing.

'I've never doubted it,' Aaron said, confidently,

'Ira and his friends are in for a big surprise. If everything goes according to plan, they'll be out of business once and for all by the time the rest of our fellow passengers are fully awake.'

Wes wished he was experienced enough to share Aaron's confidence. He hoped, too, that when the occasion arose, he would be able to steel himself to use the guns that had been bought in New Orleans.

★ ★ ★

River Pilot Stavros was nervous. When Wes and Aaron entered the pilot-house he was struggling to draw his revolver from its place in his waistband.

'I was beginning to think you weren't going to show. We're almost at the landing. In fact, I've had to slow down the boat or we'd have been there before it was light.'

'That wouldn't have done at all,' Aaron said, 'If we're too early they won't be ready for us. I want to account for every man of the gang who shows himself and I don't care whether we take him alive — or dead. One thing we can be certain of is that the first action is going to take place right here, in the pilot-house. They'll want to be sure it's them who are in command of the boat on the approach to the landing.'

'But you've said that any shooting up here is likely to alert the other members of the gang who are on board.' Wes pointed out.

'True,' Aaron agreed, 'So we need to avoid shooting if it's at all possible. Having said that, if it looks as though there's no other way, then I expect you to shoot — and shoot to kill, same as I will. But if all goes according to plan Pilot Stavros will edge the boat inshore slowly enough to draw the pirates out of hiding. That way we should get 'em all. Right now we need to hide ourselves so that Ira's men don't see us when they come into the pilot house. I'll squeeze myself into that cupboard over there . . . '

He pointed to a low cupboard that faced the door, adding, 'It'll give me a good view of anyone coming in. You get beneath that table, behind the door.'

Wes realized he was being put in what would possibly be the safest place in the pilot house if shooting erupted, but he accepted that was the way it needed to be. Aaron was far more experienced in this sort of situation.

Aaron pointed to a lantern hanging from a hook in a corner of the pilot house. Despite the already dim light it cast, he said to the pilot, 'I'm going to turn that down as much as possible. It will help keep us hidden.'

By the time dawn was bringing a faint rose-coloured light to the eastern horizon, Wes had developed cramp in his right leg, the result of crouching for so long in his hiding-place. He was about to say something to Aaron when he heard the scraping of feet on the ladder that led to the pilot-house from the deck outside.

His discomfiture forgotten immediately, Wes drew back the hammer on his Colt, the action sounding excessively loud in the confines of the

41

pilot-house and he felt that his heart rate must have doubled.

It seemed an age before the pilot house door was thrown open and two of the men Wes had seen with Ira burst in. Both had guns in their hands and the first man pointed his gun at the pilot and said, calmly, 'Don't mind us, mister. Just carry on with what you're paid to do and you'll live to tell your grandchildren how you were pilot of the *Missouri Belle* when she was taken over by river pirates.'

The pilot had gone rigid with fear when the two men broke into the pilot house. Now, in a strangled voice, he asked, 'What's happening? What are you going to do?'

'That needn't trouble you. Just carry on and do what you always do. Take the boat in to the plantation landing up ahead and berth your boat nose in, no matter what you see there.'

'Then what?' the pilot asked, nervously.

'That needn't concern you,' the river pirate. said. 'Do as you're told and in a couple of hours time you'll be taking your boat upriver again, light of a little money — and perhaps a couple of casino girls, but otherwise nothing will have changed . . . '

' . . . I don't think so, friend. Drop that gun right where you stand. Just so much as a twitch and you're dead!'

At Aaron's words the man who had been talking to the pilot looked startled, but for a moment it seemed he might ignore the Marshal's command.

Aaron was a split moment away from shooting

him when, from the other side of the pilot-house, Wes said, 'You heard him. Drop your guns — both of you — or you're dead.'

The realization that two men had guns trained on them was enough. Two handguns dropped to the deck at almost the same moment.

'Now why did you have to say that, Wes?' Aaron sounded disappointed. 'I'd have preferred two dead river pirates, but I guess this will have to do.'

Emerging from his hiding-place, Aaron spoke to the two river pirates, 'Both of you put your hands in the air and move closer together — over there, by the window.'

As both men shuffled across the pilot-house to follow Aaron's orders, Wes scrambled from his hiding place beneath the table, wondering what the marshal intended to do. He was not kept in suspense for long.

Aaron walked up behind the two men and without warning raised his handgun and brought it crashing down on the side of one of the river pirate's head. Before the man had hit the deck his companion had been dealt with in a similar fashion.

'Do you have some rope in here?' Aaron addressed the pilot.

'Yes, sir,' the nervous pilot spoke in respectful awe, 'You'll find some in the locker right by where you were hiding. If you need a knife, there's one on the shelf just here.'

As Aaron moved off towards the locker, the pilot added, admiringly, 'Jesus, mister! They never knew what hit 'em.'

43

Ignoring the pilot, Aaron located the rope and pulled it from the locker, saying to Wes, 'You tie one and I'll deal with the other. Stuff a gag in his mouth, too. We don't want either of 'em shouting out to warn the others.'

Under instruction from Aaron, Wes bound and gagged his man, putting his arms behind his back, bending his knees and securing wrists to ankles. By the time he had done, Wes's prisoner was conscious, but there had been no movement from the man Aaron had bound.

It was fully light outside now and the pilot asked, nervously, 'The landing's about a mile ahead, what do you want me to do?'

'No more than you would normally,' Aaron replied, 'Go in bow first — but take it nice and easy. Ira's men will have taken the captain prisoner and they'll make him give the order to lower the gangplank. Keep the boat far enough offshore so that the gangplank is the only way they can board the *Missouri Belle*. It's long and it's narrow. Once they're on it there's nowhere for them to go. We just don't want them jumping on board anywhere else.'

'I can see something that might just throw your plans offline,' Wes said, at the same time pointing to where a boat lay off the river bank with half-a-dozen men on board, making a pretence of fishing.

'Oh hell!' Aaron ejaculated, 'I was hoping they'd have all their men onshore. Those in that boat have only to bump against the side of the *Missouri Belle* and they can step on board and be behind our own men. You and me will have to

44

deal with them, Wes, using rifles.'

Wes nodded his acceptance of the situation. Sensing his uncertainty, Aaron said, 'I know you've never had to kill a man, Wes, but detach yourself from thinking about it — and do it right now. When things start happening men are going to die. If we don't make sure it's them, it will be us — that means you, me, and the men with Schuster. I won't go into what will happen to Lola and the women and girls on board. Keep what I've said firmly in mind. When the time comes, don't think about anything — just shoot! More men have died from thinking than from recklessness or stupidity.'

'I'll be all right.'

Wes spoke with far more confidence than he was feeling, but he knew that Aaron was speaking from experience. He would try not to let the US Marshal down.

The 'fishermen' in the small boat made no move until the riverboat began nosing in to the bank and the stage plank was being lowered — then it seemed to Wes that everything happened at once.

As the end of the narrow gangway landed heavily on the river bank an alarming number of armed men broke from the cover of the nearby trees and ran towards the steamboat. At the same time the men on board the fishing boat threw their rods into the Mississippi River and rowed in excited disorder towards the *Missouri Belle*, making for a spot just forward of the paddle-wheel, where the vessel was lowest in the water.

As they drew closer, some of the occupants exchanged their oars for rifles and began firing indiscriminately at anyone they saw moving on board the riverboat.

Aaron had left the pilot house and was kneeling by the guard rail, overlooking the river. As the first 'fisherman' set foot on the *Missouri Belle*, he was knocked backwards by a shot fired from Aaron's rifle — and so too was a second of the river pirates.

Meanwhile, as Wes was leaving the pilot-house, one of the men in the small boat fired a shot which smashed a window close to his head.

No longer wrestling with his conscience about shooting at a fellow man, Wes fired and knocked the pirate out of the boat and into the river. He and Aaron's shots both hit the fourth man — and the fifth.

The sixth and last river pirate in the boat fired off a last desperate shot which, judging from the shouts which came from the deck below where Wes and Aaron were firing, had hit one of the *Missouri Belle*'s defenders. With his last shot before needing to re-load, Wes eliminated the threat posed from this particular would-be robber.

By now, firing had erupted from a dozen separate vantage points on board the *Missouri Belle*. Most came from men who had been briefed by Schuster and were aimed at the pirates attempting to board the riverboat via the stage plank, but their colleagues travelling with Ira Gottland had shown their hand now and a number of small but desperate gun battles were being fought on board the steamboat.

The pirates attempting to board the *Missouri Belle* via the stage plank quickly realized they had not only lost the element of surprise, but were walking into a well-planned ambush. With more than half their number already killed or wounded, the survivors turned tail and tried to escape.

Only a very small number were successful. By the time the remaining survivors disappeared among the trees and all shooting had ceased, more than three-quarters of their number had become casualties. The battle was over — and more river pirates had been killed than had surrendered.

Soon, the bodies of the dead pirates were laid out on the main deck with the wounded prisoners seated behind them, watched over by Aaron's triumphant 'private army'.

The men defending the *Missouri Belle* had suffered only a single fatality. Sadly, this was ex-Confederate Captain Harrison Schuster, killed by the very last shot fired from the 'fishing-boat' in the brief but furious battle.

Checking the dead, wounded and captured river pirates, Aaron quickly discovered that Ira Gottland was not among their number and when Aaron asked if anyone had seen him, one of the wounded defenders said that after being shot, he had seen Gottland jump from the *Missouri Belle* into the river.

A passenger who had not been involved in the fighting declared that he had seen a man clinging to the side of the fishing-boat as it drifted away downriver, adding, 'Might that have been the man you're looking for?'

'It almost certainly was,' Aaron replied, furiously. 'Damn! I particularly wanted him ... the action sharpened my brain and I remembered where I had heard his name. He was in the Union army, but he never held a commission. He was a sergeant and with two privates was charged with raping a Southern girl when they raided a farm looking for food. The papers on the case came to me but he was never charged because his unit was involved in some very heavy fighting and immediately afterwards he deserted. Rumour has it that he then joined the Rebel army.'

'But wouldn't he have changed his name, in case he came across someone who had known him then?' Wes queried.

'There is no reason why he should,' Aaron replied, 'With all that was going on at the time he wouldn't have expected the report to have ever reached me. Besides, the war has been over for a long time — and the company he's keeping now wouldn't care what he'd done in the past.'

Despite the escape of Gottland and the tragic death of Harrison Schuster, Aaron expressed satisfaction with the outcome of the thwarted raid on the *Missouri Belle*.

'It will put the gang out of action for a very long time,' he said to Wes, 'In fact, I'll be very surprised if we are ever troubled by river pirates on the Mississippi again.'

'I'm sure you're right,' Wes agreed, 'But I'm

disappointed that Gottland wasn't among those accounted for.'

'That troubles me too, Wes, but don't take it to heart, I'll have a wanted notice put out for him — with a large reward. He'll be picked up, sooner or later.'

'I hope you're right, Aaron, but I don't believe you've heard the last of him.'

6

ॐ

Later that same day the *Missouri Belle* berthed at the Mississippi town of Vicksburg. Of great strategic importance during the Civil War, there was still a United States army garrison here and in response to the urgent sounding of the riverboat's steam whistle and bell it was not long before the commanding officer and a detachment of troops arrived to take charge of Aaron's prisoners and carry away the bodies of their companions.

When he learned of the desperate fight that had taken place downriver from his headquarters, Colonel Van Kleef, the officer in charge of the garrison, sent off a detail with orders to hunt down any surviving river pirates but, as Aaron told Wes, they would find no one. He had already learned that most of the river pirates had fought as Confederate 'irregulars' in the late war.

It was a term that described men who would have been outlaws even in more peaceful times. War had served to hone their skills in the art of evading capture. Heading north and west, they would vanish in the uncharted forests and uplands of neighbouring Arkansas.

When the last of the prisoners had been taken away, Aaron asked Colonel Van Kleef if there was an undertaker in the town who could provide a suitable coffin for the late Captain Schuster.

Startled, the colonel asked, 'Are you talking of Captain Harrison Schuster, son of old Silas Schuster who was a Kentucky Senator before choosing the wrong side when the war began?'

'I know very little about Captain Schuster's background, except that he was a Confederate officer, and that his family were considerable landowners in Kentucky.' Aaron replied.

'They still are,' said the colonel. 'The old Senator suffered as much as anyone during the war, losing two of his sons, who fought on opposing sides, and all his slaves too, but he's tough and is pulling things together again. If there's any justice he'll be made the next Governor of Kentucky. He's a good man, despite his wartime affiliations. I've met him a couple of times when he's passed up and down the river and I admire the man. He will be absolutely devastated by the death of yet another son. It leaves him with just one now, although I believe he has a number of daughters.'

'Harrison Schuster was a good man too,' Aaron declared. 'His help was invaluable in wiping out the river pirates.'

'Then I suggest that a letter from you to President Grant, referring to the part he played would be a practical memorial for such a man,' Colonel Van Kleef said, 'Silas Schuster would dearly love to become a political animal once more in Kentucky — and the United States would regain the services of an honest man . . . a man who is quite the opposite of a Senator who will be accompanying you with his son on the

51

Missouri Belle upriver as far as Memphis, Senator Connolly of Louisiana uses his office for the benefit only of . . . Senator Connolly. He's been in Vicksburg visiting his brother, who happens to be my administrative officer.'

As though suddenly aware that he was talking to a man who was likely to have friends in Washington, Colonel Van Kleef reverted to the conversation the two men had been having when he had suddenly launched the verbal attack on the reputation of the Louisiana Senator.

' . . . but that's all by the way. I'll have the undertaker come along to see you right away. I will also telegraph to the officer in charge of the small garrison at Cairo, upriver at the junction with the Ohio River, to say you have Harrison Schuster's body on board. That will probably be the best place for you to have it unloaded and the army will arrange for it to be carried to the family home near Mayfield with all due ceremony.'

'I'm much obliged,' said Aaron, grasping the other man's hand, ' . . . and I'll write that letter to the President.'

When the *Missouri Belle* left Vicksburg behind, the men who had taken part in the fight against the river pirates were treated as heroes — and none more so than Aaron, who shrugged off the adulation.

Replying to Wes, who had commented on Aaron's popularity after one female passenger had come to their table in the dining saloon with effusive words of praise, Aaron said, 'If you haven't learned it already, you'll come to realize folk are fickle, Wes. Today's hero is just as likely to be tomorrow's scapegoat. It's best to ignore both praise and scorn and be true to the things you believe in. When it comes right down to it, you're the one who's got to live with yourself.'

'That's the sort of thing my pa would say to me,' Wes said. 'He was very much his own man too.'

'Is he still alive?' Aaron asked. Apart from Wes's early disclosure that his father had been a gamekeeper, he had said very little about his family.

Wes shook his head, 'Neither pa, nor my ma. When she caught pneumonia and died, he went to stay with his sister in a small fishing village just as cholera arrived there. They were both buried with little more than a month between them.'

'Is that why you left to come to America?'

Wes shrugged, 'Partly, but it wasn't the only reason. The mines had fallen on hard times and there was nothing to keep me in Cornwall. A brother of ma's, who I'd once worked with, and who is my only close relative now, had come out here to a place called Harmony, in Missouri, and written to say there was no shortage of work for a good Cornish miner. I thought I'd give it a try.'

'There are easier ways to earn a living than burrowing underground like some varmint,' Aaron said.

Wes laughed, 'Such as going around looking for men like river pirates and getting shot at? You call that an easy occupation?'

'I'd say more men are killed underground in

the mines than in enforcing the law, Wes.'

'That's only because there are a lot more miners than marshals.' Wes pointed out. 'A careful miner might live to a good age.'

Aaron shrugged, 'Only if the men he works with are just as careful. You might say it's not too different for a lawman — but we won't argue about it. If ever you change your mind I'll be happy to take you on as a deputy.'

'Where will I find you?' Wes asked, 'Will you be going back up north now you've dealt with the river pirates?'

Aaron shook his head, 'That was just a sideshow, something I was asked to look at as I was passing this way. I'm on my way to the Territories. There's a shortage of law out that way, with few local sheriffs or town marshals to get on top of it.'

'And that's supposed to be safer than mining?' Wes said, quizzically, 'No thanks, Aaron, I'll stick with what I know best.'

★   ★   ★

As more and more people drew up chairs to the table and engaged the US Marshal in conversation, Wes made his excuses and left the crowded and noisy saloon. Making his way outside, he paused for a few moments, breathing in the warm but fresher air than that in the smoke-filled room he had just left. Then he headed towards the front of the vessel, where the long wooden gangway that had been the scene of so much bloodshed, stretched out at an angle of forty-five degrees, beyond the blunt bow of the steamboat.

It was dark now but from a wing of the pilot house perched atop the vessel's superstructure, the beam from a powerful acetylene lantern probed the sluggish and muddy waters as the river pilot expertly negotiated the twists and turns of the mighty waterway artery that carried life and commerce to and from the young heart of America.

It was cooler out here, but not a great deal quieter. The windows of the saloon had been thrown open to allow at least some of the heat and cigar smoke to escape, but these twin discomforts were pursued by a hubbub of talk, laughter and discordant piano music.

Wes pushed all such sounds into the background as he mulled over the happenings of what had been an extremely traumatic day.

He was surprised that the fact he had taken the lives of fellow men did not trouble his conscience at all. In fact, it affected him less than the occasion when, as a boy, he had accompanied his gamekeeper father on an expedition to kill a fox that had slaughtered chickens on one of the estate farms.

On the contrary, he admitted to feeling a certain satisfaction at seeing the bodies of the river pirates laid out in a double row on the deck of the riverboat — and this did trouble him.

Wes had been brought up to believe that human life was sacred, yet here he was gloating over the killing of so many men — albeit men to whom human life was cheap.

No doubt his father would have understood his feelings, having spent fifteen years in the army before being invalided from the service at the early age of thirty because of a wound sustained during service in Africa.

The wound had prevented Curnow senior from taking underground work when he returned to the Bodmin moor mining area, where he had been born and had worked as a boy. However, because of his skill as an army sharpshooter he was offered work as a gamekeeper at Trebartha, a large estate bordering the moor and had soon married and settled down happily.

Wes grew up to share his father's prowess with long-barrelled weapons, but there was mining in his blood from both sides of the family and he chose to work on one of the moor's copper mines.

He soon considered himself to be a highly skilled 'hard-rock' miner and looked forward to a career which would ultimately lead to him becoming a respected mine captain.

Unfortunately, mining was a fickle business, copper mining in particular being at the mercy of a great many pressures originating outside the industry. When, in the early 1870's a nationwide financial collapse coincided with a slump in the price of copper, many mines were forced out of business. Before long, the mine where Wes worked became one of them.

He might have hoped to be able to emulate his father and become an assistant gamekeeper on the estate where he had worked, but the estate owner had been a heavy investor in the mines on Bodmin moor. Although unlikely to be bankrupted, he was feeling the pinch and there was a surfeit of unemployed men seeking work. The wages he offered to Wes proved unacceptable, so Wes looked elsewhere.

A great many out-of-work miners were leaving Cornwall — leaving England — and seeking new lives in far off places that were no more than a name to most of them: Australia; South Africa; Chile; Peru; Mexico — and the United States of America.

There had been a growing exodus of miners from Cornwall to all these places over the years and it was a letter from Wes's uncle which fired his imagination. It told of the good life to be had in the lead mine communities of South East Missouri where new machinery meant mines were able to go deeper underground, creating work for experienced hard-rock miners.

The letter writer painted a glowing picture of the wages that could be earned and the standard of life that was enjoyed, declaring there to be unlimited prospects for a man who possessed a sound knowledge of mining and a willingness to work hard.

After thinking the matter over for some time, Wes decided he would leave Cornwall and begin a new life in far off Missouri.

He set off on his great adventure with a considerable advantage over most of his fellow emigrating miners. They were for the most part married men who had left behind any money they possessed to provide a meagre existence for their families until such time as they could send them more, or until they felt secure enough to call for their loved ones to come and join them in the new land.

Wes had no such commitments and during the good years of copper mining had managed to save money. He would not be leaving Cornwall through desperate necessity, but with a sense of adventure and looking forward to the opportunity to better himself.

*　★　★*

'What are you doing out here, Wes, feeling troubled about what went on this morning?'

Lola not only brought the tang of the smoke-filled saloon with her, but had been adding to it with the slim cheroot she held between two fingers.

'No,' Wes admitted. 'I feel I should be, but if I am troubled at all it's because some of the men we were fighting succeeded in escaping . . . Gottland in particular. I would be much happier knowing he was about to receive all he deserves.'

Taking up a position beside Wes and resting her arms on the top safety rail, Lola took a drag on the cheroot. Then, breathing out smoke with her words, she said, 'With sentiments like that, Aaron will make a lawman of you yet.'

Wes shook his head, 'I'm a miner, Lola, not a fighting man.'

'Tell that to the men licking their wounds in the military prison at Vicksburg,' Lola retorted. 'Aaron says you're a natural gunfighter. He

58

won't be happy until he's pinned a deputy marshal's badge on your chest.'

'Then you're going to have to get used to him being unhappy,' Wes replied, 'I'm heading for the Missouri mines and a place called Harmony.'

'We'll see,' Lola commented, enigmatically. Then, changing the subject, she said, 'There's plenty of time to get bored before you leave the *Missouri Belle*. Would you like me to introduce you to Anabelita?'

'Anabelita? Who is she?'

'She's a croupier, like me. The small, black-haired girl. She's half-Mexican too — and has taken a shine to you.'

He knew who she was talking about. Black-haired and strikingly beautiful, Anabelita was a girl who would attract attention wherever she happened to be. The most influential and well-to-do passengers on board the *Missouri Belle* were to be found at her gambling table whenever the saloon was open for business.

Grimacing, he said, 'It would take far more money than I have to be able to buy her time,' Wes said, 'I've seen the company she keeps.'

Lola's head came up and she turned to stare at him, 'You think she's a whore?'

'Probably . . . but I don't doubt that she's a very high class one.'

'Then it's just as well I haven't already introduced you,' Lola said, with an indignation that Wes found surprising coming from a New Orleans bar-girl. 'Anabelita is no angel, but she earns her money from gambling, not getting laid. If she lifts her skirt for a man it'll most probably be because she's reaching for the derringer she keeps strapped to her leg — and she's a crack shot!'

Intrigued but sceptical, Wes asked, 'Where did she learn to shoot — and to gamble?'

'Her father was a professional gambler. When her mother died he took Anabelita with him for a while. Sometimes he'd come to the saloon in New Orleans and bring her with him . . . that's where I first met her. One day, when they were down Texas way, it seems he accused a man he was playing poker with of cheating, but wasn't quick enough drawing a gun to back up the accusation. His death hit Anabelita pretty hard, but instead of going into mourning for him she asked a riverboat company to let her work on the steamboats as a croupier. They agreed — and you've seen the results for yourself. She probably knows every gambling trick in the book but has a reputation for playing an honest game. That and her looks means that she makes more money for herself — and for the company — than any other gambler on the river.'

'I'm glad you've told me about her,' Wes said, 'I'll look at her in a different light from now on and, yes, I would like an introduction to her.'

7

It had been a long and eventful day and Wes turned in early that night, with the result that it was not until the following evening he decided to follow up his conversation with Lola and visit the saloon for a while to watch Anabelita at work.

The gambling saloon was a popular place with the steamboat's passengers. Croupiers employed by the steamboat company worked at five gambling tables and a roulette wheel, a number of other tables being provided for private card games.

There was also a well-stocked bar in a corner of the saloon and this too was well frequented. As a result the air inside the saloon was hazy with tobacco smoke.

The gaming tables were busy, the largest crowd being gathered about the table where Anabelita was dealing blackjack . . . but tonight Wes sensed an attitude of unease in the mood of this particular crowd.

Although he could not at first detect exactly why this was so, he realized that others were aware of it too. Lola was operating the roulette wheel some distance away and he thought he detected a hint of concern in the glances she occasionally threw in her friend's direction.

Aaron was seated on his own behind Lola and

he too seemed to be taking a particular interest in Anabelita's table. Wes was about to cross the room to join the US marshal, when there was a sudden eruption of sound from those about Anabelita and an angry voice began protesting loudly about the last card that had been dealt to him.

'Hell . . . just look at it! What kind of card is that. I haven't had a good hand since I was dealt in. I'm losing a fortune here.' The voice sounded to Wes like that of a young man who had drunk too much.

The impression was heightened when one of the others at the table said something quietly in the angry man's ear, only to receive the retort, 'I'll back my cards with as much cash as I damn well want. All I'm asking is to get a fair deal, that's all.'

Wes moved closer to the table until he was able to see the irate young player. He remembered seeing him joining the steamboat at Vicksburg with a well-dressed and overweight older man. They had arrived late. The steamboat should have already left, but the new arrivals were obviously important and were accompanied to the levee by the Vicksburg mayor, town officials and a group of senior army officers from the local garrison.

The aggrieved young man was probably hardly out of his teens and was as well dressed as the older man who had accompanied him on board the steamboat. The flushed, lightly perspiring appearance of his face might have been caused by the heat and stuffiness of the saloon but

something about the young man's eyes confirmed Wes's belief that he had been drinking
heavily.

'I can only deal the cards as they come from
the shoe.' Anabelita spoke for the first time,
referring to the holder from which she drew the
cards dealt to the punters.

There was a murmur of support from the
others about the table, but her reply did not
appease the young man.

'Then why is it just me who is losing so much
money? You've damn near cleaned me out.'

Looking straight at the dissatisfied blackjack
player, Anabelita replied, 'It could be because
you are being reckless with your money. Perhaps
you'd do better to 'stand' occasionally, instead of
asking for another card. Had you done so you
would have won at least five or six hands, instead
of losing money. But if you are not happy with
the way I deal you should move to another table.'

Anabelita spoke perfect English but with a
Mexican accent that Wes found charming.

Not so the irate young gambler. 'I'm damned
if I'm going to walk away and leave you to gloat
over the fact that you've fleeced me and got away
with it. I'll stay right here — but I'd better start
winning . . . you hear me?'

Smiling in what she hoped might be a
disarming way, Anabelita said, 'Don't tell me,
mister. You'd better speak to the cards.'

There was a ripple of laughter from the other
players at the table but it was hastily stifled when
the disgruntled player looked about him angrily.

Turning back to Anabelita he pushed a pile of

gambling chips across the table in front of him and said, 'Right, there's my stake — now let's see you deal some cards that I can do something with.'

Shrugging with a nonchalance she did not feel, Anabelita dealt two cards from the shoe to each of the men at her table. Then she began to go around the table again, dealing the extra number of cards asked for by each man in turn.

Two of the players dropped out, surrendering their coloured counters to the dealer. Two others decided to 'stand', satisfied that the cards they held stood a chance of beating the dealer.

Then it was the turn of the disgruntled young man. With three cards in his hand, he said, 'All right, hit me again — but make it a good one.'

Anabelita drew a card from the shoe and placed it face down on the table in front of him.

Picking it up and adding it to the three he already held, the young man's expression changed to one of fury once more and he cried, 'Goodammit . . . you've done it *again!*'

Throwing his four cards face up on to the table, he said angrily, 'Look at that! If you'd dealt me a four or under I'd have won . . . but no you gave me a six.'

'You could have stood with the seventeen you held with three cards,' Anabelita said, 'I've paid out on seventeen more than once tonight.'

As she was speaking she reached out to scoop his stake towards her. Clumsily, he beat her to it, some of the chips falling off the table and landing at his feet.

'Leave it! You've taken enough cash from me

tonight. We'll play that hand again — but this time there will be no cheating . . . you hear me?'

Anabelita glanced around the room hoping to catch the attention of the man employed by the steamboat company to deal with such situations as this when they arose, but he was nowhere to be seen. She would need to handle it on her own.

The other men at the table were appalled by the young man's behaviour but Anabelita was aware none of them were likely to come to her aid. Beginning to rake in the remaining cards but leaving the stakes untouched, she said, 'I'm sorry, gentlemen, but this table is closed. I am sure you'll find places at the other tables — and good luck to you all.'

She reached out for the young man's cards but as she did so he grabbed her wrist.

'Oh no you don't. You'll play on until I've got at least some of my money back.'

His grip was causing her arm to be stretched out at a painful angle but, trying to remain calm, she said, 'Do you mind letting go of me . . . ? You're hurting my arm . . . '

'Not until you say you'll carry on dealing — even if it's only you and me playing.' As he said this, a number of the other players hastily deserted the table.

When the dissatisfied man caught hold of Anabelita's wrist, Wes had started towards the table. Now, pushing his way through the watching gamblers, he arrived in time to hear the man's reply to her pained request.

Reaching out, he took a tight grip on the

young man's own wrist, at the same time twisting it in order to relieve the pain being suffered by the dark-haired croupier.

'You heard what the lady said, you're hurting her arm. Let go.'

Recovering from his surprise but still maintaining a grip on Anabelita, the young man said, 'Keep out of it, this is none of your business.'

'I'm making it my business,' Wes retorted, increasing pressure on the other man's arm so much that the man's body twisted towards him.

The young man held on to Anabelita for as long as possible before suddenly releasing her. However, instead of immediately trying to pull himself free of Wes's grip, he fumbled awkwardly beneath his jacket with his left hand.

'Look out! He's got a gun.' The cry from Anabelita caused a stampede away from the table by the spectators attracted to the table by the altercation.

Years spent below ground in Cornish mines, wielding pick-axe, shovel and sledgehammer had developed exceptional muscle power in Wes's arms and he used every ounce of it now to twist the young man's arm sharply up behind his back, causing him to double over, his face coming into violent contact with the baize covered table top.

The revolver he was trying to draw had almost cleared his waistband but he did not have a firm grip on it and as it fell to the floor Wes kicked it beneath the table before releasing his hold on the young man who was now shouting loudly that Wes was breaking his arm.

Wes hoped the pain would be sufficient to dissuade his opponent from continuing his violence and that he would leave the saloon. Instead, he came at Wes, arms flailing like a schoolboy involved in his first fight.

Wes, on the other hand, had been drawn into more than one brawl when drunken miners from rival mines were paid out their monthly wages in the same local hostelry.

Easily avoiding the other man's wildly inaccurate blows, it took only two well-aimed punches to send him crashing to the saloon floor. Here, he lay on his back with only a twitching face muscle to show he was still living.

The noise that erupted from the crowd in the saloon was a combination of relief, approval and admiration. It died away when the overweight man whom Wes had seen board the steamboat at Vicksburg with the now unconscious young man, stormed into the saloon.

He had apparently been made aware of what was happening and, looking about him angrily, demanded, 'Who did this? Who attacked my son?'

By this time the young man was showing signs of regaining consciousness and Wes replied, 'If you mean, who dealt with him when he was about to shoot me, then I'm the one you are looking for, but . . . '

'I want this man arrested . . . *immediately*!' Raising his voice, the young man's father cut across Wes's explanation.

When no one moved to carry out his order, the large man said angrily, 'I demand that my son's attacker be locked away and handed over to the authorities when we reach Memphis.'

At this point, Aaron pushed his way to the front of the unresponsive onlookers standing about the father and his son, who was now trying to sit up.

Speaking to the older of the two men, Aaron said, 'You should be thanking this young man, not trying to have him arrested. He just saved your boy's life.'

Startled, the recovering man's father said, 'What do you mean, 'saved his life'? I am Senator Connolly, of Louisiana, and this man has just admitted attacking my son. I demand that he be locked up — immediately!'

'I know who you are, Senator, but Wesley here hit your son when he tried to pull a gun on him. That's how he saved your son's life. If that gun had cleared his belt I'd have shot him dead.'

Aaron spoke in such a matter-of-fact manner that it was a few moments before the impact of his words registered with the Senator. When they did, he could scarcely control his rage.

'You . . . you would have done what? How dare you . . . ? Who are you?'

'I'm a Federal Marshal, Senator, on my way West.'

Senator Connolly was nonplussed for only a moment. The man standing in front of him did not look like a Federal Marshal and he said, 'If you really are a marshal then I demand that you arrest this man and charge him with assaulting my son.'

'I'll be happy to do that, Senator,' Aaron said,

cheerfully, 'but if I do I will also have to arrest your son for assaulting a woman — and for attempting to draw a gun with intent to murder an unarmed man.'

Taken aback, Connolly said, 'Attempting to murder . . . ? Why, my son is hardly more than a boy. You would be laughed out of court.'

'A bullet doesn't ask the age of the man — or boy — who pulls the trigger of the gun it's fired from. It just goes ahead and kills someone. There's me; the woman your son assaulted, and a couple of dozen witnesses here who will testify against him. But you just go ahead with your complaint, Senator, and I'll carry out my duty.'

Connolly glared at Aaron for a long time before saying, 'Damn you, Marshal, I'll report your insolent manner to the Attorney-General and have your badge for this. What did you say your name is?'

'I didn't, but it's Marshal Aaron Berryman — and I don't think you will find the Attorney General accommodating. I've been appointed direct by President Ulysses S. Grant to come West and let it be known that United States law doesn't stop at the Mississippi. Any complaint from you will only remind him that the river gang we took on yesterday had been operating in the vicinity of your State without hindrance, or any action from you, for longer than a year. He might feel it time for changes to be made in order to deal with lawlessness in States along the river.'

The mention of Aaron's name had filled Senator Connolly with dismay. He was aware that Aaron had served with the United States President during the late Civil War and that the two men were close friends.

He was also aware of Aaron's formidable reputation as a Peace Officer. He realized he had chosen to lock horns with a man who probably had far more political power than he himself possessed.

'I'll take my son off to his cabin and see what he has to say for himself in the morning. I am not saying I am entirely satisfied with what has happened here tonight, but I would not question your integrity, Marshal Berryman. I'll bid you good night.'

8

⁂

When Connolly had taken his son from the gambling saloon, Wes thanked Aaron for his intervention with the Louisiana Senator, but the US Marshal made light of it.

'I expected no more and no less from Connolly,' he said. 'He's one of the most pompous men in the Senate, also one of the most insecure — and he knows it. I doubt if he's ever made a decision or put forward an original idea since the day he was elected. He bends with the wind, always chasing popularity . . . but it's something he has never managed to achieve. President Grant would be pleased to have him out, but by doing nothing Connolly makes no mistakes. He knows I am close to Grant so he'll not do anything that might upset me.'

Wes realized, not for the first time, that chance had thrown him into friendship with a very special man who had a great many influential friends.

'Would you really have shot the Senator's son had he managed to draw his gun?' He asked.

'Would you have been likely to die had he shoved the gun in your ribs and pulled the trigger?' Aaron responded. Not waiting for a reply he added, 'There's someone coming across who you'll enjoy talking to far more than to me.

I'll speak to you later about the need to keep a gun on you at all times now you're heading out West.'

Turning his head, Wes saw Anabelita heading towards them and Aaron nodded an acknowledgement to her as he made his way back to the seat he had been occupying before trouble broke out in the saloon.

When she reached Wes, Anabelita smiled at him and said, 'I want to thank you for coming to my aid just now, but I am sorry to have put your life in danger as a result.'

'It was no fault of yours,' Wes replied, aware that Anabelita was even more attractive close to than she had appeared at a distance, 'but I might not have been quite so brave had I known he was carrying a gun.'

'I do not believe that,' Anabelita replied, 'but I would not have allowed him to play at my table had *I* known. Guns are strictly forbidden in the gambling saloon.'

'Does that rule apply to croupiers too?' Wes asked, with apparent innocence.

Anabelita looked at him uncertainly for a few minutes then, with a faint hint of embarrassment, she replied, 'I think Lola has been saying far more to you than she should.'

'Perhaps,' Wes agreed, 'but, as a matter of interest, have you ever needed to make use of such a . . . deterrent?'

'Once or twice,' Anabelita admitted, ' . . . but never while I have been working.'

As Wes digested this confession, Anabelita said, 'I really am very grateful to you . . . may I call you Wes? The young man was hurting my arm very much. Had he continued to twist it for a few more minutes it is likely I would not have been able to deal cards comfortably for a few days. As it is . . . I will take the rest of tonight off. By tomorrow I will be fit and well once more.'

At that moment there was an outburst of sound from the crowd about the roulette table as a number came up on which one of the players had placed a large sum of money.

'It's noisy in here. When I'm working I don't notice it, but it's difficult to have any sort of conversation . . . shall we go outside — that's if you are quite happy to talk with me . . . but perhaps you would rather I didn't bother you?'

'You're certainly not bothering me,' Wes assured her, hurriedly, 'In fact I feel privileged to have your company all to myself — but let me buy drinks and we can take them out to the rear deck space with us.'

'Taking drinks is a great idea,' Anabelita agreed, 'but you won't need to buy them. After what you have done tonight you will not need to pay for any more drinks while you are on board the *Missouri Belle*.'

It would appear that someone had already briefed the bartender in the saloon. Pouring generous quantities of bourbon into two glasses, he passed them across the bar to Wes, explaining, 'These come with the compliments of the company, sir. We all appreciate what you did for Anabelita. She's very popular with all of us. Despite the complaint by the Senator's son, she doesn't have a dishonest bone in her body.'

'Thanks, I'll tell her what you've said about her. She'll be well-pleased.'

Anabelita had chosen to sit in an open-sided deck-space behind the saloon. Above it was the top deck of the paddle-steamer, where the pilots' house was situated.

The only light here came from the night sky, through the open sides. The lack of lanterns was intended to deter mosquitoes and other night insects that might otherwise be attracted to them.

Anabelita was waiting for him in one of two comfortable seats placed close to the stern rail. Here, noises from the saloon and the tinkling of an out of tune piano being played on another deck of the vessel were lost in the sound made by the paddle-wheel at the stern of the *Missouri Belle* as it thrashed the muddy waters of the river into a foaming wake.

There were possibly a half-dozen others sharing the deck space, but their features were lost in the darkness, their conversations impossible to be heard.

Placing a drink in Anabelita's hand, Wes warned her, 'I don't know how used you are to hard liquor, but I should take it easy with this one. The bartender is obviously a fan of yours, he's given us both enough to floor anyone not too used to drinking.'

Her teeth showing white in the darkness, Anabelita replied, 'That will be Frank. He takes a fatherly interest in me — as he did with the girl from whom Lola took over as a croupier. Sometimes, if it was quiet out here when we closed the tables the three of us would sit here for a while to slow down — and watch the sun come up if it had been a particularly long night.'

'How did you come to be gambling on a riverboat in the first place?' Wes asked. It was more to make conversation than for any other reason. Lola had already told him how Anabelita's career had begun.

'That's a very good question,' she replied ruefully. 'As a young girl I thought I was going to be a schoolteacher. At least, that's what my mother always told me. She was teaching in a Mexican school in California when she and my pa met up.'

'I believe your pa was already a gambler then?'

There was just enough light for Wes to see her head jerk up in surprise at his question. Then Anabelita asked, 'Was it Lola who told you about my pa being a gambling man?'

'Yes, she's been wanting to introduce you and me ever since we boarded the boat. She's really taken with you.'

'Lola is a nice person,' Anabelita commented. 'All she ever needed from life was to be given a break. She has it now and I believe she'll make the most of it ... but to get back to your question, yes, my pa was a gambler all his life. He knew every gambling trick in the book — and a few more he had thought up for himself. Yet, in the main, he was honest. He taught me that it isn't necessary to cheat. By studying the way a man plays his cards for a couple of hands it is possible to learn enough about him to beat him nine hands out of ten.

Those odds were good enough for him and they are good enough for me too.'

'You still haven't told me why *you're* gambling on a riverboat instead of teaching school in California,' Wes pointed out.

There was a long pause before Anabelita said, 'When I was sixteen my ma died and it hit pa hard. It took him a couple of years to recover, by which time we had lost just about everything, so he began travelling — and took me with him. When we found a respectable town I would join in a card game or two, but we would never stay long. Folk don't take to gamblers especially successful ones. Besides, most money was to be made in and around mining towns, where it was 'easy come, easy go'. Unfortunately, saloons in mining towns aren't the sort of places frequented by 'nice' young women, especially women who like nothing better than to sit down at a table with a pack of cards, taking money from men like the Senator's son you took care of for me tonight. The result was that pa eventually took me off to stay with one of his sisters who ran a respectable boarding-house in St Louis, but I didn't stay there for long.'

When Anabelita fell silent, Wes prompted, 'Where's your pa now?'

'He's gone to join my mother.'

From something in her voice, Wes felt he was about to hear something she was not in the habit of talking about very often. He was right.

'Pa died a while ago, shot after an argument in a gambling saloon in a small town in Texas. He didn't carry a gun.'

'I'm sorry,' Wes said sympathetically. 'That must have hit you very hard.'

'It did, but it was only the beginning of my troubles . . .'

Pausing to down a deep swig of her drink, Anabelita continued, 'My aunt was a pillar of her local church who had never approved of the fact that my mother was a Mexican Catholic. When she found me playing cards for money with some of her boarders she made the men involved move out of the house and find somewhere else to board. By then the money my pa had been giving her for my board and keep had run out, so she told me to leave too. I think that was the happiest day of her life.'

Wes detected the bitterness in her voice and was almost afraid to put his next question to her because he was not sure he wanted to hear her answer. Nevertheless, he asked, 'What did you do then?'

'One of the men who stayed at my aunt's house whenever he was in St Louis was a Mississippi river pilot. He was one of those I would play cards with. He told me about the gambling saloons on boats like this one and said the riverboat companies were always looking for young women to act as croupiers. I approached the steamboat company, told them what he had said and who he was, and they took me on for a trial onboard the *Missouri Belle*. I've been here ever since.'

'Well, you're obviously a great success,' Wes said, 'That can be seen by the number of men who prefer playing at your table to any of the others . . . but where do you go from here, Anabelita? How do you see your future?'

'None of us can predict the future, Wes,' Anabelita replied, 'Right now I am working at something I know and enjoy . . . at least, I do for most of the time. I also have free board and lodging, earn commission on the money I take at the tables and am able to save more than I could by working anywhere else. I don't think beyond that . . . but my drink has just about gone and yours must be too. Let me go and fetch you another.'

'No, you stay here and enjoy having nothing to do. I'll go and get them . . . '

9

When Wes woke the following morning the cabin was in darkness, although it was apparent from the curtained window that it was daylight outside.

His head felt heavy, his temples were throbbing and it took him some minutes to gather his befuddled thoughts together and realize that part of his disorientation came from the fact that he was not in his own cabin. He became aware at the same time that he was not alone in the bunk.

The body beside him stirred and the faint aroma of perfume brought memories of the events of the previous evening flooding back to him.

At that moment his sleeping partner galvanized into life. Sitting up abruptly, Anabelita groaned before saying, 'This was not meant to happen!'

The bunk was hardly the size of a single bed and as Wes struggled to sit up too he was aware that his sleeping partner was wearing no more clothes than was he.

Embarrassed, he said, 'I . . . I'm sorry, it must have been the drink.'

'Thank you very much!' Anabelita said, indignantly, 'You certainly know how to make a woman feel better about giving her all to a man.'

'I didn't mean it to sound like that . . . ' Wes was floundering and he knew it, 'I'm just . . . I'm trying to say 'sorry', that's all.'

'Is that supposed to make me feel better? Just what exactly are you sorry about?'

'Well . . . for forcing myself upon you, I suppose.'

Falling backwards to lie with her head upon the pillow once more, Anabelita said, 'If I quoted that in a courtroom do you think they would accept it as an admission of rape?'

He realized — or hoped he did — that she was teasing him now and he responded accordingly. 'I can't imagine a judge and jury of healthy, virile men taking my word against yours, so if that's what you intend doing I'd best be heading back to my cabin and getting ready to leave the *Missouri Belle* at its next call, which should be any time now.'

As he was speaking he had swung his legs out of the bunk with the bed-sheet concealing the lower half of his body. In the dim light from the curtained window he could see his clothes. Some were on a chair beside the dressing-table, others being strewn on the floor nearby.

There was no way he could recover them whilst still retaining a degree of modesty. He had just decided that modesty was a lost cause anyway, when Anabelita said, 'Are you really sorry you made love to me?'

Momentarily taken aback by the question, Wes hesitated before asking, 'Can I be perfectly honest with you?'

80

'I would prefer it if you were.'

Despite her words, Anabelita sounded uncertain and Wes felt his reply was of some importance to her.

'No, Anabelita, I'm not sorry for what we did together — and I never will be, whatever happens in the future — but I will feel guilty if you regret what happened.'

'So it *wasn't* just because you had too much to drink,' she persisted.

'No . . . but the drink did give me the courage I needed to make the first move.'

'I don't believe that! You are not lacking in courage in anything. The fight with the river pirates and the way you dealt with the Senator's son is proof of that, but if that's what you think you need, I'll make sure there is always a bottle of bourbon here, in my cabin . . . '

At that moment their conversation was interrupted by a long blast on the riverboat's steam-whistle. It was followed by a succession of shorter blasts.

'We must be approaching Memphis,' Wes said. Forsaking all modesty now, he relinquished the bed-sheet, made a dive for his clothes and hurriedly began to dress.

'What's the hurry?' Anabelita asked the question as she sat up in the bunk and watched him dressing, unabashed by the fact that she was naked from the waist up, 'You are not leaving the boat at Memphis.'

'No, but a US Marshal from Arkansas, across the river is going to be there to speak to Aaron — and he wants me to meet up with him.'

81

'Why?'

Wes was almost fully dressed now and aware of her own nakedness, Anabelita pulled the cotton sheet up about her breasts as she waited for his reply.

'Aaron believes the marshal might be able to help me find work, or at least tell me what's happening on the mines in Missouri, where I'm heading. I believe Arkansas has a border with that State.'

'It's more likely that Aaron is hoping this marshal will help him persuade you to become a deputy Federal Marshal,' Anabelita said. 'He thinks you would make a good lawman . . . and so do I. You're not a killer as many so-called lawmen are, and you can deal with difficult men — as you proved last night.'

Pulling on his boots to complete his dress, Wes glanced up to give Anabelita an arch look, 'Ah . . . but I don't suppose I could expect a similar reward every time I did something like that.'

His remark failed to provoke a response in a similar vein. Her eyes widened in disbelief and she demanded angrily, 'Is that why you think I let you make love to me? As a reward? Do you honestly believe I have so little regard for my body — and my self-esteem — that I would offer it to anyone who does something for me? Is that what you think?'

Aware that his unthinking and tasteless joke had not been well-received, Aaron said hurriedly, 'Of course not it was meant to be a joke, but it wasn't in very good taste. I'm sorry . . . I truly am.'

She was only partially mollified but just then the *Missouri Belle*'s whistle emitted another discordant and ear-splitting shriek and the riverboat slowed noticeably.

Hurriedly jumping to his feet, Wes said, 'I really must go now, Anabelita. As soon as we get underway again I'd like to have a chat with you . . . about us. You and me.'

'You mean . . . you want to give me another opportunity to show how grateful I am to you.'

Looking pained, Wes replied, 'It meant a lot more than that to me, Anabelita — and so do you, I think you know that. But I really must go now.'

He could hear members of the riverboat's crew shouting and indistinct distant replies. Hurriedly crossing the cabin floor to where she was sitting up in the bunk, he kissed her.

The kiss lingered for longer than he had intended, but a renewed outbreak of shouting from outside caused him to straighten up.

Looking down at her he said, 'I'm a very lucky man, Anabelita. I would like to stay that way.'

Hurrying to the cabin door, he opened it — and was gone.

Behind him, Anabelita sank back on the pillow. When she thought of what Wes had said, and what had happened between them she smiled . . . and it was a contented smile.

10

Once outside Anabelita's cabin, Wes discovered that the sounds he had thought to be the *Missouri Belle*'s berthing signals were, in fact, a precursor to the altercation now taking place between the riverboat's crew and the occupants of a keelboat.

A large and unwieldy craft, the keelboat was manned by men who Wes thought were even rougher-looking than Bodmin Moor tin-miners. Their vessel was being manoeuvred into a berth adjacent to that used by the riverboats and a great deal of muscle-power — and a string of ear-scorching oaths — accompanied the efforts of its ragged crew.

Wes decided to make use of the respite it offered. Hurrying to his cabin, he cleaned up and changed his clothes before returning to the deck.

A great many of the steamboat's passengers were lining the rails and watching the continuing saga of the keelboat with varying degrees of partisanship and Wes saw Aaron leaning on the rails among them.

As he made his way towards his friend someone stepped into his path and Wes recognized the young man with whom he had tangled in the saloon.

He stopped, anticipating trouble, but there was no aggression in the other man's demeanour this morning.

Aware of Wes's apprehension, the Senator's son said, 'It's all right, sir, I am not out to cause trouble. I think I did enough of that last night. My name is David Connolly and I have been looking for you in order to apologise before leaving the boat at Memphis.'

'That's fine with me,' Wes replied, 'but I don't think I'm the one you should be apologising to. It was the dealer you accused of cheating — and whose arm you were hurting.'

A contrite expression crossed the young man's face. 'I am aware of that, sir, and I am deeply sorry. It was my twenty-first birthday last week and my father took me visiting friends and relatives along the river, with the intention of making a man of me — or so he said. If by that he meant drinking myself silly every night, I guess he succeeded. Unfortunately, it didn't end there. On the way back we stopped at Vicksburg, where an uncle is with the garrison and a party was thrown for me. I had a great deal to drink and carried on when we came aboard. I know that's no excuse for my behaviour but it's the best I can do . . . and it's the truth.'

Wes believed the young man was being honest and felt genuinely ashamed of the way he had behaved in the gambling saloon. Relaxing, he said, 'Well . . . I think you might have learned there's more to becoming a man than pouring strong drink down your throat.'

'I have, sir . . . and I thank you for not

shooting me when I tried to pull a gun on you.'

Wes smiled at the young man, 'Fortunately for you I don't carry a gun, but I accept your apology and, for what it's worth, I think you're more of a man because of it.'

'Thank you, sir, I would like to shake your hand, but before I do perhaps I could ask you to give this to the woman who was dealing cards at the table?'

Handing Wes a sealed envelope, he explained, 'I've been looking around the boat for her this morning but couldn't find her. My father and me are leaving the boat at Memphis but I didn't think it would be a good idea to ask any of the crew which cabin she is in, so I wrote a note of apology. I would be obliged if you could give it to her.'

'Of course,' Wes took the envelope and slid it into a pocket.

The two men shook hands and David Connolly said, 'It looks as though we're going in now. I'd better go to my cabin and make certain everything's ready to be taken off.'

Only when the young man had hurried away did Wes realize that Aaron had moved towards him and was standing nearby, his coat unbuttoned. Wes had become sufficiently acquainted with the ways of the West to realize this would have given the US Marshal rapid access to his revolver, had it been required.

'You okay?' Aaron asked.

'I'm fine. I just had a handsome apology from the Senator's son and I think it was genuine. When I said he should be apologising to

Anabelita he said he'd tried but couldn't find her.'

Patting the pocket that held the envelope given to him by David Connolly, he added, 'He wrote an apology and asked me to give it to her.'

Aaron nodded, 'You'd better take it up to her now, there's time before we berth and you don't want to risk losing it when we go ashore . . . you know where to find her.'

When Wes looked startled, Aaron said, 'I went to our cabin before coming down here and saw your bunk hadn't been slept in. I hope this is the only apology you'll need to hand to her by the time we reach Saint Louis.'

Before Wes could express the indignation he felt at his friend's words, Aaron said, 'She's not like Lola, Wes. Anabelita is basically a good girl — and it was Lola herself who told me that. It's a rare attribute in her business and you could hurt her far more than young Connolly did.'

Biting back a retort that what he did was none of the marshal's business, Wes said, 'I'll bear that in mind . . . and talking of young Connolly, it looks as though his father is heading this way to have words with you, so I'll be off to deliver Anabelita's letter.'

When Senator Connolly reached Aaron, he frowned in the direction of the hastily departing Wes and said, 'I was hoping to have a word with your friend . . . '

'If it's something important I'll call him back for you, Senator. If not I'll be happy to pass on any message to him.'

'No, it's you I *really* want to speak to. Do you

intend taking the matter of my son's foolish escapade any further?'

Feigning surprise, Aaron said, 'Has something happened involving him, Senator? You'll have to tell me about it sometime, I don't remember a thing.'

Senator Connolly stared at Aaron uncertainly for a few moments before saying, 'I hope you mean that, Marshal Berryman. I don't think the Attorney General would approve of the type of female company kept by one of his most respected Marshals ... if he were to be told about it.'

'Is that so, Senator?' A hard expression had come to Aaron's face, although only someone who knew him well would have recognized signs of the anger that had welled up inside him. 'Do you know, you've just helped me remember what it was that happened last night. As for the Attorney General ... the last time you spoke of him to me I forgot to mention that he and I were young officers together in the Military Academy. There's not much we don't know about each other and when we get together we enjoy a chat over a drink or two about the changing habits of young men today and agree that a little army discipline might do some of them a power of good. Sometimes we're fortunate enough to have the company of the President, who is of the opinion that more often than not it's the *parents* who are to blame when a promising young man's behaviour leaves something to be desired. We all agree that some parents just aren't worth a damn! Now, if you'll excuse me, I need to go ashore to meet someone . . . someone important.'

Aaron had seen Wes heading towards him once more. The gangway had been half-lowered in readiness for berthing and, turning his back on the Louisiana Senator, Aaron went to meet him.

'Did you deliver young Connolly's apology?' He asked.

Wes shook his head, 'I think she must have gone to the washroom. I'll give it to her when we come back on board.'

Inclining his head in the direction of the departing Senator, he said, 'We both seem popular with the Connolly family this morning. Was he apologising for his son too?'

'Quite the reverse!' Aaron said, 'Senator Connolly believes in the divine right of politicians to substitute threats for apologies. I hope young Connolly grows up to be his own man — and not his father's.'

11

❧

United States Marshal Heck McKinnon was a man of about fifty years of age with a bushy, greying moustache, and his frame carried twice the bulk of Aaron Berryman. Unlike most US Marshals, he wore cowboy clothes, his gleaming marshal's badge pinned to a fringed buckskin waistcoat. He also carried two revolvers in open holsters, one on each hip.

His actions when he saw Aaron about to step onto the gangway which now linked the *Missouri Belle* to the land were as flamboyant as his appearance, bellowing a greeting that pained the eardrums of those standing closest to him.

Using his considerable weight to carve a passage through the crowd separating him from the steamboat, he reached Aaron as he stepped ashore and enfolded him in a bear hug that caused the watching Wes to wince.

Aaron merely grinned. Escaping from the embrace, he grasped the big man's hand, saying, 'Glad to see you haven't changed since we last met, Heck, and you're looking well but I'd like you to meet a friend of mine from Cornwall, in England. He was my right-hand man when we dealt with the river pirates downriver from Vicksburg.'

'We've heard all about it up here,' Heck

McKinnon said, reaching out a large hand to Wes, 'It was a reckoning that was long overdue — and by all accounts you made a good job of it. I'm pleased to meet you boy . . . and to know Aaron has someone to keep an eye on him. He's inclined to jump into things convinced The Almighty is in there on his side. So far He has been, but I'm scared that one day when he's needed The Almighty's going to be busy elsewhere.'

'Unfortunately, Wes won't let me pin a badge on him,' Aaron said, 'He's set on going mining somewhere around Harmony, up Missouri way.'

Heck McKinnon frowned, 'That's not a good idea right now. I've been called up there a couple of times to help out the Missouri deputies. The miners are mostly German and have got themselves a Union that's hell-bent on getting more money from mine owners. The owners are having none of it and are laying off the Germans and bringing in men from outside, mostly English and Welsh. It's causing a lot of trouble. There have been three murders in the last month alone, and everyone's lost count of the shootings, stabbings and brawls. If you take my advice you'll stay clear of the Harmony area, Wes. If you're serious about mining I'd suggest you head farther west — to Colorado territory, perhaps, but only if you're as handy with a gun as Aaron says you are. I was up there a few weeks ago, arresting a no-good Dutchman from Arkansas who'd murdered his family before heading West. Just about every other miner who's there claims to be from Cornwall. They're taking out a sizeable amount of gold — although most lose it again in Denver before they can put it to good use. There's money to be made there sure enough, but those who strike it rich need to be able to take care of themselves. With no law to speak of it's a case of 'every man for himself'.'

'I'll remember what you've said,' Wes replied, 'but an uncle of mine is at Harmony and expecting me to come out and join him, so I need to go there before I make any more plans.'

'We'll discuss it some more on the way to St Louis,' Aaron promised, 'right now, me and Heck have things to talk about . . . '

* * *

Wes was making his way towards the gangway of the *Missouri Belle*, when a way was cleared by the dockside officials for Senator Connolly and his son who were disembarking followed by half-a dozen ship's porters bearing heavy portmanteaus on their shoulders.

David Connolly saw Aaron and briefly raised a hand to chest height in a tentative gesture of acknowledgement.

Nearby, Marshal McKinnon saw the Senator and said wryly to Aaron, 'You've been travelling in exalted company — and Connolly would be the first to tell you so.'

'He did,' Aaron replied, 'At least, he tried, when Wes had occasion to put his boy right on a small matter of etiquette, but two can play that game. I pulled the 'I'm a friend of the President' line on him and he crawled back into his hole.'

'I've never met his son,' Heck McKinnon admitted, 'Does he take after his old man?'

'No, I think he shows promise. Wes thinks so too and he's had more to do with him than me.'

'I'm pleased to hear it,' McKinnon replied, 'but I wouldn't trust Senator Connolly any farther than I could throw him. He was a Confederate supporter when the war began, but switched his allegiance at just the right moment. As a result he not only managed to keep his own fine house and lands, but buy up those of his less fortunate neighbours. My deputies tell me he's rumoured to be sympathetic towards a band of hooligans calling themselves the *Klu Klux Klan* who go around whipping and killing freedmen ... but let's forget about Senator Connolly, we've more interesting things to talk about. I believe you're on your way West to take over as Marshal for the Territories, but stopping off at Kansas City first? Kansas City's a lively place, sure enough, but big business it taking over now they have the stockyards up and running well. The real action is taking place farther west. Cowboys are still raising hell in Abilene, Dodge and Wichita and, as I told Wes, there's money to be made in the mining camps of Colorado, with very little law to speak of.'

'That's pretty much what I've heard — and so has the President, but, although I'm likely to keep an office in Kansas City, at least for a while, I've been given a roving commission so that when I return to Washington I'll be able to give the President a personal assessment of what needs to be done to bring law and order to the

Territories — especially to Colorado. He's concerned about what's going on out that way.'

'He's every reason to be,' Marshal McKinnon agreed, 'but unless he's willing to get the army involved I can't see things changing very much. I've needed to go to Colorado Territory and Indian Country myself on occasions and they're not the most comfortable places for a lawman. Half the outlaws in the United States seem to have moved West — and to most a badge is just something to shoot at. Anyone trying to take a prisoner and bring him East needs a whole parcel of men to back him.'

'I don't plan on taking too many prisoners,' Aaron replied, 'I'm coming to look at what needs to be done. I also have one or two business ventures in mind that should keep me amused while I'm doing it.'

'So you said in your letter,' Heck McKinnon said, 'and I've looked into the prospects, like you asked me. Now, if it was me setting something up to get rich quick, I'd be looking at Colorado Territory — but I'd go no farther than Denver. West of there they'd rather shoot lawmen than bobcats. Even Denver itself isn't too healthy, the mayor and council are about as straight as the Mississippi — and a sight more dangerous.'

Aaron smiled at his fellow Marshal's assessment of life in Colorado, 'I'm not out to get rich quick, Heck. I'll be happy just to make something to add to my pension when I hand in my badge.'

'That's what I hoped you might say,' Heck McKinnon said unexpectedly, 'because I think I might have found something to interest you not too far from Kansas City. I was up that way a couple of weeks ago when I heard that Henry Scobell, owner of the Golden Gate gambling saloon in Abilene had died in a shootout. Abilene is just down the line from Kansas City and I went there to see his widow. She ran a bordello in St Louis before she married Henry and I've known her for some years. She told me she was putting the Golden Globe up for sale and heading East to find out what living like a lady is all about. She's in no hurry to sell, so I suggest you look in on her and perhaps make her an offer. The Golden Globe got itself a bad name when Henry was running the place so she's not expecting to make a fortune from selling up, but I had a look around — and was impressed. It's got a hell of a lot of potential, Aaron. If word gets around that it's you who's bought it and are running honest games, cattlemen and cowboys bringing cattle in from Texas for railroading to Kansas City will flock there — and they have good money to spend.'

While Aaron was thinking about what his friend had told him, Heck McKinnon added, 'What's more, I know two good men who would be happy to take on the job of keeping order in the place for you. One is an ex-sheriff and Texas Ranger, who's recently retired. The other's an ex-deputy United States Marshal, Pete Rafferty. He lost an arm in a fight with a gang in Indian Territory, but, one arm or not, he's a deadly shot with a rifle. They're both good men who would enjoy looking after things for US Marshal

95

Berryman in an honest establishment.'

When Aaron still said nothing, Heck McKinnon added, 'Find yourself a good manager and some honest croupiers and you could have your own little gold mine right there in Abilene, Aaron.'

'You could be right, Heck,' Aaron said, at last. 'If you are then I owe you in a big way. As for the honest croupiers . . . I think I might already have found them. I've dropped a hint or two about my plans to them, all I need do now is persuade *them* it's what they want.'

12

The *Missouri Belle* was a hive of activity when Wes made his way back on board. Freight and passengers leaving the boat were dodging incoming passengers and cargo being taken onboard, bound for St Louis.

It seemed that everyone and everything was on the move and Wes was relieved to reach the comparative calm of the deck where Anabelita had her cabin.

When she opened the door to his knock her thick black hair was glistening wet and it was evident she had just come from the shower room reserved for women passengers and croupiers.

She invited him into the cabin but he was disappointed to find Lola here too. A tray of coffee held only two cups but he was grateful to accept coffee in a glass.

Taking the envelope from his pocket, Wes handed it to Anabelita, explaining that it came from David Connolly and repeating what the Senator's son had said to him.

Pleasantly surprised, Anabelita said, 'Well, he's not the first man to give me trouble on board after drinking too much, but he's the first to say he's sorry the following day.'

She tore open the envelope which contained a single sheet of notepaper and, as she removed it, something fluttered to the floor.

Lola stooped to pick it up and, holding it up for the others to see, said, 'Hey! Why doesn't anybody ever apologise to me like this?'

She was holding up a hundred dollar note!

Astounded, Anabelita said, 'I can't accept that sort of money . . . he must have made a mistake!'

'You can't give it back to him,' Wes said, 'He and his father were among the first off the boat. They are long gone by now.'

'What does he say in the letter?' Lola asked.

Hurriedly scanning the writing on the single sheet of notepaper, Anabelita dropped her hands to her sides and said, 'It's no mistake, that's what he meant to give me — and there is a handsome apology to go with it.'

'He apologized to me too,' Wes said. 'When he's sober I think he's a good youngster — and he admitted he's not used to strong drink. He's just celebrated his birthday and his father took him on a trip to 'make a man of him'.'

'I could have introduced him to young women in New Orleans who would have done that without him touching a drop of liquor,' Lola commented, 'It wouldn't have cost him a hundred bucks either, but Senator Connolly's idea of what makes a man wouldn't be the same as that of a real man. Aaron despises him . . . where is he, by the way?'

'He went ashore to meet an old friend to discuss some business he's thinking of buying into. I'd better go outside on deck to make sure the boat doesn't leave without him, we don't seem to stay anywhere for a minute longer than is absolutely necessary.'

In truth, Wes felt inexplicably discomfited by the presence of Lola in the cabin he had shared with Anabelita the previous night. The feeling was tinged with an unreasonable resentment too. Unused to such intimacy as he had shared with Anabelita, he had wanted to speak to her alone, in order to clarify the relationship between them — if, indeed there was to be a relationship — and he fervently hoped there would be.

When he had left the cabin, Anabelita asked Lola, 'What sort of business would Marshal Berryman be thinking of going into?'

'He'd like to have a gaming house — an honest one — probably in Kansas City. A great many new businesses are springing up and a lot of money changing hands there.'

'I think he's too late to make money that way — at least, he is in Kansas City, it's been taken over by business men and they are out to make money, not spend it. It's the cowboys and cattlemen at the end of a long cattle drive from Texas who are in a hurry to get rid of their earnings in saloons, bordellos and gambling houses and they are to be found in the railhead towns, farther west.'

'Well . . . wherever, I've no doubt this friend will put him in the picture, he's a United States Marshal, same as Aaron.'

Something in Lola's manner made Anabelita ask, 'Has he asked you to go and work there for him?'

Just for a moment Lola hesitated, then, remembering that it was Anabelita who had obtained work for her as a croupier on the *Missouri Belle*, she decided she owed her the truth.

'He said he'd like me to go and work for him when he found the right place,' she admitted, 'but not as a whore. Aaron doesn't want any of that going on in any place he owns. He'd like to take on girl croupiers because they attract the men but while they work for him he says they'll deal cards and nothing else. I'd sort of manage the place for him.'

'There's a whole lot more to managing a gambling house than keeping croupiers in line,' Anabelita pointed out. 'Would you recognize a 'pasteboard pirate' or his 'capper' if you saw them working the tables?'

When Lola looked blank, Anabelita said, 'I am talking of crooked gamblers and their sidekicks. Where there's money being laid down you'll find them gathering like dogs around a bitch on heat — and trouble follows them just as surely as night follows day.'

Suddenly looking unhappy, Lola said, 'I've spent enough time in saloons to know when a drinking man is likely to be trouble, but I'm not sure I'd recognize a professional gambler.'

'You certainly wouldn't if he didn't want you to,' Anabelita agreed, 'and it's not something I could teach you in a few days — or even a few months. It comes with experience.'

After a long and thoughtful silence, Lola said hesitantly, 'Would you consider coming with me to work for Aaron, Anabelita?'

'I'm happy working on the *Missouri Belle*,'

Anabelita replied, 'I have free board and lodging and earn enough cash to be able to put some by. I'm a gambler — and I'm on a winning streak right now. Why should I want to throw it away?'

'I'm sure Aaron would make it well worth your while,' Lola replied, 'Will you at least think about it?'

Anabelita shook her head, 'There's nothing to think about. Aaron Berryman is a United States Marshal, first and foremost. Owning a gambling saloon is just something to earn him money while he's out this way. One day he'll go back East and sell up. What would I do then? Come to that, what will *you* do?'

'I'll worry about that when it happens,' Lola replied. 'In the meantime I will have done something for the first time in many years that I have no need to be ashamed of.'

'I don't have very much to be ashamed of in my life,' Anabelita said, 'and I'd like it to stay that way.' A sudden thought struck her and she asked, 'Is Wes involved in this with Aaron?'

Lola shook her head, 'No, but I think Aaron would like him to be. Would it make any difference to your decision if he was?'

'No.'

The answer was far more positive than Anabelita's thinking on the subject, but she was reassured to know that Wes's attentions to her had nothing to do with the plans of Marshal Aaron Berryman.

13

Wes had assumed he would be sharing Anabelita's cabin with her for the remainder of his nights on board the *Missouri Belle*. The assumption was dispelled that evening when they were enjoying a pre-dinner drink on the open-sided deck behind the saloon.

They were waiting for Aaron and Lola to join them when Wes broached the subject.

'Shall I stay in the saloon until gambling ends tonight, Anabelita . . . ? Or would you rather I waited in your cabin for you? Perhaps that would be more discreet.'

Giving him a direct look, she replied, 'I think you are taking a little too much for granted.'

'But . . . I thought . . . ' Floundering, Wes stopped, unable to express in words just what it was he was thinking.

Anabelita's next words dispelled any doubts he might have on the subject.

'You thought that because we slept together last night we would do the same until the *Missouri Belle* reached St Louis, when you would say 'goodbye', walk off the boat wearing a smug smile — then forget all about me?'

'I wouldn't put it like that, Anabelita. I don't think I could forget you, even if I wanted to — and I don't.'

'You will,' Anabelita said, as matter-of-factly as she could manage, then, aware he was both hurt and puzzled, she added, 'Look, Wes, what happened last night was as much of my making as it was yours. I suppose I was half hoping it would happen anyway, and the drinks did the rest. I don't regret it, but I am not a Lola, Wes, much as I like her. I can't continue to do what we did knowing it means nothing and will only last for the few days before we reach St Louis when you'll go your way and I'll go mine. We will probably never see each other again.'

Aware that Anabelita was being painfully honest, Wes wanted to tell her she was wrong. That she really did mean something to him — but he could not.

He was certainly fond of her . . . *very* fond, but he had come halfway across the world with a specific goal in mind. Something he had thought long and hard about before reaching the decision to leave Cornwall and change his life forever.

Much as he liked Anabelita, he was not ready to abandon all the plans he had made, on the strength of a one night stand.

'I suppose you're right,' he said, lamely.

'Thank you for understanding, Wes.'

In spite of her words and the fact that it had been her decision not to share her bunk with him for the remainder of the river voyage to St Louis, Anabelita felt deep disappointment that he had accepted the situation so readily. She had been attracted to Wes from the moment she had first seen him in the company of Aaron and the attraction had grown as she came to know him better.

She had nursed a forlorn hope that, somehow, their brief, albeit passionate night together might have developed into something more permanent — but it was too much to hope for. Wes was heading for the mines of Missouri, while she had a comfortable and not too onerous way of life on board the *Missouri Belle*. It had given her the security she sorely needed after so many years of uncertainty. She would not give it up easily.

'I hope it won't mean that you'll be avoiding my company for the remainder of the journey to St Louis,' Anabelita said.

Wes made his way from her cabin, murmuring words to the effect that he would enjoy her company as often as she felt in need of it and Anabelita was left alone, trying unsuccessfully to convince herself she had made the right decision about their relationship.

★ ★ ★

Only three days after her conversation with Wes, an event occurred which threw Anabelita's plans for an ordered and secure future to the winds.

It happened shortly before dawn, just as the *Missouri Belle* entered a stretch of river that was less tortuous than that so far encountered during the long voyage from New Orleans.

Stavros, the senior Mississippi river pilot, aware that he had brought the paddle steamer safely through the most dangerous section of the great river, felt confident about handing over his duties to a less experienced pilot.

However, even had he remained in the wheelhouse it was doubtful whether either he or any other pilot on the Mississippi river could have avoided the accident that occurred.

It had long been the practice of lumberjacks working in the vast forests along the banks of the Mississippi, Missouri and Ohio rivers to make gigantic, loosely knit rafts of felled timber and float them downriver.

Crewed by hard-living and hard-drinking river-men who lived in tepees on their undulating wooden platforms, the vast rafts, often an acre or more in area, would be floated down to New Orleans, to be gathered in and the timber shipped to buyers around the world.

It was a system that worked well unless something happened to cause one of the rafts to break up — and they might expect to encounter many hazards on their long journey downriver. Heavy rain in the headwaters of the Mississippi or its many tributaries could seriously affect the speed of the current and cause changes in the river's course, adding new dangers to those who travelled the river. Conversely, drought would cause a drop in water level, bringing the river's existing hazards closer to the surface.

Whatever the cause, the break-up of a raft invariably resulted in a loss of life among the raftsmen and added new and unpredictable problems to all who used the river as a watery highway.

It was one such break-up that was met with by the *Missouri Belle*, when, in a pre-dawn encounter, it suddenly found itself in the midst of thousands of errant logs, some gyrating in the grip of the inconstant current, others passively pursuing their intended course, while a few would suddenly rear from the water like frolicking river monsters.

It was one of the latter that became entangled in the river-boat's stern wheel while its companions battered the vessel's hull.

The two ton tree trunk splintered the wooden blades of the paddlewheel into matchwood, twisting the framework into a tangled metal skein.

Within seconds the suddenly paddle-less steamer was as uncontrollable as the lumber with which it was surrounded. Powerless, it was caught by the current and, gyrating slowly was carried towards the Missouri bank of the great river.

A light sleeper, Wes was awakened by the hammering of floating tree trunks against the riverboats hull. When the log destroyed the stern-wheel it sent violent vibrations through the length of the vessel and, leaping from his bunk Wes hastily pulled on some clothes, observing as he did so that Aaron was not in his bunk.

By the time Wes flung open the cabin door and staggered outside many other passengers were also awake, frightened and bewildered.

For a while the crew of the *Missouri Belle* were equally confused as those in authority, still befuddled by sleep, shouted and countermanded orders.

Wes's immediate thoughts were of Anabelita.

She had been working in the gambling saloon and after a tiring night would have been in a deep sleep when the paddle-steamer went out of control. She was likely to be even more confused and disorientated than others on board.

He made his way to her cabin, forcing his way through an increasing number of passengers who had abandoned their own cabins and were demanding to know what was happening.

Before Wes reached Anabelita's cabin the boat came to a sudden halt, sending passengers tumbling in all directions, only to begin moving again almost immediately, with a movement resembling that of a wagon traversing slowly over the surface of a pot-holed road. At the same time the sound of splintering wood emanated from somewhere deep in the hold of the shallow-draught vessel and the cry went up that the boat had struck underwater rocks.

Anabelita was emerging from her cabin when Wes reached her and in the uncertain light from a wildly swinging lantern he could see she was hopelessly bemused. Still half-asleep, she attempted unsuccessfully to tie a bow in the cord about the waist of her dressing-gown.

Recognizing Wes in the uncertain light, she demanded, 'What's happening . . . ? What's all the noise . . . and the boat . . . ?'

'We seem to have lost power . . . I think we have struck something.'

In confirmation of his last observation, the cry went up that the boat was holed and taking in water. The result was general panic and screams were added to the general hubbub on board.

'Are we really sinking?' Although not screaming, Anabelita was quite obviously frightened.

'It's possible,' Wes replied, with a calm he did not feel, 'but if the bottom of the boat is close enough to the river bed to be holed, we aren't going to go down very far. We'll be high and dry up here. Go inside and dress properly. I'll wait and come to fetch you if it looks as though there's any immediate danger.'

Wes's calm reassurance had its effect. Anabelita turned and went back inside her cabin, leaving him feeling far less confident than he had succeeded in sounding to her. While he was talking the thought had come to him that the *Missouri Belle* might have struck a pinnacle of rock rearing to a great height from the river bed. If this were so the boat's fate — and that of its passengers — might be very different to the one he had suggested.

Fortunately, the senior pilot with his vast knowledge of the Mississippi River had emerged from his cabin to take control of the situation and by the time Anabelita re-emerged from her cabin a boat had been lowered from the stricken paddle-steamer and was heading for the shore, carrying with it an anchor chain linked via a hawse-pipe to a steam winch on board the *Missouri Belle*.

It was growing lighter now and those on board the stern-wheeler were able to watch the activity of the men on the small boat. Once on shore they struggled to carry the weighty chain to a stout oak tree standing a short distance back from the river bank.

When they reached the tree the anchor chain was passed around it and secured. Then the men stood back as the steam winch started up and the chain clattered noisily, slowing as the slack was taken up and the chain tautened.

Suddenly the steam-winch took on a different sound and it was clear to those watching that it was labouring. For some minutes it seemed that the valiant efforts of the small boat's crew would be in vain. Then, with a suddenness that took everyone on board by surprise, part of the rock piercing the riverboat's hull broke away. With a horrendous sound of splintering wood the boat began to move, a combination of current and anchor chain swinging it closer to the Missouri riverbank.

There was a great deal of water in the hold of the *Missouri Belle* by now and the deck of the hull was almost level with the surface of the river but, when some of the watchers were beginning to fear it would sink even deeper, the stricken steamboat grounded and for a few moments was drawn over a comparatively flat bed of mud and gravel.

Then with the steam-winch complaining loudly and shrilly, the order was given for it to be shut off. By now the *Missouri Belle* was close enough to the bank for the vessel to be secured and within minutes the gangway was detached from its position in the bow and put over the side to link steamboat and shore.

With the *Missouri Belle* no longer in imminent danger of going down, a great cheer went up from relieved passengers and crew.

14

⤝

Although the surrounding countryside would have appeared to the casual observer to be sparsely populated, word of the *Missouri Belle's* calamity spread rapidly. Two hours after the errant tree trunk fouled the steamboat's stern-wheel, mounted men; women and children on foot and a couple of wagons were at the scene.

Most who crowded the riverbank offered genuine help and advice, but others hoped the unexpected mishap might provide some rare luxuries to improve their otherwise stark and frugal existence.

They also provided information that the railroad built with the intention of linking Belmont with St Louis passed only two miles from where the stricken *Missouri Belle* had found its last resting place alongside the Missouri State shore.

The river had changed its course since the coming of the railway and Belmont no longer existed as a potentially important riverside town, but the railroad remained.

Two other steamboats came upon the scene and their captains, observing the precarious situation of the *Missouri Belle*, approached to offer assistance but were warned off by Pilot

Stavros, lest they suffer a similar fate if they approached too close to the underwater rocks.

It was apparent to everyone on board that the *Missouri Belle* was destined to end her days settling on the river bed where she was now berthed and during that day all but a handful of passengers took advantage of the local settlers offer of transportation to the railroad, led by the *Missouri Belle's* captain who was going to St Louis to report the accident and seek instructions from the head office of the steamboat company.

Those who chose to remain on board would enjoy free hospitality for a further twenty-four hours. The crew were instructed to stay on board until the company sent another riverboat to take off whatever cargo could be salvaged.

The accident meant that Anabelita was forced to reconsider the plans she had made for her future. After a lengthy and detailed discussion with Aaron and Lola, she agreed to throw in her lot with them and go to Abilene to take up the post of head croupier at the gambling-saloon Aaron hoped to open there, following Heck McKinnon's advice.

Although Wes was present at the discussion he was neither asked for an opinion about the change in her plans, nor did he volunteer one.

Later that afternoon when the two women had gone ashore with the other croupiers to take a wagon ride to a nearby country store, Aaron and Wes were enjoying a beer together on the open deck behind the saloon, when Aaron asked, 'Do you have any views about Anabelita coming to work for me, Wes?'

Setting his glass down and apparently intent upon watching another riverboat passing, far out in the middle of the river, Wes replied, 'What I think doesn't make any difference to anyone — especially Anabelita. She'll do whatever she wants to do anyway.'

'Do I take it from what you're not saying, that you'd have preferred her to stay working on the river? That you don't approve of her coming with me and Lola to Abilene?'

'There's nothing wrong with working for you, Aaron . . . at least, not when you're around to keep an eye on things, but you're a United States Marshal with a job to do, one that will take you away from the saloon for most of the time. I know very little about gambling but from what Anabelita has told me — and from what I've seen for myself so far — where you have a combination of gambling, drinking — and guns — you've got a sure-fire recipe for trouble and, as you've said yourself, there's no law worth mentioning beyond Missouri.'

'That's why I'm heading West, Wes, to see what needs doing to bring law and order there. As for the gambling-house I hope to open . . . I intend it to set an example of how such places should be run. Heck McKinnon has recommended two good men to help me — but I'd like to think I had a man I could trust to take charge of things while I'm away. The job is yours if you want it.'

'Thanks, Aaron but as I've said many times,

I'm a mining man, I couldn't take on a job like that.'

'You could if you put your mind to it . . . and you'd have Anabelita there too.'

Aaron had hoped that the prospect of working with the attractive croupier might persuade Wes to think seriously about his offer, but it brought only a shake of his head, 'I repeat, I'm a miner and I can't see Anabelita ever settling down to the humdrum life of a miner's wife, so anything between us is in the past.'

Aaron's eyebrows arched as he said, 'I don't think I said anything about marriage, Wes.'

'You haven't, but Anabelita has made it clear she's not interested in a relationship that's going nowhere.'

Leaning forward in his chair towards Wes, Aaron said, 'If you were working together perhaps you'd have a chance to persuade her to change her mind.'

Wes smiled, 'I'll give you top marks for persistence, Aaron, and I really am flattered by your faith in me, but . . . no thanks.'

Aaron made a gesture of resignation, 'Well, I guess you are your own man, but how much of a hurry are you in to get to the Missouri lead mining area?'

'As you say, I am my own man and I'm keen to get there and settle in but I have no time-table to work to. Why do you ask?'

'Harrison Schuster's home is only about thirty miles away, across the river. Between here and there is an army garrison. I'd like to go there before sun-up tonight and ask for a gun carriage

113

and an escort to take Harrison's body home in style, it's the least I can do for him and his family. When it's arranged I intend going with it. I wondered whether you might like to come along too?'

'How long would we be away?' Wes asked.

Aaron shrugged, 'Three or four days. Five at the most, I'd think.'

Wes nodded, 'I'll come with you. Harrison was a good man, I would like to pay my last respects to him.'

'Good, I'll set off for the garrison now.'

★   ★   ★

Anabelita and the other croupiers enjoyed their impromptu visit to the Missouri country store, followed by an additional couple of hours sampling the hospitality of one of the more affluent local farmers whose family was thrilled to have a rare opportunity to entertain a group of such 'worldly' women.

Visitors were rare in this part of the State and to entertain women who regularly travelled between such sophisticated cities as New Orleans and St Louis would be the subject of conversation for many months to come.

When the croupiers eventually returned to the *Missouri Belle*, Lola was disappointed to discover that Aaron was absent in Kentucky and would not be returning to the boat that night. Nevertheless, after dinner that evening she joined Anabelita in teaching Wes to play some of the more simple card games that formed part of their repertoire. Later, the trio moved outside to the open deck where Wes and Anabelita had sat on their first night together.

In conversation both women expressed apprehension about their futures now the *Missouri Belle* was a wreck, but agreed with Wes that they could not have wished for a more satisfactory alternative than to work for Aaron.

After a couple of drinks, Lola stood up and announced that she was going to take advantage of the opportunity that offered itself of having an early night.

When she had gone, Wes and Anabelita continued to discuss the events of the day and she asked, 'Were you already awake when the *Missouri Belle* ran into the logs?'

'No, the noise of logs crashing against the hull brought me out of my bunk and I was already putting on my clothes when they wrecked the paddle-wheel.'

'That is what must have woken me,' Anabelita said, 'but I was so confused I really had no idea what was happening. Had you not been there when I ran out of my cabin I would have been thoroughly panic-stricken.'

'I doubt that,' Wes replied, 'You aren't given to panicking.'

'Don't you believe it! I can panic with the best of them when the right occasion arises.' Smiling at him, she added, 'But I think you have a calming effect on me.'

After a few moments of silence between them, she asked, 'Why were you there, Wes . . . I mean, why did you come to my cabin?'

'I knew you would have been working until close to dawn and would probably be in a very deep sleep. Like most others on board, I believed the boat was probably going to sink. I just wanted to make certain you were all right.'

Wes tried to pass off his presence outside her cabin as no more than a friendly regard for her safety, but Anabelita realized that her well-being must have been the first thought that came into Wes's mind when he woke and realized the riverboat was in trouble.

Moved by his concern, she said, 'It was certainly a great comfort having you there to explain what was happening — and to tell me what to do.'

'I'm glad.'

Strangely tongue-tied, Wes could think of nothing to add to his two word reply, until he noticed that her glass was almost empty. Standing up quickly, he said, 'I'll go and get us more drinks . . . '

He returned a few minutes later carrying a full bottle of Bourbon, explaining, 'The bartender says that anything that's left in the bar will be pilfered by the crew of the boat that arrives to take off the cargo, so we might as well make the most of it before they arrive.'

'He can afford to be generous,' Anabelita commented, 'The captain has said he's not to charge for any more drinks. That means there will be no record of exactly how much money has been taken on the voyage upriver. It will be a very profitable trip for him . . . '

She never finished what she was saying.

116

Clapping a hand to her neck, she exclaimed, 'That's the second mosquito to attack me since we've been seated out here. It's because we are so close to the riverbank. It wasn't a problem when we were in midstream. If I stay out here I'll likely be eaten alive, I'm going to my cabin.'

Trying hard not to allow his disappoint to show, Wes said, 'Oh . . . all right. I agree, they are a problem, I've been bitten myself, but what shall I do with this . . . ?'

He held up the bottle of Bourbon he had brought from the saloon.

Aware of his disappointment, Anabelita gave him a direct look. 'Well . . . we don't want to leave it here. I suggest you bring it to my cabin with you . . . '

15

Aaron made a very early start from the Kentucky army fort the next morning and reached the *Missouri Belle* not via the cross-river ferry, but on a steam launch owned by the United States military.

His early arrival, accompanied by half-a-dozen troopers from the garrison took Wes by surprise. As a result he vacated Anabelita's cabin in haste, leaving a great many things unsaid.

There was no opportunity to rectify the omission over the breakfast table which they shared not only with Aaron and Lola, but with six troopers, who enjoyed the company of the two women quite as much as the first class meal cooked for them by the excellent chef of the ill-fated *Missouri Belle*.

The recent night he had spent with Anabelita had left Wes greatly perturbed. Their first night together had been an eager physical experience, fuelled by Bourbon and a sense of novelty.

Last night had been different, even though they had drunk almost as much as on the previous occasion. In between bouts of love-making Wes had held Anabelita close in his arms and felt a tenderness towards her that he had never before experienced with any woman.

Such a feeling disturbed him. He sensed that

Anabelita might have shared the experience and he would have liked to question her about it.

The early arrival of Aaron precluded any such discussion and once the troopers had eaten Aaron was anxious to be on his way with the body of Harrison Schuster.

A soldier had been sent to the Schuster home telling them when to expect the arrival of their son's body and Aaron wanted to reach the military post in good time to ensure that all arrangements had been made to deliver the coffin with a high degree of formal dignity.

The result was that Wes had time for no more than a brief and unsatisfactory farewell with Anabelita.

She waved him off when he departed on the steam launch with the troopers and the body of Harrison Schuster and when, accompanied by Lola, she turned and disappeared in the direction of her cabin, Aaron commented, 'You and Anabelita seem to have resolved whatever differences you had. Has she been able to persuade you to come to Abilene with us?'

Irritably, Wes replied, 'I've told you, Aaron, I am a miner. There's nothing for me in Abilene.'

They were words he had repeated on many occasions but today Aaron felt there was less conviction in Wes's voice than ever before, but he kept his thoughts to himself — for now.

On the Kentucky bank of the river the coffin carrying Harrison's body was transferred to a US army wagon and the escort retrieved their horses from their waiting colleagues.

There were extra mounts for Aaron and Wes

and, belatedly, the US Marshal queried, 'I forgot to ask you before we set out, Wes . . . can you ride a horse?'

'I can sit on a horse,' Wes replied, 'but I'm no cavalryman.'

'You'll be all right,' Aaron declared, unsympathetically, 'At least, you will be tomorrow, when Columbus is behind us. I doubt if we'll manage more than a trot on the roads we'll find from then on.'

He was unable to resist adding, 'Of course, it's always possible you'll find it more enjoyable than burrowing underground like a gopher and decide to change your mind about coming to Abilene . . . '

★ ★ ★

Wes had always taken his relationship with Aaron for granted. He was a close friend, no more — although certainly no less. The degree of deference shown to the ex-Brigadier General by the garrison officers took him aback.

When he mentioned it to Aaron later that night, as they made their way together to the comfortable quarters allocated to them by the adjutant, Aaron replied, 'It took me by surprise too, Wes. I served in a wartime army, when soldiering was far more informal — and occasionally utterly chaotic. Things are different in peacetime — although having a reasonably high rank does carry with it certain advantages. I have been able to get all I want to ensure that Harrison Schuster has the sort of funeral he deserves. I am hoping it might help build a few bridges too. Kentucky could never really make up its mind whether it was for or against the Union during the war, and the outcome has still not been fully accepted by everyone. It seems some Kentuckians have been giving our soldiers a rough time.'

'How do you think Harrison's funeral might change that?' Wes asked.

'The Schuster family are held in high esteem by those who espoused the Confederate cause,' Aaron explained, 'Harrison's father is still referred to as 'The Senator', even though he was stripped of that title when he threw in his lot with the South. His opinions carry more weight than those of the Senators who represent Kentucky today. Having him on our side would mean more than all the laws passed by Congress.'

★　★　★

The determination of Aaron to make Harrison Schuster's funeral a memorable occasion was brought home to Wes the following morning, when he made his way to the parade-ground inside the stockade that had its origins in the days when early Kentucky settlers had need of such defences. He found the coffin containing Harrison Schuster's body secured to a gun carriage, alongside which was a troop of US army cavalrymen on parade under the command of a captain. They were awaiting the arrival of Aaron before setting off on the journey to the Schuster home.

121

As Wes sat his horse, admiring the immaculately turned out cavalrymen, the captain suddenly turned his horse to face the men and barked out an order, calling on them to present their arms in salute.

It was then Wes saw Aaron riding towards the drawn-up soldiers . . . but this was not the Aaron he had known on the *Missouri Belle*, or the *Northern Star*, this was Brigadier General Aaron Berryman of the United States army!

His measurements had been taken by the garrison tailor on his earlier visit to the fort and a dress uniform owned by an officer of a similar build altered to fit him. It was now adorned with the single star insignia denoting the rank of its new wearer.

Complete with white gloves carefully folded over his belt, a brand new cavalry officer's hat obtained from the tailor's store and highly polished cavalryman's boots, Aaron was a far cry from the casually dressed and almost nondescript man Wes had first seen boarding the steamship *Northern Star* in New York.

When Aaron had conferred with the captain in charge of the large troop of mounted men, he beckoned for Wes to come and join him. Wes's first reaction was to make a fatuous remark about Aaron's dandified appearance, but the comment died on his lips. This was not the easy-going friend of his shipboard days. This was a distinguished brigadier general of the United States army. A man who commanded the respect such a rank deserved.

In response to a more respectful question

122

about his transformation, Aaron repeated his statement of the previous day about Senator Schuster being a highly respected man. This would be an opportunity to show him that the United States government was ready to pay homage to any brave man who died in the service of his country, whatever his affiliations during the war that had been over for more than ten years.

'I want the Senator and everyone else who fought for the Southern cause to accept that we are all part of one great country now,' he added.

'It's a noble aim,' Wes commented.

'It's more than that,' Aaron replied, as he kneed his horse forward to take his place at the head of the column and Wes moved off alongside him, 'It's self-preservation. A great many Confederate supporters headed West after the war ended. Most are law abiding and, like Harrison Schuster, damn good fighting men. If we are to bring law and order to the territories we are going to need their help. Kentucky's motto is 'United we stand, divided we fall'. I'd like such a sentiment to take hold out there.'

The column was moving now, a flag-bearer holding the stars and stripes aloft, riding immediately behind Aaron and Wes, and a number of guidons fluttering above the mounted column proudly proclaiming the regiment to which they belonged. Wes felt conspicuous by reason of being the only man not in uniform.

16

The escort and coffin made good time and, when only a few miles from their destination, Aaron brought the troop to a halt in order to brush the dust of the journey from their uniforms and send a sergeant ahead to the Schuster home to inform its occupants of their imminent arrival with the body of a son of the house.

After inspecting the cavalrymen and supervising the placing of a Union flag over the coffin, Aaron took his place at the head of the cavalcade and they set off once more for the Schuster mansion, this time at a pace more in keeping with the occasion.

The mansion came into view when they were still at least a mile away. Surrounded by well-kept gardens, it was the most impressive building Wes had ever seen. Built of newly-white-washed stone, it had a tall, pillared facade and a myriad of windows that mirrored the rays of the afternoon sun.

News of the death of the son of the house had been telegraphed from Vicksburg to the army garrison at Columbus and relayed to the family some days before, so the immediate shock had passed. However, the family, friends and household still had their grief to cope with and

124

tears ran down the cheeks of many of those, both black and white, who were lined up in silent grief outside the Schuster home when the cortege arrived. Among their number Wes was startled to see David Connolly! He was standing close to a pretty but tearful young girl and it was quite evident to Wes that he was concerned about her.

The captain of the US cavalry troop brought his column to a halt when the gun carriage was level with the entrance to the great house and Aaron dismounted and saluted ex Kentucky Senator Silas Schuster before shaking his hand and that of a young man who was so like Harrison that Wes knew immediately he had to be Senator Schuster's only surviving son.

Wes dismounted, thankful to be out of the saddle of his unaccustomed mode of transport. Before he even had time to flex his aching muscles a black servant was on hand to take the horse from him, informing Wes that his saddle bags would be taken up to his room.

Without his horse, and having no part in the ceremonial transfer of the coffin from the gun carriage to the private chapel inside the house, Wes felt conspicuous and at a loss as to what he should do now.

He was rescued by David Connolly who hurried forward to greet him and shake him by the hand.

Grateful for the young man's intervention, Wes expressed his surprise at meeting with him again, especially as so far from his own home.

'I went to college with Harrison's brother — his only surviving brother now,' Connolly explained, 'we became close friends and I met Harrison on a number of occasions. I didn't know he had been killed and that his body was on board the *Missouri Belle*. My father knew, but didn't think to tell me until we arrived on a visit to my sister's home in Tennessee. I turned right around and came here by train to offer my condolences to the family.'

Something about the manner in which David Connolly had explained his presence prompted Wes to ask, 'Is there any particular reason why your father should have 'forgotten' to tell you about Harrison?'

'He and Senator Schuster fell out during the war. They were on the same side when it began, but my father changed his allegiance. He ended the war on the winning side, while Senator Schuster almost went under for staying loyal to the South. He managed to pull his plantation together again, but for a long time it looked as though it was the end of his political career — and my father tends to distance himself from those he considers to be among life's 'losers'.'

'So what does he think about your friendship with the young lady you were comforting when we arrived . . . I presume she is a Schuster?'

Colouring up, David Connolly said, 'My father knows nothing of Sophie. She is the youngest of the Schuster girls. There are five sisters and a brother between her and Harrison, but she absolutely adored him . . . '

Looking over Wes's shoulder, he broke off his explanation to say, with evident relief, ' . . . I think Brigadier Berryman wants to introduce you to Senator Schuster.'

The sudden change of subject took Wes by surprise and it was a moment before he realized that Connolly was referring to Aaron.

When he turned, Aaron was beckoning to him. Apologising to David Connolly for the interruption, he crossed to where the US Marshal stood with the head of the Schuster family.

When he reached them, Aaron said, 'Senator, I would like to introduce you to an Englishman, Wesley Curnow. He and your son did more than anyone else on board the *Missouri Belle* to rout the river pirates and, although it cannot bring Harrison back, it may give you and your family some small comfort to know that a bullet from Wes's gun ended the life of the outlaw who shot him.'

Grasping Wes's hand firmly, Silas Schuster said, 'Bless you, sir. I, my wife and family are honoured by your presence here. We thank you most sincerely for avenging Harrison's death and for accompanying him on this, his last journey home. You must regard our house as your home for as long as you wish to remain with us.'

Deeply touched by the grieving Senator's words, Wes replied, 'I'm the one who is honoured, Sir. Harrison was a brave man, I was privileged to know him.'

At that moment a woman's voice called out to the Senator and releasing Wes's hand, he said, 'If you will excuse me for a while, I must accompany my wife and family to the chapel to say a prayer for Harrison. I will talk to you again later and introduce you to the rest of my family.'

To Aaron, he said, 'I will send for the officer in command of your very smart cavalry to join us too. The troops will be billeted in the houses that were once occupied by senior plantation staff, and the horses cared for in the stables — I presume they will be remaining here overnight?'

'They are here to provide a guard of honour for your son, Senator and will remain for the funeral service, which will no doubt take place as soon as is possible?'

'The arrangements have all been made,' Silas Schuster confirmed. Visibly emotional, he needed to compose himself before adding, 'The minister needs only to be told when the funeral is to take place.'

With this, he turned away and made his way slowly, but with a weary dignity to where the Schuster family awaited him.

★ ★ ★

Some time later, when Wes went inside the Schuster house for the first time, he saw it was every bit as impressive as the exterior had promised, containing, as it did, artefacts and furniture that had been purchased from the cities in the eastern States of the country with little regard for expense.

He came to an awed halt in the great hall which was dominated by a grandiose, sweeping staircase and magnificent chandeliers and was still admiring it when he was joined by Aaron.

Aware that Wes was impressed by the opulence of his surroundings, Aaron said, 'It's certainly a great house, Wes, did you ever see one like it in England?'

'I saw a few fine houses — but only from the outside. I never went in, so I can't make a comparison.'

'Well, I have been in one or two that might stand comparison, but I don't think I've come across one that's grander.'

At that moment Silas Schuster came from the direction of the chapel accompanied by a tall, blonde girl who was introduced to the two men as Emma, one of his many daughters.

Sympathising with her on the loss of her brother, Aaron concluded, 'He is a sad loss to everyone, Miss Schuster. Harrison was a very brave man.'

'You actually knew him?' Expressing surprise, Emma added, 'But you are a Union officer — and a very high ranking one. Harrison fought for the Confederacy.'

'True,' Aaron agreed, 'and had the Confederacy possessed more men of the calibre of Harrison, the outcome of the war might well have been different. Fortunately, times have changed. When Harrison and I first met, only a few weeks ago, the war and our army service had ended and I was — and still am, a United States Federal Marshal. We fought together on the same side, against the river pirates.'

Entering the conversation, Silas Schuster said to Aaron, 'While we are on the subject of the late war . . . Harrison was captain of a company of Kentucky soldiers — Southern soldiers, of course. They suffered a great many casualties, but a number survived and are living in the vicinity. When they heard of Harrison's death they approached me and requested that they be allowed to attend his funeral wearing their old uniforms and showing the Confederate flag. I agreed, not knowing then, of course, that there would be a guard of honour of *Union* soldiers. It means a lot to his old comrades . . . but the last thing I wish to do on such a sad occasion is to cause an unfortunate incident. I will accept your decision on the matter, Brigadier Berryman.'

Aaron pondered the tricky situation for some time before saying, thoughtfully, 'I have no objection to men who served with Harrison attending his funeral wearing the uniform of an army that fought well and honourably for a cause in which they believed, Senator, but we are a united country now. Our country salutes only one flag — in life and in death — and that flag is the stars and stripes of the United States of America, whose soldiers are here to honour your son. He gave his life upholding the laws of that country — his country, and yours and mine too. That must be the only flag to be flown — and lowered — in his honour on the sad occasion of his funeral. However, I do understand the feelings of Harrison's former colleagues. They wish to pay homage to a man who led them into battle on many occasions beneath the banner of the Confederacy. There can be no objection if his coffin were to be draped in the flag under which he fought, as a personal tribute to a brave man.'

When Aaron's words had sunk in, Silas Schuster nodded his head in a gesture of acquiescence, 'I am grateful to you, Brigadier Berryman. I am quite certain that will be satisfactory to everyone. You are an able diplomat as well as a distinguished soldier.'

17

❧

That evening, with thirty-seven men and women gathered around a long table in the dining room of the Schuster mansion, not even the sombre occasion which had brought them all together could diminish the sheer opulence of their surroundings.

The mansion had been built in the days when the Schuster family was recognized as one of the wealthiest and most influential in the whole of Kentucky.

The family had suffered grievously during the dark days of the civil war, but the house itself had been spared the depredations experienced by many great houses. The lands belonging to the Schuster family had suffered more, having until then relied entirely upon slave labour.

However, Silas Schuster had succeeded in adapting to the new order and was reviving the family fortunes so successfully that a visitor who had known the house in the past would have found very little that was different. The plates on the table were of finest china, the dishes gleaming silver and the room was lit by candles, burning in elegant chandeliers imported from Europe.

The excellent food was served by a small army of uniformed servants who, although no longer slaves, performed their duties with a servility that Wes found more than a little disconcerting.

He was also awed by the array of cutlery lined up on either side of his plate, being used to having to deal with, at most, one each of knife, fork and spoon to serve him for the whole meal.

Emma, the Schuster daughter whom he had briefly met earlier that day, was seated to his right and she quickly realized his predicament. Immediately a course was served she would pick up the appropriate cutlery, enabling Wes to follow suit without being aware of her discreet guidance.

She also engaged him in conversation, amply compensating him for a lack of communication with an elderly and deaf great-aunt of the Schuster family, seated to his left.

Emma appeared to be genuinely interested in England and had *heard* of Cornwall, although she confessed to having only the vaguest knowledge of English geography.

When he explained that Cornwall was a narrow peninsular, with a river separating it from the remainder of England for most of the border's length, she asked, 'Does that mean that most of Cornwall is surrounded by the sea?'

Wes confirmed that this was so, adding, 'Cornwall is only a fraction the size of Kentucky and nowhere is very far from the coast. As a result the sea has always played a great part in Cornish life, even for miners like me. Tin and copper from Cornwall is shipped all over the world and some of the mines actually have workings that extend beneath the sea.'

'How fascinating,' Emma said, making her reply sound far more than a mere polite response, 'I adore the sea, I could look at it for hours without ever being bored.'

When Wes commented that Kentucky was a great distance from the coast, she explained, 'When the war began papa sent all us girls to stay with an aunt who lived on the Gulf of Mexico, in Florida. We were there for more than four years and I have never forgotten the sight of dolphins leaping from the water and pelicans tumbling from the sky into the sea, it was wonderful! Are there dolphins and pelicans around the Cornish coast?'

Wes had never heard of either but, concealing his ignorance, he said, 'The fishermen catch all kinds of fish and there are dozens of different birds, but I rarely got to the coast. The mining area where I lived and worked was about as far from the sea as is possible in Cornwall.'

'Why did you leave and come to America?'

Emma seemed genuinely interested and Wes explained, 'The price of tin and copper dropped so much that a great number of mines closed because they were losing money and miners left to find work wherever they could. Many came to America.'

Frowning, Emma said, 'I can't think of any mines around here, although I believe they dig for coal in East Kentucky. How did you and Harrison meet . . . '

Before Wes could reply he was dug violently in the ribs by an elbow belonging to the elderly woman seated on the other side of him.

When he turned to look at her, she demanded, 'How many slaves did *your* family have before those robbers from up North took them away?'

The woman spoke so loudly that the question was heard along the whole length of the long table and for a shocked moment all conversation ceased.

The question took Wes by surprise, but he replied, 'There are no slaves where I come from.'

Cupping a hand to her ear, the elderly woman said as loudly as before, 'Speak up and stop whispering. You did own slaves?'

Realizing that no matter how loudly he spoke the elderly woman would not hear, and acutely aware that everyone at the table was listening to the one-sided conversation, Wes shook his head, mouthing 'No. I am an Englishman.'

Far from satisfying the ageing Schuster aunt, the mime enraged her.

'No? *No* slaves? Who are you . . . ? Are you an abolitionist? Who sat me next to an abolitionist?'

At that moment Olga Schuster, Senator Schuster's wife, arrived on the scene. Signalling for Emma to help her, she gently eased the old woman from her seat and, ignoring her protests, said, 'Come along, Aunt Maude, it is long past your bedtime. I fear the excitement of dining with so many people has quite tired you out.'

When the elderly aunt was supported between Emma and her mother, Olga Schuster spoke to one of the servants, 'Go and find Mrs Flynn, she can put Aunt Maude to bed.'

Wes was aware that Mrs Flynn was the housekeeper and, as the old woman was assisted

135

slowly from her place at the table, Olga Schuster turned to him and said, 'Please accept my apologies for Aunt Maude's unforgivable behaviour, Mr Curnow, the only excuse I can offer is that she is ninety-seven years of age and not always responsible for her actions.'

More amused than offended, Wes said, 'No one aged ninety-seven needs to apologise for anything, Mrs Schuster. I am only sad her deafness prevented us from having a proper conversation. She must have had a fascinating life and seen a great many interesting happenings.'

As the three women passed around the head of the table, heading for the door, they passed one of the guests whose ruddy complexion owed more to strong drink than to Kentucky sunshine and Emma overheard him say in a voice that carried much farther than was discreet, 'Maude Schuster has never been backward in saying what others are thinking, especially about Yankees and their fellow travellers. Who is he anyway — and what's he doing here?'

Emma had not questioned Wes's reason for coming to the Schuster home, accepting that he was an English friend of Brigadier Berryman and she was angry that such a comment should be made about a guest in her father's house. So too was her mother, but Olga Schuster *did* know why Wes was at the dinner in the house.

Bringing Aunt Maude and Emma to an abrupt halt she proceeded to enlighten the boorish speaker.

'Wesley Curnow is neither a Yankee, nor a Northerner, Mr Kidd, he is a guest of the Schuster family . . . an honoured guest. You should make an opportunity to have a talk with him. I seem to remember that *you* too were once with Harrison when he was involved in a battle, so you will have something in common . . . or perhaps not!'

With this final enigmatic remark she continued on her way with Aunt Maude and Emma, leaving the indiscreet speaker uncomfortably aware of the smirks of the men around the table.

It was well known that when he had been *Lieutenant* Kidd, with Captain Harrison Schuster's troop during the war, they had run into a Union army ambush, during the course of which Harrison had been wounded. Kidd had fled from the scene and ridden back to the main army carrying news of the ambush and of Harrison's probable death.

The party that hurried off to verify his information returned — with Captain Harrison Schuster and his troop. They had stood their ground and eventually put the Union soldiers to flight.

It had taken Kidd a long time to live down his actions on that day and he did not care to be reminded of it.

Emma had listened to her mother's castigation of the discourteous guest with great interest, but her curiosity concerned Wes's part in the action in which her brother had been killed.

18

❧

'Had you ever killed anyone before the fight you and Harrison had with the river pirates, Mr Curnow?'

The question was put by Emma as she and Wes sat on the low stone surround of the flagged terrace where the Schuster's and their guests were enjoying a light breeze after the heat of the dining room.

'I would rather you called me Wesley, or Wes,' he replied, 'but the answer to your question is 'no', although I have seen many men die violent deaths during the time I worked in mines.'

Emma shuddered, 'I can't think of anything worse than having to work under the ground . . . but that would have been very different to what happened on the Mississippi. How did you feel about actually pointing a gun at someone, pulling the trigger and seeing him fall, knowing you had killed him?'

Taking care over his words, Wes said, 'I *had* thought it would trouble me but, as Marshal Berryman said to me before the fight, 'If you pause to think in such a situation it will likely be the last thought you ever have.' They were shooting at us and we firing at them. My only regret is that I didn't shoot one particular bandit *before* he fired at Harrison . . . but there was a lot of shooting going on at the time.'

'*Marshal* Berryman . . . ? Oh yes, the brigadier. I forget that he is also a lawman. Killing must come naturally to a man like him.'

'He is no stranger to shooting, or being shot at,' Wes agreed, 'but I don't think he takes any pleasure from it. He is a lawman and takes his work very seriously, but he's a good man. Harrison both liked and respected him.'

'Poor Harrison. He survived a horrible war, only to be killed in a gunfight that really had nothing to do with him.'

Wes had taken an instant liking to Emma and, aware that she was very close to tears, he said, 'Had he not taken such a prominent part in fighting off the river pirates a lot of innocent men would have died — and I dread to think what would have happened to the women on board. Yes, it is tragic that Harrison was killed, very tragic, but he died a hero's death. That's why Marshal Berryman was so determined it should be recognized as such by the United States. He is sending a full report to your President about Harrison's part in eliminating the gang.'

After a lengthy silence, Emma said, 'Thank you for saying what you have about Harrison. Papa says he has invited you to stay here with us for a while, I do hope you will. This is a wonderful estate, I — and my sisters, of course — would love to show you around.'

'It's very kind of your father — and you and your sisters — but I am expected at the lead mines in Missouri and it's time I began earning a living again.'

139

Wes was aware that what Emma meant was that she would enjoy his company for a while longer. During the evening she had made that as clear as propriety would allow. He was tempted to stay if only for that reason, but there could never be anything serious between them, their backgrounds were so very different. Besides, he believed he could never feel entirely comfortable staying in such sumptuous surroundings.

'But . . . you will stay for a while?'

'That depends very much on Marshal Berryman. Everything I own is on board the *Missouri Belle* and he knows more about what is likely to happen to the boat than I do.'

'Of course! I was forgetting that your boat was wrecked on the river. You have had a very adventurous introduction to America . . . '

The conversation turned to the last minutes of the *Missouri Belle*'s life as a Mississippi riverboat and they were still talking about it when they were joined by David Connolly and Sophie.

The Louisiana Senator's son did not seem at ease with the subject of their conversation, and Wes realized he feared something might be said about the trouble he had brought upon himself in the riverboat's gambling saloon. However, it was not long before the talk turned to England and what life was like there and David Connolly was able to relax.

Before long, they were joined by Emma's other sisters and her brother and were soon discussing the various social functions they had

140

enjoyed, comparing the merits and demerits of Kentucky and Louisiana society. It made Wes more aware than ever of the insurmountable differences in his way of life and theirs.

The gathering of mourners at the Schuster mansion ended for the night when Olga Schuster rounded-up her daughters, reminding them that the following day would impose an emotional strain upon the whole family and they should ensure a good night's sleep in order to cope with all that the day would inevitably bring.

Before she went off with the others, Emma had once again pressed Wes to remain at the house when the funeral was over. She eventually extracted a promise from him that he would seriously consider the matter.

Wes was not enthusiastic about remaining here, in Kentucky, especially if, as was certain, Aaron would be leaving within the next day or two. Emma was a very attractive, kind and thoroughly likeable young woman, but she lacked Anabelita's worldliness, and her obvious wealth actually frightened him.

He believed his own appeal to her lay in the fact that he was not an American and came from a different background to any of the other men she knew.

He wished he had been able to speak to Aaron about his plans, so that he might use them when Emma next brought up the suggestion that he extend his stay at her home. Unfortunately, the US Marshal was heavily involved in discussions with Silas

Schuster and some of the older guests about United States politics and the talk looked as though it would continue until well into the night.

He decided he would follow the example of the female members of the Schuster family and go to bed.

19

❧

The funeral of Harrison Schuster was a solemn but impressive ceremony on a day that Wes thought should have been dull and grey to suit the sombre occasion. Instead, it was warm and bright with not a cloud to be seen in the soft blue sky and the refrain of Kentucky songbirds beyond the open chapel windows at odds with the solemnity of the service.

Ex-Confederate soldiers, wearing grey uniforms that had probably fitted no more comfortably when they were issued to owners who were more active then, entered the chapel in ones and twos. Some appeared embarrassed by the presence of the immaculately turned out US cavalrymen, drawn up at the rear of the chapel. Others were rigidly defiant of the blue-uniformed representatives of an army which had emerged victorious from the hard fought Civil War.

Incorporated in the service were glowing eulogies from Harrison's one-time commanding officer and also from a sergeant who had served in Harrison's company and had known him from boyhood.

There was a ripple of resentment among the grey-uniformed contingent when, at the request of Silas Schuster, Aaron was called upon to say a

143

few words in honour of the deceased.

The dissent did not die away until Aaron had slowly climbed the three wooden steps to the pulpit and paused, hands on the edge of the octagonal structure, looking out over the congregation. When he had their full attention, Aaron began.

'On this sad occasion we are here to mourn a very special man. A man with such strong beliefs that he once put his life on the line to fight for what he believed in, wearing the grey uniform that is in evidence in his honour today. The cause for which he fought lost the war — although I can vouch for the fact that there were many times when it was a close run thing.

'However, being on the losing side did not leave Harrison Schuster a bitter man, nor did he wish to live in the past, still fighting the war with words, if not deeds. Harrison was aware that the future — a great future — lay in being part of a united country. The United States of America. He became a committed supporter of that country — our country, yours and mine.

'When we were on board a ship together, bound from New York to New Orleans, only days before his death, we would often talk about that future and I was greatly impressed by his enthusiasm. Yes, he was proud of being a Kentuckian — and rightly so — but he had grasped the much loftier concept that we are no longer 'Southerners', or 'Northerners'. We are all *Americans*, equal citizens of The United States of America.

'I was so impressed by his enthusiasm for all

144

this entailed that it was my intention when we eventually parted company to write to President Ulysses S. Grant and recommend that Harrison be made a United States Marshal.'

Aaron's revelation brought a gasp of surprise followed by murmurs of both approval and dissent from sections of the congregation.

Waiting until the sound died away, Aaron continued, 'Sadly, it was not to be. Harrison lost his life upholding the law of this great country of ours. Let our lasting tribute to him be that we are all so inspired by his example that we too would be willing to make the same sacrifice for our country, the *United* States of America, should the need arise — although I pray to God that it will never be necessary.'

There was silence in the chapel when Aaron returned to his seat, his war-wounded leg troubling him as he descended from the pulpit more than it had when he climbed the steps, but Silas Schuster gave him an approving look as he passed him by.

After the singing of a hymn and final prayers from the minister, the grey-uniformed pall bearers took up the coffin once more and, closely followed by the grieving Schuster family, led the sombre procession along the aisle.

As they neared the doorway, Wes caught sight of a strange figure standing at the rear of the chapel. He had not seen him before at the mansion — and would certainly have noticed him had he been there.

No taller than Aaron, the newcomer was dressed in buckskin trousers and a fringed and well-worn buckskin jacket. He was by no means a young man and although it was difficult to accurately guess his age from what little of his weathered face could be seen between a heavy grey beard and hair of the same colour that hung down to his shoulders, Wes thought he must be at least sixty.

Aaron caught sight of him at about the same time and Wes was startled when the Marshal's head came up in sudden recognition. Leaving the slow moving cortege, he hurried across the chapel and clasped the unkempt stranger in a warm embrace.

Wes was about to drop out of the procession too when, after only the briefest exchange of words, Aaron took the buckskin-clad man by the arm and despite his obvious reluctance, hurried him to the place he had left in the procession, walking beside Wes.

Aaron made no attempt to introduce his companion to Wes until they were outside the house and making their slow way to a small, walled cemetery at the side of the mansion, where the dismounted US cavalrymen were drawn up beside an open grave. Here, in the briefest of introductions, he said merely, 'Wes, this is Charlie Quinnell — better known as 'Old' Charlie. Charlie, meet Wesley Curnow.'

The two men shook hands and Wes was aware that Old Charlie was attracting a great deal of attention from the mourners. It was hardly surprising, his grab was quite unlike anything Wes had ever seen before and it was apparent his dress was considered equally unusual by

146

everyone except Aaron.

The burial service was brief but moving. The flag carried by the US cavalrymen was lowered and the soldiers brought to attention as Harrison's coffin was lowered into the ground. Then, as the Schuster women expressed their grief, a salute was fired over the grave by a small guard of honour.

The ceremony over, mourners and soldiers together made their way to the terrace at the back of the house, where food and drink were laid out on tables.

As family friends gathered around the Schusters, Silas left them and made his way to where Aaron and Wes stood with Old Charlie, in order to learn who he was and what he was doing at the funeral.

Once again it was Aaron who made the introductions, but this time he added, 'Charlie is an ex-mountain man, ex-plainsman, trapper and hunter — and frontiersman. He scouted for me when I was stationed in the Territories with the army, but when I was called back to Arkansas we lost touch with each other.'

Shaking hands with Old Charlie, Silas Schuster said, 'I am pleased to meet you, Mr Quinnell, but what brings you to Kentucky — and how did you learn that Brigadier Berryman was here?'

'I didn't know he was,' Charlie replied, 'I was on my way back from the East, where Bill Cody had persuaded me to go with him to take part in some damn fool show he was putting on for city folks who had never so much as smelled an

Indian. He said I'd make more money in a month than in a year of hunting, out in the Territories. He might have been right, but making a fool of myself in front of a crowd of gullible Easterners wasn't for me. I packed it in and me and my mule decided to go back to where we both belong. Along the way I learned Cap'n Schuster had been killed and was being buried nearby, so I came to pay my respects. I kept him and his men in meat when they were fighting up on the Kansas — Missouri border.'

Shaken out of his customary composure, Aaron said accusingly, 'You fought for both sides in the war, Charlie?'

'No, General.' Fingering the hairs of his substantial beard away from his lips, Charlie added, 'I was a *hunter*, not a fighting man. The only men I fight are Indians — and then only if they're too riled up to listen to reason.'

'If you knew my son then you are welcome in my home, Mr Quinnell. As for fighting . . . I don't think there will be any of that going on here today!'

Silas Schuster inclined his head to where the men wearing uniforms, both blue and grey, were helping themselves from the laden tables and chatting amiably to each other.

'Some of the men from the Columbus fort are veterans,' Aaron said, 'They'll have respect for men in grey and will no doubt be quite ready to swap yarns about battles they shared — and the incompetence of some of the officers who led them.'

'Well, speaking as an outsider who saw the

148

fighting from both sides, I don't think they'll be talking about either you or Cap'n Schuster, General,' Charlie said.

'In that case shall we go and join them, Gentlemen?' Silas Schuster suggested, adding, 'I hope you are hungry, Mr Quinnell, there is a great deal of food to be eaten up.'

Fingering his beard once more, Charlie replied, 'The only way I could get here in time for the funeral was to ride all night, Senator. Right now I could eat my mule — if it wasn't that I've ridden all the meat off her bones . . . '

20

❧

The United States cavalry from Columbus left the Schuster mansion that afternoon. Wes had thought he and Aaron would leave with them but, as Aaron pointed out, they could not possibly reach the ferry to take them across the Mississippi before darkness fell and as they were riding government cavalry horses they would need to make arrangements for them to be returned.

Aaron felt it would be better to put their departure off until the following morning. It would enable him to send a note to the garrison commanding officer asking him to make the army steam launch available to take them direct to the stricken *Missouri Belle* and at the same time have someone waiting at the river bank on the Kentucky side to take the horses from them.

Reluctantly, Wes was forced to fall in with his friend's plans.

One of the reasons he would rather not have spent another night at the Schuster mansion was because he realized Emma was infatuated with him — or, to be more realiztic — with the man she imagined him to be. He believed she would probably have been attracted to any man who came from another land and seemed different to those who had so far been part of her life. He enjoyed her company but was embarrassed by her attentions, largely because of the huge social gap existing between them.

After dinner that evening, the guests and family split into groups. The older women sat chatting together on domestic matters while the older men settled down with their drinks to talk of the political and business news emanating from the more settled Eastern States.

All were subjects of which Wes had no knowledge. As a result, he spent the evening in the company of the younger mourners, among whom were the Schuster girls, their sole remaining brother John, and David Connolly.

Wes found John Schuster to be a very likeable young man. He was both shy and quiet, but Wes had little opportunity to get to know him better because Emma was loath to allow him out of her sight, or even to share his company with anyone else.

On one of the rare occasions when Emma left the group, Wes was talking with David Connolly and Sophie Schuster when the Louisiana Senator's son asked whether Wes intended remaining at the Schuster mansion for a while.

When Wes replied that he would be leaving the next morning, Sophie asked, 'Does Emma know?'

'We haven't actually spoken of it,' Wes replied, 'but she knows I am anxious to get to Missouri and begin working again.'

'She is going to be very upset,' Sophie commented, explaining, 'I've never seen her take to anyone in the way she has to you.'

151

'I'm convinced that's only because I am not from around here ... and because I knew Harrison. It's obvious she was very fond of him.'

'We all were,' Sophie said, 'and I hope you are right about Emma, but you are the first man in whom she has ever shown a serious interest. You should be very flattered!'

'I am!' Wes lied, although he felt more uncomfortable than flattered by what he believed to be only a passing infatuation on Emma's part. However, Emma was not only an attractive young woman, she was also kind-hearted and had done a great deal to ensure he did not feel completely out of place in the opulent surroundings in which he found himself at the Schuster home, he had no wish to hurt her in any way. Nevertheless, no matter how real her feelings for him were, a romance between them was out of the question.

'Emma is probably the nicest girl I have ever met,' he said, honestly, 'but there could never be anything more than friendship between us. She will find someone who works at something more rewarding than mining — and that's what *I* am ... a miner.'

'I think you are destined to be something more than that,' David Connolly said unexpectedly, 'as I am certain Marshal Berryman would agree. I overheard him saying as much to Senator Schuster earlier this evening. He believes you have the temperament to one day become a great Marshal ... '

Emma's return brought that particular conversation to an end and, shortly before midnight,

Olga Schuster, perhaps fearing her girls might be Cinderellas, gathered them together saying it had been a very trying day for them all. Ignoring the protests, from Emma in particular, that they were no longer children, she ushered them off to bed.

Emma's protest had been to no avail, but she succeeded in turning her back on her mother for a few moments and holding Wes's hand tightly while saying 'Goodnight' to him. When she had gone he realized, guiltily, that he had still not told her he would be leaving early the next morning.

When the girls and their mother had gone inside the house, David Connolly, John Schuster and a couple of other young Kentuckians announced their intention of going to the billiard room. Wes was invited to join them but Aaron was beckoning to him from across the terrace. Making his apologies to the others, Wes went to join his friend.

Old Charlie was seated beside Aaron and, although seemingly out of place among the well-dressed company, the buck-skin-clad plainsman did not appear at all ill-at-ease. Sitting back comfortably with a glass of whisky in his hand, he was saying little, preferring to listen rather than talk.

Wes too remained as a listener until one of the Kentuckians asked him, more from politeness to bring him into their conversation than with any particular interest, what had brought him to America?

When Wes replied that he was on his way to

Harmony, in Missouri, to join an uncle in the mines there, another of the group asked, 'When did you last hear from this uncle of yours?'

'The letter would have been written quite a few months ago,' Wes replied, 'I didn't make up my mind to come to America for some time after I received it then needed to make the arrangements for travelling.'

'I think you'll find things have changed a great deal on the Missouri lead mines since the letter was written.' The man who had asked the question said, adding, 'I have a business interest in one of the mines and was there only ten days ago. A great many German miners have been coming into the mines in recent years and are now in enough strength to begin flexing their collective muscle. They have formed a 'Union' of miners and begun action to have their pay raised. They walked out on their employers for a while and there was a great deal of trouble when Cornish miners were brought in to take over the work — I believe you are from that part of England?'

When Wes confirmed that he was, the Kentuckian shook his head, 'The Germans eventually won the day and are back at work now — but they have never forgiven the Cornish miners. Indeed, there was so much trouble between the two that most of the Cornish have moved on elsewhere. I suspect your uncle was probably among their number.'

This was disturbing news for Wes. He had come all this way on the assumption that there would be work for him at Harmony. There had been no hint in his uncle's letter of impending trouble with other miners.

'It doesn't sound like good news,' he admitted, 'but having come all this way I need to go there to find out what is happening and, if my uncle has moved on, where he is now. He'll certainly be on a mine somewhere. Like me, mining is all he knows . . . but perhaps the trouble with the Germans didn't extend to all the mines around Harmony?'

'It didn't in the beginning,' said the Kentuckian, 'but I think you'll find it does now. This 'Union' of theirs has a stranglehold on every mine in the area. It's become so bad that I intend selling my interest there — but the way things are looking I doubt if I'll be able to find a buyer.'

Wes agreed with the Kentuckian that his prospects for work at Harmony was a cause for concern, but until he went there and learned what was happening he could not change the plans that had brought him all the way across the Atlantic from England.

21

❧

Wes and Aaron were up before most of the house guests the following morning but, early as they were, Emma was already downstairs waiting for Wes.

She greeted him accusingly with, 'You never told me you were leaving early this morning. Mama mentioned it to me when we were on the way to bed. I crept downstairs after the others had gone to sleep, hoping to speak to you, but you were with papa and his friends. If I had come down this morning and found you were gone I would have been very unhappy.'

'I knew my going would make you unhappy but there had been enough unhappiness in your life for one day, so I said nothing.'

It was no more than a half-lie. He had thought that if he told her he was leaving so soon there would have been an emotional scene and he would have found that hard to deal with.

'Would you have just ridden off without even saying 'goodbye'?' Emma was only slightly mollified by his words.

'No. At least . . . I was going to leave a note saying how much I had enjoyed your company and to say I wished we had met in happier circumstances.'

This was the truth. In fact, he had already

written the note. It was in his pocket and he had read it four or five times before leaving his room. He was glad he would not now need to give it to her. He had been unable to make up his mind whether it might give her false hope that he really did care for her and was likely to come back one day — perhaps when he had made more of a success of his life.

He was also aware that the note would make it clear to anyone reading it that he had received only a very elementary education.

Thankfully, she seemed to accept his excuses and the arrival of her mother with an announcement that breakfast was ready to be served put an end to that particular conversation.

Emma sat next to him at the breakfast table but her mother was seated on his other side and the conversation was centred on Aaron's appointment as US Marshal for the Territories and what it was likely to entail.

When asked what help he would have to bring law and order to such a vast and notoriously violent area, Aaron cast a glance at Wes before replying.

'I was hoping I might persuade a certain young Englishman to come there and give me a hand, but he sees his future in mining and not in law enforcement, so I guess I will just have to manage as best I can.'

'Perhaps it is not too late for him to change his mind.' Silas Schuster had been listening to the conversation and he added, 'Judging by what was said last night there is little future in the lead

157

mining industry — especially for an English-man.'

'That's quite true,' Aaron agreed, 'So I'll keep a job open for him, just in case.'

Wes merely smiled and said nothing. He felt he had already made his views quite clear to Aaron.

Emma had taken in what was being said and, before everyone had finished eating she rose from her chair and going to where her father sat, whispered in his ear at some length.

As she whispered, he first frowned, then looked thoughtful and eventually nodded, whispering something to her in reply.

A delighted Emma kissed him on the cheek before hurrying to her mother and whispering in the ear farthest away from Wes.

Her mother arrived at a decision in a much speedier manner than had her husband. When she too nodded, a jubilant Emma hurried from the breakfast room, leaving her father to apologise for Emma's rudeness to the others seated at the table, saying, 'I am quite sure you will excuse such bad manners when the reason for it is revealed and you will not have to wait for too long.'

When Emma returned to the breakfast room some minutes later she was carrying something wrapped in a coloured cloth. Bringing it to the table and flushed with scarcely contained excitement, she stood by Wes's chair and addressed all the guests at the breakfast table, saying, 'As a great many of you will know, it would have been poor dear Harrison's birthday next week and, because he had worked harder than anyone to help restore the Schuster plantation to its former glory, Papa and Mama wanted to buy him something special as a present. We all discussed what it should be and when we were agreed, Papa had something especially made for him in Connecticut and shipped here. Sadly — very sadly — Harrison never saw it . . . '

Here Emma's voice broke and it was a few moments before she recovered sufficient composure to continue, 'I have had a talk with Papa and Mama and they both agree it would be appropriate for the present to be given to the man who shot his killer — and who one day might become a Deputy United States Marshal and put the present to good use. We all believe Harrison would have approved.'

Turning now to Wes, she said, 'It is something I am certain you will enjoy owning, Wesley, but I hope you will never need to use it! Does that sound contradictory . . . ? Well, when I give it to you, no doubt you will understand what I mean.'

When she lifted the towel from the present that had been bought for Harrison there was a gasp of admiration from those seated about the table as she handed Wes a Colt .45 calibre revolver, nestling in a soft leather holster — but this was no ordinary revolver. The gun-metal blue of the steel contrasted with a tooled ivory butt to make it a beautiful, if deadly, weapon.

Taken aback, Wes expressed disbelief, 'This is for me? But . . . it's beautiful!'

Glancing up he saw Emma looking at him

expectantly and, rising to his feet, he kissed her. As she coloured up, he said, 'It's a present that Harrison would have truly appreciated. I echo Emma's words and hope I am never called upon to use it — but, if I *am*, I will try to use it in a manner that would have had Harrison's approval. Either way, it is something I will always treasure . . . always. Senator . . . Mrs Schuster . . . Emma, thank you very much indeed.'

22

Riding away from the splendid mansion with the Schuster's present affixed to his belt, Wes looked back when they were almost out of sight of the house and saw Emma still standing outside the impressive entrance of the mansion. He waved and received an immediate and energetic response.

Wes was in the company of Aaron and Old Charlie. The mountain-man had not put in an appearance for breakfast and when Wes asked him about his absence, Charlie replied, 'I've never been able to get along with the fancy ways folks like the Schusters have of eating — nor with their manner of living, come to that. I slept in the stable, close to my mule, and got coffee and grub from the kitchen. That way I could use just my knife and fingers to eat without upsetting anyone.'

Remembering his own confusion when confronted with an array of cutlery at the first meal he had taken in the Schuster mansion, Wes said, 'They do seem to use far more knives, forks and spoons than I'm used to. If Emma hadn't been there to help me I'd have made a fool of myself at eating times.'

'You've got time to learn fancy ways, boy . . . I ain't and Aaron tells me the girl has taken a shine to you,' Old Charlie commented, 'Says it's because of her you've got that fancy six-shooter you're carrying. Can you use it?'

'Aaron taught me how on the boat from New York,' Wes confirmed, 'Although I used a rifle against the river pirates.'

Aaron had been listening to their conversation and now he said, 'He's better than average with a rifle, Charlie, and knows how to point a pistol and pull the trigger but he wouldn't stand a chance against most men who carry a handgun.'

Ejecting a stream of tobacco juice to one side of his mule, Old Charlie said to Wes, 'Until you can handle that gun better than anyone you're likely to meet up with, I suggest you keep it tucked away, boy. Men wearing fancy guns are targets for those who like to think of themselves as 'gunmen' — and a great many of 'em really are handy with a gun.'

'I won't be going anywhere looking for trouble,' Wes declared, 'As for wearing it . . . I've only got it on now to please Emma. I'll take it off when we get a little way from the house.'

Nodding his approval, Old Charlie cut a piece from a twist of tobacco using a knife he carried in a sheath on his belt — but which Wes thought would not have been out of place in a butchers' shop. The tobacco safely ensconced in his cheek, he said, 'Keeping it out of sight is a good idea . . . at least, for now, but Aaron tells me you're on your way to Missouri mining country, around Harmony. If you're looking to keep out of trouble then you're heading in the wrong direction. You won't need to *look* for trouble there — it'll come and find you for sure. A friend of mine from way back is County Sheriff there, least, he was when I last met him, but he was born and brought up in America. So many German miners have come in during the last year or two they'll be wanting one of their own to take on the job. It's certainly not the place for an *English* miner. From what I've heard they've all been forced out and gone to find work farther West.'

'I've heard the same,' Wes admitted, 'but I wrote and told my uncle I was coming out to him at Harmony and in the last letter I had from him he said he was looking forward to meeting me there. He might, or might not still be around waiting for me, but if things are as bad as you say and he's moved on, he'll have left word of where he's gone. So I really have no alternative but to go there and find out.'

Old Charlie shrugged, 'You must do what you think is for the best — but you'd do well to put that fancy gun out of sight before you get there lest someone takes a shine to it.'

On the way to the river, Wes learned a great deal about Old Charlie and the adventurous life he had led. Some of the details came from anecdotes told by Aaron of the days when the old mountain-man hunted food to feed Union soldiers who were engaged in fighting Confederate irregulars, or Indians — sometimes both — on the plains of the Western frontier.

The old man was quite happy to reply to the many questions put to him by Wes about the things he had seen and done, but he rarely volunteered information.

Nevertheless, before they arrived at the river Wes had learned that Old Charlie, now in his sixties, had been born on a desperately poor homestead in the mountains of South Carolina, one of a great many brothers and sisters. He had helped his father to scratch a precarious living until he ran away at the age of sixteen to go trapping with a party of Frenchmen in the Rocky Mountains.

Later, he became a buffalo hunter on the Great Plains, was a guide to some of the wagon trains heading for new lands in the West, then hunted for meat to feed both Union and Confederate armies in the 1860s.

In between such varied activities Old Charlie alternately fought Indians and lived, apparently quite happily, among them.

He was now heading west once more, this time to the mountains of Colorado to try his hand at the one thing that seemed to be missing from his adventurous life — prospecting for gold.

Much of his life story was already known to Aaron, but Old Charlie had been able to fill in one or two gaps in his knowledge and Aaron asked now, 'Trying something new is fine, old-timer, but what happens if you're successful and strike it rich? Will you go back East and live out the rest of your years in luxury?'

Charlie spat out juice from the latest wad of tobacco, but this time it was a gesture of disgust. 'I wouldn't go back East if I found a nugget as big as a tepee! The East ain't for me — especially not the cities. There's so many folk packed into 'em that there's not enough air to go around for everyone. Breathe in and all you get is what someone else has just breathed out!'

Wes did not know how accurate Old Charlie's description was of city air, but he was inclined to accept it. During the short time he had spent in New York he had thought there was a taste in the air and it was not pleasant.

'What would you do if you suddenly struck it rich?' He asked.

'I'd buy myself a young Indian wife — a Pawnee, perhaps. They're good homemakers and have been taught how to grow food to fill a man's belly. Then I'd take her to part of the Territories where settlers haven't yet reached, get me a piece of land in good hunting country, and have a few hogs and maybe a cow. I might do that anyhow. It's about as much as any man could want when he gets to my age.'

Wes thought it a simple enough ambition but wondered what a young Indian woman would think of such an arrangement. He could think of no young woman of his acquaintance who would be happy to cut themselves off from others in such a way, even with a younger man. He doubted whether an Indian woman would be any different.

23

When the trio eventually reached the *Missouri Belle*, Anabelita was greatly relieved to see Wes. After greeting him warmly, she said, 'Lola and I were expecting you last night and feared something might have happened to you both.'

Pleased that she had missed him, Wes explained, 'There wasn't time to make arrangements to get back here after the funeral, so we had to leave it until today — and we've brought an old friend of Aaron's along with us.'

'Is he an army friend?' Anabelita asked, without any particular interest.

'No, he hunted for Aaron and his soldiers during the war. He's quite an old man who seems to have done all sorts of things but he doesn't care too much for the company of others. He's been a trapper, a buffalo hunter, fought with Indians — and now he's on his way to Colorado to look for gold.'

'Searching for gold in Colorado's not likely to suit a man who likes to be on his own,' Anabelita commented. 'Half the world must be there doing the same thing . . . but forget Aaron's friend — forget everyone else for a while. I really have missed you, Wes. I'd show you how much right now, but you'll need to wait until tonight. The captain's back from St Louis and Lola and I are helping make an inventory of everything left on board that can be used again.'

'Surely there are others on board who could be doing that.'

'There *should* be,' Anabelita agreed, 'but while you, Aaron and the captain were away most of the crew left the boat and a great many things that should have been on the inventory went with them — including all the drinks from the saloon. Fortunately, the captain had kept the only key to the liquor store with him and it wasn't touched, but now he's opened it up to those of us who remained on board. Every night will be a party night until a company steamboat arrives to take off whatever's worth salvaging.'

Old Charlie joined Aaron and the others on board the *Missouri Belle* for drinks that evening, but he declined an invitation to remain on the steamboat until the others were taken off. Instead, he went ashore after enjoying an alcoholic evening with them, explaining that he and his mule would find somewhere out in the open away from the river. He declared that folk not only attracted trouble, but mosquitoes as well.

When Old Charlie had gone, Wes commented to Aaron, 'I wish he had stayed around longer, he's probably one of the most interesting men I've ever met and there can be few men who know more about America and its people. I would like to have spent more time talking with him.'

'You might still have the chance,' Aaron said. 'you remember him saying that he has a friend who is County Sheriff up that way? Old Charlie's decided that as he'll be so close and almost certainly won't be passing this way again it would be a pity not to find time to visit him.'

Breaking into a smile, Aaron added, 'He's taking his mule on the train and sharing a box-car with it. He prefers the mule's company to that of folk he doesn't know. They make a good pair, the mule is as cantankerous as Old Charlie himself.'

★   ★   ★

That evening, as Wes, Aaron and the two women sat drinking on the open-sided deck, Wes could not help thinking of the time he had spent at the Schuster mansion, and comparing Anabelita with Emma.

He realized that not only had Emma lived a far more sheltered life than the steamboat gambler, she had also been brought up to conform to a standard of behaviour that was expected of girls in the society to which she belonged.

Anabelita had no such constraints. She lived her life according to the standards she set for herself.

While Emma was probably the nicest young woman he had ever met, and one of whom he could have become very fond, Wes knew that such a way of life would not have proved acceptable to either Emma, or her family.

The way he felt about Anabelita was very different. So different that he would not allow himself to spend too much time thinking about it.

★　★　★

It was three days before a company steamboat arrived from St Louis and edged gingerly alongside the *Missouri Belle*. The three days had passed very pleasantly for Wes and Aaron. They helped Anabelita and Lola with the not too onerous task of taking the inventory of salvageable items but Wes and Anabelita also found time to take walks along the river bank and get to know each other better, in more relaxed circumstances than at any time before.

The captain of the stricken vessel and his remaining crew members were quite content to have a United States Marshal and a man who had helped fight off river pirates with them on board the marooned ship to help protect them should the need arise and they lived well.

With the arrival of the other steamboat, things on board changed immediately. Within twenty-four hours the *Missouri Belle* was no more than an empty shell. On the final morning even the beds that had been slept in by the remaining occupants were removed.

It was time for Aaron, Wes and the two croupiers to leave too.

Wes realized it was not going to be easy to say goodbye to Anabelita. Since returning to the *Missouri Belle* after his visit to the Schuster mansion she had become increasingly important to him, even though he could see no place for her in the future he had mapped out for himself. He had certainly never intended that he should feel this way about her.

Despite this, an inborn Cornish stubbornness prompted him to reject yet another suggestion from Aaron that he forget his plans to go to Harmony and come to Abilene with him and the two women instead.

'It would make Anabelita very happy,' Aaron pointed out. 'She's fallen for you, Wes, and you don't need me to tell you that she is a very special lady.'

'I don't need anyone to tell me,' Wes said, irritably, 'but I have promised to go to Harmony — and that's where I'm going.'

Accepting defeat, Aaron shrugged, 'Well, I can at least tell Anabelita that I tried my damnedest to get you to come with us. If you change your mind you know where you can find her, but if it's your feelings for Anabelita that cause you to change your mind then don't leave it too long. Abilene's a cattleman's town. Some of the ranchers who come up from Texas with their herds are very rich men, with a lot to offer any girl who takes their fancy.'

'They'll be able to offer her more than I ever will, so if the right man came along she'd be a fool to turn him down.' Wes spoke with a magnanimity he did not feel, adding, 'As you say, she's a very special woman, while I am a miner — and, right now, an out-of-work miner. From all I've been told I could stay that way for a long time. I'm not exactly a prize catch, for *any* woman!'

'You're no longer in England, Wes, so try to stop thinking like a damn fool Englishman! This is America, a land that's brimming over with opportunity — for everyone. You were probably a miner in England because everyone else around you was one. It doesn't mean you *have* to do the same thing here. In America you look around, see what it is you *really* want to be, then go out and get it. I've told you that you only have to say 'yes' and I'll make you a deputy US Marshal right here and now. You could also take over looking after things at the gaming-house I intend opening in Abilene. Then again, you could go back to the Schuster plantation and ask Silas Schuster to take you on. Do that and you'd end up marrying Emma and becoming a very rich man. Dammit, man, there are thousands of young men out there who'd bust a gut for the opportunities you have right now — and one woman, at least, who'd go along with whatever you decided to do. So don't tell me — or yourself — that you're no more than an out-of-work miner. You can be whatever you want to be. The choice is yours.'

24

Wes and the others reached the main St Louis to Iron Mountain railroad travelling on a twice weekly branch-line train which served those living on the many outlying farms in the area. Here they parted company.

It was not an easy parting for either Wes or Anabelita. As a professional gambler Anabelita was used to concealing her feelings and she did so today — but with the greatest difficulty. She kept her face turned away from the others so that only Wes saw the tears that welled up in her eyes before the train she was on pulled away, heading for St Louis, leaving Wes to wait for one that would carry him in the opposite direction — to Harmony.

Since Wes's return from the Schuster plantation he and Anabelita had spent each night together and she had made use of every wile available to her in an attempt to persuade him to change his mind and travel to Abilene with her and the others.

The most she had been able to achieve was a promise that if Peter Rowse, Wes's uncle, was no longer in Harmony and had left no message for him, Wes would make his way to Abilene, find Anabelita, and discuss the future with her.

To Anabelita it sounded as though he had

made up his mind they would not be seeing each other again. She would never know how close he came to changing his mind whenever he looked at her.

★   ★   ★

When the train on which Wes was to travel came along and he climbed on board he began to wish he had gone with Anabelita and the others.

The train was comprised of ore trucks with the addition of a single passenger 'carriage' at the rear of the train, immediately ahead of the brake van. It was, in fact, a boxcar, from which sections of the side-panelling had been removed.

The seating consisted of half-a-dozen bench seats placed around the perimeter of the floor space and all were occupied, albeit loosely.

As none of the seated men seemed inclined to move up and make room for him, Wes dropped the bag containing his possessions on the floor and sat down beside it.

The men in the carriage were dressed in clothes Wes instantly recognized as those worn by miners and they fell silent when he climbed on board. When the train jerked into motion they began talking together again in a language he did not understand, but took to be German.

Once, one of the men tried to engage him in conversation, but when he indicated he did not speak the other man's language no further effort was made and he was ignored for the remainder of the journey.

When the train juddered to a halt some of the

men alighted and, although Wes repeated the name 'Harmony' to those remaining, they pretended not to understand what he wanted.

Fortunately, the brakeman came along and when Wes put the question to him he proved to be an American, saying, 'There's no station at Harmony, friend. This is Potosi and as close as you are going to get.'

Gratefully, Wes picked up his bag and alighted from the train. Standing beside the track he asked the brakeman, 'How far is Harmony from here?'

The brakeman shook his head, 'I've never been there, but I believe it's about fifteen miles, or so.'

When Wes expressed dismay, the brakeman said, 'There's a store a little way into town. They run wagons up to the mines. You could ask if they have anything going to Harmony.'

Thanking him, Wes made his way from the railroad station as the train clattered into motion once more.

The owner of the general store proved more helpful than had the German miners. In reply to Wes's question, he said, 'I've got a couple of wagons leaving for Harmony within the hour. You're welcome to a ride on one of them — but do you have friends there?'

'I hope so,' Wes replied, 'I've come all this way to meet my uncle, he's a miner there.'

'An *English* miner?' There was incredulity in the storekeeper's voice.

'Well, yes . . . although he would no doubt prefer to be known as a Cornishman.'

'How long is it since you heard from this uncle of yours?' The storekeeper asked.

'I suppose he must have written his last letter to me about eight or nine months ago. Why do you ask?'

Ignoring the question, the storekeeper said, 'I doubt if he's still there. A great deal has changed on the mines around Harmony in the last twelve months. So many Germans have come in that they've taken over most of the work on the mines, ousting miners from other countries. They've also formed themselves into trade unions — militant ones at that. A while ago they all downed tools in a bid to get more money from the mine owners. The owners' answer was to bring in workers from outside. There was a whole lot of trouble for a while before the Germans were forced to go back to work if they didn't want to see their families starve. A great many of the miners brought in by the owners were Cornishmen, so unless you have someone influential there you'd do well to stay well clear of Harmony. Around this area Cornishmen are about as popular as weevils in a cookie factory.'

'You're not the first person to tell me that,' Wes admitted, 'but I wrote and told my uncle I was coming. It's just possible he stayed on to wait for me. If he did he'll be having an uncomfortable time. I need to go there and find out.'

'I don't think you realize just how bad things are up there,' the storekeeper said, seriously. 'Men who fall foul of the unions don't find it merely 'uncomfortable'. Their problems are more likely to prove terminal.'

Pointing to where the Winchester bought by Aaron for Wes at New Orleans was strapped to his bag of belongings, the store-keeper added, 'I see you've got a rifle there. While you're in Harmony I suggest you keep it loaded and have it close by — day and night.'

With these words of warning the storekeeper left the store and went outside to check the wagon yard. When he returned to where Wes had been thinking over what he had been told, the helpful store owner said to him, 'The wagons are just about ready to leave. If you haven't changed your mind you'd best get out there.'

Assuring the storekeeper that he was still intent on travelling to Harmony, Wes thanked him for his assistance and was making his way from the store when the man called after him.

'Seeing as you're not going to see sense, I suggest you check in at the Eastern Promise hotel in Harmony. It's run and staffed by Chinese. They don't care where a man comes from, or what colour he is. Just so long as you're able to pay your way they'll give you as good a room as you're likely to find anywhere.'

25

Harmony was a typical American mining town although the hastily erected houses raised when lead was first discovered in the area had been largely replaced by more permanent structures and the streets were cleaner than any of the mining towns and villages Wes had known in Cornwall. It was a result, the wagoner told him — albeit grudgingly — of Germanic influence upon the town.

The same wagon driver set Wes off outside the Chinese hotel and expressed thanks for the few coins Wes gave him to buy himself a couple of drinks when the wagon had been unloaded.

The diminutive and elderly hotel proprietor's Chinese name was Nieh Tei, which had been corrupted by early English occupants of the town to 'Nitty'. As Nieh Tei preferred to be known as 'Joe', he inevitably became known as 'Nitty Joe'.

Nitty Joe went out of his way to make Wes welcome in his establishment. There seemed to be few other guests and Wes thought it highly probable that most other Harmony hotels catered for Germans, leaving Joe to tend to the needs of the few non-German visitors to the small mining town.

Wes was given a front room overlooking the

street and although this was quite noisy when the window was open, the hotel itself was quiet and after a passable meal Wes went to bed and enjoyed a good night's sleep.

Next morning at breakfast he got into conversation with a garrulous travelling salesman who worked for a Chicago footwear company, visiting various town and mining stores taking wholesale orders.

He was exactly the type of man Wes had been hoping to meet with. After listening to a lecture on the impossibility of the Germans allowing him to work in the lead mines in the area, Wes persuaded him to draw a passable map of mines in the vicinity for his use.

Armed with this, Wes set off after breakfast to find Peter Rowse — and also sound out the possibility of finding work in the area.

It soon became apparent to him that the reports he had heard of the German attitude towards English miners had not been exaggerated.

At the first two mines his search for Peter Rowse met with a 'don't know and don't *want* to know' response and while a tentative inquiry about the possibility of being given work provoked incredulity in the first mine office and anger in the second, when he broached the subject at the third he was actually threatened with violence and forced to leave the mine in a hurry.

At the fourth mine, that afternoon, the mine manager was more reasonable and spoke more English than had the Germans on the other mines. It turned out he had attended the Camborne school of mines in Cornwall and had actually learned some of his skills working in Cornish mines.

He had not known Peter Rowse, but gave Wes the useful information that many miners who moved from the area left details of their intended destinations in the post office in Harmony, where a record was kept of such information.

The helpful mine manager also warned Wes that another strike was imminent with the first men coming out that very night. At such times tempers boiled over and because of previous strike-breaking activities by Cornish miners he suggested Wes should obtain the information he wanted and leave Harmony at the earliest opportunity, explaining that when news that a Cornish miner was in the town reached the ears of union officials, as it most certainly would, they would seek him out and forcibly evict him from Harmony.

Wes was told this was an action the union men had taken on many occasions during their previous strike — and with ever-increasing violence.

Thanking the helpful mine manager for his information and the warning, Wes tramped back into Harmony, aware that he could not reach the town before the doors of the post office closed for the day. However, the office was not far from his hotel and he decided he would go there first thing the next morning and plan his future actions according to the information he received.

One thing had already become increasingly

certain. He would not find employment as a miner in Harmony and if his uncle was no longer here there was nothing to tie him to this particular area.

Indeed, if there was no message from the family member, he could go anywhere. Even to Abilene!

★ ★ ★

When Wes reached the Chinese owned hotel he found 'Nitty' Joe in a state of some excitement. It seemed from what Wes was able to gain that someone from the sheriff's office had come looking for him, with a message.

The hotel owner could tell Wes nothing more than this. Puzzled, Wes made his way to the sheriff's office, only to find it locked and no one there.

An old man, crippled from years spent underground in the lead mines and suffering from a more recent excess of alcohol was seated on the boardwalk nearby. He told Wes the sheriff had sworn in a number of deputies and gone to the mines in anticipation of trouble when miners came off the late shift and the strike began.

Wes decided to return to the hotel and have another early night, ignoring what was going on in the mines around the town. He was not aware that his presence in town was known and had been rekindling the still smouldering resentment against non German miners — Cornishmen in particular — who had been called in to break the earlier major strike.

26

The following morning, Wes had finished his breakfast and was contemplating the map drawn for him by the travelling salesman, trying to make up his mind whether he should go to the sheriff's office before visiting more mines, when he heard raised voices in the reception hall outside the restaurant.

The owners of the voices sounded angry and he could also pick out the loud and excited sing-song voice of the hotel's proprietor.

Rising from his seat he had reached the doorway to the reception area when he was confronted by more than a dozen men he took to be miners, with a voluble and agitated 'Nitty' Joe berating them in an unintelligible mixture of English, Chinese and German.

Among the miners Wes recognized the man who had made a half-hearted attempt to engage him in conversation on the train to Potosi.

The miner recognized Wes at the same time and excitedly pointed him out to a squat, heavily-built man who appeared to be the leader of the group.

The heavily-built man spoke to Wes in German but, well aware that the men had not come to the Eastern Promise to welcome him to Harmony, Wes said, 'I'm sorry, but I only speak

English and, if you'll excuse me, I have things to do.'

He made to pass through the group but the miner's leader stepped into his path. Jabbing a finger towards Wes, he demanded, 'What are you doing in Harmony, Englishman?'

Wes's inclination was to tell him to mind his own business but before he could reply 'Nitty' Joe intervened. Stepping between the two men, he spoke excitedly to the German, 'Mister Curnow guest in hotel. He good man . . . no make trouble.'

The glance the German miner's leader gave to the hotel owner was brief and contemptuous. Returning his attention to Wes, he said, 'I asked you a question. You have been to the mines asking about work. We will not have Englishmen come here for work when we have called a strike. You are not welcome.'

'I came here looking for a relative,' Wes retorted. 'I am still looking for him. My asking what work is available was incidental, but I am a miner.'

'You are not a miner here — and you will not be. We had trouble with Englishmen coming here to work when we called our last strike. It will not happen again. You will leave today.'

'I will leave when I've found out what I want to know about my uncle,' Wes retorted. 'Now, if you'll excuse me . . . '

He moved to bypass the Union leader but the German moved too, blocking his path and the other miners closed in around him.

Once again the Chinese hotel proprietor tried

182

to head off possible violence. Pushing in front of Wes, he pleaded with the German, 'Please . . . no trouble. I want no trouble my hotel.'

'Then you should be more particular about who you allow to stay here . . . now get out of the way.'

With this, he reached out and, taking a grip of the front of the cotton jacket worn by the diminutive Chinese, he lifted him off his feet and flung him to one side, where he crashed heavily against the reception desk and fell to the ground.

'There was no need for that,' Wes protested, 'He's an old man.'

'You are not,' the German miner replied, 'and you are next.'

'I'm not looking for trouble,' Wes said. Even as he was speaking he stepped back into the doorway of the restaurant so that none of the miners could come at him from behind, or from either side.

'Then you should not have come to Harmony,' the miner's leader said, taking a pace towards him.

Wes was deciding whether he should strike the first blow, or turn and make a dash for a window in the restaurant, when suddenly 'Nitty' Joe appeared from behind the reception counter — and in his hand he held a double-barrelled percussion sporting rifle.

What he intended doing with it was never put to the test. One of the miners, more quick-witted than his companions, grabbed the barrel of the gun and forced it downwards, pointing at the floor.

Suddenly, the contents of one barrel discharged, creating a hole in the floor that left no one in doubt what it would have done to a man, or men, had it been fired in their direction.

The miners' union leader was furious. Wes was forgotten for a moment as he turned on 'Nitty' Joe. 'You think you would shoot me, eh?' he shouted.

The miner who had caused the gun to discharge had now taken possession of it and another miner had pinioned the owner of the weapon from behind, holding him in a grip from which the puny Chinaman had no possibility of escaping.

Taking the gun from the man who held it, the Union leader addressed 'Nitty' Joe, 'Perhaps now I shoot *you*.'

The miner who held the hotel owner, aware that if his prisoner was shot, he too would at least be wounded, hurriedly protested the situation to the union leader and, swinging the gun away from his frightened intended victim, the man pulled the trigger.

The shot shattered a very large mirror decorating a wall of the reception area. Before the last of the glass had fallen to the ground the union leader was swinging the gun around to strike the helpless little Chinaman a savage blow across the face with the barrel. Before he had recovered from the pain of the blow, he had been struck on the other side of his face with a return swing of the gun.

This was the moment when Wes should have taken the opportunity to run back through the restaurant and follow the example of the three guests who had been taking breakfast in the restaurant when trouble erupted. Opening a window, they scrambled outside as quickly as they could.

Instead, Wes took a couple of paces into the reception hall as the miner holding the hotel proprietor released his hold, allowing his bloody-faced captive to fall to the floor.

'That wasn't necessary,' Wes said angrily to the man who had struck the blows, 'Joe's an old man who was merely trying to prevent trouble in his hotel.'

'If you had not been here there would have been no trouble,' was the reply. Then, with a gesture to his companions, he barked an order in German.

Wes was immediately seized and held by two of the miners. Swaggering up to him to stand with his face close to Wes's, the union leader said, 'Perhaps you are right, he is too old to have any sense . . . but you are not. You will leave Harmony — now!'

'I've already told you why I am in Harmony. As soon as I've learned where my uncle is I'll leave and go to a place where miners are happy to spend their time doing what they're paid to do, and not go around beating up old men.'

The German union leader smiled sadistically, 'No, you will go today, as soon as I have shown you it is not only old men we beat.'

Standing back from Wes he struck him hard across the face with the flat of his hand, then gave him an equally forceful back-handed blow.

He repeated this four times and Wes tasted blood on his lips, but he remained defiant. 'Perhaps you'd care to ask your friends to release my arms so I might return the compliment.'

The union leader smiled again, 'By the time your arms are released you will not feel like doing anything to anyone.' He drew back his hand to strike once more, but before he could do so Wes kicked him hard in the groin.

The German bully let out a grunt of pain, but the kick had failed to put him out of action and Wes was still held fast by the miners.

Angry now, the union leader said, 'You will suffer for that, Englishman. You will suffer very much . . . '

'I don't think so.' The loud voice carried no trace of an accent. 'You've had all the fun you're going to have for today, Kauffmann.'

The speaker was a tall, grey-haired man with a five-pointed star pinned to the left breast of his jacket. Stepping around the side of the group of miners, he spoke to the two men holding Wes.

'Let him go.'

Instead of obeying the order, they looked uncertainly at their leader.

The new arrival reacted angrily, 'Damn you! I said release him — now! Otherwise I'll arrest you and take you back to the county gaol in Potosi to stand trial for assault and battery, unlawful detention . . . and anything else I think of along the way.'

The two men holding Wes were in no doubt that the lawman meant what he said and they hurriedly released him.

Wes put a hand to his mouth and his fingers came away bloody. He gave the man who had hit him an angry glance, but said nothing. Instead, he went to where 'Nitty' Joe was sitting up groggily, holding both hands to his face.

Behind Wes, his rescuer said to the Union leader, 'I see you are up to your old tricks again, Kauffmann. Didn't you learn anything the last time you went on strike?'

'Yes, County Sheriff Marlin,' Kauffmann replied, 'We learned not to allow any strike-breaking Englishmen in to Harmony — and to collect enough money from miners when they are working to carry them over the time they are on strike.'

The proprietor of the Eastern Promise was sitting up now, his swollen face obviously painful, but he waved Wes away, repeating, 'No trouble . . . No trouble!' when he tried to examine it.

He was less dismissive about his shattered mirror. Pointing to it he was close to tears and unleashed a torrent of Chinese. Wes, who had overheard what Kauffmann had said to the County sheriff, said, 'Since the union has no money problems I suggest they make a collection among the members who are here to pay for a new mirror for Joe. It was his pride and joy.'

'That sounds a good idea to me and, as County sheriff, I think you should volunteer the money, Kauffmann. Otherwise I am going to have you all lodged in gaol until we can organise a court to try you and order you to pay. Tell your members, Kauffmann, just in case there is anyone here who doesn't understand American.'

County Sheriff Marlin was aware that Harmony's town sheriff was German himself — and also an ex-miner. If the union members were arrested and turned over to him they would remain in custody only until he left town.

Kauffman was aware of it too and if the County sheriff was intent upon a showdown, he would eventually be the winner, yet the German was not ready to capitulate right away.

'What happened was an accident.'

Wes snorted scornfully, 'Just as Joe's face was an accident! You're a bully and a coward, Kauffmann. You wouldn't last five minutes if you were representing Cornish miners.'

'You are *Cornish?*' Kauffmann's surprise was genuine. 'Had I known I would not have wasted a shot on the mirror. In fact if anyone here is carrying a gun I'd be happy for him to use it on you anyway, County sheriff or no County sheriff.'

'I wouldn't advise anyone to take that seriously. This here's a buffalo gun and one shot would put a bullet through as many as six men — even if they are as thick-skinned as some of you.'

The voice was that of Charlie Quinnell. Standing up, away from 'Nitty' Joe, Wes could see the old mountain-man standing in the hotel doorway, holding his long-barrelled buffalo gun in a deceptively casual manner.

The Chinese hotel proprietor, still seated on the floor, pleaded, 'Please . . . no more trouble. Too much trouble already.'

'I'm inclined to agree with Joe,' Sheriff Marlin said to Kauffmann, 'I suggest you set an example to your men by being the first to make a generous donation towards a new mirror for the Eastern Promise. Put the money on the counter, where we can all see what's being given. That way nobody will want to appear mean.'

After a brief discussion with his fellow miners, Kauffmann put a number of coins on the counter. When he looked up and saw the frown on Sheriff Marlin's face he dug in his pocket to add more. The other miners followed suit, albeit with considerable reluctance.

When the last man had contributed his donation, Kauffmann asked curtly, 'We can go now?'

'Yes . . . No! The sight of all that money has reminded me of the reason I came to Harmony this morning.' Shaking his head in mock disbelief, Sheriff Marlin added, 'I just can't believe I forgot in the first place . . . A bank was robbed in Potosi during the night and the gang which did it split up afterwards. My deputy's heading a Potosi posse following some of 'em who were heading west. I came to Harmony to raise a posse to try to catch up with the others, who set off heading for the mountains up this way.'

Believing he had a much needed opportunity to hit back at the County sheriff and regain some of his credibility as leader of his union, Kauffmann said, incredulously, 'You came to Harmony to ask us to help *you* catch bank robbers? No, Sheriff Marlin, you have never tried

189

to hide your contempt for miners — *German* miners. Now you will realize the contempt they have for you. You will not find one man in Harmony to join your posse. Not one. We all have other things to do.'

Wes thought Sheriff Marlin seemed surprisingly unconcerned at Kauffmann's almost gleeful statement but the reason soon became clear.

Shrugging his shoulders, the tall sheriff said, 'Oh well, I can't go after them by myself. Go get your things together, Wesley. You won't find your friend here, in Harmony, but he'll no doubt have left a message for you in the post office. They've tried to keep a record there of where miners are heading when they leave Harmony. We'll call in on the way back to Potosi. You can stay at my place for a while until you decide what you're going to do with yourself.'

While he was talking, Kauffmann and his fellow miners were making for the door, at least some of their self-esteem restored. As they were about to leave, the sheriff called out to their leader.

'By the way, Kauffmann, I wouldn't count on there being any money around to give to your men while they're on strike. The bank that was robbed last night was the Union Bank — your bank. The robbers went to the manager's home first and took him and his keys along with them. There were so many men involved they were able to take away every cent the bank held. It's the biggest

190

robbery we've ever had in these parts, probably the biggest in the whole of Missouri ... but don't let me hold you up. As you told me, you and your miners have things to do ... '

27

'Was there really a raid on the Union's bank last night?' Wes put the question to County Sheriff Howard Marlin as the three men made their way to the post office from the Eastern Promise.

'There was a raid sure enough,' Marlin replied. 'They cleaned the bank right out.'

The sheriff had already told Wes that Old Charlie had been staying at his home in Potosi for some days and had told him of Wes's intention to go to Harmony looking for his uncle.

Aware of the impending strike and knowing the German miners' hatred of Cornishmen, Sheriff Marlin had telegraphed to the Harmony sheriff's office, intending to ask him to warn Wes of the danger he faced. Unfortunately, the Harmony sheriff was out of town and the ageing deputy who took the message did not appreciate the seriousness of the situation.

'Because of that, Charlie and I would have come to Harmony this morning anyway. The bank robbery meant that we started off earlier, that's all.'

'I'm glad you did,' Wes said fervently, 'You saved me from a bad beating, at the very least . . . but shouldn't you be going after whoever robbed the bank? If I can hire a horse I'll be happy to come along with you.'

Sheriff Marlin shook his head, 'I'm not too anxious to become involved in it — for a couple of reasons.' Suddenly smiling, he added, 'I've asked Kauffmann and his miners to provide me with a posse. If they're not concerned about losing their money, I don't think I should bother too much.'

'You said there was more than one reason for not going after them,' Wes prompted.

'That's right. The truth is, my term of office ends in a couple of month's time. With the increased German influence in the county I'm not likely to be re-elected, so, if it's an honest-to-God bank robbery I have no intention of risking my life for folk who don't want me looking after the law for them anyway.'

'What do you mean, 'If it's an honest-to-God bank robbery'?' Wes was puzzled.

'Well, I've heard that someone's been hiring outlaws to come into Missouri from the Territories. Now, there's no range war brewing here and I couldn't think why anyone would want to hire such men. I think last night's raid on the Union bank gave me the answer. The mine owners know as well as I do that the last strike failed when the miners had no money left to feed their families. Kauffmann knows it too, that's why he had his union open their own bank to hold the money he's been docking from the men to form a strike fund. Without it, a strike is doomed before it begins.'

'You mean ... the mine owners would actually hire outlaws to rob a bank in order to stop men from striking? That's unbelievable!' Wes was incredulous.

'You may find it hard to believe, Wes, but this is America and it's a young country. Men — especially powerful men — make or break laws as it suits them and some mine owners are men with influence far beyond the State of Missouri. They wouldn't allow small fry like Kauffman — or even a County sheriff to stand in their way.'

Giving Wes a wry smile, Sheriff Marlin added, 'Besides, to be perfectly honest, Kauffmann has been a pain to me and the Federal Marshals ever since he took over the Miners' Union. He uses the law when it suits him and flouts it when it doesn't. Anything likely to put him out of office is all right with me — lawful or not. If I learn the names of any of the men involved in the bank robbery I'll have 'wanted' notices put out for them, but I have no intention of risking my skin at this stage of my career just to get Kauffmann out of a hole he's dug for himself.'

Wes thought that Aaron might have taken a very different line had this been a case which involved him, but he kept his thoughts to himself. Sheriff Howard Marlin had rescued him from possible death. He would always be in his debt for that.

The senior clerk at the Harmony post office was German but, unlike Kauffmann, he treated Sheriff Marlin with a deference that bordered upon obsequiousness. He produced a large, leather-bound ledger in which was entered in alphabetical order the names of hundreds of miners who had moved on from Harmony in the last couple of years, together with their intended destinations.

It took him no more than a couple of minutes to find an entry for 'Rowse, Peter'. Running a finger across the page, he said, 'Ah yes, here we are! He left Harmony bound for Denver in Colorado, some four months ago. Unfortunately there is no forwarding address but . . . ' and here he looked at Wes, ' . . . if you are Wesley Curnow, from Cornwall, there is a letter in the other office for you. I will go and fetch it right away.'

Disappearing into a back room, he appeared a few minutes later with an envelope upon which Wes's name was written in bold letters.

Tearing open the envelope, Wes read the letter that was inside then turned to Howard Marlin and Old Charlie. 'He's gone to Denver, right enough — and so have a great many of the Cornish miners he was working with here. He says there's gold to be found there and that men are making fortunes, some within days of arriving. How far away from Harmony is Denver?'

'Far enough away for you to need to do a whole lot of thinking about it.' The reply came from Old Charlie, 'But if Howard knows where we can hire a horse for you we'll go back to his place in Potosi and talk it over there. I'm on my way to Colorado too . . . but it might be that my way of travelling wouldn't suit you.'

28

෨

Sheriff Howard Marlin had a very pleasant home
on the outskirts of Potosi where he and his wife,
Nancy, had brought up a family of two sons and
a daughter. The children had now left home to
make lives of their own, but it seemed they often
returned to visit their parents and Wes gained an
impression that it was a close and affectionate
family.

Nancy came from pioneering stock and
understood the ways of some older mountain-
men but she would not hear of Old Charlie
sleeping in the stable with his mule. Instead, she
allocated him a spare room in which was a bed
and a wardrobe, but very little else.

In spite of half-heartedly grumbling about
'women always trying to change a man's ways',
Old Charlie settled for this and actually
appeared to enjoy being spoiled for a while. He
even gave the sheriff's wife a mountain-man's
ultimate accolade when he told Howard he was a
lucky man and couldn't be better looked after
had Nancy been a squaw!

The day after Wes's arrival at the house, when
the three men were seated in the garden,
Howard Marlin said to Wes, 'Charlie tells me
that one of Senator Schuster's daughters gave
you a fancy six-shooter while you were in

Kentucky. Perhaps you'd let me see it some time?'

'I'll go and fetch it now,' Wes replied, 'but it was a present from the whole Schuster family, not from a particular daughter.'

When Wes had gone to fetch the gun, Howard Marlin commented, 'The boy's a mite touchy on the subject of Schuster's daughter, did something happen there?'

'Nothing that shouldn't have happened,' Old Charlie replied, 'One of the younger girls took quite a shine to him. Wanted Wes to stay on at the Schuster place.'

'He could have done a whole lot worse,' Howard replied, 'There's both money and influence in that family. More than he's ever likely to make from mining.'

'That's what Aaron Berryman was always telling him — but Aaron had his own plans for the boy. Reckons he'd make a real good deputy. As for the Schuster girl . . . Wes hankers after a girl who deals cards on the riverboats. At least, she did. Now she's on her way with Aaron and another girl to work in a gambling-house he hopes to set-up in Abilene. I'll give the girl her due though, she seems to feel the same way about Wes, and she also has the reputation of running an honest game.'

'Hmm! Honest or not, she'll never be able to give him the sort of life the Schuster girl could.'

'No doubt about it, but I don't think he felt any more comfortable in the Schuster home than I did. It's so big a man could get lost in there

'. . . but here's Wes now, with his fancy six-shooter.'

When Wes arrived at the garden table where the two men were seated he was rather self-consciously wearing the leather gun-belt to which was attached the holstered Colt revolver.

When he handed it to the County sheriff, Howard weighed it in his hand and turned it this way and that before saying, admiringly, 'Now this really *is* a fine handgun, Wes. It's got the right balance for a working six-shooter, plus one or two gewgaws that would appeal to a young man — but how well can you handle it?'

'I've never used it,' Wes admitted.

'But you have fired a handgun?'

'Yes . . . but I handle a rifle better.'

'Aaron said Wes needs to get some practice in with a pistol,' Old Charlie said, 'and I've told him if he's ever going to wear that fancy six-shooter he'll need to be able to shoot better than the men he's likely to meet up with, especially if he's planning to join up with that kinsman of his at a mining camp in the Territories.'

'No doubt about it!' The sheriff agreed. 'Some of these fancy gunmen would kill a man just to get hold of a gun like this.'

'I don't intend wearing it,' Wes explained, 'I never asked for it in the first place.'

'Ask for it, or not, you've got it now,' Howard Marlin said bluntly, 'and going where you're heading you'll need to be like everyone else and carry a handgun, so it might as well be this one, but you'll need to learn how to use it properly.

I'll set up a couple of cans on the fence at the bottom of the garden and we'll see how well you can shoot. Do you have ammunition for it?'

When Wes admitted he did not, the sheriff said, 'The gun's the same calibre as mine and I have plenty of ammunition in the house. I'll fetch some when I go in to find the cans.'

When he came from the house, Howard Marlin was wearing his own gun-belt and revolver and carrying a box of ammunition. Setting up three empty cans and a bottle on the garden fence, he returned to Wes and loaded his gun for him. Then, standing back, he said, 'Okay, now let's see you shoot 'em all off.'

Wes fired four shots before one of the cans tumbled to the ground. The fifth shot missed. Taking careful aim and steadying his hand, he succeeded in hitting another can with his last shot.

'Hm! It's the first time you've ever fired the gun, so I suppose it's not too bad.'

It was evident to Wes that the sheriff was trying not to appear too critical. Old Charlie was less kind.

'Trouble is, had he been shooting at men and not tin cans, they wouldn't have stayed sitting on a fence waiting for him to take aim and try again.'

'True, but how's your aim these days, Charlie?'

Instead of replying, the old mountain man reached beneath his buckskin jacket and pulled out a percussion revolver. Raising his arm to shoulder height, he fired off two shots. The first sent the remaining can spinning from the fence, the second shattered the bottle.

Still holding the smoking pistol in his hand, he stroked his beard and looking at Sheriff Marlin, said, 'There's my answer, Howard. Now I'll stick the cans back on the fence and we'll see what you can do.'

Walking the length of the garden, he picked up the three cans and placed them back on the fence, with a gap of about a yard between them. He was still in the act of turning to return to the others when Howard Marlin drew his gun and, seeming hardly to take aim, fired off three rapid shots, each sending a can tumbling from its perch.

The first of the shots must have passed very, very close to Old Charlie but, grinning broadly, he said, 'You always were something of a showman, Howard. Seeing as how you're so close to retiring, perhaps you'd like me to put in a good word for you with Buffalo Bill. I reckon you'd get on real well with him.'

It was a good-humoured exchange and when the two men had returned to their seats and taken up their beers once more, Wes shook his head, ruefully. 'I have a lot to learn about shooting with a revolver, but if you like to stand the cans up again I'd put up a better showing with a rifle.'

Old Charlie shook his head, 'A rifle's fine to earn a living with, as both Howard and I've done in the past — and to kill food too, but if you want to stay alive where you're going then you need to be able to use a handgun — and use it well. I don't know about you, but I won't be staying here more than another couple of days. We'll have to see just how much Howard and I can help you improve in that time.'

29

*

The day after Wes's first practice with his gift revolver, he received an unexpected and welcome surprise. Sheriff Marlin had been out of the house for some hours and when he returned he sought out Wes who was seated on the back porch with Old Charlie after yet another session with his new toy.

Seeing the holstered gun on the table in front of him, the sheriff said, 'How's the practice coming along, Wes?'

It was Charlie who replied, 'We won't be running out of cans just yet, but if we stay in your home much longer there'll be enough bullets beyond the fence to open up a lead mine.'

'Well, I just happen to have something here for Wes that will buy enough bullets to serve the Mexican army.' With this, Sheriff Marlin placed a wad of notes on the table beside Wes's revolver.

Startled, Wes demanded, 'What's this for?'

'It's a thousand and two hundred dollars, your share of the reward money that had been posted for the outlaws you put out of action, one way or another, on the Mississippi. Most were wanted in more than one State. Apparently when Marshal Berryman met up with the Arkansas US Marshal he gave him a list of the outlaws and the names and addresses of those who had helped deal with them. The wheels were set in motion and authorisation given for the reward money to be paid out — or some of it. I believe there's more to come, so make sure you let me know when you get to wherever you're going from here.'

Wes was both surprised and relieved to receive the money. He had been concerned that if he did not soon find work he would need to start being careful how he spent the remaining money he had brought from Cornwall. He now felt he possessed a small fortune.

★ ★ ★

That evening, as Wes, Old Charlie and their hosts finished eating, Wes arrived at a decision. Addressing Nancy, who was seated at the table directly opposite to him, he said, 'Nancy, you and Howard couldn't have made me feel more welcome in your home had I been family and I really do appreciate it, but I think it's time I moved on to find my uncle and get settled into my new life over here.'

Both Nancy and her husband were protesting that he was welcome to stay for as long as he wished, when Old Charlie interrupted them, saying, 'You know, I was about to open my mouth to say exactly the same thing, when Wes beat me to it! It's been good to see you again after all this time, Howard, you too, Nancy. There'll be many a time when I'll think about you both and be happy for you and what you've got here, together, but you've both known me long enough to understand how restless I get when I'm surrounded by folks with ways that ain't mine. It's time I moved on too. Besides, if I don't give that mule of mine work to do real soon she'll be so fat and lazy she'll be no good to anyone.'

'Now wait a minute . . . ' This from Howard, ' . . . Have you two been cooking this up between yourselves? If you have, you can forget it. Nancy and I both enjoy having you here. You give us new things to talk about to keep us from growing old before our time.'

'Good! Wes and I'll write to you from wherever we happen to be and you can call in the neighbours to spend evenings talking about us and our news. No, Howard, like I just said, you and Nancy have given us everything a man could want from friends and I know Wes appreciates it every bit as much as I do . . . but it's moving on time for both of us . . . '

Old Charlie was interrupted by a knocking at the front door of the house. When Nancy answered it, she called back that there was a query at the County Sheriff's office for her husband.

When the Sheriff left the house with the caller, Nancy said to Wes and Charlie, 'Howard shouldn't be long. While he's gone I'll be clearing the table and washing up. You two take a couple of beers out on the porch and we'll join you when he gets back.'

When the two friends had carried their beers to the porch and settled back in their seats, Wes said, 'I've been thinking, Charlie . . . now I have a bit of money to see me along for a while, I think I might head for Abilene before going on to Denver.'

'Well now, why aren't I surprised? Mind you, if I had a woman in Abilene who looked at me the way I seen that half-Mexican girl look at you, maybe I'd be doing the same. Still, I'm a mite disappointed. I've been thinking too and I came up with an idea that could turn you into a tolerable gunman by the time you reach Colorado.'

'What is this idea of yours?'

Old Charlie had fascinated Wes with his reminiscences of a way of life that, if not already gone forever, was fast disappearing. It would not be long before there were no men like him left. He wanted to hear what he had intended suggesting.

'It doesn't matter now,' Charlie replied. 'You probably wouldn't have gone along with it anyway.'

'Tell me what you had planned and I'll tell you what I think of the idea. I'm not tied to getting anywhere at a particular time, especially now I have a bit more money to help me last out.'

Old Charlie's pleasure showed — and it made Wes feel guilty. He had pushed the old man into telling him what he had planned more out of curiosity than for any other reason. Now he saw it really mattered to him.

Wes realized that, despite his companion's oft-expressed aversion to human company, he was a lonely old man. It was possibly the knowledge that he was growing old and the thought of dying alone somewhere . . .

'You really want to know?' his companion's question jolted him out of his thoughts.

'I wouldn't have asked you otherwise,' Wes lied.

Leaning forward in his seat eagerly, Old Charlie said, 'You seem to be interested in the old days of the frontier, so I was going to give you a chance to learn about it for yourself. To see how we lived then . . . and at the same time get in some practice with that fancy six-shooter of yours.'

'I don't quite follow you, Charlie. How are you suggesting I might do all this?'

'By going to Colorado *my* way. By forgetting all about rail-roads and riverboats and travelling across country, shooting our meat as we need it and perhaps buying another mule to carry whatever other supplies we might need — with perhaps a few trinkets as presents for any Indians we meet up with along the way.'

Wes had very real doubts about Old Charlie's idea and the two men were still discussing it when Howard returned, his business having taken less time than anticipated.

He asked what the two men were looking so serious about and when Wes told him, the sheriff shook his head. Addressing Old Charlie, he asked, 'When was the last time you made a journey like that, old man?'

'What's it matter?' Charlie retorted, stung by being called an 'old man'. 'It's a journey I've made many times — or journeys like it.'

'That's not what I asked,' Howard persisted. 'Have you made that particular journey since the war ended?'

'No, but . . . '

Interrupting him, Howard said, 'When you went East with Buffalo Bill, did you travel with your eyes closed all the way?'

'I didn't need to, I travelled in a box car with Nellie — my mule.'

'So you didn't see very much of the country through which you were travelling?'

'I saw enough to know I didn't like it. Too many folk for my liking.'

'That's what I'm trying to say to you, Charlie. Times have changed — and they've changed fast. Dammit, old-timer, surely I don't have to tell you that? You've brought old Nellie all the way from the East. Were you able to ride her cross-country?'

'Not very often,' Old Charlie admitted, 'There were too many homesteaders sitting on a couple of hundred acres and making out they owned the whole blame country. I had to travel on their roads . . . but that was the East and it's always been like that.'

'That's just it, Charlie, it *hasn't* always been like it and it's no longer just in the East that things are that way. The frontier's been moving west so fast we haven't been able to keep up with it. There are so many folk in Missouri now that a buffalo couldn't move ten paces without treading on someone.'

As he listened to Howard talking, Wes was watching Old Charlie's changing expression. Now he asked the sheriff, 'How far west would a man like Charlie need to travel before he got to the sort of country he's looking for?'

The county sheriff thought for a while before replying. 'Well now, Missouri's pretty well settled, so too is East Kansas — and the Kansas Pacific railroad has hatched out a heap of homesteads clinging to it like a string of toad spawn almost all the way to the Smoky Hills.'

Wes had no idea where the Smoky Hills were but he was beginning to form a mental picture of the land that lay between the town where he now was and the mining area in Colorado to which Peter Rowse and the other Cornish miners had gone.

Speaking to Howard, he asked, 'How far is it from here to Abilene?'

The question took the county sheriff by surprise but, after only a moment's thought, he replied, 'About four hundred and fifty miles, I reckon. Why . . . ?'

Instead of replying, Wes asked him a second question, 'How about the distance from Abilene to Colorado?'

'To Denver, where your uncle has gone, must be much the same distance, I guess . . . but why do you ask?'

'Because I've just had an idea,' Wes replied.

Turning to Old Charlie, he said, 'You want to go overland to Colorado and I've decided to go by train. Now, why don't we meet each other halfway, Charlie? Why not travel by train to Abilene together — through the country that's already settled and fenced off — then, once we've reached Abilene and I've had a chance to talk to Anabelita we could go on to Colorado — but this time travelling the way you say you want to? Along the way you could teach me what you think I ought to know about using a handgun.'

Old Charlie's immediate reaction was to turn down the suggestion outright. Shaking his head vigorously, he said, 'Me and Nellie travel across Missouri on a train? No, boy, it would be more than either of us could bear. You take the train to wherever you want to go, me and Nellie'll take our own time getting to Denver and I'll look you up when we get there.'

Sheriff Howard Marlin now came into the discussion on Wes's side, saying, 'Wes's suggestion makes a whole lot of sense, Charlie — as you'd agree if only you'd think about it. Missouri's a settled State now, with sheriffs, town marshals, deputies and policemen every way you turn. You come through their territory trying to live the way you did forty, thirty — or even twenty — years ago and you'll get yourself arrested. It wouldn't matter to them that you've been a trapper, a scout for the army, or a mountain man. To them you'd be a hobo, someone with no work and no home and they'd throw you in gaol. Is that how you want to end up, Charlie? Getting yourself arrested because you don't belong any more to the world in which folks like them are living?'

Sheriff Marlin shook his head, 'I don't think so. You just put your mind to what Wes has suggested and you'll see that it makes a whole lot of sense. He's giving you an opportunity to do what it is you want to do for perhaps a last time — and enjoy his company while you're doing it. Given the choice, I know what I'd do.'

30

❧

'I don't know why I let you talk me into travelling on this damned contraption! If the Good Lord had meant us to get around like this he'd have made us with wheels instead of feet and laid rails all over his earth.'

Wes grinned at the grumbling of his companion, 'Having wheels for feet and going around on rails would have been all right for bandy-legged old timers like you, Charlie, you'd have been quite comfortable going around with a wheel on each rail, but it might have proved hard on the rest of us.'

The two men were talking on the ore-train that ran from Iron Mountain, as it rattled and swayed its way along the track that would take it to St Louis.

The attack on the Union Bank in Potosi had produced the result predicted by Sheriff Howard Marlin. Faced with the prospect of having no money to sustain their families, the miners had gone back to work, ignoring the exhortations of Kauffmann and the other union leaders.

Whoever had planned and executed the bank robbery, the result had certainly done a great favour to the mine owners. The miners' union had suffered a humiliating defeat and it would be many years before they regained the absolute power they once held over their members.

There were very few miners on the train, but the ride was no more comfortable for passengers than it had been on Wes's previous journey.

'How much longer do we have to put up with this misery?' Old Charlie was grumbling once more.

'We should arrive in St Louis in another fifteen minutes, or so. We'll then have a couple of hours on our hands to get to the Kansas Pacific station, buy a ticket and get the train to Abilene. You'll find it more comfortable once we're on board a proper train.'

★   ★   ★

Wes's hopes that boarding a main line passenger train would satisfy his travelling companion were soon shattered. The Kansas Pacific line was popular with settlers heading west and the long carriages were packed with men, women and children — a great many children. Most were immigrants to the United States, with their belongings. These new arrivals to the country were particularly excited to be coming towards the end of the greatest adventure of their lives.

Even Wes, inured by virtue of his sea voyage to America to the chatter and presence of a surfeit of fellow beings, found so much loud and unintelligible conversation difficult to endure. Old Charlie declared it to be intolerable.

Taking his bedroll, the old mountain-man decamped at the first stop, announcing that he would spend the thirty hour journey with Nellie, his mule, in the boxcar at the rear of the train.

Unfortunately, Nellie was even less enamoured than her owner with the accommodation offered by the Kansas Pacific railroad — and with the equines brought on board the train at Jefferson City to share her accommodation.

She threw a tantrum.

Soon after the train arrived at Sedalia, the conductor came through the carriage calling for 'Wesley Curnow'.

When Wes identified himself, the conductor asked, 'Are you a friend of that cantankerous old-timer who's dressed up like a 'squaw-man'?'

Wes did not know what constituted a 'squaw-man', but he thought he recognized the description of a 'cantankerous old-timer'.

'If you're talking about Charlie Quinnell, yes, I'm a friend. We're travelling to Abilene together, but he decided to spend the journey with his mule in the boxcar at the rear of the train.'

'You might be travelling to Abilene, but your partner isn't ... leastways, not on this train — unless he agrees to shoot that mule of his!'

'Shoot Nellie?' Wes was aghast. 'He'd shoot you — or even me before he'd do that. But what has Charlie, or his mule, done to upset you?'

'The old-timer's done nothing — apart from giving me a lot of lip — but that mule of his ... The Kansas Pacific spent a lot of money fitting out a boxcar with stalls to accommodate horses in damn near as much comfort as the passengers. It's worked out well for as long as I've been conducting on this line — until that mule came on board. The brute has kicked out one side of its stall, bit the ear off a deputy marshal's horse and lamed a top rodeo horse that's on its way to perform at the Kansas City fair. It's a good thing your partner has agreed to leave the train here, at Sedalia. If he hadn't, the railroad would have taken him — and his mule — before the court in Kansas City.'

Wes was appalled, but his primary concern was not with the rodeo horse, or the Kansas Pacific railroad.

'How far are we from Abilene?' He asked the question as he began gathering belongings from the rack above his head.

Shrugging his shoulders nonchalantly, the conductor replied, casually, 'Somewhere about two hundred miles or so, do you have a horse in the boxcar?'

When Wes shook his head, the conductor said, 'Then I guess you've got a long walk ahead of you.'

★ ★ ★

By the time the cattle town of Sedalia was behind them, Old Charlie's mood had undergone a dramatic change. From being angry and resentful of the threats made against Nellie and being thrown off the Kansas Pacific train, he now looked about him appreciatively. 'This is the way a man should travel in America, Wes. Sniffing God-given air and admiring what the country has to offer, not shut up in some prison-on-wheels with a crowd of strangers who have no appreciation of the country they're

213

travelling through and who just want to get to where they're going so they can make it exactly like the place they've been in such a goddam hurry to get out of!'

Wes shifted his bulk in a bid to make himself more comfortable on the unfamiliar cowboy saddle, which was all that had been available at the Sedalia stables from which he had purchased the mare he was riding.

Advice on the purchase had been given by Charlie who succeeded in driving a hard bargain with the stable owner. The old man was well pleased with the beast, telling Wes he now owned as fine an animal as any he was likely to come across during his travels in the Territories.

Settling down in his saddle once more, Wes asked, 'How long is it going to take us to reach Abilene, Charlie?'

'We'll be there in about a week,' the old man replied.

'A week!' Wes repeated bitterly, 'I'll arrive to see Anabelita, dirty, tired out and . . . ' shifting his weight again, ' . . . most probably saddle-sore. The train would have got us there in another fifteen hours, or so.'

'So? What's a week out of a lifetime? By the time you reach Abilene now you'll be more suited to life in the West than when you started out — and if you travel on to Colorado with me you'll be able to hold your own among the best — or the worst — of the gunmen you're likely to come up against there.'

'I've no intention of 'coming up against'

anyone, Charlie, certainly not with a gun in my hand.'

'Then I suggest you turn right around now and go back East. Where you're heading a man needs to prove himself and earn respect from others if he's to survive. Aaron says you have guts and are a good man to have around when there's trouble. He knows men, so I'm happy to go along with that, but out in the Territories you'll need to prove it to men who ain't so easy to convince — and unless I can teach you how to do it you'll not live very long.'

BOOK 2

1

❧

Anabelita, Lola and Aaron boarded a Kansas Pacific railroad train from St Louis a week before Wes and Old Charlie made their abortive journey along the same line.

It was a much less crowded train than the one boarded by the two men. A special immigrant train had been provided by the railroad company the day before. Lacking many of the amenities of a scheduled train, it had nevertheless attracted many miners and settlers heading west, aware they would be saving a great deal of money by travelling in such a Spartan fashion.

Anabelita had become increasingly quiet since leaving the stranded *Missouri Belle* and, soon after the train set off, when Aaron had gone to spend an hour in the saloon car Lola tackled her about her lack of conversation.

'Are you all right, Anabelita? You've hardly said more than a few words since we left the river.'

Anabelita started, as though her mind had been far away when Lola spoke. Gathering her thoughts together, she replied, 'Haven't I? I'm sorry, Lola, I don't mean to be rude, it's just . . . oh, I don't know! I suppose I believed that my life had pretty well settled down while I was working on the *Missouri Belle*. Now everything is up in the air again.'

'Is it the fact that you are going to work for Aaron now . . . ? Or does it have more to do with parting company with Wes?' Lola asked the question casually, but she studied Anabelita's face closely for a reaction.

She had forgotten she was speaking to a very accomplished poker player. Without changing her expression, Anabelita lied, 'It's the change in my way of life, I guess. I like to plan my life as much as I can. It's just not possible right now.'

'We can none of us tell exactly what's going to happen in the future, but I think we can both rely on Aaron to look after us. He won't let us down.'

'I'm sure he won't . . . at least, not intentionally. But he's first and foremost a United States Marshal whose work is out in the Territories. It doesn't exactly make him the most secure of employers.'

Shuddering involuntarily, Lola said, 'I'd rather not think about that, Anabelita.'

Reaching out, Anabelita gripped her friend's arm, sympathetically 'I'm sorry, Lola, that wasn't very tactful of me.' After a few moments, she added, 'When I get really depressed I wish I had led a 'normal' life and ended up with a safe home and a family, like most women. But had we both done that we would never have met men like Aaron or Wes, would we?'

'In the long term that might have been for the best,' Lola said enigmatically, 'At least, it would have been for me. Aaron is an important man . . . a friend of the President, no less. I am nothing more than a bar girl . . . a whore! One day he'll go back East to his own kind, leaving me to go back to mine. But I accepted that when I let myself fall for him and I'll make the most of him while I can. It's not every woman who is lucky enough to have someone like Aaron come into her life.'

Lola was not in the habit of expressing her feelings quite so openly and, giving Anabelita an embarrassed, lop-sided smile, she added, 'We haven't done too well in our choice of men, have we? There's me saying Aaron's too good for me and Wes believing he's not good enough for you!'

Startled by Lola's words, Anabelita demanded, 'What do you mean . . . ? Whatever gives you the idea that Wes doesn't believe he's good enough for me?'

'Aaron told me,' Lola replied. 'It seems Wes told him he could never see you settling down to life as the wife of a miner.'

'Since the question of marriage has never come up, I don't think Wes had any right to say who I would, or wouldn't settle down with. For all he knows I might be ready to settle down with anyone who will have me.'

Anabelita's reply puzzled Lola. She thought about it for a few moments before asking, 'Are you pregnant?' She put the question hesitantly, fully expecting her friend to be indignant at such an impertinent question.

Instead, Anabelita shrugged, 'I don't know.'

The reply astonished Lola. 'You don't know whether you're expecting a baby? There can't be any doubt, one way or the other, surely? You either are, or you're not!'

'I've never been particularly regular,' Anabelita replied, 'and I'm only a couple of weeks overdue.'

Showing very real concern, Lola said, 'But ... what if you are pregnant? You can't take up work in a frontier town gaming house in that condition.'

'Why not? It won't even show for about six months — and what else should I do? Retire on what little money I've got put by, only to discover it's a false alarm? No, Lola, I'll carry on with whatever Aaron has planned for us and decide what to do when I know one way or the other.'

When Lola remained silent, Anabelita said, 'You won't say anything to Aaron about it?'

'Of course not, but in all fairness to him I think you should tell him as soon as you know for certain — for his sake and for yours. He'll no doubt be able to get in touch with Wes ... '

'No!' Anabelita spoke fiercely, 'I don't want Wes to know anything about this ... even if there is something to know. I hope he will come back to me sometime soon, Lola. I think I want it more than anything I have ever wanted in the whole of my life, but it needs to be because he loves me, not because he believes it is what he should do. If he returns to me because someone tells him I am expecting his baby I will never know for certain. If he comes back to me of his own accord then I will tell him. I will also tell him how I feel about becoming a miner's wife ... but all that is in the future. I am glad I have told you, Lola, you are a good friend and I wasn't happy not saying anything to you but let's not talk about it again until I am certain whether or not I am having Wes's baby.'

2

&

The next day was a Saturday and, late in the afternoon, as the train slowed on the approach to the Abilene depot, Lola and Anabelita made a final check to ensure they would leave nothing behind when they disembarked.

Both women were excited to be arriving at their destination — but their enthusiasm was not shared by Aaron. The US Marshal had been led to believe that Abilene was a thriving and exciting railhead town, where cowboys, cattlemen, buyers and their many hangers-on made it a rowdy and free-spending town. What he was seeing through the train window did not justify such a claim.

There were extensive stockyards, it was true, but they were standing empty with a neglected air and what could be seen of Abilene itself gave the newcomer an impression of a sleepy and rather tired town.

It was not at all what Aaron had been expecting. At this time of day a railhead town should have been bracing itself for a night of riotous entertainment. Abilene did not look like a town where a man could make his fortune by opening a gambling house.

At that moment the conductor came through the car and Aaron commented to him on the

224

lack of activity to be seen through the car window.

'Things in Abilene certainly aren't what they used to be,' the conductor agreed ruefully, 'There was a time when there'd be nigh as many folk waiting to meet the train as there were steers in the pens we've just passed. Trouble is, too many newcomers brought fancy ideas in from the East and they didn't care for the smell of the cattle — nor the cowboys. Thing got so bad that the Texan cattlemen persuaded the Sante Fe railroad to lay track into Dodge. When they did, the cattlemen moved the stockyards there too. I tell you, if it wasn't for all that's going on out in Colorado the Kansas Pacific would be in deep trouble and it'd be hardly worthwhile stopping in Abilene at all. There's only six of you getting off the train today and I doubt if there'll be that many getting on.'

Lola and Anabelita had been listening to the conversation with increasing concern. When the conductor moved on Lola asked, 'If all he says is true, what are we going to do, Aaron? If there are no cattle coming in there's going to be very little money around to spend on gambling.'

Aaron could only agree, but he said, 'Let's not get too depressed about it right now. We'll find a hotel, book ourselves in and I'll check out how much truth there is in what the conductor had to say. Things might not be quite as bad as he makes out although I must admit there doesn't seem to be very much going on in Abilene right now.'

Booking in to a hotel posed the trio no problem. Aaron had already inquired about which of the town's establishments was most suitable for the two women and had learned that the best of them was right opposite the railroad depot. Here he booked a room for Lola and Anabelita to share and another for himself.

When he had seen the two women settled in, Aaron set off to find the town sheriff. He had no trouble locating his office on the town's dusty and tired-looking main street, but the sheriff was not here.

A one-armed man sitting in the office cleaning a shotgun informed him that the town's premier lawman was out of town with his wife, attending a relative's wedding in Kansas City.

'Then I guess things must be pretty quiet around here right now,' Aaron commented.

Shaking his head, the one-armed man said dejectedly, 'Mister, things are so quiet in Abilene that if anyone so much as sneezed, it'd likely make headlines in the next day's newspaper.'

Aaron smiled, 'I'll remember to tiptoe around town and make sure not to blow my nose . . . but am I right in thinking you're Pete Rafferty?'

'That's me, Mister, but you have an advantage over me . . . '

'I'm sorry, I should have introduced myself when I came in . . . ' Extending a hand, he said, 'I'm Aaron Berryman, a friend of Heck McKinnon.'

The one-armed man's lackadaisical air disappeared immediately. Scrambling to his feet still clutching the shotgun, he seemed momentarily at a loss what to do with the weapon. Eventually laying it upon the table, he grasped Aaron's right hand in an awkward grip with his own left and said, 'It's an honour to meet you, Marshal. Heck telegraphed that you'd be coming this way, but he didn't say when, or why.'

'I'm on my way to the Territories,' Amos explained, 'but thought I'd like to set up a little personal business venture right here in Abilene first. At least, that was my intention. I came to look at a gambling saloon called the Golden Globe. Heck said you might be able to help me out.'

Rafferty grimaced, 'I could have helped you, Marshal, but not any more. You've arrived in Abilene a little too late. The Golden Globe burned down a couple of weeks ago.'

Startled by the news, Aaron asked, 'Burned down . . . ? How did it happen?'

'The only person with the answer to that question is Kate Scobell, who owned the place . . . but she ain't around any more. She was arrested on suspicion of burning the place down so she could claim insurance on it, but a slick lawyer got her released and no one's seen hide nor hair of her since then. Rumour has it she's taken off and gone East.'

Looking sympathetically at Aaron, Rafferty added, 'All this might have come as a nasty shock to you, Marshal, but take it from me, you've had a lucky escape.'

227

When Aaron asked him to explain what he meant, Rafferty said, 'The days when money was easy come, easy go in Abilene, are over. There's not one gaming-house in town that's making money any more. Most have already closed. You'll have seen the empty stockyards as you came in. Cattlemen have taken their money to Dodge City and until something comes in to take their place folk are going to need to tighten their belts — and I know what I'm talking about, Marshal. Time was when six deputies were hard put to keep order in this one street alone. Now they've all been paid off and the sheriff is able to go out of town to a family wedding, leaving a one-armed man without a badge to look after the town while he's away.'

'Well, according to Heck McKinnon you're more than capable of doing just that, but finding Abilene so quiet has come as a big disappointment to me . . . '

Aaron told Rafferty the story of the wrecking of the *Missouri Belle*, explaining, 'I brought two of the women croupiers along to Abilene with me.' Making no mention of Lola's past, he added, 'They're both straight players and I was looking forward to buying the Golden Globe, setting it up as an honest house and asking you to keep order in it while I was away. Now I suppose I'll need to take a look at Dodge.'

'Dodge City is no place for women, Marshal — leastways, not unless they're whores. My brother came through here from Dodge only last week, heading home to Missouri. He says it's already wilder than Abilene ever was and reckons there's no more than a couple of decent women there right now. As for gaming-houses . . . big men from the East have moved in and put the opposition out of business — some of 'em permanently. If you were likely to be around all the time you might be able to do something about it, but it's no place to leave two women while you go about your government duties. No, Marshal, if I was thinking of starting up some such business I'd turn my back on cattle towns. I'd go way out West — to where you're heading anyway. To Colorado. It's still a Territory, although I've heard it said it won't be too long before it's given Statehood . . . but you'll know that already. Miners are striking it rich around Denver and flocking into town looking for ways to spend their earnings. Yes, sir, If I was intending setting up a gambling saloon — one with an honest game and two women who weren't whores working the tables, I'd head for Denver. A miner who struck it rich passed through here only last week and said men from the diggings will pay good money just for the chance to look at a decent woman. That's where there's money to be made, Marshal — and you'd always be somewhere near at hand to see that things were going just the way you wanted. I'm so sure that's the place to be that if you decided to take your chances there and wanted someone to be around to keep order for you, I'd up sticks here and come along with you.'

3

At the hotel that evening when Aaron told the two women the worrying information given to him by Pete Rafferty, Anabelita was particularly concerned.

'What do we do now?' She asked, 'I've given up everything to come along with you, Aaron.'

'I realize that, Anabelita, that's what I want to discuss with both you and Lola. It's come as quite a shock to all of us but, according to folk I've spoken to in Abilene, everything happened so suddenly that moving the stockyards from the town took them by surprise. There had been rumours for some time about the demise of the stockyards, but business was booming so no one took them seriously. Then, one day, it just happened. Cattle and cattlemen didn't need to come to Abilene any more because the railroad had gone down the trail to meet them.'

'Are you suggesting we do the same?' This time the question came from Lola.

'No . . . ' Aaron replied, before adding honestly, 'I did think about it, but it would mean going too far out of the way from my real work out here.'

Leaning towards them and sounding more enthusiastic, he said, 'Mind you, this could prove to be a blessing in disguise . . . for all of us.'

'How?' Anabelita demanded, unconvinced. 'Lola and me came with you to work in a gambling parlour that's been burned down, in a town where there's no money and Lola and I have nowhere to work. I can't see how that's a good thing for any of us.'

His enthusiasm increasing, Aaron replied, 'Think what might have happened had we got here earlier, bought the Golden Globe, and I'd gone off to carry out my duties as a United States Marshal leaving you to run a gaming-house. Now that would have been a real calamity for every one of us, especially me. I would have lost all my cash and not been able to help either of you. As it is I am able to finance either, or both of you, to go to wherever you think will best suit you — that's if you want to go your own ways after you've listened to what I have to say.'

Aware that he had the full attention of both of them, Aaron continued, 'I still intend setting up a gaming-saloon — an honest one — but in a place where there's real money being made by men who are just looking for places in which to spend it. I'm talking about Denver.'

Anabelita looked at Aaron sceptically, 'I've never heard of this 'Denver', but it sounds a lot like a place the Spaniards used to talk about . . . I believe they called it 'El Dorado', a place where everything was made of gold. The trouble is, such a place has never existed — or, if it did, no one's ever found it.'

Leaning back in his chair once more, Aaron gave Anabelita an amused smile, 'You know, you're not so very wrong, Anabelita. Denver may not quite be an 'El Dorado', but the wealth that's being spent there comes from gold. Men are flocking to the mines around the town in their thousands.'

'Oh? And will they all become millionaires and go home happy — after spending a percentage on the gaming tables, of course, or are the great majority going to be disappointed when they find nothing and either starve or turn to crime in order to stay alive? It sounds to me as though this Denver might turn out to be an even wilder town than the new railhead town of Dodge.'

Aaron was not particularly surprised by Anabelita's response to his suggestion that they should try their luck with a gambling saloon in Denver. After all, she had given up what was comparatively secure work on the Mississippi River to come with him. Colorado was still a Territory and few women thrived on frontier life . . . but he had brought *two* women to Abilene.

Turning to Anabelita's companion, he asked, 'What do you think about the idea, Lola?'

'I can't say I'm exactly jumping for joy at the thought of going further west than we are now,' Lola replied honestly, 'but I've less to lose than Anabelita and I don't have enough experience to go back and get a croupier's job on the river or in any other place that's half-respectable. If you're willing to take me on to Denver on my own I'll come with you — because I trust you . . . but I would be a whole lot happier if Anabelita came too. There's a great deal about gambling that she knows and I don't.'

Appealing to her friend, she pleaded, 'Won't

you give it a try, Anabelita . . . for me?'

While Lola had been talking, Anabelita's thoughts had been of what concerned her even more than the shock of finding there was to be no work waiting for her in Abilene. Her reply to Lola's plea reflected this thinking.

'What happens if Wes comes here looking for me, only to find we've moved on to somewhere else?'

Lola had said nothing to Aaron about Anabelita's suspected condition, but he was a shrewd man and he asked now, 'Is there any particular reason why he should come looking for you?'

'No *particular* reason,' Anabelita lied, 'but I do think a hell of a lot of him and I believed he was coming around to feeling the same way about me. Everyone we've spoken to about the place he was going to in Missouri has said that things there are bad — especially for English miners. I thought that if he couldn't get mining work he might come looking for me to see what he might do in Abilene.'

'The way things are here he'd be no luckier finding work than in Missouri,' Aaron commented, 'but if you decide to come with us I'll send a telegraph to the County Sheriff of the Harmony area asking him to find Wes and tell him where we've gone. Not only that, just in case he's already left and is on his way here, I'll leave a message at the Abilene sheriff's office too. If Wes comes here I'll make certain he learns where we've gone. You can be quite certain of that, Anabelita. I'd like to make Wes a deputy United

States Marshal to help me out with what's going to be a tough task in Colorado. So, you see, I have a keen interest in that young man too!'

Anabelita could not tell Aaron that she believed her interest in Wes's future movements was even more urgent than those of the United States Marshal, albeit of a far more personal nature.

It concerned her whole future — and that of the child she was almost certainly carrying, the child that was hers and Wes's.

She also realized that if Wes did not turn up, she would be able to rely on more support and help from Lola and Aaron than she was likely to find if she abandoned them now and returned to work back East, where she knew very few people well enough to ask for their help.

Making up her mind, she capitulated. 'All right, if you leave word for Wes where we've gone, I'll come to Denver with you . . . '

4

In Denver, Colorado, Aaron and the two women
with him, found all they had expected to find in
Abilene — and much more. It was early evening
when they arrived accompanied by Pat Rafferty,
and the streets surrounding the downtown
railroad depot were thronged with men, women
and children — but mostly men.

Among them were a number of cowboys, but
the majority were men wearing a garb that Wes
would have recognized immediately as that
adopted by miners. Many spoke with an accent
he would also have recognized and it thrilled
Anabelita to hear them speak in the way he did.
She wished he could have been here with her to
hear it for himself.

Aaron looked about him and beamed. 'Now,
this is more like it, there's a healthy aroma of
money in the air . . . '

At that moment there was an eruption of noise
from somewhere along the street, accompanied
by a number of gunshots and a woman began
screaming.

When Aaron seemed unconcerned by the
sounds, Anabelita said to him, 'Something's
happening along there. As United States Marshal
shouldn't you find out what it is?'

To her surprise, Aaron shook his head. When

she appeared confused, he explained, 'Denver's a frontier town. If I got myself involved in every little altercation that occurred I'd just be wasting government money. Besides, it looks to me as though Denver has got itself a police force . . . of sorts. It's standing right across the street and is no doubt paid by the good citizens of Denver to keep the peace. If he's not concerned by whatever's going on I'll mind my own business.'

Looking across the street Anabelita saw a man wearing a blue uniform with a silver badge pinned to the left breast of his jacket. He was standing with his back to the disturbance, unconcernedly chatting to two men, both of whom to Lola's experienced eyes appeared to have been drinking.

The four travellers had an amount of luggage with them and Aaron said to the one-armed man, 'Will you look after the girls and the baggage for a few minutes, Pat? I can see a sign for the Denver Hotel up the quieter end of the street. It's the hotel recommended by that talkative carpetbagger on the train, but this isn't Abilene. If it's as good as he said, then it's likely to be full. There's no sense lugging everything up there only to have to take it somewhere else.'

'Go ahead.' Rafferty grinned, 'I don't think we'll be bored while you're away.'

His comment was in response to an upsurge of sound from the street in the opposite direction to the Denver Hotel. Now it was mainly cheering and hooting and as they all looked in that direction they were in time to see a horse and rider emerge from the entrance to the saloon.

The rider was wielding a six-gun in one hand and a bottle of whisky in the other.

Across the street from the railroad depot the uniformed policeman had turned to see what was happening, but was now in conversation with his two companions once more.

Aaron and Pat exchanged glances, then Aaron shrugged and set off to walk to the Denver Hotel.

As Pat and the two women talked together the crowd outside the saloon farther along the street gradually drifted away. The town policeman was still talking to his companions, but one of them had begun taking an interest in Anabelita and Lola.

He said something to the others which caused all three men to look across the road before he sauntered across the thoroughfare towards the newly-arrived trio.

Dressed in none-too-clean cowboy clothes, the man wore a revolver in an open holster at his hip and as he drew closer, it became evident his face had not felt the touch of a razor for a week or more.

'Uh-ah! Here comes trouble,' Anabelita commented softly to Lola.

Stopping in front of the two women and ignoring their one-armed companion, the cowboy said, 'Howdy, girls, you just arrived in town?'

The aroma of stale whisky which was breathed out with his words was the least offensive of the odours he brought with him and neither woman made any reply.

Undeterred, the cowboy spoke again, 'If you're

looking for somewhere to stay I can take you to a hotel that's as cheap as any you're likely to find in Denver.' Beaming at Lola, he added, 'Not only that, they'll ask no questions and if you're looking to set yourselves up in business . . . well, you couldn't find anyone better than Archie Leveridge to look after your interests.'

'You're being offensive, friend,' said Pat Rafferty, 'I think you'd better back off and return to your friends. They seem more amused by you than we are.'

Looking contemptuously at the one-armed man, the cowboy said, 'Stay out of this — unless you want to lose the use of the arm you've got left.'

Pat Rafferty did not carry a handgun and his shotgun was strapped to his bag, which was on the boardwalk with the other luggage.

As he began to sidle towards it, the cowboy lifted his revolver from its holster and said, 'Don't even think about it, Mister. You'd be dead before you laid a finger on it.'

While he was threatening Rafferty, Anabelita whispered to Lola, 'Move in front of me . . . quickly!'

Startled, Lola said, 'What . . . ? Why . . . ?'

'Just do it!' Anabelita hissed, in such an authoritarian tone that Lola did as she was told immediately and Anabelita reached beneath her skirt so swiftly that no one around her was even aware of the move.

'Get over there, away from that bag,' the cowboy gunman motioned Pat Rafferty away with a wave of his gun.

238

'Look, cowboy, just go on your way and leave us alone. These are two respectable ladies and we're all waiting here for a friend to return, then we'll be going about our business.'

'Is that so? Well, the ladies have just found themselves a new friend and I'm sure we'll all know each other a whole lot better by the end of the evening — but so neither of 'em will feel left out I'll call my partner to come over and join us.'

As he was speaking the cowboy signalled to the man who still stood speaking to the Denver police officer on the far side of the street and when the man started to walk towards them he spoke to Rafferty once more.

'Now, go on your way and leave these 'ladies' to enjoy the company of two real men.'

'If it's all the same to you, I'll stay where I am and keep the ladies and their luggage with me.' Pat Rafferty was hoping that if he could only keep the other man talking for long enough, Aaron would return, but it seemed the gunman had other ideas.

'I've asked you real nice to go away, but I'm running out of patience with you, Mister. I'm going to count to five . . . if you're not gone by then you won't be going anywhere . . . ever!'

Looking straight at Pat Rafferty, the cowboy began counting. 'One . . . two . . . three . . . four . . . '

The revolver came up and there was the sound of a shot . . . but the cry of pain that followed came from the cowboy and not from Rafferty. The revolver he had been holding dropped to the ground and he staggered backwards, clutching his shoulder, his expression one of agony and disbelief.

As Anabelita stepped from behind Lola, smoke still trickling from the barrel of the small revolver she held in her hand, the wounded cowboy began screaming, ' . . . She shot me! The goddam bitch shot me . . . '

While all this was going on, the friend who had been invited by Leveridge to join the anticipated party with the two women had looked on uncertainly. Now, seeing Anabelita holding the diminutive pistol, he began to draw his own pistol from its holster.

Whether or not he would have used it was never put to the test.

Aaron had been returning from the Denver Hotel when he saw a crowd gathering about the place where he had left Pat Rafferty with the two women and he began hurrying. As he neared the spot he heard the sound of a shot, fired from a small calibre weapon and he broke into an awkward run.

Pushing his way roughly through the gathering crowd he was in time to see Leveridge's friend drawing his revolver. At the same moment Pat Rafferty dived for the shotgun strapped to his bag and the cowboy hesitated, uncertain whether to shoot at Anabelita, or the one-armed man.

Before he reached a decision a hand came over his shoulder and the muzzle or a revolver barrel was pressed against his right temple. He froze as Aaron's voice said, 'Just so much as twitch your trigger finger and you'll lose what little brain you might have. Drop your gun — and be quick about it.'

The cowboy dropped his handgun as though it had suddenly become red-hot. Aaron promptly kicked it towards the women and Lola hastily picked it up.

A push from Aaron sent the disarmed man staggering across the road to where the uniformed Denver police officer was now supporting the wounded cowboy who had his back to a store front and appeared to be about to slip to the boardwalk.

While Aaron was being appraised by Pat Rafferty of what had occurred, a second uniformed man pushed his way through the crowd. He too wore a badge on the breast of his jacket, but the wording on it displayed the word 'Chief' and Aaron rightly assumed he commanded the Denver police force.

Addressing the officer supporting Leveridge as 'McAvoy', the newly-arrived police chief demanded to know what was happening.

Lowering the wounded man to the boardwalk, officer McAvoy explained, 'There's been a shooting, Chief.' Pointing to Anabelita who had returned her .22 revolver to it's holster, hidden beneath her skirt, he added, 'She shot this man for no apparent reason.'

'That's a lie!' Pat Rafferty said, heatedly, ' . . . and you damn well know it because he was talking to you before he came over here and started insulting the two women who are with me — something you seemed to find highly amusing at the time. When I told him to get lost he drew his gun and threatened to shoot me if I didn't go away by the time he counted to five. He'd got to four and was raising his gun when Miss Jones shot him. She saved my life.'

The police chief digested this for a moment, then turned to McAvoy. 'Is this true?'

The officer shook his head, 'I didn't see anything of the sort . . . and I know Mr Leveridge. He's not the sort of man who'd bother women that way.'

'Leveridge . . . ? Now that's an unusual name.' This from Aaron, 'His first name wouldn't happen to be Archibald, I suppose?'

Glaring at Aaron, McAvoy replied, 'His name is Archie . . . but what's it got to do with you?'

'Well now, Archie Leveridge isn't a man who any lawman should claim for a friend — although any one involved in law enforcement should know the name. A wanted poster went out to all sheriffs' and marshals' offices — including those in the Territories — declaring that a certain Archibald Leveridge is wanted in Missouri with others for holding up a stagecoach and making off with a cash box and a couple of bags of United States mail. Most of the others have either been killed or captured, but Leveridge managed to evade arrest, in spite of the fact that he has a seven hundred dollar reward on his head. Two hundred put up by the governor of Missouri and five hundred by Wells Fargo. I think Miss Jones can rightly claim that reward. I suggest you lock Leveridge up in your cells, have a doctor look at his wound, then ship him off to Jefferson City to stand trial — but if I

242

were Chief of Police here I'd want to know how come one of my officers is so friendly with a wanted outlaw and was ready to take his part when he knew damn well that he started all the trouble here in the first place.'

Angrily, the Denver police chief demanded, 'Are you trying to tell me how to do my job, Mister . . . ? Who the hell are you, anyway?'

Pulling his coat open to reveal the five-pointed US Marshal's star pinned to his chest, Aaron replied, 'I'm Aaron Berryman, United States Marshal for The Territories. If I remember the notes I made before heading out West, you'll be Chief Jack Kelly.'

Momentarily taken aback, Kelly made an attempt to retrieve his badly dented authority, 'If a US Marshal came to Denver, I'd like to think I'd be the first to know — but what's happened here is a local matter, not a Federal one. If Officer McAvoy has decided to arrest this woman then she stays arrested.'

'I don't think so, Chief Kelly. As it happens, you are the first to know I'm here, but from what little I've seen of your town so far, you're not likely to be the last. Colorado has applied to President Grant to be given Statehood and admission to the United States of America. The President has sent me here to check on whether Colorado is ready to become a State; is capable of maintaining law and order without help, and whether I think Denver should become the State capital. I haven't been in Denver for half-an-hour yet, but already I'm beginning to doubt whether any of his questions can be answered in the

243

affirmative. As for the rest . . . among Leveridge's crimes, he's wanted for stealing US mail from a Wells Fargo stagecoach. That's a *federal* offence and I'm a federal marshal. What's more, I'll personally shoot anyone who tries to arrest Miss Jones — and that includes you and McAvoy. She's disabled a wanted and dangerous criminal and is due a reward for doing it. Now, get Leveridge into gaol and have him sent off to Missouri at the first opportunity. Mr Rafferty, me and the women are off to the Denver Hotel and that's where I'll be should you want me.'

Aaron was a diminutive, almost insignificant man but he seemed to grow in stature as he spoke and it would have taken a braver man than either Police Chief Jack Kelly, or Officer McAvoy to try to stop him from leaving with his small party.

Besides, Pat Rafferty had unstrapped his shotgun from his bag and neither of the Denver policemen doubted that he would use it to good effect if they made a move against his companions.

5

❧

For the next few days Aaron was kept busy in his role as US Marshal for The Territories, meeting officials of the various areas and settling in to the office allocated to him by the Colorado Territorial governor.

He learned there was great dissatisfaction in Denver with Police Chief Jack Kelly and considerable disquiet about some of the men he had appointed as officers in his police force. McAvoy, in particular, was known as a blustering bully, inclined to use his fists too readily on men who were too drunk to retaliate.

Because he did not trust Kelly, Aaron swore in two recently retired army sergeants as temporary deputy Marshals and despatched Archie Lever-idge in their custody to Jefferson City, Missouri. They carried with them a note from Aaron, explaining that the wanted man had been shot by Anabelita and claiming on her behalf the posted reward for his capture.

Aaron quickly became aware there was great potential in Denver for making money — either honestly or otherwise. When thousands of miners had flocked to the Rocky Mountain gold-fields seeking their fortune, dubious brothels and gambling saloons followed in their wake to cater for their masculine needs and relieve them of their hard-won gold. Denver grew up around them.

Brothels and gambling houses still existed in present-day Denver, but the town's authorities had succeeded in containing them inside an area that was studiously avoided by Denver's more recent 'respectable' residents.

Gaming houses and saloons did exist outside this section of the town, but they were run along more acceptable lines, tolerating neither rowdiness nor vice and frowning upon discernible dishonesty.

Although he was kept busy on government business, Aaron still found time to pursue his intention to open a gambling saloon. For a while it seemed unlikely he would succeed, but when Anabelita and Lola were becoming restless, and Pat Rafferty despondent about his own prospects, Aaron was told of a building that had been built as a theatre but had functioned as such for only a brief period of time.

It seemed that the owner-builder had left Denver in a great hurry when the husband of the woman he had run off with from somewhere in the East, came to town seeking them both.

The property had been left in the hands of a lawyer with instructions to sell the theatre for whatever he could obtain and send a banker's draft for the amount to a secret address.

Aaron took Anabelita, Lola and Pat along with him to inspect what was on offer and each of them was impressed with the theatre's potential. A certain amount of work would need to be done before it became fully operational, but it was less than Aaron had anticipated and the gilt and chandeliers inside the building excited both women, who went around pointing out each new feature as it was found.

Pat Rafferty was impressed too, declaring the stage to be an ideal place from which chips and money could be safely issued and from where he would be able to oversee most of what would be going on in the gaming room.

The matter was clinched when the lawyer showing them around mentioned that he knew an excellent carpenter who could construct all the furniture Aaron would need in order to transform the theatre into a superior gambling emporium.

Aaron decided his new venture would be called the 'Thespian Club' and the lawyer told him it was likely to become the second largest such establishment in Denver. The number one gaming-house in Denver was owned by a man named Vic Walsh, who had arrived from the East with a great deal of money to invest in his own gambling venture.

The lawyer knew little about Walsh's background, but told Aaron he had earned a reputation for himself as running a respectable business, even though he was credited with forcing a number of less scrupulous establishments to close their doors, the owners leaving town in an unexplained hurry.

As Walsh had let it be known he intended Denver should gain a reputation as the West's centre for honest gambling, he was given credit for their hasty departures.

It seemed he neither denied nor admitted responsibility for ridding Denver of such establishments, but the more cynical of the town's residents pointed out that business at Walsh's Palace was booming as a result of the demise of his rivals.

A couple of days before the advertised opening of the Thespian Club, Aaron was in the Marshal's office, catching up on paperwork, when a man was shown in by one of the deputies who occupied the outer office. Dark-haired and of stocky build, the man introduced himself as Vic Walsh in a dialect that Aaron recognized as being the same as that spoken by Wes. It seemed Walsh was a Cornishman.

Extending a hand to Aaron, Walsh said, 'I'm pleased to make your acquaintance, Marshal, I'm the owner of the Palace.'

'I know who you are, Mr Walsh — I also recognize your accent. Unless I am mistaken your early life was spent in Cornwall, in England.'

Temporarily taken aback, Walsh recovered quickly, 'That's very astute of you, Marshal, but you've no doubt met many Cornishmen since you arrived in Denver, we form the backbone of a great many American mining communities.'

'I met up with a Cornishman before my arrival in Denver, Mr Walsh. Wesley Curnow and I travelled together from New York to New Orleans on the ship that brought him from England. He is a miner, but on the steamboat coming upriver to St Louis he handled himself so well when we were attacked by river pirates that I had hoped to make him a Deputy Marshal and bring him out here with me.'

Walsh appeared impressed, 'I heard about the way you dealt with the river pirates, Marshal and was very impressed, but I wasn't aware a Cornishman had been involved with you.'

'Well, you know now,' Aaron said, 'but take a seat, I don't suppose you've come here to chat about your countrymen, or to welcome me to Denver. You'll no doubt have something to say about me opening up the Thespian Club in opposition to your Palace.'

'I sincerely hope we're not going to be in opposition, Marshal, I'm rather hoping the Thespian Club and the Palace will complement each other and that, together, you and I will be able to shut down the sleazy gaming rooms that give gambling such a bad name . . . '

Correctly interpreting Aaron's sceptical expression, Vic Walsh said, 'I don't know what you might have heard about me, Marshal, but I'd like to tell you myself exactly where I stand, so there can be no misunderstanding between us. I am an ambitious man and will move heaven and earth to further that ambition, but I am also an *honest* man, something that can on occasion prove a weakness as well as a strength. You know yourself that you'll never be able to prevent men from gambling and, like me, you've decided to make money from their requirements — and why not? If we don't there are many others who will and most in this part of the world are dishonest. They are out to make quick money and get out when their honesty is questioned. I am not such a man

— and I don't believe you are, either. If you were, you wouldn't be such a well-respected United States Marshal and I wouldn't be here talking to you as I am. I think we both know that a man who runs an honest house can make more money in the long-term than a crooked gambler will ever see. I am in Denver to stay, Marshal. I have made it my home and I have my sights set on becoming Mayor. One day, when Colorado is a State and Denver its capital I might even look to Congress and the Senate.'

Aaron's gut reaction was that Walsh was trying too hard to portray himself as an honest man, but he said, 'There's nothing wrong with a man having ambition, Mr Walsh, but you're counting on a great many things that haven't yet happened. If Colorado is to be admitted as a State and Denver made its capital, both need to prove they're fit to be given what they want. Quite frankly, where law and order are concerned I, for one, am going to need some convincing!'

Leaning forward in his chair, Walsh said, 'I wouldn't argue with you about that, Marshal — but with me as Mayor — and with your backing — everything could change. There are a great many honest folk in Denver who are aware that things are not going to change while brothel keepers and crooked gamblers are pouring money into the pockets of the present mayor and too many of the city councillors. We had an election last year that should have got rid of the Council's rotten core, but gamblers and prostitutes went to the polls by the cartload. I swear there were more of them than there are registered residents in the town. The result was we finished up with the same Corporation — and the same problems. I am determined it won't happen again. It's not going to be easy, but I'm going to do my damnedest to make Denver a place to be proud of.'

Reserving judgement on his visitor, Aaron remained cautious. 'I'm glad you came to see me today, Mr Walsh and if you run the Palace as I intend running the Thespian Club we'll have the foundation for the gambling Mecca you hope to have in Denver. As for the rest, if you can provide me with records of the last election and they're as false as you claim, you might make it to Mayor sooner than you think — and if Wesley Curnow ever makes it to Denver, as I hope he will, you could do worse than have him — a fellow Cornishman — as your next police chief.'

BOOK 3

1

❦

'If we'd shot that damn mule of yours when she went berserk and upset the conductor on the Kansas Pacific, we might have arrived and found them still here.'

Wes was more than half-serious. He and Old Charlie had reached Abilene only to learn that Aaron, Anabelita and Lola had left for Denver days before with Pat Rafferty. Irritably, he placed the blame for missing them squarely upon the old mountain-man's mule.

Old Charlie understood Wes's disappointment, but he was hurt by his comments about his mule. 'That ain't no way to talk about Nellie, Wes. She just didn't like the company she had on the train. Come to think of it, I didn't care none for it myself. Besides, according to the deputy they only stayed in Abilene for one night. They'd left before we even stepped onboard the train.'

Aware that Old Charlie was right and that he had upset him unnecessarily, Wes said grudgingly, 'All right, so it wasn't Nellie's fault and we'd have missed them anyway, at least we can take the next train to Denver and catch up with them in a couple of days . . .'

'Catch another train . . .? No, sir!' Shaking his head vigorously, Old Charlie declared, 'Me and Nellie have had enough of trains to last us both our lifetimes — and you still need more practise with that pretty six-shooter of yours before you meet up with the men you're going to come up against in Colorado Territory.'

Wes looked at the old man with an expression of disbelief. 'You're not suggesting we ride all the way to Colorado?'

'I'm not *suggesting* anything, I'm *telling* you that if you don't get in more practice you'll be shot dead by the first man who pulls a gun on you. I'm not saying you can't handle a rifle well enough. I'll go as far as to say you can use it as well as any man I've known. If you and I had met years ago we could have made a fortune hunting buffalo — but you need more work with a handgun, boy. I reckon another ten days should do it — if you work at it hard enough.'

'Ten days! Is that how long it would take to ride to Denver?'

'I reckon . . . give or take a day or two.' Old Charlie was aware he was being dishonestly optimistic. Denver was some four hundred miles away across Great Plains country, where Indian bands still hunted buffalo — and white men — and where the weather was notoriously unpredictable. A horseman would be fortunate to complete such a journey in twice the time.

Unaware that a ten day estimate was likely to prove wildly inaccurate, Wes seriously considered what the old frontiersman had said. He was aware of his shortcomings when it came to using a handgun, but he learned fast and was quickly mastering what Old Charlie considered to be an essential skill.

Although he believed the 'frontier' Old Charlie had known in his young days probably no longer existed, Wes actually enjoyed mastering a gunman's skills and the old frontiersman was both interesting and knowledgeable about the vast continent over which they were travelling.

In addition, and despite Old Charlie's eccentricity and occasional irascibility, Wes had grown fond of him. He decided that, as Anabelita was not expecting him, a few extra days would make little difference.

'Are you sure you'll be able to find your way to Denver, Charlie?'

The old man spat a stream of tobacco juice into the dust of the street in disgust. 'Boy, I guided wagon trains along the Smoky Hill trail before anyone knew there was a trail there — and I've fought Kiowa, Comanche, Cheyenne and Arapaho for the right to do it. Not only that, I kept most of Colonel Butterfield's relay stations in buffalo meat when he was running his stage line to Denver. Then, when the railroad was being laid I kept their gangs fed — though there's many times now I wish I'd let 'em fend for themselves. It might have meant there'd have been no railroad and we'd all be the better for it.'

Ignoring Old Charlie's views on the benefits, or otherwise, of progress, Wes said, 'If you really *do* know the way to Denver and it's only going to take ten days then I'll go along with you — but if you're telling me wrong I'll take off for the nearest railroad station and leave you out there on your own.'

'If that's meant to be a threat you're well wide

of the mark, boy. I've spent more time on my own than I have being crowded by folk and I like it that way. The only reason I'm inviting you to come along with me is because I believe you have the makings of a frontiersman — although you'd never have survived as a mountain-man — and I'd like to make sure you stand a chance of staying alive before I turn you loose.'

★   ★   ★

Their cross-country trek began well enough. Old Charlie had Wes practising hard with his revolver and when they came across a rattlesnake Wes drew the gun and shot the snake with an accuracy and speed that so delighted the old man he skinned the snake and made bands for his own battered headgear and for the wide-brimmed hat he had insisted Wes bought in the first store they came across after being thrown off the train in Missouri.

Nine days after leaving Abilene they arrived at Fort Hays. Declaring that he had 'had a bellyful of army forts' Old Charlie ensured they stopped only long enough to replenish their stores and buy more ammunition before setting off again.

Thirty-six hours later Wes expressed his increasing concern at the lack of signs of civilisation about them. If Denver was the bustling place they had been told it was, there should have been others heading for the town.

Instead, they had now reached country which appeared devoid of all human life, even though Wes thought it good farming land which should have appealed to settlers in close proximity to such a busy place.

When he questioned Charlie, the old man avoided giving him a direct answer, saying only that settlers would reach this part of the land 'soon enough'.

It was not until the following day that Wes learned the truth.

They were following the course of the Smoky Mountain River, heading westward, when they heard the unmistakable sound of horses coming along the trail behind them.

This was uncertain country and, as a precaution, the two men took cover behind some bushes, a short way from the river. They remained in hiding until the riders came into view and proved to be a large troop of cavalry riding at a sharp canter.

When Charlie and Wes showed themselves, the captain leading the troop brought his men to a halt. To Wes's surprise the officer and Old Charlie appeared to know one another well.

Shaking hands with him, the Captain said, 'I heard you had been to the fort, Charlie. I was sorry to have missed you then but I'm even happier to have met up with you today. You are just the man I need.'

'When the army's told me in the past that I'm needed it's always spelled trouble. I don't suppose that's changed. What is it this time?'

'Same as it was the last time you and I rode together, Charlie . . . Indians. A messenger from Fort Larred came riding in hell-for-leather late yesterday. Seems a whole mess of Cheyenne and

Arapaho have got themselves het up over something and gone on the warpath. They've raided a few farms down Larred way and are heading north hoping to join up with Sioux and Northern Cheyenne who are giving the cavalry the runaround. Fort Larred doesn't have enough troops to go chasing after them so they've asked for help from Fort Hays. I've been sent out to try and head the war party off. Trouble is, although we have enough men at Fort Hays, we took over garrison duty there only a month ago and there's no one who knows the country, but if I remember right, you know the Plains country better than most.'

'I wouldn't argue with that,' Old Charlie agreed. 'Had an Indian woman when I first came this way . . . this was Cheyenne country in those days and I'd hunt buffalo for her people. Did the same for the army, as you know. Country ain't the same nowadays though, too many settlers and not enough buffalo. It was better in the old days.'

'I've heard a lot of old-timers say the same, Charlie, but none of us can turn back the clock — and right now we haven't got time enough to discuss it. We need to head the Indians off before they get among the settlers farther north. Once there they'd cause havoc.'

Listening to the cavalry captain, Wes had become increasingly concerned and now he queried, 'These Indians . . . are there a lot of them? Enough to attack Denver?'

The captain looked at Wes with an expression of bewilderment and Old Charlie said hurriedly,

'He's a greenhorn, new from England. I'm showing him something of the country.'

'Then I suggest you get him a map — and fast!'

Turning his attention to Wes, the captain replied to his question, 'It's certainly a large party. The largest we've had on the loose for some years, but if it's Denver you're heading for, then you'll find the railroad no more than nine or ten miles north of here. I suggest you head in that direction and take a train to Denver. You'll be safe there from . . . from these Indians, anyway. Like I said, they're heading north and Denver is more than two hundred miles to the west.'

Wes looked at the captain in disbelief before rounding on Old Charlie. 'Is he right? Is Denver still two hundred miles away?'

Old Charlie's embarrassment was evident and he mumbled, 'Could be . . . I'm not too good on distances.'

'You told me we'd reach there in ten days,' Wes pointed out, his anger fuelled by the amusement exhibited by the troopers within hearing of the exchange, 'That was eleven days ago. Now I learn that there's two hundred more miles to go. You lied to me, Charlie.'

'It's just taken longer than it should have,' Old Charlie said, lamely, 'Your horse losing a shoe set us back, you know that . . .'

He was evading the truth as Wes was fully aware . . . but the captain cut in on their altercation, 'You'll need to settle your difference some other time, there are lives at stake out there

261

on the Plains. You know this country better than any other white man, Charlie, and can follow a trail as well as an Indian. I need you — and those unsuspecting settlers with their women and kids need you even more.'

'I can't just leave Wes out here on his own, Captain. Like I told you, he's a greenhorn.'

'You won't be leaving me, Charlie, I'm leaving you! Point me in the direction of the railroad, Captain, then you can take Charlie to go and find your Indians or to any other place you like. I'm catching the next train to Denver.'

'Like I said, the railroad is due north of here, about eight or ten miles and you should come to the small town of Lauraville before you get there.'

Turning to a trooper with a number of yellow stripes on the sleeve of his uniform, the cavalry captain asked, 'Do you have an issue compass on you, Casey?'

By way of reply the veteran trooper pulled on a piece of cord hanging from a breast pocket to reveal a compass attached to the end of it.

'Good! Give it to this young man in case he forgets where north is.'

When it looked as though the veteran cavalryman might object, the captain added, 'I'll write you a chit to draw another when we get back to Fort Hays.'

The sergeant handed over the compass, but now it was Old Charlie who was not happy. 'The boy's new out here, captain. I feel responsible for him.'

The sharp edge of Wes's anger had evaporated

as quickly as it had erupted and now he said, 'Don't worry about me, Charlie. You heard what the captain said, there's no one out here can help him more than you and I believe him. You take care of yourself and come and find me in Denver when you've sorted this out.'

'I'll surely do that,' Old Charlie promised, but he still had misgivings and, as Wes turned away, he called out after him.

'Don't forget to keep that fancy six-shooter of yours hidden away when you reach Lauraville. You're good enough now to hold your own against ninety-nine out of a hundred men you're likely to meet up with — but the hundredth will always be waiting out there somewhere.'

'Come on, Charlie, we've got some riding to do.' The cavalry captain spoke impatiently. 'Perhaps you should have given your mule to your pal and taken his horse . . . '

Old Charlie was still berating the cavalry officer for his suggestion when Wes rode off, heading northwards, while the cavalry troop cantered off along the Smoky Hill trail.

2

❧

Lauraville was larger than Wes had expected it to be. The reason for its size was that when the railroad was being built Lauraville was founded as a stores depot for goods and material brought from the East for building the railroad and supplying those employed on laying the track.

But Lauraville's heyday was in the past. Many houses were tumbling down and others deserted now, although a surprising number were still occupied. Towards the centre of the sprawling town, narrow streets and narrower alleyways spread out on either side of the main street in which were located an over-abundance of well-patronised saloons.

As Wes would learn, the reason for there being so many men in town was because it was generally believed a branch-line was being planned from here to link the Kansas Pacific Railroad with another to the north of the State. As a result a great many prospective labourers had flocked to the town hoping to find employment when work began on the new railroad.

Taking over many of the empty and apparently ownerless houses, they spent their time drinking, quarrelling, fighting and stealing anything that might be sold for the price of a drink.

Wes quickly learned that Kansas Pacific trains no longer called at Lauraville. Instead, they now stopped at the town of Trego, farther to the West, where there was a tank for refilling their boilers. He was also informed he had missed a Denver-bound train by only hours — and the next one would not be coming through for another three days.

Rather than ride on to Trego, Wes decided he would spend that night, at least, in Lauraville.

He was riding along one of the alleyways off the main street, following signs to a livery stable, when he heard the sound of men's raucous laughter coming from an alleyway intersecting the one along which he was riding. It was interspersed with the voice of a young woman pleading to be left alone and allowed to go home.

Commonsense told him that whatever was going on did not concern him and that he should go on his way and ignore the pleas, but the girl sounded terrified. When her cries continued unabated he suddenly made up his mind and turned into the alleyway from which the sounds were coming.

Almost immediately he came upon an open space surrounded by broken posts and planks, indicating that this had once been a small corral belonging to a now derelict barn.

There was also a well-worn path running across it, evidence that it was now used as a short-cut between alleyways.

Within this space a young girl of no more than fourteen or fifteen was trying to escape the attentions of two horsemen, one of whom had used a lariat to lasso her, tightening the rope whenever she tried to escape the attentions of the second man who was leaning from his horse and attempting to grab her whenever she came within reach. It appeared to Wes they were trying to get her inside the nearby derelict barn which lacked a door.

At first glance Wes had thought the girl was black, but as he drew closer her features reminded him of some of the Indian women he had seen at Fort Hays. He thought her parents were probably from both these races.

As he reached the scene the girl collided with one of the men's horses and fell to her knees. As she struggled to her feet, the man reached down and took a grip of her hair, causing the girl to scream.

Both the horsemen wore revolvers in open holsters attached to belts which had cartridges nestling in loops for most of their length. Wes realized that these were not ordinary cowboys, but probably experienced gunmen. Nevertheless, drawing his rifle from the scabbard hanging beside his saddle, he said, 'I don't think she likes that, friend. Let her go.'

The two men looked at Wes and although he was carrying a rifle across the pommel of his saddle, they saw he was not wearing a gun belt and both decided he posed no particular threat.

Without releasing his hold, the man gripping the young girl's hair said, 'This is not your game, mister. Back off and mind your own business.'

As the man was talking, Wes had swung his

gun until it pointed in the speaker's direction and suddenly it fired, the bullet passing so close to the horseman's head that he instinctively jerked it back, at the same time releasing his grip on both the girl and his lariat.

Due to the practise Wes had put in during recent weeks, his horse had become used to the sound of a gun being fired at close range, but the horses of the other two men were startled. As their riders worked to bring them under control, the young girl wriggled loose of the noose pinning her arms to her sides and, pushing past Wes, ran away along the alleyway.

The man who had roped her was the first to bring his horse under control and angrily reached for his revolver.

Wes fired a second shot from his rifle, but this time he had it to his shoulder and the man's hat flew from his head, to be trampled on by his still skittish horse.

'That's the second bullet I've wasted on warning you,' Wes said, more easily than he felt, 'I'll not waste another.'

His rifle moved momentarily to cover the second man and he called out, 'Keep your horse close to your friend's — and your hand well clear of your gun.'

The gunman instantly put his hands out to the side of his body.

Still watching him, Wes returned his attentions to the man who had lost his hat. 'Undo your belt and drop it to the ground . . . with the gun still in the holster.'

When the man hesitated, Wes peered down the

sights of his rifle meaningfully and the man obeyed his instruction immediately.

'Now draw your rifle out — nice and slowly — and drop that too.'

When the man began to protest, Wes snapped, 'Just do it — and quick, I'm beginning to get an urge to pull this trigger and put an end to this.'

The rifle followed the revolver and belt to the ground.

It was then the turn of the second gunman and while he followed the same routine, his companion said to Wes, 'You're going to regret this, Mister. Robbing a man of his guns is as bad as stealing his horse — and they hang men for that.'

'I'm not stealing 'em,' Wes replied, greatly relieved that the incident had not resulted in serious gunplay, 'You'll be able to collect them from the sheriff's office. I'll leave 'em there as soon as I've found where it is. Now, as we have nothing more to talk about I suggest you take yourselves out to the main street. I'll watch until you get there, to make sure you don't bother any more young girls along the way.'

The two men rode away scowling but saying nothing to each other. As they reached the main street one of them looked back and even with the distance between them Wes could see his venomous expression and realized he had made a serious enemy.

Gathering up the men's weapons, he led his horse in the direction indicated by the livery stable signs.

He had not gone far when the girl who had

been molested by the two gunmen turned into the alleyway ahead of him. She was accompanied by a black man who wore a silver sheriff's star pinned to the breast pocket of his shirt.

Excitedly, the girl said something to her companion who immediately increased his pace, drawing ahead of the girl.

As he neared Wes, he pulled out a revolver and called, 'Hold it right there . . . and drop those guns to the ground.'

Startled, Wes dropped the guns he was holding. Just then the girl caught up with the sheriff and said, 'This isn't one of the men I was telling you about, Pa! He's the one who came along and made them let me go.'

The sheriff looked uncertain for a moment, then, holstering his revolver, he said, 'I'm sorry, stranger, but I was so het-up by what my little girl told me you're lucky I didn't shoot you. Instead, I'd like to shake your hand.'

Putting his words into actions, he introduced himself as Sheriff Eli Wolfe and, pumping Wes's hand added, 'I reckon I owe you.'

Mildly embarrassed, Wes said, 'I'm glad I came along when I did. They were giving her a bad time.'

'They're lucky it was you and not me who happened upon 'em. I'd likely have shot first and asked what they thought they were up to afterwards. Would you happen to know who they were?'

Wes shook his head, 'I'd never seen them before, but then, I'm not from around here. Anyway I took their guns and told them they could get them back from your office if they felt so inclined, so you might well meet up with them later.'

Peering at the revolvers in their open holsters, the sheriff said, 'These belong to gunslingers, not your everyday cowboy, yet you took their guns away from them. Who are you, stranger, should I know you?'

Wes shook his head, 'The name's Wes Curnow and I'm just a miner from England who came to America looking for work and fell in first with a Marshal Berryman and then with an old man who liked to be known as a mountain-man. Between them they had me practising handling guns. I guess it paid off today.'

While Wes was talking the Sheriff's expression became one of incredulity and, dismissing talk of the two gunmen for the moment, he said, 'You know Marshal Berryman . . . ? Brigadier General Aaron Berryman?'

Wondering yet again whether there was anyone in America who did not know Aaron, Wes replied, 'That's him. We travelled together by ship from New York to New Orleans, then up the Mississippi to St Louis. You've heard of him?'

'I've done more than that! I served with him during the war. I was a sergeant in the First United States Coloured Cavalry. After we'd had some hard fighting at Swift Creek, he stopped to say, 'Well done, Sergeant', to me. That was just about the proudest moment of my service . . . '

Bringing his thoughts back to the present, Eli said, 'We'll find time to talk about Brigadier Berryman later. For now I'd like to find the men who scared the living daylights out of my Tessa. She thought they were going to do some harm to her.'

'I thought so too, Sheriff, and they didn't take kindly to my taking their guns away. But if they come to your office to collect 'em you'll be able to learn more about who they are.'

The Sheriff shook his head, 'If they really are gunmen the first thing they'll do is get hold of new weapons, they'll feel naked without 'em. I don't suppose you happened to get their names?'

'No, but I'd say they were probably brothers, they certainly looked alike.'

'I heard their first names,' Tessa said, unexpectedly. 'One was called Ike and the other Clint.'

Her father looked alarmed, 'It sounds like two of the Denton brothers — and they're all wanted men. The Sheriff at Salina sent word down the line that they were heading this way with a couple more men they've been running with. They're trouble . . . *big* trouble.'

To his daughter, he added, 'You're mighty lucky this gentleman came along when he did, girl. The Dentons rode with Quantrill who showed no mercy to anyone, man, woman or child. From all I've heard they're no better now than they were then.'

Speaking to Wes once more, he said, 'I'll put word about that they're around, but most lawmen in these parts would rather not meet up with them. You were lucky too, Wes, but you'll need to be on your guard. The Denton's don't forgive easily and they'd as soon shoot a man in the back from some dark alley, as any other way . . . Where are you staying in Lauraville?'

'I don't know yet,' Wes confessed. 'I've only just got into town. I was on my way to put my horse up at the livery stable and look for a cheap hotel when I ran across Tessa being tormented.'

'I thank The Lord you did, but you don't want to be wandering about town after upsetting the Dentons . . . ' He hesitated for only a few moments before adding, 'We've got a spare room at my place, why don't you put up there. I reckon the Wolfe family owe that to you.'

When Wes hesitated uncertainly, the Sheriff's daughter pleaded, 'Please say 'yes'. If you don't I'll not sleep for worrying that those men will be looking for you because of what you did for me.'

Wes realized she was probably right and he was not anxious to have his untried skill with a handgun put to the test against two such experienced gunmen.

'Thank you, Sheriff, that's very kind of you.'

Tessa, obviously delighted, said, 'I'll run on home and tell ma you're coming and help her get the room ready.'

She ran off ahead of them and Wes said, 'She seems to have got over the shock of her ordeal at the hands of the Dentons.'

'That's thanks to you too,' Eli said, 'She's excited at the thought of having you in the house . . . We don't get many visitors.'

'I can understand that,' Wes said, 'There can't be many places more remote than Lauraville.'

Eli fell silent, as though weighing up something in his mind. Arriving at a decision, he said, 'It's not just because Lauraville is a frontier town, or even that a great many of those passing through fought for the South during the war and resent the town having a black Sheriff. I also happen to have a Cheyenne Indian wife. Even many of those who fought for the North can't stomach that. As a result life's hard for Tessa and she has few friends.'

Wes knew little about the distinctions between the various Indian tribes, but he had been in the country long enough to know the strength of feeling against Indians in general.

'If things are so bad why did you settle here?' he asked.

Eli shrugged, 'I guess one place is as good — or bad — as another for a family like ours. When I first saw Lauraville I intended passing straight through, as we had with so many other places. At the time I was in a wagon with Noni, my wife, and Tessa. We were heading east in the hope of finding a better life among more tolerant people than were coming to the Great Plains. I stopped my wagon outside Lauraville and Noni was cooking something for us to eat when I heard a whole lot of shooting coming from the town. I grabbed up my rifle and it was lucky I did because two men riding on one horse came hell-for-leather out of Lauraville. When they reached my wagon they demanded my horse. When I refused to give it to 'em they pulled their guns on me. I shot one dead and wounded the other. Might just as well have shot him dead too because when a posse arrived from town they lynched him anyway. Seems they'd run the sheriff out of town before robbing the bank and killing a cashier. One of the posse was Lauraville's mayor. He asked where I'd learned to shoot and when I told him I'd been a sergeant in the Union army cavalry he said I was just the man Lauraville needed as Sheriff. Not everyone agreed with him but so many lawmen had come and gone from town that no one thought I'd last anyway. That was more than two years ago. The mayor has long gone, but somehow I stayed on.'

'Why?' Wes queried, 'Why stay doing such dangerous work if the town doesn't really want you and Tessa is unhappy here?'

'That's a good question,' Eli said, rubbing his chin ruefully, 'It's something I ask myself many times, but where else am I likely to be given a house and three hundred dollars a month, as well as extras for executing warrants for the Territorial court — and occasionally arresting someone with a reward on his head? I won't be a Sheriff for ever but by the time we need to move on we'll be able to go east by train and have a whole lot more money to start a new life than we had when we arrived in Lauraville . . . but here we are at my place. We'll put your horse in the stable at the back before we go in. That'll give Noni a bit more time to ready herself, then I'll take you in to meet her.'

3

๑

Sheriff Eli Wolfe's home was sparsely furnished but everything was spotlessly clean, as was his wife, Noni. She was an attractive woman with fine features and much younger than Wes had imagined she would be.

During conversations with Eli over the next twenty-four hours he would learn that she and Eli had met shortly before the late Civil War when as a runaway slave he had been given succour by a small band of nomadic Cheyenne Indians, led by Noni's father.

Tessa had been born in the year the war began, when Noni was only fifteen years old, but it was perhaps inevitable that Eli should go off to fight for the anti-slave Union army of the North. By the time the war between the divided States ended and Eli located the small Cheyenne group once more Tessa was a bright little four year-old who had seen her father on only two very brief occasions.

The war over, the army turned its attention to the 'Indian problem', rounding-up or hunting down bands of Indians who roamed the lands of the West that were soon to be thrown open for white settlement.

For some years Eli and his wife's Cheyenne family group roamed the Great Plains, Eli's skill with a rifle providing them with meat and fighting off the occasional band of desperadoes attracted to the Territories by the absence of any formal laws.

Eventually, when the army intensified its heavy-handed campaign against the Plains Indians, shipping whole tribes to reservations, Eli decided to head east with Noni and Tessa and seek a new life for them all.

Being Sheriff of a frontier town was not the easiest way to earn a living but, as Eli had said, he doubted whether he could make more money elsewhere.

★   ★   ★

Wes soon became aware that Noni spoke very little English, although she seemed to understand most of what was said to her in this language. He realized that her life in a frontier town was a very lonely one and must be in sharp contrast to the one she had known with her own people on the Great Plains.

She and Eli spoke to each other in Cheyenne. Tessa was fluent in the Indian language but she also spoke excellent English and Wes learned she could read and write although she had attended school only after coming to Lauraville, where the attitude of other pupils towards her had not made learning any easier. The school had now closed, due to a lack of pupils, the teacher leaving town just ahead of a lynch mob after getting not one, but two pupils pregnant.

That evening, Eli went off to carry out his

evening check of the town before handing over to the two night-time deputies who dealt with those who drank too much, or caused a disturbance, only calling on Eli if things got out of hand, or a crime was committed that required his attention.

Wes was seated on a rocking chair on the back porch when Tessa came to him carrying an open, coverless book and, somewhat uncertainly, asked whether he was able to read.

When he affirmed he could, she pointed to a word in her book and asked him what it meant.

The word was 'Invocation' and was in the title of a poem by Walt Whitman, the book being a collection of poetry by American poets.

Fortunately, as a child Wes had for many years attended a Wesleyan chapel where the word was a favourite with one particular circuit preacher. 'It's a call to God for help . . . a sort of a prayer,' he explained.

Before handing the tattered book back to her he read the short poem and said, 'That's a nice poem, where did you get the book?'

'A drunken miner who pa had in his cells for a night left it behind.' Suddenly animated, she added, 'Do you like poetry? I love it. I wish I knew enough words to write some myself.'

Aware that this was an intelligent girl who was frustrated by her lack of education, Wes said, 'If you're able to read and make sense of poetry you're doing a whole lot better than most people. Why don't you try writing poetry using the words you do know? You'll probably end up surprising yourself by finding out you know far more words than you realize.'

Tessa shook her head and some of her passion ebbed away. 'I've tried doing that but I just get upset because I don't know the words that say what I *want* them to say.'

Aware of her frustration, Wes said, 'Well, while I'm here, if you come across any more words you don't know, come along and tell me. If I know the meaning we'll see how many words we can think of between us that mean the same thing.'

Some of her enthusiasm returned momentarily, but disappeared again quickly. 'Thank you, Wes, but you won't be here for very long, will you?'

'No, I'm on my way to Colorado and will be catching a train in the next few days.'

'Do you *have* to go? . . . I mean, is someone waiting for you there?' She tried to make it sound like a casual question, but she was a young girl totally lacking in guile and Wes realized that in common with her mother, she too was lonely and he was probably the first man apart, perhaps, from her father, with whom she had ever discussed any of her problems.

The last thing he wanted to do was to hurt her in any way. Deciding to make no mention of Anabelita, he explained, 'My uncle is in Colorado and he's my only living relative. I was supposed to meet up with him in a mining town in Missouri, but by the time I arrived there he'd moved on, leaving me a note saying I was to look for him in the mines around Denver.'

'What will you do when you've found him?' Tessa asked.

'Find work on the mine with him, I hope.'

278

They were still talking together when Eli returned from downtown Lauraville and saw Tessa squatting on the porch at Wes's feet, listening enthralled as Wes told her about Cornwall and the people who lived there.

Eli commented to Noni that Tessa and Wes seemed to be getting along very well.

'Of course!' Noni replied, 'She regards him as a hero for saving her from those two men. He is also a good-looking young man and Tessa is of an age to find such a man very attractive.'

Eli frowned, 'She's too young to be thinking about men. She's still no more than a child.'

Noni gave her husband a pitying look, 'She is almost fifteen, the age I was when I gave birth to her.'

'That was different . . . we were following the ways of your people.' Eli pointed out.

'So?' Noni retorted, 'Tessa is her mother's child and I was younger than she is now when I met you, but I know how I felt — and you do too.'

Refusing to admit his wife was right, Eli said, 'I still say she is far too young to be thinking about such things. I will be keeping any eye on them — and you must too.'

★ ★ ★

The day after Wes's talk with Tessa, he and Eli went to the Sheriff's office to check whether there were any telegraph messages about the Indian raiding party. Wes had got over his anger

279

with Old Charlie and was concerned for the mountain-man.

There was a telegraph message for the Sheriff and although it shed no light on the whereabouts of Old Charlie, it *did* throw Wes's plans into confusion. Word had been received that the railroad had been cut somewhere out on the Great Plains, between Trego tank and Denver.

The message failed to make it clear exactly what had occurred and whether the break in the line was the result of Indian depredations, or some other phenomenon. All that was certain was that there would be no trains going to Denver for another week, or ten days.

Leaving Eli in his office, Wes walked back towards the Sheriff's house feeling depressed. Along the way he passed the large cabin that Eli had pointed out to him as once being the Lauraville school building. The door had been shut then but it was now open and Wes could hear the sound of movement inside.

Acting upon an impulse, he turned in to the building and found an old man sweeping out the one-time classroom.

The sweeper looked questioningly at him, but said nothing and Wes was the first to break the silence.

'Hi! I saw the door open and wondered whether the school was about to open up again?'

'Why d'you want to know? You a teacher, or something?'

'No, I'm just passing through but I'm staying with Sheriff Eli Wolfe and was talking with his daughter about the time when there was a school here. She's very keen on learning.'

'Don't suppose she's the only one. Having a school again would appeal to every youngster in Lauraville — not that there's so many of 'em left now, but if that's what they're looking for they'll need to find somewhere else to put it. I intend turning this place into a meeting room for men . . . and for women too, if they've a mind and can afford to hire it. It'll be a popular place and well away from the noise of the saloons along the main street.'

'You own the building?' Wes expressed surprise. The old man looked as though he could not even afford a respectable set of clothes.

'I do — and I've got the deeds to prove it. I own a whole lot more places in Lauraville too. I made my money cobbling boots for the railroad men when they were laying the track, and I didn't throw it right back into the pocket of any saloon-keeper, neither. I saved it and when everyone ran off out of town, I bought up the places they left behind. Some I got for no more than ten dollars. Others weren't registered anyways, so I just needed to pay for the land. Nothing might be worth much right now, but one day it's going to make me a fortune.'

'I hope you're right,' Wes said, 'A man who's careful with his money deserves to do well. Pity about the school, though.'

He turned to leave but the old man called after him, 'This girl belonging to the Sheriff . . . can she read?'

'She surely can,' Wes replied, 'I think it's something she enjoys more than anything else.'

'Then you can tell her there's a whole lot of books here. She can have any of the big ones for a dollar apiece and the little ones for fifty cents.'

Expressing an interest, Wes said, 'Can I have a look at what you've got?'

'Help yourself. They're in that cupboard, over there.' The old man pointed to a rough-wood cabinet in a corner of the one-time schoolroom.

Opening the door of the rustic piece of furniture, Wes saw shelf upon shelf of books, stacked in a haphazard manner. Among them he was delighted to see a large leather-bound book, embossed with gold lettering which proclaimed it to be a *Complete and Universal English Dictionary*.

Excited, Wes lifted it down. It was exactly what Tessa was in need of. 'I'll have this from you for a dollar,' he said, happily.

'Ah now, it looks a mighty fine book to me and that's real fancy leather. I reckon it ought to be worth a lot more than a dollar.'

Wes realized that the old man thought he had set his prices too low . . . but while they were talking he had been looking at the titles of some of the other books. He saw a number of volumes of poetry, together with text books and a couple that he thought must be novels, although he knew nothing about them, or their authors.

Still holding the dictionary, he said, 'I think one dollar is a fair price for this one, there won't be many folk in Lauraville who'd want to buy it but I tell you what I'll do. I'll give you *five* dollars if you let me take this one, and all the smaller books that I'm able to carry away in my arms.'

When the old man seemed uncertain, he pointed out, 'This one book is pretty heavy, I'm not going to be able to carry many more. I reckon you stand to gain by the deal — and with five dollars you can probably buy yourself another half a house, or even a plot of land.'

As he was talking, Wes was fishing in his pocket for a coin. Pulling out a gold half-eagle, he proferred it to the other man.

For a few moments the avaricious schoolhouse owner weighed up the deal, then he reached out, took the coin and said, 'It's a deal . . . but no more large books, make sure the rest are small ones.'

When Wes left the old schoolhouse he was staggering beneath the weight of the books he was carrying, but was well-satisfied he had obtained value for his money.

Arriving at Eli Wolfe's house he tripped over the doorstep and dropped a couple of books from his load. The sound brought Noni from the kitchen and when she reached him he was trying unsuccessfully to pick up the fallen books, succeeding only in dropping more.

Picking them up, Noni replaced them on top of the load he was carrying, but she looked puzzled.

Aware that she understood far more than she was prepared to admit, Wes explained, 'They're books from the old school. I just bought them . . . for Tessa.'

Noni's delight was evidence that she understood. Beckoning for him to follow her, she led the way to Tessa's bedroom, at the back of the house.

She pushed the door open to reveal Tessa writing, seated at a home-made piece of furniture that served as both dressing-table and desk.

Tessa was startled by the unexpected invasion of her privacy, but Noni was already excitedly explaining in Cheyenne the reason for the intrusion and Tessa's expression became one of delight.

'You bought the books for me?' She asked Wes, in disbelief.

'That's right.'

Dumping the books on the bed and shaking circulation back into his arms, he picked up the leather-bound volume, 'This is the one I'm most pleased about. It's a dictionary. It will be able to explain all the words you come across for which you don't know the meaning. Once you've learned how to use it you'll be able to find all the words you need to write your poetry.'

Tessa was delighted with her unexpected gifts, but even more pleased that Wes cared enough to buy them for her. With a squeal of delight she flung herself at him and after hugging him gave him a kiss that expressed far more than gratitude.

At least, that was how it appeared to Eli. He had just stabled his horse and was walking to the house and, unaware of Noni's presence in the room he saw, through the open bedroom window, Wes with Tessa.

4

❧

'I'm sorry, Wes, but I know what I saw. It's enough that I'm willing to believe you wouldn't have taken things any further with Tessa. If I thought different I'd be doing more than talking to you now . . . but I still want you out of my house tomorrow.'

Eli was taking his customary late evening walk around town and had asked Wes to accompany him. Along the way he told Wes what he had seen through the window of Tessa's bedroom — and expressed his strong disapproval.

More than once during the Sheriff's diatribe Wes had opened his mouth to speak, only to shut it again for fear of angering the other man. When he did finally speak, he said, 'It's your home, Eli, and of course I'll leave if it's what you want, but I don't want to go away with you thinking ill of me or of Tessa. She was talking to me yesterday about how she wished she'd been able to get more schooling so she would know the meaning of a lot more words. On my way back to the house after leaving your office today I saw the man who owns the old schoolhouse. We got talking and he mentioned there were still some books inside. I had a look at them and found a dictionary — the very book that Tessa wanted, so I bought it, together with some of the others, and gave it to her. She was so delighted with them that she gave me a 'thank you' kiss. That's all there was to it. If you don't believe me ask Noni, she was in the room at the time.'

Taken by surprise, Eli exclaimed, 'Noni was there?'

'Of course. I certainly wouldn't have gone to Tessa's bedroom otherwise.'

Eli realized he had been too quick to jump to a wrong conclusion, but he was unused to admitting he was wrong — to anyone.

'Like I told you, Wes, I'm ready to believe you wouldn't take advantage of Tessa, but she's a young girl with no experience of men and you're a hero to her. She might well do something she'd regret later, especially as you'll be out of her life for good in just a few days time. I think you should go sooner, rather than later.'

Wes was sorry to be forced to leave the Sheriff's home in such circumstances but he told himself if he was Tessa's father he would probably have made the same decision and in his heart Wes knew Eli was right.

Tessa had kissed him in excited gratitude, but he had been aware the gesture was intended to show him more than the innocent appreciation of a child. He said, 'I'll have my things packed and leave in the morning, Eli.'

★ ★ ★

'Do you *really* need to leave today, Wes? I . . . me and ma, will be sorry to see you go — and I know pa enjoys having you around.'

A very unhappy Tessa was posing the question. Wes was leaving the house later than he had intended. He had waited in the hope that he could pack and go while Tessa was out of the house, but she did not go out, so he was forced to announce his imminent departure to her and her mother.

On the verge of tears, Tessa was standing in the doorway of his room, watching as he checked the gunbelt and revolver that been a present from Emma Schuster. He did not intend wearing them but thinking about the Indians who were somewhere about, he decided to place the revolver on top of the contents of a saddle bag, where it would be close at hand should it be needed.

'I've enjoyed being here with you all,' Wes replied, 'It's reminded me of what life as part of a happy family is all about, but it's time to move on. I need to find work and earn some money.'

'Couldn't you find something around here . . . ?' Even as she spoke Tessa realized there was no employment to be had in the vicinity of Lauraville.

Desperately trying to think of something, she said, 'You could be a schoolteacher and open the schoolhouse again. You'd be a good teacher, I know you would.'

Wes smiled, 'I don't know enough to be a teacher, Tessa. Besides, I was talking only yesterday to the man who now owns the schoolhouse. He said there aren't enough youngsters in Lauraville to make a school worthwhile. Even if there were, he's got other ideas for the building.'

Tessa would have continued her pleading but at that moment they heard a boy's voice shouting urgently 'Mrs Wolfe ... Mrs Wolfe ... Come quick.'

Noni was at the back of the house and it was Tessa who ran to the door. She hardly had it open before the boy declared breathlessly, 'My grandpa works at the Four Horseshoes saloon. He said I was to run and tell you to come quick. The Denton brothers have got the Sheriff there. He thinks they're going to kill him ... '

As Tessa screamed, Wes snatched up the gunbelt and revolver from his open saddlebag. Pushing past the near-hysterical girl, he called, 'You and your ma stay here. I'll deal with it.'

Wes had seen the Four Horseshoes saloon on the town's main street but as he sprinted along an alleyway towards it, at the same time buckling on the gun-belt, he had no plan of what he would do when he reached it.

Turning on to the street, he saw a crowd of excited men on the boardwalk, milling around the doorway of the saloon, all eager to secure a place from which they could see over the shoulder-height swing doors.

Wes had almost reached the saloon when there was the sound of a shot from inside. It was immediately followed by another — and then a third.

Drawing his gun, Wes charged into the crowd of uproarious onlookers. Those who did not immediately scatter were roughly shouldered out of his path. As he hit the swing doors there was another shot from inside accompanied by raucous and drunken laughter and he heard the shouted word . . . 'dance!'

When the doors crashed open he took in the scene inside the saloon. A hatless and dishevelled Sheriff stood shakily in the centre of the saloon floor, upturned chairs and tables nearby indicating there had been a desperate fight and Sheriff Wolfe's bloody face was grim evidence that he had taken a beating.

Three men stood around him. Two were the gunmen from whom he had rescued Tessa. The third could have been the twin of one of them and it was he who was holding a revolver.

Taken by surprise at Wes's unexpected arrival upon the scene this man still had the presence of mind to fire a shot at him. Fortunately it went wide, punching a hole through one of the flimsy saloon doors.

The cry of pain from an onlooker on the boardwalk, hit by the bullet, went unheard inside the saloon as a second shot rang out. This one came from Wes's gun — and it did not miss its target. The Denton brother staggered backwards dropping his six-shooter before tripping over an upturned chair and falling to the floor.

While this was happening one of the two remaining Denton brothers had drawn his own gun and fired at his brother's killer.

Wes felt a pain in his left arm above the elbow but it did not prevent him from returning the fire and a second Denton brother fell to the floor where he lay twitching uncontrollably.

The third of the Denton's was slower to react

than his siblings and by the time he drew back the hammer of his Colt, Eli had pounced on the weapon dropped by Wes's first victim and fired from a crouching position.

The heavy bullet shattered a bone in the remaining Denton's shoulder and he spun around, dropping his weapon which was promptly kicked away by Wes.

'Are you all right, Eli?' Wes put the question as the Sheriff checked to confirm that both the fallen brothers were dead.

'Thanks to you . . . yes.' Eli confirmed.

The wounded Denton brother had dropped to one of the few chairs in the saloon that remained upright, and was bent double and moaning, either from pain, or awareness that he had just lost two brothers.

'Do you want any help getting this one to gaol?' Wes asked.

'No, but send someone to find the doctor and get him down to the gaol to fix him up, I don't want him cheating the hangman.'

'Fine, I'll leave you to it.' So saying, Wes left the saloon, those crowding the doorway standing aside respectfully to allow him through.

Wes had left the saloon in what appeared to be unseemly haste. Only he knew that it was necessary if he were not to show himself up in front of Eli and the Lauraville onlookers. As it was, he barely made it to the nearest alleyway before throwing up.

When he stood upright once more, gulping air into his lungs, he tried to tell himself his reaction had nothing to do with the knowledge that he had just killed two men — although it had been far more personal than his involvement in the battle with the river pirates.

He decided it was because he had come so close to death himself — and he was far more aware now of pain not only in his arm, but in his side. The Denton brother's bullet had grazed his ribs before passing through the fleshy part of his upper arm, and the latter wound was bleeding profusely.

Nevertheless, he succeeded in hiding his wounds from Tessa and her mother when he met them in a shadowed alleyway. They were hurrying towards Lauraville's main street despite his instructions that they should both remain in the house.

'Eli . . . ?'

The agonised one word plea from Noni showed the fear she felt for her husband more eloquently than a hundred words might have done.

'He's all right. There's been a gunfight, but Eli's fine. You'll find him in the Sheriff's office. He's taking a prisoner there . . . '

To Wes's relief and unaware of his problems, they were running towards the lawman's office before he had finished talking. He was able to make his way to the Wolfe home and awkwardly bind his wounded arm in an effort to stem the bleeding before saddling his horse and riding out of Lauraville.

5

❧

Wes's gunshot wounds were worse than he had realized and the movement of his horse did not help. The ride to Trego took him three hours and by the time he arrived at the railroad town he had lost a lot of blood and the pain in his side equalled that of his arm.

Finding a hotel close to the railroad depot, he put his horse in the care of the hotel's ostler and booked in. However, the bloodstains on his clothes did not pass unnoticed and when a concerned hotel manager commented upon them Wes said only that he had been hurt a few hours before and the ride had exascarbated his injuries.

The manager suggested Wes should have the Trego doctor look at it and try to stem the bleeding, adding that the doctor was one of the finest they had ever had in the town and would call to see Wes at the hotel if he so wished.

Wes hesitated over the suggestion for only a short time. The wound *did* hurt and he had lost so much blood that he was beginning to feel light-headed. He agreed to have the doctor sent for.

Doctor Strauss was a five-feet-nothing fussy little German who had spent enough years as a frontier doctor to recognize bullet wounds when he saw them.

Tut-tutting over the furrow along Wes's ribs, he used a pair of tweezers from his medicine bag to extract a fragment of bone, saying as he worked, 'It is painful, is it not?'

'It's painful,' Wes agreed.

'Be grateful you have pain,' said the diminutive doctor. 'Had the bullet passed between your ribs you would be feeling nothing. You would be dead!'

'Thank you, Doc, I'll lie here enjoying the pain and thinking how lucky I am.'

'Hah! You play with fire, you get burned, eh? The other man . . . he is hurt too?'

'The two I shot are both dead. Another one, shot by the Lauraville sheriff, was hurt but will probably live long enough to hang.'

'So you are a gunman who is on the side of the law, eh? It is a rare breed this far west.'

Aware that the doctor doubted the truth of his explanation, Wes said, 'I'm not even a gunman, I'm a miner. I just stepped in to help when Sheriff Wolfe got into trouble.'

'Admirable!' said the doctor, with more than a hint of scepticism, 'You are so helpful to this sheriff, he does not even call for a doctor to tend your wounds? For this you have to leave Lauraville and come all the way to Trego.'

Wes felt it unnecessary to reply and the doctor asked no more questions — but he did not keep the information he had already gained to himself.

An hour after Doctor Strauss had left the hotel there came a knock upon the door of Wes's room. Without waiting for an invitation, a man wearing a sheriff's star entered. Seating himself in a sprawling attitude in an armchair, he introduced himself as Sheriff Murray.

Coming straight to the point about his reason for the visit, Murray said, 'I've just been talking to Doc Strauss. He told me he'd patched up a couple of bullet wounds for you and that you picked them up helping the Sheriff over at Lauraville . . . I've forgotten his name for the moment.'

Wes did not believe that Sheriff Murray had forgotten the name, but was merely testing the truth of his story.

'It's Wolfe, Eli Wolfe, and yes, there were three gunmen causing a bit of trouble for him. They'd managed to disarm Eli and were in a saloon trying to make him dance. They'd have killed him once they'd had their fun.'

'Instead, you killed them, or so the doc said.'

'I killed two of 'em, but only after they'd shot first. One missed me . . . the other didn't. While this was happening, Eli picked up a gun and wounded the third. I believe all three were wanted men.'

Making no comment on Wes's story, Sheriff Murray asked, 'What did you say your name is?'

'I didn't, but it's Wes Curnow.'

'You figure on staying long in Trego, Curnow?'

'Only until the line to Denver's open again. I'll be catching the first train out.'

Rising from his chair, Sheriff Murray said laconically, 'Fine. I reckon we'll be meeting again before you leave town.' With this, he left the room.

Wes sank back on his bed aware that he had not seen the last of Trego's Sheriff.

⋆ ⋆ ⋆

Wes was right. Exhausted by his long ride, the loss of blood from his wounds, and the attentions of Dr Strauss, he fell into a deep sleep only to be awakened a couple of hours later by Sheriff Murray's robust shaking.

'Wake up, Curnow . . . wake up.'

'Uh? What is it . . . ?' For a moment, Wes could not place where he was and, momentarily forgetting his wounds, he tried to sit up in a hurry — only to suffer for his efforts. 'Ouch! What is it . . . ? What's going on?'

Seeing Sheriff Murray, with a deputy standing behind him, Wes sank back on the bed once more. 'What is it this time, Sheriff?'

'We've got a change of lodgings for you. We're putting you behind bars in the Sheriff's office.'

Startled, Wes demanded, 'What for? What am I supposed to have done?'

Coming as close to a grin as he knew how, the stern-faced Sheriff said, 'You don't need to go reaching for your six-gun, we've fixed up a comfortable bed for you — and the cell door won't be locked. It's for your own good. I telegraphed Eli at Lauraville and asked if he knew you. He's come back to say he owes his life to you. He also said the two men you killed were Denton brothers. Now, had you told that to me I'd have taken you to my office right away — for your own safety.'

Puzzled, Wes asked, 'Why? I know there was a third brother, but Eli shot and wounded him. He's got him locked up in Lauraville.'

'Maybe so — but there's more than three Dentons. They're like gophers, just when you think you've cleared 'em out you look round and find another one behind you. There's a fourth brother — I think his name is Gideon, who was here in Trego. He might *still* be here, although nobody's seen him for a couple of days. He was with a couple of cousins and another man who might well be the leader of the whole bunch because one of my deputies says he seen a 'wanted' notice for him. He can't seem to find it now, but that's hardly surprising. Back East, if a man's wanted they reckon he'll be heading this way sooner or later and send us a notice. If we kept 'em all we'd be able to paper the walls of every house in Trego.'

Wes gave Sheriff Murray a weak smile. The medicine given to him by Dr Strauss had obviously been intended to help him sleep and he was feeling drowsy, nevertheless, he thought of Eli who needed to uphold the law in Lauraville without any help.

'We ought to warn Sheriff Wolfe about him. This fourth Denton, or perhaps the leader of the gang, could show up there and try to break his brother out of gaol. Do you have a name to give him for this wanted man?'

He expected to be given a short 'yes' or 'no' answer, neither of which should have meant anything to him. Instead, Sheriff's reply caused

Wes to sit bolt upright, the pain of his wounds suddenly forgotten.

'He's not known to any of us hereabouts. His name is Gottland . . . Ira Gottland.'

6

❧

'Now, tell me more about this man Gottland.'

Wes and Sheriff Murray were seated in the Trego Sheriff's office. Behind them, a narrow bed had been made up in one of the iron-barred cages that formed the Trego lock-up.

After Wes had admitted knowing Ira Gottland, the Sheriff had said Wes could tell him more when he was safely ensconced in his gaol office.

Now, nursing a mug of coffee, Wes told Sheriff Murray of meeting Gottland in New Orleans and the subsequent events upriver that involved him, Aaron and the river pirates.

'This Gottland sounds as though he's both bad and clever,' the Sheriff mused, 'It's a combination that spells trouble. I'll have my deputies inquire around town and see what they turn up.'

Looking quizzically at Wes, he added, 'One way or another you've had yourself quite a time of it since you arrived in America.'

Managing a weak grin, Wes said, 'You haven't heard the half of it, Sheriff. Throw in a riverboat wreck and a run-in with striking German miners and you'll be getting close.'

'It seems you can use a gun too, where did you learn that?'

'My pa taught me how to handle a rifle,' Wes

298

replied, 'but I'd never even seen a handgun until I came to America. Aaron Berryman showed me how to use one but it was an old mountain-man named Charlie Quinnell who kept me practising until he thought it was safe to leave me alone out here.'

'You know Old Charlie as well?' Sheriff Murray had been impressed when he learned that Wes knew US Marshal Aaron Berryman, but mention of Charlie really animated him. 'I first met Old Charlie when I ran away from home to go trapping,' Murray said, 'He taught me to shoot as well and we hunted buffalo together for a while. He was more of a father to me than any kin I ever knew. How did you meet up with him? Last I heard, he was heading east with Buffalo Bill Cody.'

'The East didn't suit him . . . ' Wes told him of his own meeting with the old frontiersman and of their journey across Missouri and Kansas that culminated in their meeting with the US cavalry and Charlie going off with them in search of Indians, adding, ' . . . The cavalry were from Fort Hays. I don't know whether he'll go back there with 'em when they've sorted out the Indians, but he and I were both heading for Colorado. Unless something happens to that bad-tempered mule of his he'll be riding it across the Great Plains.'

'We had a telegraph to say a whole parcel of Cheyenne and Arapaho braves were trying to make their way North to join up with the Cheyenne and Sioux up that way and a trainload of soldiers went through here, heading west, but

I never imagined Old Charlie would be involved. He should be past all that by now.'

'I wouldn't say that to his face if I were you,' Wes warned. 'He doesn't look upon himself as growing old. He's even talking of taking a young Cheyenne wife somewhere along the way.'

Shaking his head in rueful admiration, the Sheriff said, 'He'll never change — but, talking of men with Cheyenne wives Eli said in his telegraph that he'll be riding here tomorrow morning to see you.'

★ ★ ★

Sheriff Eli Wolfe left Lauraville at sun-up the following morning and was in Trego in time to share the breakfast brought to the lock-up for Wes and Sheriff Murray.

Wes was relieved Eli had not brought Tessa to Lauraville with him, the thought of such a possibility had kept him awake during the night although he had been dozing when Eli walked in.

The Lauraville sheriff was dismayed to see Wes's weakened state. Shaking hands, he said, 'Hell, Wes, why did you run out on me the way you did?'

'Run out on you? It was your idea I should leave, remember?'

Sheriff Murray, who had been given only an outline by Wes of his reason for leaving Lauraville, waited with considerable interest for Eli's reply.

Looking sheepish, Eli said, 'That was before

300

my run-in with the Denton's. You saved my life, Wes, you must know that. They'd already told me I was going to die after they'd had a 'little fun' with me. As for Tessa . . . she was upset because I'd come so close to being killed, but I swear she was even more upset when she found out you'd left Lauraville. It's as much as I could do to stop her from riding out with me this morning.'

'Then it's just as well I left when I did, Eli. Tessa's a great girl, she's prettier than most and will grow up to be a bright and intelligent woman — but she's still not much more than a child.'

'I think she'd take issue with you on that, Wes — and her mother certainly would. Noni's taken to reminding me that she was no older than Tessa when she gave birth to her.'

'That's as may be, Eli, but although I like Tessa — and I do like her a lot — I don't have the same feelings for her that you have for Noni. The last thing I would want to do is take advantage of the way she feels about me, she deserves better than that.'

'I appreciate your concern for her, Wes, though neither she nor Noni would agree with either of us — but I've got something here Noni gave me for you to put on those bullet wounds of yours. It's an ointment the Cheyenne women use on wounded braves — and it really works, believe me. Noni's treated me with it twice now so I can vouch for it at first hand. I've got something else that should make you feel better too. There were hefty rewards out for the

Dentons — and they're yours. I hadn't got the ready money at Lauraville and anyway, before I got the telegraph from Sheriff Murray I wasn't sure where I'd find you, so I telegraphed the US Marshal's office in Denver, asking Marshal Berryman to look out for you and pay the reward money when you arrived.'

'That reminds me,' said Sheriff Murray, who had been following their conversation, 'I telegraphed Marshal Berryman in Denver too. One of my deputies has learned a great deal about Ira Gottland. A rumour is going around that he and the Denton's were here because they'd planned to board a train travelling from Denver and rob the passengers and the boxcar of the gold that most trains from Denver carry to the East. The plan was never carried out because the army put men on board all trains in case they were attacked by the Cheyenne and Arapaho who are on the loose. Then, when the line was cut, out on the Great Plains, they gave up the idea altogether and the gang split up for a while. Gottland and Gideon Denton, with a couple of others left Trego on a train carrying a repair gang and some railroad parts up to the break. Once there they'll transfer to the railroad on the other side and catch a train on to Denver. They've been boasting about easy pickings up in the gold-diggings around that way. They left word for the other Denton brothers to join them there. Of course, they won't be doing anything of the sort now, but there's no doubt that they'll get to hear of your part in the killing of the two Dentons in Lauraville. Gideon will be out for revenge, so you'd better make sure you're up to dealing with him by the time you reach Denver, Wes. As sure as Hell's hot you're going to one day have to deal with Gideon Denton in the same way you did with his brothers.'

7

Crossing the Great Plains on the train, Wes marvelled at the sheer vastness of the landscape. He almost wished he was traversing it on horseback in company with Old Charlie, ruefully conceding that his late partner might have already located the Indians for the cavalry and be in Denver before him.

The railroad link with Colorado had opened nine days after Wes's arrival in Trego, but the first few trains en route for Denver had been so packed with passengers that it was another week before travel on the Kansas Pacific returned to normal and Wes was able to board a westbound train and enjoy any degree of comfort.

By this time his wounds had healed so well that even a usually sceptical Doctor Strauss admitted that the Cheyenne ointment probably contained a constituent unknown to qualified medical practitioners and which possessed positive healing qualities. He had written a letter to Eli Wolfe asking if his wife would provide him with the formula.

Eli duly obliged, but Noni knew only Cheyenne names for the various herbs and plants she had used and they meant nothing to the frustrated doctor.

Despite Wes's rapid recovery, he had not fully

shaken off the effects of the Denton's brother's bullet and was ordered by the doctor to stay clear of trouble until he was fit once more.

★ ★ ★

As the train slowed on its approach to the Denver station, Wes was excited at the thought of meeting with Anabelita . . . but he was apprehensive too. It had been more than a month since they were last together. Much had happened in his life since then and no doubt a great deal had occurred in hers.

There was always the possibility there might be another man in her life . . . but this was something he had no wish to dwell upon. The first thing he needed to do was find out where she and the others were.

He had already decided he would begin his enquiries at the United States Marshals' office. Even if Aaron was not there, someone should be able to tell him where he and the two women were staying.

Only minutes after the train came to a halt all Wes's misgiving disappeared. Waiting until the majority of the passengers had disembarked, he was stepping from the train carrying his bag when from somewhere among the crowd about the train he heard a woman excitedly calling, 'Wes . . . Wes . . . over here!'

He recognized the voice immediately and looking over the heads of the crowd could see Anabelita literally jumping into the air in her efforts to attract his attention.

305

Waving an acknowledgement, he pushed his way through the throng and in the moments before she threw herself at him he saw a widely smiling Lola standing beside her, accompanied by a one-armed man.

He had no time to wonder about the absence of Aaron before he was caught up in Anabelita's excited embrace.

For much of the journey on the Kansas Pacific train he had been silently rehearsing what he was going to say to her when they met again, but he had imagined it would take place in the privacy and quiet of her room somewhere, not in Denver's crowded railroad station.

'It's good to see you again,' he said, lamely, ' . . . but how did you know I'd be arriving on this train?'

'A telegraph message was sent to Aaron's office. He's away at the diggings in the mountains, but Pat brought it to us . . . '

'Pat?' Wes queried.

'Yes, he came from Abilene with us, come and meet him . . . Oh, Wes! There's so much to tell you . . . but it's absolutely wonderful to be with you again . . . '

After greeting Lola, who was almost as effusive as Anabelita, Wes was introduced to Pat Rafferty. Informed that Wes had a horse and saddle in a horse box at the rear of the train, the one-armed man said he would collect them and take them to the stable at Aaron's house.

Reluctant to lose sight of Anabelita for even a moment, Wes thanked Rafferty and said, 'Shall we all make our way to the horse box, so I can show Pat which is my horse? She was chosen for me by Old Charlie and we've travelled a great many miles together. I've grown quite attached to her.'

'Where is Old Charlie?' Lola queried, 'Did you spend much time together?'

'There were times when I thought it was too much,' Wes said, ruefully, 'but to be honest we got along well enough most of the time. We parted company on the Smoky Hill trail, this side of Fort Hays, when he went off with the United States cavalry, chasing Indians. I've since heard they caught up with them and was hoping to find him here, in Denver.'

Anabelita was more familiar with the geography of the West than most women — or men — and she said meaningfully, 'It sounds as though you have a lot to talk about too . . . but it can wait, I'm just so happy you're here . . . '

As she was speaking she gripped his left arm, above the elbow and squeezed it hard in affection causing him to let out an involuntary cry of pain.

He apologised immediately, but Anabelita was concerned, 'What's the matter, Wes . . . what did I do?'

'It's nothing. I hurt my arm a while ago . . . it's almost better now, but still a bit tender.'

'What do you mean, you hurt your arm? Let me see.'

'No.' Wes said firmly. Then, aware that she would not allow it to rest there, he confessed, 'It's a bullet wound. It grazed my ribs too

. . . but it's caused no permanent damage. I'm as right as rain now.'

'No you're not. I thought you looked pale when I first saw you getting off the train and decided you hadn't been well. I wasn't wrong, was I?'

She was interrupted by the quiet voice of Pat Rafferty who had overheard the conversation. He asked, 'Does this have something to do with the reward that Aaron's been authorized to pay you for the Denton brothers?'

When Wes nodded, Pat said, 'I believe you saved the Federal government the cost of a hangman for two of them?'

'I had no alternative,' Wes said, defensively, 'They both fired first — and one shot came close to settling things in their favour.'

'I wasn't criticizing you,' Pat said, hastily, 'Far from it, their demise was long overdue, but too many men — good men — have tried to get the better of them, and failed.'

'Unfortunately, I believe there's still another brother to be accounted for,' Wes said, 'Sheriff Murray said he'd heard he was somewhere in Colorado and had telegraphed the news to Aaron.'

'That's right, we're talking of Gideon Denton. We missed him at the station and last we heard he was heading for the diggings up in the mountain with Ira Gottland and a few others of a similar ilk. That's why Aaron has gone up there.'

'Is Aaron up there on his own?' Wes asked anxiously.

'It's how he prefers to work most of the time,' Pat replied. 'Besides, he hasn't found anyone here to deputise yet.'

Concerned, Wes asked, 'How far away are these diggings?'

Anabelita decided she had heard enough. 'If you're thinking of going up there to help Aaron you can forget it until I've seen that arm of yours and you've had it looked at by a doctor, right here in Denver. The last thing Aaron wants is to have to look after you as well as tending to his own business.'

'I need to go up there to look for my uncle,' Wes pointed out. Then, aware that Anabelita was genuinely concerned for him, he said, 'but you're right, of course. I need a few days to be certain my arm has healed properly. Do you know of somewhere in Denver where I can stay in the meantime?'

'Yes,' Anabelita replied, 'in the house Aaron bought for all of us to stay in. It's immediately behind the Thespian Club — Aaron's gambling house — and was built to house actors and actresses who came to Denver to play in the Thespian Club when it was a theatre. Each of us have a room and there's one for you too . . . if you want it. Come along, we have a lot of catching up to do . . . '

8

The house Aaron had bought backed on to the Thespian Club and was the largest in its street. Although accepted as being in a 'respectable' location, it was only just outside the sleazy area of brothels; dance halls; pleasure parlours and the disreputable 'gaming rooms' which usually incorporated the other three categories.

It was a part-wood, part-brick structure and when first built must have been an imposing building, but time and the failure of the fortunes of the theatre had taken their toll. However, compared with the properties Wes had seen in Lauraville, it was positively palatial.

When Wes entered the house with the two women, Lola immediately made an excuse to leave him and Anabelita on their own.

Wes was carrying a saddle-bag containing most of his belongings and when he asked where he should put them, Anabelita replied, 'I'll show you. Your room is next to mine,' adding meaningfully, 'There is a connecting door — with a key on my side. Take your bag into your room and while I'm opening the door you can take your coat and shirt off and let me look at that bad arm.'

'There's no need for that,' Wes protested, 'It's almost healed now.'

'Is that why you winced when I touched it back at the railroad station?' She retorted. 'I'll see you inside your room.'

When they met inside Wes's room he had taken only his coat off and said, 'I'll just roll my sleeve up . . . '

'No you won't,' Anabelita said firmly, 'You said the bullet had grazed your ribs. I'll check on that too.'

Giving her a quizzical look, Wes said, 'I think you're just using my wounds as an excuse for me to take my clothes off.'

He was undecided whether the look she gave him in response to his only partly facetious remark was confirmation or not.

Her next words left him in no doubt. 'Do you really need an excuse for that, Wes?'

He removed his shirt, hopefully, but any thoughts of immediate romantic activity were put on hold when Anabelita saw the barely healed scars, the one that had carved a path across his rib looking particularly angry.

Deeply concerned, she said, 'The wound on your rib looks as though it needs some attention, Wes . . . ' Suddenly wide-eyed, she added, 'An inch or two to the side and it might have killed you . . . '

'That's what the Trego doctor said,' Wes agreed, 'but the Lauraville sheriff who was also involved in the shooting has a Cheyenne wife. She made up an Indian potion to put on it and it did the job well. Unfortunately, I haven't been able to apply any of it since yesterday and the constant movement of the train meant it got rubbed and is a bit sore. I'll put some of Noni's ointment on it now, that'll soon fix it.'

'No . . . *I'll* put it on,' Anabelita said, firmly, 'and something to protect the wound, as well . . . ' Suddenly, coming as much of a surprise to her as it was to Wes, tears welled up in her eyes and she said, 'I was so worried about you, Wes, even though Aaron told me I shouldn't be. He said Old Charlie would see that no harm came to you . . . but I was right to be worried. Where was he when you were shot?'

Abruptly, she began dressing Wes's wounds, as much to cover her emotions as for medical reasons.

Deeply touched by her very real concern for him, Wes said, 'Charlie did look after me, Anabelita. In fact he and his friend the County sheriff probably saved my life when I got in trouble in Harmony. Mind you, just *being* with Old Charlie was a whole adventure in itself! He wasn't with me when I was shot because the United States cavalry had taken him off to help them hunt down some Indians who'd gone on the warpath out on the Great Plains, but he'd made me practice using a handgun for hours on end every day we were together. It definitely gave me the edge when I met up with the Denton brothers, so I guess he saved my life twice over . . . but my shooting days are over now. When I find my uncle I'll go back to being a miner again . . . but tell me what you've been doing since you left the *Missouri Belle*. No doubt Aaron made certain you and Lola didn't get into any trouble.'

Anabelita had almost completed her task now and she thought of all the things she *could* tell him about her life since they had last met. But she had other things in mind . . .

★ ★ ★

Later that evening and despite Wes's sleepy protests, Anabelita slipped out of bed declaring she intended having a shower-bath before going to the gaming saloon to perform her duties as a croupier.

When Wes suggested the Thespian Club might manage for one night without her, she disagreed with him. 'No, Wes, Aaron would probably give me the night off if he were here but there's a lot of competition from Vic Walsh's Palace gambling house just along the road. We need to work hard if we're to catch up with him.'

'Was this Walsh unhappy about Aaron opening up a rival gambling place in Denver?'

'He says he's not and he's gone out of his way to tell Aaron that having another well-run gaming house here will actually attract gamblers to Denver, but I'm not convinced. Walsh is just too good to be true. He's also a very ambitious man. When some of the backstreet gaming houses became too successful they mysteriously lost customers and went out of business very quickly. Rumour has it that Walsh was responsible. Having said that, he has gone out of his way to be friendly with Aaron — and made it clear he would like to be even friendlier with me.'

Showing immediate interest, Wes demanded, 'What do you mean . . . has he been pestering you?'

313

Childishly pleased at his reaction, Anabelita said, 'No, Walsh is far too subtle for that, but he sometimes comes calling to chat to Aaron and if he's not around and things are quiet he will stop and chat with me. He's always interested to know how the Thespian Club is doing, but he's asked me a couple of times to have dinner with him at the Palace and doesn't seem too put off when I decline his invitation. He has also dropped some very strong hints that should I fancy a change he would be willing to offer me work in the Palace at more money than I am getting at the Thespian Club — and that isn't the action of a friend. I told Aaron, but he only smiled and said I shouldn't hold that against him and that if I'd been working for Walsh when we first met he'd have tried to take me from the Palace.'

'Perhaps he's right,' Wes suggested, but Anabelita shook her head.

'No, Walsh wants to give everyone the impression that he's a good and generous man but I don't think he is. He has obviously got a lot of money, although no one seems to know where it came from in the first place. If you want to learn more about him why don't you pay him a visit? He is from Cornwall, the same as you. He even talks like you.'

'I might do that,' said Wes, ' . . . but not tonight. I think I'll stay right where I am until you finish work.'

★   ★   ★

314

Those employed in gambling saloons would often work right through the night hours and Anabelita was no exception.

The morning after his arrival, Wes left her sleeping and took a stroll around Denver. He soon became aware that the Thespian Club and its fellow gambling emporium, the Palace, were on the fringe of an extensive vice area where even at this early hour women and girls stood in doorways and sat at open windows trying to lure any passing man inside with the offer of 'a good time'. Most wore the white 'brothel gown' that was generally recognized as a symbol of their calling.

After about half-an-hour spent walking unmade but more respectable streets closer to the edge of town, Wes made his way back towards Aaron's house. As he was passing the Palace he heard a voice hurling abuse at someone Wes took to be a cleaner.

There was no mistaking the man's Cornish accent and Wes paused to catch a glimpse of the voice's owner. He did not have long to wait. A small, bearded man who reminded Wes vaguely of Old Charlie appeared in the wide doorway of the gambling establishment, his rapidly moving feet hardly touching the floor as he was propelled along by a stocky and powerfully built man who had a hold on the back of his collar.

Once outside the doorway, the older man's feet lifted off the ground and he was thrown clear of the boardwalk to land in the rutted dirt street and given the warning, 'If I ever see you here again I'll scat you so hard with something

315

your eyebrows will tickle your collarbone.'

Climbing painfully to his feet and staggering as he tried to regain his balance, the ejected man complained, 'You owe me wages for cleaning up this morning.'

'The only thing you've cleaned up this morning is my whisky. You've drunk enough of that to pay two men's wages and if you don't get on your way right now I'll drill a hole in you that'll drain most of it right out of you.'

It was said with a ferocity that sent the old man scurrying away non-too steadily along the street.

'That was as good a Cornish warning as I've heard for a long time,' Wes said to the man who stood watching his departing ex-employee weaving an erratic course from the front of the Palace.

'So . . . you thinking of taking sides?' came the aggressive reply.

'No, I've had enough of fighting other men's battles for a while,' Wes replied. 'I was only saying it was good to hear a Cornish voice again, even if it was raised in anger.'

'You must be new in Denver,' the other man retorted, 'Otherwise you'd have noticed that half the voices you hear in town speak with the same accent, but I haven't got time to stand here chatting . . . not unless you want a job as a cleaner in the Palace?'

Wes grinned, he realized he was talking to the owner of the Thespian Club's rival gambling saloon, 'Thanks . . . but no, Mr Walsh. I'm a miner and I don't think Marshal Berryman would forgive me if I went to work for anyone else.'

While Wes was talking Walsh had rudely turned away and was walking back inside the Palace. Now he halted and swung around. 'You know Aaron and you're Cornish? Are you the one he came up the Mississippi river with from New Orleans?'

'I am. It wasn't a voyage I could forget in a hurry.'

Vic Walsh's off-hand manner underwent an immediate change and he became almost effusive as he advanced towards Wes, his hand outstretched, 'I am very pleased to meet you . . . 'Wes', isn't it? Come inside to my office and we'll have a drink together. Whereabouts in Cornwall are you from . . . ?'

Walsh led the way to his office, talking all the while of Cornwall, but when Wes said he was from Bodmin Moor, in central Cornwall, Walsh said he was from farming stock on the coast in a remote part of the south east of the county.

When Wes queried what had brought him to America, Walsh replied that there was no more money to be made from farming in Cornwall than there was from mining.

Once in the Palace owner's office and drinks had been poured, Walsh turned the conversation to gambling and he asked how the Thespian Club was faring.

Wes was able to reply truthfully that he had not been in Denver for long enough to learn anything and had not yet seen Aaron, who was away on 'Marshal's business'.

317

'Word is going around that the Thespian Club is doing well and I'm pleased for Aaron,' Walsh declared, 'I'd like to see gamblers flocking to Denver because they know they'll get an honest deal here. If they do, they'll come again and bring their friends with them. That's why Marshal Berryman is so good for business. He's known to be scrupulously honest and he brings respectability to a profession that's been given a bad name by the two-bit gaming rooms associated in the past with Denver and the mining camps around the town.'

There was much more in a similar vein, but far from being convinced that Walsh was an honest man on a crusade to make gambling respectable, Wes left the Palace wondering why Walsh felt it necessary to work so hard to project himself as a pillar of respectability.

9

❦

Aaron returned to Denver five days after Wes's arrival in the town and was delighted to see him again. He had been visiting various mining camps around the Rocky Mountain towns of Central, Black Hawk and Idaho Springs. Wes was pleased to learn that on his travels he had met with Old Charlie, who had gone straight to the mountains after parting company with the cavalry on the Great Plains.

When the initial euphoria of their reunion had worn off and the two men were having a meal with Anabelita and Lola in the Thespian Club's eating room, Aaron said, 'I called in at my office on the way here and read the telegraphs from the sheriffs at both Trego and Lauraville. They gave me some idea of what you had been up to in their part of the world. I always said you had the makings of a first class lawman, Wes. I only wish I could have found someone like you to accept an appointment as Deputy US Marshal up in the mining camps. No one is prepared to take it on . . . but I can't say I really blame them. Matters are totally out of hand up there. In fact, the situation is so bad I'm considering getting the army involved.'

'That's not good,' Wes agreed, 'I need to go up that way to try to find my uncle — but I'll be going as a miner and not as a deputy marshal,' he hastened to add, before Aaron could suggest another role for him.

'Don't be in too much of a hurry to make the journey,' Aaron said, 'It's chaos up there right now. The only hotels — and I hesitate to call them that — let out beds, not rooms, cramming as many as they can into every available space. A man who takes a bed is lucky if he gets any sleep with all the noise and movement going on around him and as soon as he gets out of the bed it's rented out to someone else. I suggest the best hope you've got of finding this uncle of yours is to put a notice up in the Thespian Club and as many hotels in town as you can, asking if anyone has news of him. It's more likely to have results than going up there looking for him. There are so many diggings in the mountains you could search for ever without finding him.'

With her mouth full of food, Anabelita could only nod vigorously in agreement with Aaron's suggestions and he continued, 'I remembered you telling me your uncle's name is Peter Rowse and I asked about him whenever I was in the company of miners, managers or owners, but learned nothing. Old Charlie might have more success. After taking a look at the crowds in the mining camps, he and that mule of his took off for more remote areas of the Rockies — and there are thousands of square miles of some of the most remote country you're ever likely to find anywhere.'

Wes told Aaron of his relief to know that Old Charlie was safe, telling him of their meeting with the cavalrymen and the officer's insistence that Charlie accompany them in their pursuit of the Indians.

He added, 'While I was in Trego I heard that the Indian war party was much larger than had been first thought. I was worried he might have run into serious trouble.'

Aaron merely smiled, saying, 'Trouble comes as natural to Old Charlie as eating and drinking but he found the Indians for the cavalry and after only a very brief fight persuaded them to give themselves up and let the army escort them back to their reservations. All this happened not more than a hundred miles north east of Denver, so Old Charlie left the cavalry to go their way and had an uneventful ride to the diggings. He was concerned about you though. Felt he'd let you down — but he wouldn't tell me exactly how.'

When Wes enlightened Aaron, Anabelita was horrified, 'No wonder Charlie wouldn't tell you what he had done,' she said to Aaron, 'It was unforgivable of him to ride off and leave Wes in the middle of nowhere, not knowing the country and with Indians on the warpath. With friends like that I was right to be worried about Wes.'

Aaron was far more relaxed about Old Charlie's apparent abandonment of Wes. 'Fortunately, Wes not only came out of it well, but succeeded in earning more money in rewards than you and Lola will earn in a year of dealing cards — even though I pay you both well.'

'He almost got himself killed doing it,' Anabelita retorted, ' . . . or hasn't he told you

321

about being shot? But Lola and me need to start work, so we won't be able to stay to hear the true story of what happened . . . or learn more about the Cheyenne woman who made up the ointment that helped his wounds to heal.'

Abruptly changing the subject, she asked, 'Will we see you in the gaming room today, Aaron?'

'I'll be there before long,' Aaron replied, 'but I want to have a chat with Wes first.'

When the two women had left the room, Aaron poured drinks for himself and Wes before leaning back in his chair and saying, 'I have a couple of things to tell you that I wouldn't mention in front of the women . . . but, first, how are you getting along with Anabelita? She's missed you while you were away and, as you've probably gathered, she was very worried about you.'

'I've missed her too,' Wes confessed, 'More than I thought I would — but you said you had things to say that you didn't want Anabelita or Lola to hear . . . ?'

'Yes . . . although I'd first like to say I wasn't aware you'd been wounded. Had I known I'd have come to find you — and I'm quite sure if Anabelita had known she'd have been with me.'

'She's already said as much herself . . . but what is it you want to tell me?'

'I didn't tell you everything I learned while I was up at the mining camps and making enquiries about the uncle you came out here to join up with . . . I am right in thinking his name is Peter Rowse?'

When Wes nodded, impatient for more

information, Aaron continued, 'There was no news of him in any of the major mining camps, or the towns that are springing up there. The closest I came to learn anything came from an old prospector who thought he'd heard the name among a group of miners high in the Rockies up beyond Leadville . . . but I stress, Wes, he only thought he'd heard the name and to go up there and attempt to find him would be sheer madness. The country he's talking about is beyond belief. It's more than eleven thousand feet high for a start, which means you need to breathe twice to get any air at all into your lungs and there are ravines and gulches where you could hide a couple of armies without them ever being found. If you do meet up with anyone the chances are that you'd recognize them only if you'd studied the Wanted notices.'

'Are you trying to tell me I should give up looking for my uncle?' Wes queried, 'There's no way I'm going to do that. He's the reason I came to America.'

'I'm not saying that, Wes, but I think you should concentrate on talking to your fellow Cornishmen right here in Denver. Most have spent time up in the mountains and could have met up with him at some time or another. Don't go into the Rockies until you have a positive lead to follow up, a lead from someone willing to take you there. A mountain-man like Old Charlie, perhaps. I'm not exaggerating the dangers, Wes. The Rockies are no place for greenhorns, there are more skeletons lying up there than you'll find in Arlington cemetery.'

Wes had never heard of Arlington cemetery, but he realized what Aaron was trying to tell him . . . and the Marshal was still talking, 'I'll have some posters printed and put up around Denver asking for news of him. We'll put a couple up in the Thespian Club and I'm sure Walsh will do the same in the Palace.'

Wes thought about what Aaron had said and Anabelita loomed large in the decision he reached, 'Alright, Aaron, I'll give it a try . . . for a couple of weeks, anyway.'

'Good!' Aaron's relief and delight were unfeigned, 'That will please Anabelita — and I do like to have a happy staff . . . '

Then, on a more serious note, he said, 'There's one other thing I didn't want to mention in front of the girls, Wes. I know from the reward authorisation Sheriff Wolfe tele-graphed to me that you saved his life by killing two Denton brothers and helping him take a third into custody. You've made the Territories a whole lot safer by what you did but, unfortunately, there's another brother at large and he was up at the diggings when word reached him of what had happened. It seems he went wild, swearing to kill whoever had done it. I tried to find him, but he'd left for Lauraville, swearing to avenge the deaths of his brothers. There are likely to be other kin with him. They've been terrorising the mining camps and many will be on the Wanted list. I telegraphed the US Marshal in Topeka, the State capital of Kansas, and had him send a couple of deputies to Lauraville, with orders to stay with Sheriff

Wolfe around the clock, but the surviving Dentons will learn soon enough that *you're* the one who actually shot the others and they'll come looking for you. I'll have Pat keep a close eye on you and I'll try to do the same, but we don't want to frighten the girls too much.'

While the import of the danger Wes was in sank home, Aaron asked, 'Did you kill the Denton's with a rifle, or handgun?'

'A revolver,' Wes replied, 'The one given to me by the Schusters.'

'Good,' Aaron nodded his approval, 'Old Charlie told me he'd taught you how to handle it — and that you'd learned well. Now you'll need to carry it with you at all times . . . '

When Wes began to protest, Aaron waved him to silence, 'You must, Wes. You've killed two Dentons and they're a large and close-knit clan. They'll be out to gun you down. Until we have them all in custody you need to be able to protect yourself — but the danger goes far beyond the Dentons. The two men you killed were well-known and wanted gunmen. You shot them both in a fair fight — that makes you a better gunman than they were. From now on there's a strong possibility some ambitious youngster will set out to prove he's better than you and if he's had enough to drink it won't matter whether or not you're armed. Merely killing you would be something to brag about.'

While Wes was digesting this latest warning, Aaron stood up. Clapping Wes on the shoulder he unexpectedly smiled. 'Like it or not, Wes, and with or without a badge, you're one of us now.

But before you hurry away to buckle on that gun belt, shall we go and tell Anabelita that you're likely to be staying in Denver for the foreseeable future?'

10

As Aaron had predicted, Anabelita was overjoyed
to know that Wes would be remaining in Denver
for the foreseeable future, but she could not
allow her feelings to show immediately because
the gaming saloon was filling up and she was
dealing blackjack. Nevertheless, she determined
that Wes would be left in no doubt of her delight
when they were alone later that night.

In the meantime, Wes and Aaron joined Pat
Rafferty on the stage of the Thespian Club where
he sat with a rifle resting on his lap, keeping a
watchful eye on the players.

They were here when Vic Walsh entered the
room. Looking about him, the owner of the
Palace waved when he saw Aaron and Wes and
made his way towards them.

Raising a hand in salutation to Wes, he greeted
Aaron enthusiastically. 'I heard you were back,
Marshal. I thought I'd come across and make
sure you were all in one piece.'

Looking puzzled, Aaron asked, 'Is there any
particular reason why I might not be?'

'Well, in a job like yours you go out looking for
trouble and never know when you're likely to
find it — especially when it concerns the Denton
gang. Did you find any of them?'

'Neither hair nor hide,' Aaron said easily,

'They've made such a good job of disappearing it's almost as though they know I'm looking for them.'

'How about this man, Gottland . . . any sign of him?'

Aaron shook his head, 'Not a thing. He's probably long gone.'

'Well, like you said, perhaps they've got wind that you're after them. You know better than I do that we don't need a telegraph out here for news to travel fast.'

'Some news does, but some don't' Aaron replied, 'Take Wes, here. He's been trying to trace the whereabouts of a kinsman who came out here mining. He's searched for him from Missouri to Denver and had me asking after him up in the mining camps in the Rockies, but he's proving as elusive to him as the Denton gang is to me. I'm having a poster printed and put up in here. We wondered whether you'd do the same in the Palace?'

'Of course I will,' Walsh said, effusively, 'Wes mentioned his uncle to me when he was in my place a few days ago and I've already been asking around, but with no success so far . . . but, much as I'd like to, I can't stop here talking, I've got staff problems in the Palace, but when I heard you were back I wanted to make sure you were all right. I'll just say 'Hello' to the girls, then get back. Why don't you both come over for a drink a little later?'

When Walsh was talking to Anabelita, Pat left the stage to talk to a punter who seemed uncertain what he was expected to do in a gaming saloon. With no one else within hearing distance, Aaron said to Wes, 'I gather you've already made the acquaintance of your fellow Cornishman, what do you make of him?'

When Wes hesitated, Aaron said, 'I'd value your opinion, Wes, it could be important.'

Aware from Aaron's manner that this was more than a casual question, Wes thought carefully before replying. 'In all honesty, I'd be hard put to find a reason for not liking the man, but the truth is . . . I don't.'

'That's exactly the way I feel . . .' Aaron broke off to wave at Walsh who had left the table where Anabelita was dealing and turned at the doorway to look back before leaving the gaming room. ' . . . Did he give you any details of what he did in Cornwall, or why he left?'

'None. He asked where *I* came from and when I told him, he said his family were farmers from a part of Cornwall I know nothing about. Similarly, he seemed to know little about Bodmin Moor and nothing at all about mining. That's not particularly significant, of course, not everyone in Cornwall is involved in mining, but he seemed to be avoiding saying anything about his life before he came to Denver . . . in fact, before he came to America.'

Then, aware that he really knew nothing about either Walsh's character or history, Wes added, 'I'm probably maligning the man. It could simply be that he prefers to keep his personal life private.'

'Perhaps . . . but I don't think so, Wes — and neither do you. You have a good lawman's mind, you really should be wearing a marshal's badge!'

During the next two weeks Wes became familiar with Denver, occasionally hiring a horse and buggy and taking Anabelita with him to explore the surrounding countryside.

One day, when he had the buggy he organised a surprise picnic for her. They went a couple of miles from the town, choosing a quiet spot beside a stream to stop. There had once been a wooden shack here and the outline of a small garden could still be traced.

Wes laid out the cloth for the picnic and produced an appetising array of food prepared specially for them in the Thespian Club's kitchen.

Anabelita tried to appear enthusiastic but she ate so little that a disappointed Wes eventually asked her whether she felt ill.

'No, I'm not ill, Wes, I'm just not feeling particularly hungry . . . but don't let it spoil the day, I really am enjoying being out here with you and don't let me stop you from eating, you've produced a wonderful spread. I'm really sorry I can't do justice to it, but I'm happy enough . . . truly.'

Wes felt guilty to be eating when Anabelita was having nothing, but he said, 'It's probably the result of spending so many hours in that smoky gaming room, it can't be good for you.'

'I'm used to it by now, Wes. After all, I've spent most of my life in smoky gaming rooms.'

'Then what is it, Anabelita? . . . No, don't tell me it's nothing, I've been watching you for days, that's partly why I planned this picnic today, to get you out in the fresh air for a while. Sometimes you're as pale as a ghost and when you came back from the washroom yesterday I could tell you'd been sick, even though you assured me you hadn't. Is there something wrong with you that you're not telling me about? Are you ill? Have you seen a doctor?'

'There's no need to see a doctor . . . and I am not ill.'

There was a long silence between them, during which Anabelita realized she would be unable to keep her secret for very much longer — and she might never have another opportunity like this to reveal the truth to Wes.

Making up her mind, she met his concerned gaze with a direct look and said simply, 'I'm pregnant, Wes. I'm expecting your baby.'

'You're WHAT!?' Her statement shook him to the core and he looked at her with an expression of total disbelief before asking, 'Are you *sure*?'

'I wish I wasn't, Wes . . . but there can be no doubt about it.'

Still thoroughly bemused, Wes asked, 'How long have you known?'

'I suspected it soon after leaving the *Missouri Belle* and it became certain as the weeks passed.'

Gathering his senses together, Wes queried, 'When do you think it happened?'

'I couldn't say for certain, but I think it might have been on that very first night we spent together on the *Missouri Belle*.'

'Then there certainly can't be any doubt by now . . . does anyone else know?'

'Only Lola, but Aaron will have to be told soon, it's only fair to him after he brought me all this way to work in his gambling saloon.'

'It will certainly upset his plans,' Wes said, 'but that's not the most important thing right now. You are.'

The silence that followed was broken by an unhappy Anabelita, 'I really am sorry, Wes, I should have tried to stop it happening.'

'You can't take all the blame ... ' Wes succeeded in giving her a weak smile, 'After all, I had something to do with what's happened. The question is, what do we do now?'

Anabelita was more heartened by the 'we' in Wes's question than he would ever know but much as she loved him — and she knew she really *did* love him — she had given the future a great deal of thought since her condition had become a certainty and had made up her mind about her future — hers and the baby's.

'You don't need to do anything about it, Wes. I have enough money put by to keep me and the baby for at least a year. By then I'll be able to work again and I think Aaron will take me back in the Thespian Club.'

'You'd go back to gambling? What will happen to the baby while you're working?'

'I've thought of that too. I'll bring in a young Mexican girl to act as a nurse-maid, there are many of them in New Mexico and Texas who are desperate for such work. They are cheap and reliable and, of course, it helps that I also speak Mexican ... '

Glancing beyond Wes as she was speaking, she suddenly broke off to say, 'There are two riders heading this way.'

Turning around, Wes saw two horsemen approaching at a slow trot from the direction of the mountains. As they drew closer Wes could see that both were dressed in the manner of cowboys — and each carried a holstered revolver.

'Stay close to the buggy,' Wes said to Anabelita. 'I'll be on the other side with the rifle to hand.'

The riders slowed when they neared the picnickers and it was apparent to Wes that they were commenting on the presence of Anabelita.

He felt uneasy at their appearance. Unshaven and unkempt, their clothes were stained and dusty and he hoped that when they neared the picnic spot they would remain downwind.

The two men rode up to the buggy and stopped, taking in the scene without dismounting before one addressed Anabelita, saying, 'Well now, ain't this cosy. Is it a private party, ma'am, or can two hungry travellers join in?'

'It's private, friend,' Wes said, 'and we're not looking for company.'

The two men had given Wes only a casual glance when they arrived, focussing their attention upon Anabelita. Now the one who had spoken to her looked at him dismissively, 'I don't remember asking you . . . 'friend'. I was speaking to the lady . . . although I don't know many ladies who'd risk any reputation they might have

333

by riding out so far from other folk with a man.'

'No,' agreed Wes, aware that the cowboy was deliberately goading him, 'I don't suppose you do . . . but then, you won't have met many real ladies.'

The cowboy frowned, not certain whether or not Wes had intended an insult. He decided he *had*. 'I don't think you and me are going to get along with each other,' he said, edging his horse closer to the buggy.

'Then I suggest you go on your way and find someone more understanding,' Wes said, bringing up the rifle which had been hidden in the buggy and at the same time levering a cartridge into the breech.

The cowboy pulled his horse to a halt and Wes tensed, anticipating a move towards the gun at his belt, but his companion said, 'There ain't no need for that, mister, Jericho don't mean no harm. He's just not used to being around folk. Besides, neither of us has eaten for two days. I guess the sight of all your food's made him a mite mean.'

'Then I suggest you ride on to Denver and find yourselves a meal,' Wes said, the Winchester pointing unwaveringly at 'Jericho's' midriff, 'but I wouldn't turn a hungry man away when we have more than we can eat. Anabelita, hand them up a couple of sandwiches — but don't get between them and my gun.'

Listening to the conversation, Anabelita had been prepared at any moment to reach beneath her skirt for the small-bore pistol she kept there. Now she snatched up a couple of sandwiches and passed them up to the cowboy closest to Wes.

Taking them from her, he said to Wes, 'We have some unfinished business to settle if ever we meet up again.'

Before turning his horse away, he said to Anabelita, 'You heard my name. If ever you feel like doing something more exciting than sitting in the middle of nowhere, eating sandwiches, just ask after me in Vic Walsh's Palace, in Denver. He'll know where you can find me.'

With the Winchester held ready for use, Wes watched as the two cowboys rode away, but neither turned around and whether or not their talk of having nothing to eat for two days had been the truth, they made short work of the sandwiches.

When they had passed from view, Wes and Anabelita packed up the remains of their food and left the picnic spot, following the same route as that taken by the two intruders.

He and Anabelita had much they should have been talking about, but Wes was on edge, especially whenever they approached any spot where the men might be waiting in ambush for them.

As a result, nothing had been resolved by the time they reached Denver and the house behind the Thespian Club.

11

⚜

That evening when Anabelita and Lola had left for work at the club, Wes was telling Aaron of he and Anabelita's encounter with the two cowboys. When he mentioned that the one referred to as Jericho had told Anabelita he could be contacted through Vic Walsh at the Palace, Aaron suddenly became very interested.

'This Jericho . . . did you get a surname for him?'

Wes shook his head, 'No, it was sheer luck that we got a first name. I thought our meeting was going to end in a shoot-out. Why do you ask?'

'Jericho is an unusual enough name to stick in the mind and I believe I've seen it on one of the Wanted posters piled up in my office. Let's go there and see if we can find it.'

On the way to the United States Marshal's office, Aaron explained why he was particularly interested in the man who had been instrumental in bringing Wes and Anabelita's picnic to a premature end.

'It's the fact that this Jericho knows Walsh,' he said. 'You and I both believe the image Walsh is working so hard to project of himself is too good to be true.'

When Wes agreed, Aaron explained, 'I've made a few enquiries about our Mr Walsh — but it wasn't easy. He's remarkably vague about what he was doing before he came to Denver but when he was in my office one day I found some old posters advertising a well-known singer who had appeared at the Thespian Club when it was a theatre. Forgetting his usual caution, Walsh mentioned that he'd seen her on stage on a number of occasions . . . in Chicago. From that scrap of information I deduced he'd probably lived in that city for some time, so I wrote to the United States Marshal there, sending a photograph of Walsh and asking what, if anything, he knew about him. I had a reply today.'

'You managed to get hold of a photograph of Walsh?' Wes was genuinely surprised. He felt a man with something to hide would have been very careful not to have a photograph taken of himself.

'It was taken when the Palace had its official opening. Walsh was photographed with a group of the dignitaries who attended the ceremony.'

'Has the Marshal in Chicago recognized him?'

Showing a rare moment of excitement, Aaron replied, 'Yes — but not as Vic Walsh. He said he was known in Chicago as Victor *Walsingham*, a downtown jeweller from Cornwall, who sold up and left the city more than a year ago — after suspicion had fallen on him of receiving stolen jewellery. Nothing was ever proved and Walsingham — or Walsh — is known to have made a couple of return visits to Chicago since then. Another most intriguing piece of news the Chicago Marshal gave me is that the Pinkerton Detective Agency is also interested in Walsh

— and has been for some time. They are awaiting information from the police in England about him.'

'Why should a private detective agency be interested in him?' Wes queried.

Aaron shrugged, 'It's an internationally recognized agency. He's probably come to their notice as a result of some inquiry they are carrying out. What is certain is that they'll be able to learn far more about Walsh than I ever could, so I've got in touch with them and asked to be kept informed of anything they learn.'

'Talking of being kept informed of things . . . '

Before beginning work that evening, Anabelita and Wes had returned to the subject of her pregnancy. She was not yet ready to discuss the future with Wes but had agreed that should an opportunity arise he might tell Aaron of her condition. Aaron had just given him such an opportunity and he proceeded to tell him now of the conversation that had taken place between him and Anabelita on their eventful picnic.

Aaron was not as surprised as he might have been, saying, 'I've thought for a while now that she hasn't been her usual self and suspected it probably had something to do with you.'

'It has everything to do with me,' Wes admitted, 'and now I need to get it sorted out.'

'That shouldn't be too difficult,' Aaron said, 'You're both free to do whatever you decide. Have the pair of you discussed it at any length?'

'Anabelita had only just told me about it when Jericho and his fellow gunman appeared on the scene,' Wes explained, 'The thought that they

338

might be hiding behind a bush waiting to jump out at us dominated both our thoughts on the way back to Denver. We haven't had much time to talk about it since then, but from what she said when she gave me the news, she plans on getting a nursemaid to look after the baby and coming back to work for you.'

'Is that what you want?'

'It's too soon to know exactly what it is I want,' Wes admitted, 'It still hasn't properly sunk in — but marrying Anabelita and having a family is an idea that could grow on me — although I'm not sure it's what she wants. Besides, as I think I've mentioned before, I can't see her settling down to life as a miner's wife.'

'I think that would depend very much on who the miner happened to be,' Aaron pointed out, 'Although I can understand any reasonable woman thinking twice about such a life. Quite apart from the filth and squalor of a mining camp, you can find your way to any one of them by stopping and listening for the sound of miners coughing their lungs up — those who've managed to survive roof falls and blasting accidents. I swear there wasn't a day passed while I was up there when I didn't need to take my hat off in a mark of respect for at least one funeral cortège. Besides, you haven't been down a mine for many months now and have had a chance to see what else the world can offer you — and a wife and family. I'm not in the habit of giving unasked advice, but I'm giving it now. Don't put your work before the chance of happiness with a good woman and a family. It's one of the most important things in life, Wes, take it from me.'

Wes was going to question whether it was a lesson that Aaron had learned the hard way, but something in his friend's expression stopped him.

Instead, he said, 'You might be able to sell the idea to me, Aaron — but I'm not sure Anabelita thinks the same way.'

12

Old Charlie rode into Denver the next morning, missing seeing Aaron by less than an hour. The US Marshal had taken the train to Kansas City in order to attend a meeting there of Western marshals.

The news that the old mountain-man brought with him would ultimately have a considerable influence on Wes's future — but this was not the reason he was uncertain of the reception he would receive from the man who had been his cross-country travelling companion. The truth was that Old Charlie still felt guilty about the manner of his parting from Wes.

His relief was evident when Wes showed delight at meeting his old friend again but the mountain-man's expression changed when, aware that he would go to great lengths to avoid populated areas, Wes asked what had brought him to Denver.

'I came because I have news of your uncle . . . ' When Wes showed delight, Old Charlie added, hurriedly, ' . . . It's not good news, Wes. In fact, it's as bad as it could be . . . worse, even.'

Wes did not want to believe him. He had crossed the Atlantic specifically to join his uncle and travelled halfway across America to find him.

'What is it, Charlie . . . ? What have you heard?'

Old Charlie shook his head unhappily, 'I'm afraid it's not hearsay, boy. You see . . . I was with him when he died and was able to tell him you'd come out here to join him and that we'd both been looking for him. He said for me to tell you he always knew you'd make it to America — and he gave me this for you . . . '

He pulled a flat oilcloth pouch from inside his shirt. Travel-stained, it was incongruously tied with a length of bright scarlet ribbon.

Distressed by the news he had been given, Wes took the package from the old mountain-man and asked, 'What is it, Charlie?'

'It's papers for a registered claim up in the Rockies. It's a nice piece of land, Wes, right by a river. Your uncle was working it for gold with three partners but two of them are dead too.'

'What did they die of, Charlie? Was it an accident? Sickness . . . ? The weather?' He put the last question because there had been talk of early snowfalls on the higher peaks of the mountains. Those who spoke of it recalled the men who had been trapped by snow and died in past years.

'It was none of them, Wes,' Charlie replied grimly, 'They had a visit from a bunch of killers. I heard the shooting when I was up near their claim looking for a homestead site for me and a young Cheyenne squaw I'd bought from her father . . . that's her ribbon around the pouch you've got in your hand. I went to find out what the shooting was all about. Lucky for me the

342

Denton gang had rode off in the opposite direction, or I wouldn't be here talking to you now.'

'The Dentons . . . ? Are you sure, Charlie?'

'It wasn't my say-so, it was your uncle's. He was still alive when I got there. Two of his partners had been shot dead, the other one was lucky, he'd gone off to bank the gold they'd already found. He got back just as I'd finished burying the others and was carving your uncle's name on a cross I'd made from some wood I found around the place. According to him, your uncle and the others must have been murdered for the sake of killing because there was nothing of value around the place. He'd taken all their gold to the bank and there was nothing else . . . at least, not much, but your uncle apologised to you in almost his last breath. He said he'd promised you the photograph of his wife and her sister — your mother — that he kept in the back of his watch. One of the Denton gang took that from him. I got the feeling he was more upset about that than what had happened to him.'

For a few moments Wes thought he would make a fool of himself in front of the old mountain-man but although his throat felt tight enough to choke him, he managed to tell Charlie that the stolen piece was a gold inscribed watch, presented to his uncle for rescuing six miners and leading them to safety after a roof fall at the three hundred fathom level in a Cornish mine. Wes added that he had valued the photo of his wife and sister even more than the watch. 'It was a cruel thing to do to a dying man,' he declared,

343

adding, 'Where do you think the Dentons were heading when they left the claim?'

'Deeper into the Rockies,' Charlie said, 'but there's no sense trying to go after 'em. They'll show up again before long for sure. Prospectors up in the mountains live in constant fear of a visit from them, and managers of even some of the largest mines are just as scared they'll one day come calling.'

'How many are there in this gang?' Wes asked.

'I've heard it said there are more than twenty, but they mostly go around in groups of about half-a-dozen when they're raiding a small prospecting camp, joining up only if they're taking on something bigger, or when they intend raising hell in one of the mining towns.'

'Are you going to tell Aaron about what happened up in the mountains, Charlie, and get him to go after them?'

Even as he was asking the question, Wes knew Aaron would never be able to raise a posse willing to go into the mountains to track the killers of three unknown prospectors . . . especially if they were told they were hunting the Denton gang. Besides, such killings were all too common out here in the Territories.

Old Charlie was talking again, 'Any time you fancy going up into the Rockies to visit your Uncle's grave I'll be ready to take you — but don't try to locate it on your own, you'd never be seen again.'

'How will I be able to contact you?' Wes asked.

'You won't,' came the blunt reply, 'but if you take the mine railroad up to Black Hawk and head west out of town, after a couple of hours you'll see three peaks standing up over the ridge. Head for the right hand one and you'll soon recognize some of the features shown on the map you've got with the papers on the claim. Just keep riding towards the claim and I'll know you're coming . . . no, don't ask me how I'll know, I just will.'

Making no attempt to question him about how he would know, Wes asked, 'Will you be staying in Denver for a while now, Charlie?'

'You know better than to ask me a question like that, boy. Me and towns don't agree with each other. Besides, there's a squaw waiting up there for me. She's one of the most patient women I've ever come across but she won't wait for ever.'

★　★　★

Later that evening, Old Charlie joined Wes, Anabelita and Lola for a meal in the Thespian Club's eating-house, but he was not comfortable eating in company and said he intended returning to the mountains as soon as he had bought a few stores to help him and the Cheyenne girl he called 'Usdi' get through the winter months.

When Anabelita asked whether Usdi was happy living in such a remote spot, Old Charlie replied, 'I haven't asked her. Even if I did, I don't think there are any Cheyenne left who are old enough to remember what happiness is. I'll make sure she's well-fed and clothed and has all she needs to run a home the way she wants. I'll even take back a few gewgaws from town to please her. There's not much more any Indian woman expects from life.'

13

A few hours after Anabelita had gone to work in the Thespian Club, Old Charlie came to find Wes to tell him he was about ready to leave for the Mountains.

Wes had been thinking a great deal about what the old mountain-man had told him and, making a spur of the moment decision, he said, 'Can you put off leaving for an hour, Charlie?'

'I *could* . . . but only if you give me a good enough reason.'

'If you wait until I'm ready, I'll come with you. I'd like to look at my uncle's grave and check on one or two things I've been thinking about. I just need to throw a few things into a saddlebag and tell Anabelita where I'm going.'

Old Charlie was secretly delighted that Wes would be accompanying him to the mountains, but looking shrewdly at him, he asked, 'These things you've been thinking about would I be right in guessing that they have more to do with that card-dealing girl from the *Missouri Belle* than anything else?'

'Maybe,' Wes admitted, 'Although it has to do with mining too. I might decide to give something else a try . . . I don't know yet.'

'That's the trouble with the women a man meets up with when he's east of the Territories,'

347

Old Charlie said philosophically. 'They can always find something about a man that needs changing. You should have let me find a squaw for you, boy, they accept a man for what he is and let him get on with his own life.'

About to spit out tobacco juice, Old Charlie remembered where he was. Walking to the open window he sent it into the street below before saying, 'I suppose we all want different things from life. When you're good and ready come and find me. I'll be in the stable, with Nellie.'

'Oh, before you go I want to give you this.' Wes held out the oilcloth pouch that had belonged to his uncle.

Looking at it in puzzlement, Old Charlie asked, 'You want me to look after it for you?'

'No, Charlie, I want you to keep it. To have the claim. I'm not a prospector and I don't want to become one. You once told me it was something you've always wanted to do, so now's your chance. Do what you want with it, it's yours.'

Trying to hide his delight, Old Charlie said, 'Thank you, boy. I'll speak to your late uncle's partner and find out whether he means to stay up there working, with me to help him. Now, you go off and get yourself ready, but don't be too long I want to get clear of Denver as soon as I can. You'd better bring a couple of blankets with you too — and the warmest clothes you have. Make sure they're good and thick. Winter's coming close and it drops to below freezing up there come sundown.'

Wes did not doubt the old mountain-man. From Denver it was possible to see the snow that capped the tallest peaks of the Rockies and in recent days it had been gradually creeping lower.

Having decided to give the claim to Old Charlie and no longer having any obligation to return to mining, realization had come to Wes that he was now his own man. He could do whatever he wished with his life . . . for himself and for Anabelita. But first he wanted to pay his respects to the man who had been the brother of his late mother.

'How long will it take to get to this claim, Charlie?'

'If we set off real soon we can snatch a couple of hours sleep when we're clear of Denver and be within striking distance of my cabin soon after nightfall tomorrow. That's the time I want to arrive, so I need have no fear of having the Denton's or any other good-for-nothings learning where I'm living.'

'Is that a truthful estimate of how long it's going to take, Charlie — or is it another 'We'll be in Denver in ten days' sort of story?'

Looking abashed, Old Charlie said, 'We'll be there when I've said . . . as long as we beat the snow.'

★   ★   ★

Anabelita was not happy with Wes's news when he called in at the Thespian Club to tell her what he intended doing.

'You be careful up in the mountains, Wes — and it's not only the Denton's you need to look out for. If your uncle hadn't still been alive when Old Charlie found him the deaths would have been blamed on the bands of Indians who roam the Rockies. They have no reason to respect the lives of those who claim to have bought 'rights' to lands where they and their people have lived for hundreds of years.'

'I don't think you need worry about that, Anabelita,' Wes said, 'I'll be with Old Charlie. There's little he doesn't know about Indians.'

'I still wish you weren't going,' Anabelita said unhappily, 'but you must do what you need to do — just take care of yourself, that's all.'

In truth, it was not only the dangers that Wes might encounter in the mountains that concerned her. She realized that up there he would probably be meeting miners . . . men who either earned a living, or were trying to make a living doing the work with which Wes was familiar and that he had come to the United States to continue. She was afraid that being with such men might persuade him to remain in the Rockies and not come back to her in Denver.

14

Old Charlie had not lied to Wes about the time it would take to reach his cabin in the Rocky Mountains — but he had said nothing about the precarious route they would need to travel in order to get there.

Darkness was descending on the mountains when they were approaching the upper slopes and the hair on the back of Wes's neck began to rise when the old man pointed out the track which could just be discerned clinging to the side of a sheer cliff rising thousands of feet above them.

It made it no easier when Old Charlie insisted they continue the journey after dark, declaring that a man was safer travelling in the mountains when it was impossible for any of those on the look-out for vulnerable travellers to see them.

As Old Charlie had earned the right to be called a 'mountain-man' and had managed to survive to a venerable, if not entirely respectable old age, Wes accepted his decision. Although never entirely at ease, he chose to be grateful that, although the moon and stars were a help to them as they picked their way along the precarious mountain-side tracks, the night cast shadows that made it impossible to see the awesome depths of the canyon whose wall they were traversing. Some time after midnight, when they had left the narrow cliff-side track, Old Charlie led the way through a narrow defile in the mountains that would have been hard to locate even in daytime.

After pushing and pulling Old Charlie's mule and Wes's horse over numerous piles of fallen and broken rock, the two men came out into a narrow, uneven valley. Here, hidden among the pines was a small timber cabin that in daytime would show it was newly-built from trees felled from the pines and which had not yet had all the gaps between logs caulked with mud.

Pausing when still some paces from the door, Old Charlie emitted a number of shrill whistles. At the third signal, a female figure appeared at the doorway of the cabin and Wes could see that it was an Indian woman.

'Let her take your horse,' Old Charlie said, 'She'll turn it loose and it'll find good grass up here and come to no harm. There's only one way in and out and no horse is going to try to climb those rock falls. There's no fear of wolves, either, they don't come up this way. As for grizzlies . . . I've shot out all that were here.'

Handing his horse to the care of the silent Indian woman, Wes entered the cabin and was relieved to find a fire burning in the fireplace. His hands were so cold they had become numb and his ears were tingling painfully.

He was seated beside the fire on a pine log stool, with a steaming mug of coffee in his hands when Usdi returned from attending to the horses and immediately began to cook venison in a pan,

352

at the same time making a hash of potatoes mixed with a vegetable he failed to recognize.

Usdi spoke no other language than Cheyenne, so the only way he could show appreciation for her cooking was to eat every scrap and it proved to be no hardship.

She was older than Wes had imagined she would be. He guessed her to be in her early thirties but she still showed signs of the beauty she must have possessed as a younger woman.

Although she had been awakened in the middle of the night to cook for her man and someone who was a total stranger to her, she seemed not to resent it. In fact, at no time did Wes see her show any emotion whatsoever.

After the two men had eaten she made up a hay bed covered with blankets for Wes in a corner of the room. Then, after adding a number of logs to the fire, she and Old Charlie went to bed in a small, doorless room situated at the other end of the simple cabin.

★　★　★

The next morning, after a substantial breakfast, Wes set off from the frost-dusted valley with Old Charlie, heading for the claim where his uncle had died and was buried.

The place proved to be much closer to the cabin where he had spent the night than Wes had envisaged. Once they had made their way through the narrow defile and Old Charlie had reconnoitred the immediate vicinity to ensure no one was around to see them emerge, they rode

353

for no more than forty minutes before arriving at the more accessible and smaller mountain hollow that was the last resting place of Cornishman Peter Rowse.

They were met by a cautious man who had obviously been panning in the stream which ran through the small valley. He had run into a small and ramshackle cabin when he heard their approach and now emerged pointing a shotgun menacingly in their direction.

Recognizing Old Charlie, his relief was apparent and he greeted the old mountain-man warmly, saying, 'It's good to see you again, Charlie. I haven't spoken to a soul since I last saw you, and when I heard you coming I was afraid it might be some of the Denton gang returning.'

'If they were to come back now you couldn't have anyone better than the young man I've brought to meet you, Daniel. This here's Wesley Curnow. He shot and killed two of the Denton brothers in Lauraville, when they were trying to make the sheriff dance to the tune of a six-gun. He also happens to be the nephew of your late partner, Peter Rowse . . . Wes, meet Daniel Pike.'

Grasping Wes's hand, the prospector said sorrowfully, 'I'm sorry your uncle isn't alive to greet you, Wesley, there was hardly a day passed when he didn't wonder whether it was going to be the day you'd arrive from the Cornwall he hoped one day to return to as a rich man. He thought a whole lot of you.'

'And I of him,' Wes replied, 'but . . . where is he buried?'

Pointing to where three primitive crosses stood sentinel over three small mounds of earth rising above the grass at the foot of a tall bluff, Pike said, 'Charlie made your uncle's cross, I did the same for the other two.'

Wes walked over to the three graves and was moved by the care Old Charlie had taken in carving his uncle's name on the horizontal bar of the cross marking his grave.

Dropping to his knees beside it, he tried to remember the words of some of the prayers that had been said at funerals of his mother and father and victims of mine disasters, but could think of nothing that suited either the manner of his uncle's death, or the place where he had been wounded and left to die. Eventually, he simply clasped his hands together and mumbled all the prayers he could remember them reciting together in the Wesleyan chapel on the edge of Bodmin Moor.

Rising to his feet when he had done, he saw Old Charlie and Daniel Pike poring over the papers he had given to the mountain-man.

Throwing Wes a sympathetic glance, Pike said, 'Do you feel easier in your mind now you've been able to visit Peter's grave?'

'I'd feel a whole lot better if I knew his killers were going to be caught,' he replied.

'There's little chance of that,' the prospector said, 'You'd never learn which of the gang did it . . . Not that it makes any difference, they're all as bad as one another. There's not one of them that doesn't have at least one murder to his name. I'd say you've already done enough to avenge Peter — but that reminds me, I've a few of his things here, though they're mainly clothes, the Denton's made off with anything of value.'

'You keep any that you might be able to use,' Wes said, 'but are you going to stay up here after what's happened?'

'I had half a mind to move on,' Pike said, 'but Charlie says he'll come and help me to work the claim, going back to his own place each night. I'll get me a dog to keep me company at night and warn me if anyone comes around . . . but that reminds me, there's money in the bank down at Central. A quarter of it was Peter's, but it's yours now. Do you have a bank I can put it in for you when I go down to Central and have the money belonging to the others sent on to their families?'

'Not at the moment,' Wes replied, 'but next time you go there, draw out whatever you think was due to Uncle Peter and Charlie can bring it to Denver next time he comes there.'

'Do you reckon you'll be staying in Denver long enough for me to get it to you?' Old Charlie asked.

'I don't plan moving on just yet, Charlie, so I guess the answer is 'yes'.'

'There's no accounting for taste,' Old Charlie said, sarcastically, 'but Denver's quieter than some of the mining camps up this way.'

'Talking of mining . . . ' Wes addressed Daniel Pike, 'What are they taking out of the ground around here? I wouldn't have thought there was enough gold to make it worth the expense of working a deep, hard-rock mine just for that.'

'You're probably right,' Pike replied, 'Just lately they've been making the most of whatever comes out of the ground but there seems to be far more silver than they realized was in the ground.'

'I thought that might be so,' Wes said, 'I was looking at some of the waste taken out of your claim here. If you ever decide you've taken out all the gold there is to be had you might be able to interest one of the big companies in buying you out.'

'That might be good news for the future,' Old Charlie said, 'but when we've taken out all the gold that's here I hope Daniel will have enough money to do everything he wants and can go away and forget all about the claim. I've found a place that will keep me happy for the few years I've got left. I don't want to share it with no clattering mine and a whole bunch of noisy, quarrelling miners. Remember that, Daniel, when the gold runs out.'

15

꧁

Accompanied by Old Charlie, Wes left the hidden mountain valley before dawn the day after visiting the grave of his murdered uncle. It was a cold, crisp morning and Wes was glad to be wearing a heavy coat.

The two men rode in single file until they left the narrow, shelf-like mountainside path behind. By this time it was light enough to see the land about them. Dropping back to ride alongside Wes, Old Charlie pointed to three jagged peaks rising above the mountain ridge far to the right of the path they were on.

The sun was not yet high enough to be seen, but its rays had reached the three peaks, painting their mantles of snow a vivid red that was so bright no artist would have dared depict it on a canvas for fear of being ridiculed.

'Have you ever seen anything like that, boy?' The old mountain-man demanded.

When Wes admitted he had not, Old Charlie said, 'That's what I see most every morning when I open my door and walk outside. What's more, I can stand and admire it for as long as I please without having some damn fool making a noise, or grumbling about the cold, or some such. It's why I'm a mountain-man, boy, and why I'll never be as happy anywhere else.'

'The Rockies are truly awesome, Charlie,' Wes agreed, 'but it would be a hard life for a woman — and a lonely one, too.'

Wes had learned during his time with Old Charlie that spitting out tobacco juice was his way expressing disapproval of something he had seen or heard. He showed his irritation at Wes's words now.

'Like I've said before, there's a whole lot more to life than having fancy things in a home and having to share the breath of thousands of other folk. I know where I'd want to be, even if I was unfortunate enough to be a woman.'

Wes was inclined to agree with Old Charlie's sentiments when they approached a large but impermanent mining town lower down on the slopes of the Rockies. Wes could smell it when they were still a mile away. It was the aroma of industry, habitation and poor sanitation. A town that had far outgrown its primitive amenities.

As they drew nearer the stench became so bad that Wes baulked at even entering the town and he told Old Charlie he intended bypassing it with as much speed as possible, and so the two men parted company.

The road to Denver was well marked from here but despite Old Charlie's aversion to most forms of human habitation, he needed to go into the town to buy a number of items needed at the mountain cabin if he and Usdi were to survive the fast approaching winter.

★ ★ ★

Wes reached Denver late that evening and after putting up his horse made his way to the Thespian Club gambling saloon where Anabelita was busy dealing cards.

He thought she looked tired but when she glanced up and saw him her delighted expression caused the players at her table to swing around to learn what it was that had so clearly shattered the sangfroid manner she adopted when dealing cards.

It was another half-an-hour before she was able to arrange for a trainee croupier to deal in her place for a few minutes and take Wes to the croupiers' rest room. Here she could greet him away from the gaze of the Thespian Club's gamblers.

'I didn't expect you back so soon,' she said breathlessly, breaking away from his enthusiastic embrace. 'When I told Aaron you had gone off to the mountains with Old Charlie, he said he doubted whether we would see you again for weeks. It made me quite depressed.'

'Aaron is back in Denver?'

'That's right, he arrived earlier today and was disappointed you weren't here. I think he has something to tell you. I have no idea what it is . . . but I am glad to have you back, Wes.'

Her declaration signalled another warm hug then, suddenly apprehensive, she asked, 'Did you see your uncle's grave — and meet with any Cornish miners while you were up in the mountains?'

'I saw his grave, yes, and learned that it must have been a cold-blooded killing . . . but I'll tell you all about it when you finish work and we are able to talk without needing to worry about anything else. We have a lot to talk about . . . but where is Aaron now? I want to speak to him about what I've learned . . . is he at the house?'

'No, he said he had some work to do at the Marshal's office. If you see him will you tell him Vic Walsh came to the Thespian Club asking after him last night, I forgot to tell him when I spoke to him earlier. Walsh asked after you too, but I think it was really Aaron he wanted. I told him you were both out of town and likely to be away for some time. When he learns you're both back in Denver he'll think I was deliberately misleading him.'

'I don't think you need worry too much about what Walsh thinks,' Wes said dismissively, giving Anabelita a brief moment of guilty pleasure in the belief that Wes was showing just a hint of jealousy that Walsh had been talking to her, ' . . . I don't suppose he had anything of importance to say to either of us.'

'No, it was probably nothing more than he said to me, that he was taking a trip back East. He asked whether there was anything he could bring back for me.'

'Is there anything you asked him to get for you?'

'There was nothing I could think of that I wanted . . . but I must be getting back to my table, Rosie is new here and hasn't been left on her own before.'

'Of course, but try to finish early and we'll have a long talk then . . . I've missed you.'

Anabelita flashed him a happy smile but as she turned to go a sudden thought came to Wes, 'This trip Walsh is making . . . did he say when he would be leaving?'

Turning back to him, Anabelita said, 'What day is it today . . . Friday? He's catching the early train tomorrow morning.'

16

Aaron was writing at his desk when Wes entered the Marshal's office. He was pleased to see him, commenting, 'I'm surprised to see you so soon, Wes, Anabelita said you'd gone up to the mountains with Old Charlie and she didn't expect to see you again for a while. She told me about your uncle. I'm sorry to hear what happened to him, I know finding him meant a great deal to you.'

'It was Old Charlie who brought me the news, he heard the shooting and when he got to the claim my uncle was still alive — but only just. He told Charlie it was the Dentons who did it. While I was in the mountains I met his partner who was lucky enough to be away when the raid happened. He said it must have been murder for the sake of it because there was nothing of value at the site.'

'We'll discuss the Denton's in a minute, Wes, but what are your plans now? Anabelita said your uncle left you his claim, are you going to use it and try your luck at prospecting?'

'I'm a miner, not a prospector, Aaron. My uncle left me a bit of money too and it will come in handy while I make up my mind about the future. I don't fancy the sort of life my uncle was living, so I've given the claim to Old Charlie and after smelling the air around one of the mining camps up there in the mountains I'm not at all sure I want to go back to mining. I certainly wouldn't even think of taking Anabelita up there.'

Showing sudden increased interest, Aaron asked, 'If you don't intend working the claim and are not going back to mining, what will you do?'

Wes shrugged, 'I'll find something, there's no real hurry. I'll talk it over with Anabelita before making up my mind.'

'While we're on the subject of life-changing moves . . . Senator Schuster and his son were in Kansas while I was there, but he's no longer ex-Senator Schuster, he's *Governor* Schuster of Kentucky now. Standing with the support of the President he swept the board in an election held only a couple of few weeks ago.'

'Did the letter you wrote to the President about the way in which Harrison Schuster died influence his support for Harrison's father?'

'I think it might have helped,' Aaron admitted, 'The Governor certainly thought it did. He told me that the United States Marshal for Kentucky is retiring very soon. He said he would ask for me to be appointed if I wanted the post.'

'It would certainly be easier than being US Marshal for the Territories,' Wes pointed out.

'Perhaps,' Aaron said, enigmatically, 'But I don't think an ex-Union brigadier would be popular with everyone in that part of the country. Besides, President Grant sent me out here to try to bring some law to the Territories, I have no intention of letting him down. The

Governor asked after you and was very impressed when I told him how you'd put the gun the Schusters gave you to good use. They had trouble with the Dentons in Kentucky soon after the War. When I mentioned that you'd been wounded in the gunfight the Governor's son said it was a good job his sister, Emma, hadn't heard about it, or she would have been on the next train to Lauraville. It would seem she's very disappointed not to have heard anything from you.'

Wes gave a smile that was tinged with relief, 'She's a nice, warm and caring girl,' he said, 'Any man, myself included, would find it easy to become very fond of her, but I'm glad she *didn't* know I'd been shot.'

Aaron was aware that Wes was thinking of the embarrassment her arrival would have caused, in view of Anabelita's condition, but he had other matters he wanted to talk to Wes about.

'While I was in Kansas I learned some very interesting information about Vic Walsh,' he said, 'Very interesting indeed. As you know, the Pinkerton Detective Agency has also been checking up on him and they might have uncovered the secret of where he got the money to start up as a big-time gambling entrepreneur here, in Denver. They have certainly discovered he didn't start life as Vic Walsh — or even as Victor Walsingham, the name he used when he had a jewellers business in Chicago and was suspected of handling stolen jewellery.'

'Are they sure all these names they're throwing around are one and the same man?'

'No doubt about it,' Aaron said jubilantly, 'I showed the Pinkertons the photograph I have of Walsh and they confirmed it.'

'Did you learn why the Pinkertons began taking an interest in him in the first place?' Wes asked.

'It was because of someone that they — and we — would like to see brought to justice. It seems Walsh handled a great deal of the jewellery taken off River steamboat passengers . . . *on behalf of a certain Ira Gottland!*'

Wes's interest quickened immediately, but Aaron had not finished talking. Leaning forward in his chair, he said, 'I have left the best until last, Wes. As Walsh is so obviously a Cornishman, the Pinkerton's made enquiries about him in that part of the world. They came up with some very interesting information indeed . . . Not about Vic Walsh, or Victor Walsingham, but a Victor Waller, son of a good family from Cornwall. He was apprenticed to a jeweller in Plymouth, which I believe is just across a river from Cornwall. He did well there and became a trusted employee . . . until the jeweller went to London for a few days leaving Waller in charge. When he returned Waller had disappeared — and so had most of the jeweller's stock! Rumours were rife that he'd gone to Europe . . . to Canada . . . to Australia, but then a number of the more valuable pieces began to surface right here, in America — *in Chicago!* The Pinkerton's found evidence linking the jewellery to Walsingham . . . or Walsh . . . or Waller, whichever name you prefer but, of course, they could take no action on anything he had done in England.'

Wes's mind had been working overtime while Aaron had been talking, now he said, excitedly, 'And we know that Gottland is here in Colorado now — and tied in with the Denton gang!'

'That's right, and the Dentons hold up stage coaches and take jewellery from the passengers.'

'But what does Walsh, or whatever his name is, do with the jewellery? He can't sell it around here.'

'He doesn't. We know that he's made a couple of return visits to Chicago, he obviously sells it on while he's there.'

Something Anabelita had said suddenly hit Wes like a stone. 'Walsh was asking Anabelita when you and I were expected back in Denver. When she told him you were expected to be away for some time he said he was going to Chicago on business.'

Now Aaron was interested. 'When?'

'Early tomorrow morning.'

'That soon! He must be catching the same time train I took to Kansas. It leaves at seven o'clock. No matter, I'll be there to have a look at what he's taking with him.'

'You can't do it alone, Aaron, what if he has someone — one of the Denton's — with him? I'll come with you.'

'I'd appreciate that, Wes, but I can't let you help me out on something like this unless you have an official status. I'd need to swear you in as a deputy marshal.'

Aware that Aaron had long wanted him to

become a deputy marshal, Wes said, 'I'm not so certain I *want* that.'

'It has to be, Wes. If it comes to a gunfight, I want it to be quite clear that you are acting with the law on your side. It will just be for this occasion . . . if that's what you really want. You'll be able to resign whenever you like.'

'You're quite certain of that?'

'Of course . . . Now, let's work out exactly what we're going to do . . . '

17

Anabelita did not finish work at the Thespian Club gaming room until after three o'clock in the morning and she was not amused by Wes's announcement that he needed to be up by five-thirty that morning.

'You have only just come home,' she pointed out, 'We have spent so little time together. Can't you put off whatever it is for another day?'

'I'm afraid not,' he said, 'Aaron wants me to help him out with something that won't wait.'

'Aaron wants . . . ? To do what? Can't he find someone else to do whatever it is — and what is it that is so important anyway?'

Wes weighed up whether or not to tell Anabelita what was happening — and decided he would. He wanted her to be in a receptive mood when he spoke about their future.

He ended his explanation with, ' . . . it was you who told me that he's leaving for the East this morning — and Aaron is very grateful you did. Had we not known, Walsh, or whatever his real name is, would have got rid of anything likely to incriminate him while he was in Chicago.'

Still finding it hard to believe that Walsh was the criminal Wes had said he was, Anabelita said, 'Is Aaron quite sure of all this, Wes? I don't like Walsh, but he is an important man, here in

369

Denver . . . and if he *is* so friendly with the Dentons isn't he likely to have one or more of them with him?'

'It's possible, I suppose, although he wouldn't like to be seen with any of them, but Aaron would like me to be with him, just in case. He's made it all official by swearing me in as a deputy United States Marshal. It's something he's been trying to do since we first met, but I've said I'll only wear a deputy marshal's badge until Walsh is safely behind bars.'

Still concerned, Anabelita said, 'You must watch Walsh carefully, Wes, he carries a Derringer strapped to his leg, below his right knee.'

'How do you know that?'

Aware that Wes suspected she and Walsh were friendlier than they in fact were, she said, 'He came into the Thespian Club one night after he had been drinking and was at his obnoxious worst. He kept making lewd remarks about wanting to see where it was I kept the gun I'd used to shoot that man on the day we arrived. When I ignored him, he said he didn't know why I was being so coy because he didn't mind showing me his . . . and he did.'

'Thanks for warning me, Anabelita, I'll tell Aaron but I'm sorry this has come up tonight, I wanted to speak to you about the future . . . yours and mine — and the baby's.'

Trying to sound off-hand, Anabelita said, miserably, 'What is there to talk about? Once Walsh has been arrested I've no doubt you'll be going up into the mountains mining or prospecting and I'll stay here until I can no longer work then go off and have the baby. That's all there is to it. I know you've offered to make an honest woman of me, Wes, and I do appreciate that, but I couldn't live in a mining camp — and I certainly wouldn't want to bring a baby up in one.'

'I agree wholeheartedly with you about the mining camps. I passed close to one up in the mountains and couldn't stand the stench, even from a distance but now my uncle is dead I have no commitment to mining and I'm not particularly interested in prospecting. Aaron told me a little while ago that here, in America, a man can try his hand at just about anything and succeed. I thought I might do something new, but I wanted to discuss it with you and decide on something we would both be happy with. Although you talk of going your own way, it's my baby too you're having, Anabelita. I like to think we could become a family, either here, in Denver, or anywhere else you'd rather be.'

'You mean . . . be married?'

'Yes.'

Anabelita was silent for some time before saying, 'You want me to give up gambling?'

'Only if that's what you want. I have some money — and there's more that my uncle left to me in a bank. There are also one or two rewards still due to me. We could always go off and set up a small gaming-house — or perhaps go in with Aaron. He might feel like expanding when Walsh is put away, as he certainly will be.'

Again there was a thoughtful silence before

371

Anabelita spoke again. 'You don't *have* to marry me, Wes, I can manage well enough on my own. I've worked it out . . . '

'I *want* to marry you. If I didn't I could have ridden away from Denver when you first told me about the baby. I didn't, and the more I think about it, the more I like the idea of us being married.'

'That's all very well, Wes, but you haven't asked me if I want to marry you.'

'But . . . you're having my baby.'

'That's right and the baby will come whether we are married or not. If that's the only reason for wanting to marry me, then the answer is 'no'!'

It was quite apparent to her that Wes had never considered the possibility that she might not want to marry him . . . but he was thinking about it now.

'The baby *isn't* the only reason I am asking you to marry me, Anabelita. I couldn't ask you before because I had absolutely nothing to offer you. I don't have a huge amount now, but I feel I can make something of myself for the sake of you — and the baby — and will enjoy doing it.'

'I appreciate what you are saying, Wes, and I know you *will* make something of yourself. I have never doubted that, but there is more to marriage than that — far more. For instance, I don't think I have once heard you mention the word 'love'.'

Taken aback, Wes said, 'Do I need to actually say it to you?'

With a typical positiveness, Anabelita gave him a categorical 'Yes!'

'Very well. Anabelita Jones, I love you . . . now will you marry me?'

Shaking her head in mock despair, Anabelita said, 'How could any woman refuse such a romantic and spontaneous proposal.'

Choosing to ignore her sarcasm, Wes asked, 'Can I take that as a 'yes'?'

'I suppose you can! In fact . . . I think I would quite enjoy being Anabelita Curnow. Yes, Wes, I will marry you . . . so now you must take great care when you go off with Aaron this morning. You have a future wife and unborn son or daughter to come back to.'

18

'What if we find nothing on Walsh?'

Wes put the question to Aaron as the two men waited in the telegraph office at the railroad station for the arrival of the owner of the Palace. From here they could see both the approach road and the passengers waiting to board the Kansas-bound train.

'I'd rather you hadn't said that,' Amos replied, 'The same thought kept me awake during the night. It really shouldn't have, I doubt if he'd write a letter of complaint to President Grant. The worst that could happen is that I'd lose a self-appointed 'friend'. He might even decide to move on from Denver and take another name, leaving me with a monopoly on gambling!'

'Knowing what we do, couldn't we arrest him anyway?'

'For what? Sure, he's suspected of crime by me and by the Chicago police and the Pinkertons are interested in him, but none of us can provide proof that he is, or even has been, involved in anything criminal.'

'What about the things he did in Plymouth, in England?'

'He could have committed a dozen murders there, Wes, but we still couldn't charge him for them in the United States. No, we need to find some evidence against him today.'

Although Wes was keyed up by the thought of what would take place when Walsh arrived, his thoughts kept returning to Anabelita's acceptance of his somewhat tardy proposal of marriage. He wanted to tell Aaron about it but this was not the right moment.

Every so often his hand went to the United States deputy marshal's badge pinned to the shirt he wore beneath his coat. It gave him an unexpected thrill — but he was determined it was not a feeling he was going to become used to.

The train had just arrived at the station and Aaron passed a comment about Walsh missing it if he did not soon put in an appearance, when Wes saw the Palace owner emerge from an alleyway leading from the direction of the establishment above which he lived. Walking unhurriedly, he was accompanied by a man Wes recognized as one of the Palace doormen.

Leaving the telegraph office hurriedly, Aaron and Wes intercepted the two men before they mingled with the other passengers who had surged forward to board the train.

Walsh was obviously startled by their sudden appearance, but he recovered his composure quickly, greeting them and saying, 'I am surprised to see you, I thought you were both out of town.'

'So I believe,' Aaron replied, 'but I returned yesterday having received some very disturbing news, as a result of which I am afraid I am going to ask you to open that travelling bag you are carrying.'

His eyes narrowing, Walsh said, 'Do you mind telling me why?'

'Not at all, you have a right to know. I have received information that you are in possession of stolen goods.'

'It's an absolutely absurd accusation,' Walsh blustered. 'Who told you?'

'That doesn't matter, but perhaps you would like to prove them wrong by opening the bag and showing me what's inside?'

The item in question was a semi-rigid leather bag fitted with two locks.

'I would like to oblige you, Aaron, but I can't remember exactly where I have put the key — and the train is about to depart.'

'Then unless you find the key pretty damn quick and show me what's in the bag the train is going to go without you.'

The guard began calling, 'All aboard . . . All aboard . . . '

Walsh made an attempt to push past the US Marshal and board the train, but Aaron blocked his path. It looked as though the Palace doorman would interfere at this point but, allowing his coat to fall open to show his badge, Wes called on him to stay where he was.

When the doorman moved in closer with the obvious intent of pushing him aside, Wes drew his gun. Pointing it at the doorman, he said, 'I'd rather not use this, but I will if I need to.'

The doorman came to a sudden halt and in a last act of desperate bravado, Walsh held the bag out towards Aaron, 'Look . . . I need to catch this train. Take the bag and we'll sort everything out when I return.'

'No! I want you *and* the bag.' Taking Walsh by the arm, Aaron propelled him, still carrying the bag, away from the train. Wes followed, gun in hand, leaving the doorman standing by the track as the train pulled away.

The two men and their prisoner made their way to the US Marshals' office and as Walsh still refused to hand them a key, Aaron broke open the locks and pulled the bag open.

Much to his relief it contained a large quantity of personal jewellery.

Exchanging a jubilant glance with Wes, Aaron addressed Walsh, 'I'd say this is quite a haul, even at the deflated price that stolen jewellery fetches. Where has it come from, Walsh?'

'I take it in from the punters when they can't pay their gambling debts.'

Lifting out a necklace set with diamonds and emeralds, Aaron said, 'You have lady punters in the Palace?'

'It was probably bought for a wife or sweetheart but some unlucky gambler never got as far as home with it.'

At that moment a sleepy Pat Rafferty arrived at the office carrying his rifle. He explained he had been woken by Anabelita who told him Wes had gone with Aaron to arrest someone. She had been so concerned about him she wanted Pat to come to the Marshal's office to make sure all was well.

Asking the one-armed man to remain with Walsh for a few minutes, Aaron left the room and went to the outer office with Wes. Here he said, 'I hoped Walsh might talk if we found the jewellery on him, but he's too damned clever. We've got the jewellery and too much of it is obviously taken from women for his story to be true. In due course we'll be able to prove it's stolen, when the owners are traced, but I can't hold him until that happens. I'm going to have to let him go.'

'We can't do that, Walsh is as guilty as hell. Let's have a proper look through the bag.'

Going back into the office where Walsh was sitting at ease in the marshal's chair, engaging Pat in apparently unconcerned conversation, Wes took the bag and tipped its contents onto the large desk in front of the Palace owner.

Suddenly Wes's stomach turned over and he reached out and picked up a gold watch. When he opened it a photograph of two smiling women stared up at him. It was his mother and her sister.

Giving Walsh a look that startled him, Wes said angrily, 'I'd like you to do me a favour, Walsh. Reach for that gun you have strapped to your leg, beneath your trousers. I want you to do that so I can justify shooting you like a dog, just as the Denton gang did my uncle when they took this watch from him.'

Genuinely frightened now, Walsh said, 'I don't know what you're talking about . . . and I've made no move towards my gun . . . you can prove that.' He directed his plea to Pat, who had been startled by Wes's angry words.

'You know *exactly* what I'm talking about,

Walsh. Three men died on my uncle's claim up there in the Rockies, and all the gunmen went away with was this watch. My uncle's watch.'

'Can you prove it was his, Wes?' Aaron's voice broke into the tension caused by Wes's words.

Holding the watch out to Aaron, Wes said, 'The photographs in the back of the watch are of my mother and her sister — my murdered uncle's wife. Take the photograph out carefully and you'll find an inscription there. It reads 'Presented to Peter Rowse, September 1865. For Bravery'.'

The other men in the room waited with bated breath as Aaron carefully removed the faded photograph and exposed the inscription underneath.

'You're right, Wes. That's exactly what it says and I know the way you must be feeling about the killing of your uncle. Would you like Pat and me to leave the office? We'll come back in when we hear you shoot Walsh for trying to escape.'

'You can't do that . . . that's murder!' Walsh was genuinely terrified. When no one appeared moved by his plea, he said, 'Look, I admit I got the jewellery from the Dentons and I knew it was probably stolen. I'll make a statement to that effect, if that's what you want, but I swear I never knew they'd killed anyone to get it. I wouldn't have touched it if I'd known that.'

'A statement would be handy, I suppose,' Aaron said, 'but I'm not fussy, I'd just as soon save the country the expense of carrying out a trial. It's your call, Wes. Would you like Pat and me to leave the office?'

Looking at the heavily perspiring Palace owner, Wes considered what Aaron had said for what seemed to Walsh an interminable time, before saying, 'Take his gun from him before I change my mind, Pat. Aaron can take this statement he's so anxious to make. I'd rather think of him spending the rest of his life behind bars, than enjoying a moment's satisfaction in shooting him.'

19

❦

Once again Aaron was faced with the fact that no Federal cells were available in Denver for prisoners arrested by United States marshals and their deputies. He was obliged to place the many aliased Walsh in the care of the suspect Denver police chief, in his downtown lock-up.

When the police officer on duty saw the marshal's prisoner, he was horrified. 'I can't lock up Mr Walsh. He's one of Denver's most important citizens . . . a personal friend of Chief Kelly!'

'I suggest your chief chooses his friends with more care,' Aaron retorted. 'Walsh has been arrested for knowingly receiving stolen property — some of it the proceeds of murder. He's made a statement admitting his guilt. I'm placing him in your custody only until I can arrange for him to be conveyed to a Federal court.'

'You put him in the cell yourself,' said the representative of Denver law, handing a ring of keys to Aaron, 'I'm off to find Chief Kelly . . . '

Aaron lodged Walsh in an empty, cage-like cell, then, performing a task that should have been carried out by the absent policeman, he entered Walsh's details in the police office's prisoners' ledger.

He had just completed this task when Chief

Kelly stormed into the office followed by the officer who should have been guarding prisoners.

Angrily confronting Aaron, Kelly said, 'What's this I hear about you arresting Mr Walsh and demanding he be put in my lock-up?'

'It's exactly as you heard it, Chief,' Aaron replied amiably, 'He's admitted to having knowingly handled property that is the proceeds of robbery and murder. Until I'm able to have him taken before a Federal Judge I am placing him in your care. It's all quite uncomplicated. You'll receive the usual fee for accommodating a Federal prisoner, no more and no less.'

'This is preposterous!' The police chief blustered, 'Vic Walsh is a highly respected member of this community and has done a great deal to rid Denver of some of the more undesirable riff-raff who found their way into our town.'

'I don't doubt it,' Aaron said, 'Mr Walsh, or Mr Walsingham, or Waller — you can take your pick of his names — is choosey about those he tolerates. One day it will be marshals and police chiefs, another time it will be men like the Denton gang and river pirates. Take care of him for the United States government, Chief, I'll be back to collect him from you as soon as I can make arrangements to get him out of the Territory.'

Arresting Walsh was only the beginning of that day's excitement. The result was that the party Aaron had planned when Wes announced his proposed marriage to Anabelita needed to be put on hold.

Within an hour of Wes telling the news to his friend, Old Charlie arrived unexpectedly and came to the US Marshal's office with news that the Denton gang had come down from the more remote snow-bound heights of the Rockies and taken over a large cabin in a remote canyon not far from the mining camp where Charlie had parted company with Wes the day before.

The mountain-man had gone to the mining camp with the stated intention of buying winter stores but after meeting up with some of his companions from earlier days he had spent a long evening carousing instead of returning home to Usdi.

During the course of the night's revelry the saloon in the mining camp had been visited by a few of the Denton gang and Old Charlie learned of the gang's new hideout.

In view of what had happened to Wes's uncle and the threat made by Gideon Denton to avenge the death of his brothers, Old Charlie decided that Wes and Aaron should know that the gang was now no more than twenty miles away, so this morning he had ridden into Denver to warn them.

Wes and Aaron were grateful for the warning but the US Marshal was not concerned solely for the safety of his friend. When word reached the outlaws of Walsh's arrest — and Aaron knew it would be carried to them very quickly — they would undoubtedly consider it in their interest to make a surprise sortie into Denver and break Walsh free from gaol.

'How many outlaws are at this hideout, Charlie?' he asked.

'Your guess is as good as mine,' Old Charlie replied. 'The Denton gang is bigger than most in the Territories, but I doubt anyone's ever stopped to count 'em. What difference does it make?'

'A lot, Charlie. There's no way I can raise a posse to go against them, but if I could prove it really is a very large gang I might be able to call on the army for help.'

After a few moments thought, he asked, 'Would it be possible to get close enough to their hideout to make a head count of them?'

'I know the canyon where they have their cabin and you just might be able to get close enough — if you was to know where to go, but you wouldn't last long if they caught you scouting around trying to find a hidey-hole.'

'Well, seeing that you know the lay-out of the canyon can you tell me of such a place?'

'What you're really saying is, will I take you there and show you the right spot?'

'I can't think of anyone I'd trust to do it better, Charlie.'

The old mountain-man shook his head, 'There must be something about me that makes army men — and one-time army men — think I'll do any damn-fool thing to help 'em out when there's trouble brewing, or when they intend stirring some up.'

'Well, will you do it,' Aaron persisted.

'Only because it's you who's asking,' Old Charlie replied, 'When do you want to go?'

384

'How soon can you take me?'

'Well, seeing as how we don't know too many of the gang and there could even be some of 'em right here in Denver, we'd need to set off quietly after dark and get hidden up by sunrise. We can't risk meeting up with any of 'em along the trail . . . '

'Good, that's settled then,' Aaron cut in on the old man's observations, 'We'll leave tonight. How long will it take to get there?'

Old Charlie groaned, 'I was hoping to get back to my cabin and sleep off last night's hangover when I left here.'

'Since when have you needed to do that . . . ? What time shall we meet up, Charlie?'

'We'd best be leaving about midnight. That will give us plenty of time to get there, hide the horses and find a good hiding place up among the rocks. Perhaps even manage an hour's sleep before dawn.'

Turning to Wes, Aaron said, 'Will you be coming along with us, Wes?'

'Just try leaving me behind,' Wes replied, 'I have a personal interest in this, Aaron . . . besides, I haven't handed my badge back yet, I'm still a deputy and I suppose you might say this is part of my duty, but I doubt whether Anabelita is going to forgive me for neglecting her for another night.'

20

❧

It was a chilly night, although not as bitterly cold as when Wes had gone with Old Charlie to his mountain cabin and tonight a near full moon and a myriad of stars made travelling easy — too easy, according to the mountain-man. He pointed out that if they were able to see everything about them, they could be seen by anyone on the look-out for strangers.

Fortunately, they met with no one and the only sound they heard was the occasional mournful howling of an apparently lonesome wolf.

Long before the sky showed even the slightest hint of dawn the three men had settled themselves in a spot among the boulders of the Rocky Mountain 'foothills', blending in with their surroundings as best they could, their horses tethered in a hollow some distance away, hidden from the sounds made by any riders who might be making their way to the outlaws' hideout.

As Old Charlie explained to Wes, sound travelled for an incredible distance in the rarefied air of the mountains — and even the so-called foothills where they now stood were more than six thousand feet above sea level. The outlaws occupying the cabin that was still lost in the shadowed canyon would be able to hear the slightest sound made by the trio.

His caution was not misplaced. When a hint of dawn was showing in the east one of the outlaws left the cabin in order to relieve himself. The sound of the door closing behind him sounded like a rifle shot, startling Wes who had begun to doze.

The next sound was an oath from the same outlaw when he scraped his shin on the handle of an axe that had been left embedded in a pine log close to the cabin.

'That sounded as though he was almost within touching distance,' Wes whispered, in awe.

'Remember it,' Charlie replied in an equally soft voice, 'They'll be able to hear us just as clearly.'

There followed a lengthy period of waiting, during which Wes found himself wondering what Anabelita would be doing, back in Denver. She would no doubt be sleeping after her night's work at the Thespian.

She had been unhappy about him coming on this trip, fearing he would be placing himself in danger, yet again. It had not helped when one of the gambling saloon's patrons had asked her whether it was true Aaron and Wes had arrested Vic Walsh.

When she replied warily that she believed it was so, the punter shook his head doubtfully, 'Berryman may be a US Marshal, but Walsh is a big man in Denver with some very dubious friends who won't take this lying down. I hope the Marshal knows what he's doing.'

Anabelita had reported the conversation to Wes before he left Denver with Aaron and Charlie.

★　★　★

Aaron had brought a pair of field glasses with him and as the sun rose behind the Rockies he began scanning the cabin in the canyon. It was reasonably large, with stables extending the whole length of the rear of the building and a corral beyond this.

He began counting the men as they emerged from the cabin and after a while, he said, 'I've counted fifteen outlaws so far, but twenty-four horses have been released into the corral, so there are probably more.'

'Even fifteen are more than the three of us can tackle,' Wes said, 'and, as you say, some are probably still asleep in the cabin. Do you see anyone you recognize?'

'Not yet,' Aaron replied, 'I'd let you have the field glasses but first I want to try to make as accurate a count as I can . . . just a minute, there's someone I *do* recognize. *It's Ira Gottland!* He's obviously riding with the gang now, probably as their leader. If we could only take them all we'd have ourselves quite a haul and make Colorado a hell of a lot safer for law-abiding folk.'

'What's Gottland doing?' Wes asked.

'He's just gone round the back of the cabin, to the corral,' Aaron reported, 'He seems to be checking the hoofs of the horses . . . '

As he was speaking, Old Charlie nudged him, without saying anything and, when the marshal turned to him, pointed in the direction of the canyon entrance where two men were approaching, apparently from the Denver direction.

Their arrival brought more outlaws from inside the cabin and Aaron said, 'There are twenty-one of them now, and the new arrivals will make twenty-three. They'll all be used to handling guns, so that's a whole lot of fire power to go up against.'

The two latest arrivals pulled their horses to a halt and had an animated conversation with the outlaws who crowded around as they dismounted.

Suddenly, one of the men broke away from the others and, running towards the corral, began shouting before he reached it, his excited words carrying clearly to the three watching men.

'Ira . . . Ira . . . Gideon and Curly are back . . . and they've done it. They've killed the Marshal and that English partner of his!'

The three watching men looked at each other in bewilderment. It was Wes who put their feelings into words, 'What do they mean, they've killed the Marshal and an Englishman. Who are they talking about?'

'I think they're celebrating killing *us*,' Aaron replied, adding grimly, 'but we're not dead, so who have they killed? We've seen what we came here for. I think we ought to head back to town and find out.'

★ ★ ★

It had been an unexpectedly quiet night in the Thespian Club and Lola and Anabelita spent much of the time chatting to each other.

'Have you and Wes decided when you're going to be married?' Lola asked.

'We've hardly had enough time together for me to agree to marry him,' Anabelita complained. 'Since Aaron succeeded in pinning a deputy's badge on Wes I've hardly seen him. I can see why Aaron's never found time to marry.'

Observing Lola's sad, albeit fleeting expression, Anabelita immediately apologised. 'I'm sorry, Lola, that was unthinking of me.'

'It's all right,' Lola replied, trying to appear unconcerned, 'I've never expected Aaron to even think of marrying me. I may have given up being a whore, but no matter where I go there's always going to be some man who knows me for what I once was. It's enough that Aaron wants to be with me. He's looking after me better than anyone ever has. I'm happy enough just being what I am to him.'

'I know,' Anabelita said, deeply regretting her unthinking words and trying to undo what she had said, 'He's told me so . . . he's told Wes too.'

Her face lighting up, Lola said, 'Has he? He's a good man, Anabelita. I know you wouldn't agree, but I wish he had Wes with him all the time. I worry about him going off on his own against some of the outlaws out here. They'd rather shoot a lawman than talk to him.'

'I believe you. Look, it's going to be absolutely dead in here tonight, why don't we close our tables and have an early night? We've both lost sleep with the comings and goings of our men . . . Aaron wouldn't mind.'

Lola agreed and telling Pat what they were doing, the two women left the Thespian Club and made their way to the house, chatting happily.

In the house they had a drink and talked together for half-an-hour before turning in.

Across the road from the house a man who was standing outside the Nugget saloon watched the lamps in their rooms go out and went inside to tell Gideon Denton, who was downing whisky at the bar.

Anabelita did not know how long she had been sleeping before she was woken by her own coughing and she tasted smoke. At the same time the door to her room was flung open and a panic-stricken Lola fell inside, a rapidly growing cloud of smoke entering with her.

'Anabelita . . . quick, put something on and get out . . . the house is on fire.'

Struggling out of bed, Anabelita snatched a coat from behind the bedroom door. It belonged to Wes, but she put it on as quickly as she could, at the same time asking, 'Where *is* the fire?'

'I don't know, I could hear it crackling away downstairs, but there's so much smoke it's difficult to know what's happening.'

While they were speaking they had reached the head of the stairs, but flames were leaping up towards them. It was apparent there would be no escape this way.

Coughing and choking, Lola said, 'The fire must have started in the hall . . . we'll go to Pat's room. It's farthest away from the hall and we can get out of his window and drop into the street.'

They felt their way along the passageway, eyes streaming and having increasing difficulty in breathing. Both women were barefooted and could feel the heat coming up now through the flimsy floorboards.

They reached a recess in the passageway and, trying to keep the terror she felt from her voice, Lola said, 'This is Pat's room . . . Stay with me, Anabelita.'

Opening the door, and gripping Anabelita's hand so tightly that it hurt, Lola led the way into the smoke-filled room. Groping her way to the window, she fell over Pat's bed along the way.

Although they were now some distance from the downstairs hallway it felt even hotter in here and pulling back the curtains the two women could see flames from the whole ground floor of their house reflected in the Nugget's windows across the street.

Fumbling for the catch of the sash window, Lola eventually found it and, sliding it back, lifted up the window.

No sooner had she done so than the window in the room below them exploded with a frightening crash and there was a deafening roar as flames erupted from the gaping hole left behind, reaching as high as the window sill where the two women cowered.

At the same time they heard a frightening crackle behind them and flames began to show themselves through the dry wooden floorboards.

'We have to get out, Lola,' Anabelita said, her eyes red and smarting from the smoke. 'Climb out of the window, hang from the sill and drop. It will probably hurt your legs when you land, but you'll be safe.'

Frightened of staying, yet even more scared of dropping through the flames onto the unseen boardwalk below, Lola said, 'No, you go first . . . I'll follow you.'

There was no time to argue, the flames showing through the floor of the room had taken hold of the dry timber now, fanned by air being sucked through the shattered window of the downstairs room.

Climbing awkwardly through the window, Anabelita edged herself over the sill, well aware of the strain she was putting on her stomach, and hoping that what she was doing would not harm her baby . . . Wes's baby.

As she edged farther over, weight and gravity took command. Twisting awkwardly, she managed to grip the window sill and a moment later was hanging full length from it.

As she looked down, trying to see the boardwalk through the smoke, there was a sudden sharp crack which Lola took to be something from within the inferno. The next moment Anabelita was gone, disappearing into the smoke.

'Anabelita, are you all right?'

As Lola leaned out of the window and peered down through the smoke there was another crack, just like the first — but Lola did not hear this one.

She slipped back into the burning room, a bullet hole drilled expertly in the centre of her forehead.

21

When Wes, Aaron and Old Charlie neared Denver, riding hard, smoke was still rising from the charred ruins of the house behind the Thespian Club and as they drew closer the smell of the devastating fire hung heavily in the air about the town.

Not daring to voice their thoughts, they turned their horses into the street where the house had been — and their worst fears were immediately realized.

Where the house had once been there was now no more than a heap of smouldering rubble, with only a skeletal framework of blackened timbers remaining at the end of the site farthest away from where Pat Rafferty's room had once been.

'Oh God . . . Anabelita . . . ' Wes spurred his horse forward to where bystanders stood in sombre groups, gaping at the scene of devastation.

As Wes leaped from his horse, the smoke-grimed figure of Pat broke away from one of the groups and hurried to meet him, his face distorted in anguish.

'Pat . . . Where's Anabelita? Is she all right?'

Aware that a grim-faced Aaron was making his way towards them, Pat said, 'I'm sorry, Wes, there was nothing I could do. I was still in the Thespian Club when the fire was discovered. Anabelita and Lola had gone off early because there was hardly anyone in the club gambling. She's in Welensky's ... ' He named the undertaker whose establishment was in nearby Market Street, ' ... We can't begin looking for Lola until things have cooled down.'

The one-armed man was close to tears, but Wes was tortured by his own thoughts. 'Was she caught in the fire ... ? I mean ... How did it happen?'

'She didn't suffer, Wes ... ' Appearing increasingly distressed, Pat added, 'but she wasn't killed by the fire, in fact she was making her escape from an upstairs window ... but ... someone shot her in the back as she was about to drop to the boardwalk.'

'Shot her?' The question came from Aaron before Wes was able to speak. 'Who shot her ... and *why*?'

'I can't answer that,' Pat replied, deeply distressed, 'but someone said the shots came from an upstairs room of the Nugget.'

'You say you're still looking for Lola?' a grim-faced Aaron asked, 'Do you believe she and Anabelita were together when the fire began?'

'I don't know,' Pat replied, 'They certainly left the Thespian Club together — and more than one person has said there were two shots fired from the Nugget, although only one hit Anabelita.'

'You think the other one might have been aimed at Lola ... ? Perhaps if she was at the window from which Anabelita was dropping?' Aaron was allowing none of his anguish, or anger, to show.

'I think it must have been, Aaron. Men have been scouring Denver for her without result. We're waiting now for the remains of the house to cool down, so we can sift through what's left. I'm absolutely devastated that this should have happened. You trusted me to take care of them . . .' His voice broke and he could say no more.

Aware of Pat's torment, Aaron said, 'Don't blame yourself, Pat, this was carefully thought out. The targets were not the girls, but Wes and me — and we believe we know who did it . . .'

He told Pat of the arrival of Gideon Denton and 'Curly' at the outlaws' cabin, and the information that had been shouted to Ira Gottland.

'What time would that have been?' Pat asked, regaining some control of himself.

'Soon after dawn. When was the fire discovered?'

'The alarm was raised at about two o'clock, but the fire had really taken hold by then. I tried to get into the house by the back door but the flames drove me back. I think the whole ground floor was ablaze. It must have been about that time that Anabelita was shot. To be honest, there was so much smoke around that whoever shot her wouldn't have been able to tell whether they were shooting a man or a woman — and Anabelita was wearing your coat, Wes. It must have been the first thing she found when she woke up and realized the house was on fire.'

396

'Was Chief Kelly around when all this happened? Does he know about Anabelita?' Aaron put the question to Pat.

'I never saw him at the fire and I ran to his office when Anabelita's bod . . . when Anabelita had been taken to Welensky's, but Kelly wasn't there. The officer on cell duty said he'd gone home right after releasing Walsh.'

Startled, Aaron said, 'Chief Kelly released Walsh *before* Anabelita was found?'

'He must have done,' Pat declared.

Aware of Aaron's thoughts, Wes said, 'That means that Gideon Denton, thinking he'd shot both of us must have gone straight along and told Kelly.'

'Not only that,' Aaron pointed out grimly, 'For Kelly to be in the police office at that time of night means he must have been expecting the news. We'll have a few words with Chief Kelly — but not until we've re-arrested Mr Vic Walsh.'

Turning to the one-armed man, Aaron's composure almost cracked when he said, 'Have the ashes of the house searched as soon as you can, Pat — and let me know as soon as you find anything.'

'I'll stay and give Pat a hand,' Old Charlie had remained silent until now. 'You and Wes go off and get Walsh. You won't want me around when you find him.'

★ ★ ★

When Aaron and Wes arrived at the Palace, a servant girl told them that the Palace owner had packed hurriedly and caught the morning train heading east out of Denver.

'He's escaped . . . yet again!' Wes exclaimed angrily.

'He hasn't got away yet,' Aaron said, 'We'll call in at the telegraph office on our way to speak to Chief Kelly. I'll send a message to Sheriff Murray at Trego, asking him to board the train and take Walsh off there. He'll have no problem. Most of the passengers on board will be able to point Walsh out to him.'

On the way to the telegraph office the two men needed to pass the charred remains of the house once again. There was still a large crowd of sightseers gathered outside and they appeared to be having an impromptu meeting with Old Charlie and Pat in their midst.

When Aaron and Wes were sighted word went around the crowd and a man Aaron recognized as Denver's Mayor, Solomon Colville, flanked by two of the Denver councillors hurried to meet them.

'Here comes trouble!' Aaron said, grimly 'but I'm not in any mood to humour them.'

However, the mayor and his companions were about to spring a big surprise. Acting as their spokesman, the mayor said, 'Marshal, we . . . myself and the Denver council, deeply regret the tragedy that occurred during the night, resulting in the loss of your home and the very sad death of at least one of your staff. She was, so I am informed, a personal friend of both you gentlemen.'

'She was more than a friend, Mayor,' said Wes,

bitterly, 'We were to be married and it wasn't just a sad death, it was cold-blooded murder. It's also probable that we are going to find the body of another murdered woman in the ruins of the house.'

'So I believe,' said the mayor. 'You have my deepest sympathy and that of my colleagues . . . but am I right in thinking you know who perpetrated these acts, Marshal?'

'I do,' Aaron said, 'We actually witnessed them boasting about it when we were watching an outlaw camp early this morning. Unfortunately, there were more than twenty of them and only three of us, so we were unable to do anything about it right then — but it would seem that your chief of police was aware of what was going to happen some time before the event. We're on our way to arrest him now.'

The Denver mayor was visibly shaken. 'Chief Kelly has been less than efficient in maintaining law and order in Denver . . . but I was unaware of his involvement in anything dishonest.'

'Well you are now,' Aaron said curtly, 'So if you'll excuse me and my deputy we'll be doing what should have been done by you and your council a long time ago . . . Come on Wes, let's go.'

He turned to leave, but Mayor Colville said, 'Wait, Marshal. Do you intend going after the murderers and the gang to which they belong?'

'I intend to hunt them down and see that each and every one of them receives the punishment he deserves — but you'll pardon me if I don't tell you, or anyone else in Denver, what my plans are.'

Colville adopted a pained expression, but he said, 'I fully understand your mistrust of us, Marshal, but this is a frontier town in a raw and largely untamed Territory and perhaps we have been far too tolerant towards the lawless element in our midst. Nevertheless, every man in this town deplores the coldblooded murder of a woman. If you intend forming a posse to go after these outlaws I can promise you the support of every able-bodied Denver man — and I include myself in that number.'

Aaron looked speculatively at the mayor before saying, 'We'll put that to the test, Mayor, but before you commit yourself I think you ought to know I won't be taking you off on a futile jaunt that you'll be able to joke about at one of your evening parties. I know where these outlaws are hiding-up and that's where we'll be going — and I'm talking about the *Denton* gang. They will neither run, nor give themselves up. They'll fight — and they'll fight hard. I'm telling you this so that any man who volunteers knows exactly what to expect. I'll take as many armed men as are willing to come with me — and I'll be ready to move from here in exactly one hour from now. Go back and tell the others of the situation and let's see just how many men match up to your fine opinion of your fellow Denver citizens.'

★ ★ ★

Chief Kelly was not in his office when Aaron and his two companions arrived there. A nervous young police officer, the only person in the office, told them he had put in an appearance earlier that morning but had returned to his home, feeling 'unwell'.

As they made their way to the chief's home, the three men were joined by Pat, who, like the others, was carrying a rifle and had a revolver holstered on his belt.

Each of them had been up all night and they were tired, but, grim-visaged, they were determined to have a show down with Kelly. They were a daunting quartet for the chief's wife to have to face when she opened the door to them.

She repeated the policeman's story that her husband was too unwell to be at work, but Aaron cut her excuses for him short.

'I understand your concern for your husband, ma'am, but insist that I speak to him. Tell me where his bedroom is and I'll go there on my own while these three men keep you company.'

When she protested, Aaron brushed past her and tried two doors in the single storey building before finding a bedroom where the police chief lay in bed with the bedclothes drawn up to his chin.

Wasting no time on polite conversation, Aaron reached out and pulled the covers from the 'unwell' police chief. Looking down contemptuously at the fully dressed man, Aaron asked, sarcastically, 'Are you so ill you are too weak to even remove your boots, Kelly? Well, it means there'll be no time wasted in getting dressed. You're coming downtown with me. There should soon be some men waiting for you there.'

'You wouldn't be party to a lynching, Marshal

you couldn't do that. I swear I didn't know anything about any women being killed.'

'Of course you didn't,' Aaron said with a stony expression that terrified the police chief more than had he showed anger, 'You thought it was me your friends had shot, after setting fire to my place. That's why you released Walsh, a Federal prisoner. As for lynching . . . if there's any hanging to be done it'll be by order of a judge, not an unlawful mob. No, I've some work for you to do. You'll find this difficult to believe, Kelly, but the good citizens of Denver have volunteered to form a posse to bring in the Dentons. I think they'd like you to join them. On reflection I'll rephrase that. I insist that you come along with us, so I suggest you get well right away, strap on your gun and come along with me before my deputy comes in here to fetch you. In case you don't already know, he was planning to marry the girl who was shot dead and he's a little short on forgiveness and understanding right now.'

When Aaron, accompanied by the others took Chief Kelly to meet the posse, he was taken aback by the number of armed and mounted citizens awaiting his instructions.

Wes estimated that at least fifty men were volunteering to take on the Denton gang. It was unprecedented. Aaron warned them they were going to besiege the outlaws in their canyon cabin in the Rocky Mountain foothills and he was determined that every man in the Denton gang would be taken 'dead or alive', but not a man dropped out of the posse.

He next asked how many of the posse had fought, on either side, in the Civil War which had been over for more than ten years. When three-quarters of their number raised their hands he knew he had a force he could at least count upon not to run when the first shot was fired.

Pat Rafferty had wanted to be included in their number but Aaron asked him to arrange for a couple of days supplies and blankets to be sent up to the men of the posse, after which he wanted him to supervise the gruesome task of locating Lola's body in the remains of the burned-out house.

When all had been arranged it was a grim and unnaturally silent band of men who rode out of Denver soon after noon that day, but — with one exception — every one of them was determined that the menace of the Denton gang would be eliminated from Colorado Territory once and for all.

22

On the way to the outlaw's canyon hide-out, Aaron questioned Old Charlie in detail about the geography of the area. He was told there was another way out of the canyon, but it was by means of a narrow defile in the canyon wall, only just wide enough to allow horsemen to squeeze through in single file and it would necessitate scrambling up a steep slope strewn with rocks that had tumbled from the peaks above in order to reach it.

Old Charlie added the information that, as it was at the far end of the canyon from the cabin and not easily seen, it was possible the outlaws did not know of its existence.

Even if they did, he believed it would be possible for a single posse-man armed with a repeating rifle to be positioned at any one of a number of vantage points above the narrow defile and prevent the whole gang from escaping along this route.

When they reached the canyon, Aaron sent Old Charlie off with eight of the posse-men to seal off this possible means of escape for the Denton gang.

The remainder of the posse-men were stationed at the mouth of the canyon to prevent any attempt to escape this way and Aaron placed them in such a way that a fusillade of bullets could be poured into the gang if they attempted a cavalry-type charge on the besiegers.

Satisfied he had done all that was possible to contain the Denton gang, Aaron and Wes made their way to the vantage point they had occupied during the previous night, in order to count the horses in the corral. If a large number of outlaws had left the canyon during their absence and returned unexpectedly, they could pose a serious threat to the posse.

Much to Aaron's relief there were now twenty-six horses in the corral, the animals belonging to Gideon Denton and his companion being added to the original number.

He had arranged that Old Charlie should join them here when the mountain-man had placed the posse-men to his satisfaction in the defile. While they were waiting, Aaron looked at Wes's gaunt and tired features and asked, 'How you feeling, Wes?'

Shaking his head wearily, Wes replied, 'When we got back to Denver and found . . . found what had happened I felt a sense of unreality and my mind was numbed. It's still numb, but feeling's coming back now and letting the pain through. I'm finding it hard to come to grips with it, Aaron. This time yesterday Anabelita was alive and as happy as I've ever seen her. We'd talked things through . . . talked about the baby . . . about getting married and becoming a family. We had so much to look forward to, but now . . . ?'

Wes stopped abruptly as the stark reality of

what had happened to Anabelita, and all that it meant, hit home fully for perhaps the first time. Raising his glance to Aaron's face, he said, 'But you'll have a good idea of how I'm feeling. You and Lola . . . '

He failed to finish what he was saying, but Aaron understood and they were both silent for some time. It was Aaron who broke the silence, saying, 'It's strange, Wes. I've met many bar-girls in my life, but there's not one I've remembered for more than an hour after I'd got on my horse and ridden away from her. Lola was different, there was something in her I've never found in any other woman. I think I once said to you that if she hadn't been a whore she'd have made someone a good wife. It's easy to say now, but I'd been thinking more and more lately about the sort of wife she'd make and there weren't many arguments — not real, important arguments — I could make against it, especially when I saw how excited she got when you and Anabelita decided to marry. You and me might get some satisfaction from seeing justice done on their behalf, Wes, but it's not going to bring either of 'em back to us.'

Trying unsuccessfully not to dwell upon how happy Anabelita had been at the thought of their future together, Wes was relieved when Old Charlie arrived to report that he had placed the posse-men in position along the defile.

Dismounting from his mule and seating himself Indian-style on the ground beside the two men, he said, 'Well, we're all where we should be, Marshal, what do we do now, go in and take 'em by surprise?'

'There's no way we could do that, Charlie. We'd never reach the cabin without being seen and they'd pick us off like pigs in a pen. No, we'll negotiate, like civilised men should.'

Wes and Old Charlie looked at Aaron as though he had suddenly taken leave of his senses. It was the mountain-man who put their thoughts into words.

'This is the Denton gang we're talking about, Aaron. Since when have they behaved like civilized folk? I doubt if they've even heard tell of the word.'

'I don't doubt it for a moment, Charlie, but I think we ought to at least try — and we have just the man with us to go in and do the negotiating for us . . . Chief Kelly.'

Now it was Wes who challenged Aaron's reasoning, 'He's not likely to even try to persuade them to give themselves up. He's been in their pockets for so long he wouldn't dare risk them being taken alive and telling what they know about him. He's far more likely to join up with them and give them some idea of what we are planning to do.'

'So? Either way he's a loser. One way he might just finish up as a live loser. The other way he'll be dead with the rest of 'em.'

23

❧

Chief Kelly rode up to the outlaws' cabin holding aloft an empty rifle, to which was attached a white handkerchief supplied by Denver's mayor. To the casual observer it would have appeared the handkerchief was fluttering in the breeze, but the air was still and the movement was caused by the chief's nervousness, his shaking hand transferring movement to the improvised 'flag of peace'.

Kelly had good reason to be nervous, he had been tolerated by the Denton gang in the past only because he could occasionally prove useful to them, setting gang members free on the few occasions when a Denver police officer had the courage to arrest one of them for misbehaving in the town, and turning a blind eye to the more serious crimes they committed in the surrounding countryside. However, now there was a United States Marshal in Denver, Kelly's usefulness to the gang did not amount to much.

Aware that he was probably being covered by a great many guns, the frightened chief began shouting out his peaceful intentions long before he reached the outlaws cabin but he felt no less threatened when Ira Gottland came to the doorway holding a rifle in his hands.

'What d'you reckon you're doing coming here

waving a flag, Kelly, it's not Thanksgiving for a while yet?'

'This is no celebration, Ira,' the police chief declared, 'We're all in deep trouble. Marshal Berryman is out there with a posse from Denver. He's sent me in under a flag of truce to say you're to give yourselves up or he's coming in to get you.'

'What are you talking about? The marshal's dead — and that Englishman too. Gideon killed them.'

'No he didn't.' Terrified of contradicting the outlaw leader, Kelly continued hurriedly, 'Gideon certainly burned the marshal's house down, but he shot one of the women Berryman brought to Denver from the riverboat. He probably shot the other woman too because she hasn't been seen since.'

Turning back into the cabin, Gottland shouted angrily, 'Did you hear that, Gideon? You didn't shoot no marshal or interfering Englishman, you killed two women and now Berryman's out there with a posse. He's sent this snivelling police chief to call on us to give ourselves up.'

Coming to the doorway, Gideon Denton was scowling. 'You sure Kelly's telling the truth, Ira? You don't think he's brought a posse up here to trick us into giving ourselves up, just to get the glory . . . that and a hefty reward?'

Breaking out in a cold sweat, Kelly protested, 'I wouldn't do nothing like that, Ira, you know I wouldn't.'

'Do I? I *thought* I did, but you've come up here with Marshal Berryman, calling on us to give ourselves up . . . and I'm suddenly not so sure any more.'

'I didn't come here because I wanted to, I swear! The marshal came to my home and pulled me out of bed, telling me I was in trouble for letting Vic Walsh go. I didn't want to come. I've got a lot to lose too if he stays alive. Look, I'll stay here with you and help fight the marshal and his men off.'

'We don't want you here,' Ira said. 'As for the marshal . . . you tell him that if he wants us he'll need to come in and try to take us — but he'll need to bring the army and an artillery piece in with him. He's never going to take us with a posse, no matter how big it is.'

'I'll tell him that, Ira and I'll try to persuade him and the posse to go back to Denver. Whatever happens, you won't find me firing at you. If he makes me shoot then I'll aim up in the air, you can count on that.'

Fearing for his life, here in the canyon, Chief Kelly turned his horse and dug his heels into the horse's flanks . . . but he did not get far.

The horse had not even got into its stride when Gideon Denton threw up his rifle and fired. Kelly fell forward onto the neck of his mount before slipping sideways, causing the horse to turn and come to a halt.

'What did you do that for?' Ira Gottland demanded of Gideon Denton, 'He was going back with a message for the marshal.'

'We'll tie him on the horse and send him back dead,' Denton said, callously, 'That'll give

Marshal Berryman and his posse all the message we need give.'

He had hardly finished speaking when one of the men crowding around Chief Kelly's horse fell to the ground and a split second later the sound of a rifle shot echoed around the canyon.

Suddenly, all thoughts of using the dead chief of police as a gruesome message were forgotten as outlaws ran to the cabin, dragging their wounded companion with them.

★　★　★

Aaron and Wes, with Old Charlie and two of the posse-men had returned to their position on the canyon edge look-out spot, over-looking the outlaws' cabin by the time the slow-riding Denver police chief arrived at what would be his final destination.

When Kelly was shot from his saddle, Aaron asked Old Charlie if he felt he could hit one of the outlaws with his large calibre rifle.

'The way they're bunched it'd be like putting a shot into a herd of buffalo,' Old Charlie declared. 'It might even down two or three of 'em.'

His subsequent shot downed only one and he fumbled the cartridge when re-loading, with the result that by the time he got off a final hasty shot the outlaws were fleeing back to the shelter.

He fired a third time, but the outlaws were already inside the cabin and it only resulted in the door being slammed shut.

Old Charlie's fire was returned from the

windows of the cabin, but the outlaws did not possess a weapon with the range of his large-bore buffalo gun and the bullets fell short.

Further shots from Old Charlie's rifle shattered a window before stout wooden shutters were swung into place inside them.

'What do we do now?' Wes asked.

'That depends,' Aaron replied, 'How many bullets do you have for that gun, Charlie?'

'Enough to last out a lengthy siege,' was the reply, 'and there's plenty more in my saddlebags.'

'Good! Start picking off their horses in the corral.'

When Wes protested that such a course of action was extreme, Aaron retorted, 'So is shooting women. We're dealing with unprincipled killers, Wes, and I don't intend to let a single one of 'em escape. Start shooting, Charlie.'

The old mountain-man had downed five of the unfortunate animals before the outlaws realized what was happening and returned a fusillade of wasted shots.

Eventually, one outlaw, braver or more foolhardy than the rest flung open the only door of the cabin and ran around to the corral with the cabin between him and the three men in position above the canyon. His intention was to open the stable door so that the horses might find sanctuary inside.

He died against the still closed stable door and Old Charlie completed his heartless cull of the hapless horses.

'What now?' Wes asked, aware that it would soon be dark.

'We wait,' was Aaron's reply, 'In the meantime you and I'll go and warn the men guarding the path at the end of the canyon to be on their guard in case anyone attempts to escape that way. They can work in two shifts, half of them sleeping while the other half stay on guard at the canyon end of the defile. They'll be hidden from view but with a nearly full moon tonight they'll see anyone coming towards them. You remain here, Charlie. You should be able to see if there's any movement around the cabin and I want you to shoot, even at shadows — and put the occasional shot through a window. I want to keep the outlaws awake all night.'

24

The outlaws were aware of the defile at the far end of the canyon and during the night Ira Gottland sent two men to check whether the posse-men also knew of its presence. Both were shot dead as they approached the defile, the sound of the shooting telling Gottland all he needed to know.

It was a cold night but a wagon had reached the posse-men with a load which included blankets. As a result, most, including Aaron and Wes were able to snatch a few hours much needed sleep.

A relief was detailed to take over from Old Charlie, but the mountain-man refused to allow anyone else to use his gun, declaring that sleep was something he could either take or leave. He proved it by wrapping a blanket around himself and keeping up an intermittent fire on the outlaws' cabin for the whole night long.

The next morning, when coffee and a meal of bacon and beans were being dished out from the wagon, Denver's mayor, speaking on behalf of the other posse members asked Aaron whether he intended keeping the posse in situ around the canyon in an attempt to starve the outlaws into surrender, or whether they were likely to attempt an assault on the cabin at sometime. He pointed out that many of the posse-men had businesses in Denver that could not be neglected for too long, adding, 'We are not trying to wriggle out of our civil obligations, Marshal, but we have no way of knowing how much food and water the outlaws have inside the cabin. They could hold out for days . . . perhaps for weeks.'

'That's true,' Aaron conceded, 'but right now I can think of no alternative. An attack on the cabin would be costly in lives — our lives — so that can be ruled out. I think we're just going to have to keep them bottled in and hope they don't have ample supplies.'

Wes had been listening to the conversation and now he said, 'I have an idea on what we could do, Aaron. It came to me in the night and I wondered why we hadn't thought of it before. If it works it would be paying the gang back in kind for what they did in Denver.'

'Go ahead,' Aaron said, 'Let's hear it.'

'Well, the stables are attached to the back of the cabin and, with winter coming on, they'll no doubt be stacked with hay . . . right?'

'You mean, if it was fired it would set light to the cabin too? But your idea needs someone to get there and set fire to it.'

'I'll do it,' Wes said.

For a moment it seemed Aaron would raise some objection. Instead, he said, 'When would you do this, tonight?'

'Why not today . . . right away? We don't need to wait until nightfall because the windows are all at the front of the cabin. Anyone approaching from the rear couldn't be seen. I could enter the canyon from the defile with, say . . . a dozen men? They could take up positions close to the cabin with a clear view to either side of it while I went on and set fire to the hay, running back to join them once the hay was well alight. Meanwhile, when you and the rest of the men at the mouth of the cabin see the smoke begin to rise you could come into the canyon, remaining out of rifle range until the fire drove the outlaws out. They'd be caught in the middle with no place to go. While all this was going on Old Charlie would be where he is now and use his buffalo gun to help out in whatever way he thought best.'

'It *could* work,' Aaron mused, thoughtfully, 'It would certainly bring things to a head — and quickly.'

'Then let's give it a try right away,' Wes said. 'I'll go to the far end of the canyon with a few men, picking up the rest there. On the way I'll stop and tell Old Charlie what's happening.'

'Right, Wes, we're on . . . but don't take any unnecessary risks. I know how much you want Gideon — but so do I and it will be a sour victory if anything were to happen to you. Tell Old Charlie his support is going to be critical. He's to fire at anyone who appears in the cabin doorway. When there's no stopping the outlaws, he's to shoot at those most likely to pose a threat to the posse-men.'

★ ★ ★

Old Charlie took his instructions without showing any emotion, saying simply. 'Get on and do what needs doing, boy, I'll be up here looking out for you.'

The posse-men at the defile were, on the whole, far more excited than Old Charlie about the forthcoming action. Their enthusiasm contradicted the generally accepted feeling in Denver that the town's men would never form part of a posse and hunt down those who lived outside the law.

When Old Charlie saw Wes and the posse-men moving along the canyon from the defile, he began firing at the door and windows of the outlaws' cabin in a bid to keep the occupants occupied while Wes's plan was being carried out.

His ploy worked only until the Denver posse-men began to fan out to cover the sides of the cabin. There was a rifle shot from inside the log-built building and a bullet passed close to the advancing men.

Wes immediately ordered them to drop to the ground using whatever cover they could find in the treeless but rolling floor of the wide canyon.

Speaking to the nearest posse-man, Wes said, 'That shot must have come from the cabin ... but there are no windows at the sides! How do they know we are here?'

'They've picked away the mud between the logs,' came the reply, 'Fortunately, the cabin appears to have been well-built, which means there won't be a great deal of space between the timbers. All that the men inside will be able to do is spot us through a peep-hole, then poke a rifle barrel through and fire without being able to aim properly.'

'It doesn't make the bullets any less lethal if they hit anyone,' Wes commented, 'Tell the others to pull back to where they can see the cabin sides, but can't be shot at from anyone in there. I'm going forward to the stable now.'

Wes reached the stable at a run but, once inside, he discovered to his dismay that the back wall of the stable was also the back wall of the cabin! Anticipating that the posse might try to creep up on them from this direction, the occupants had already picked away spy-holes in the mud between the logs — and the outlaws were able to use their revolvers here.

However, Wes had made his way to the stable for a purpose — and he was determined to carry it out.

The hay was stored in a small room at one end of the stables and, although a number of shots were fired at him through the wall of the cabin, Wes reached it safely. Fortunately, the holes between the logs had been made at a height convenient for the men inside to spy through and Wes realized that by wriggling on his stomach along the base of the log wall he would be below their line of fire and able to place hay against the bottom of the cabin wall in comparative safety, but he could hear the men inside the cabin scraping away at the mud between the lower layers of logs and knew it was going to be a race against time.

Eventually, he was satisfied he had placed sufficient hay against the wall of the cabin to start an effective blaze, especially when soaked with oil from a couple of lamps he found in the stable.

Unfortunately, the oil had a pungent smell that reached the nostrils of the outlaws. When they realized what was happening gunfire from inside the cabin increased alarmingly.

Hastily striking a match, Wes threw it on to the hay. It ignited immediately and when the flame reached the paraffin it ignited with a roar that left the outlaws in no doubt about what was happening.

Wes rose to his feet to run outside, but before he reached the door disaster struck!

One of the outlaw's bullets hit him behind and above his knee, bringing him to the ground and he heard a jubilant voice shout, 'It's the Englishman, Gideon. I've brought him down!'

The cry was answered by another voice, saying, 'Don't shoot again . . . he's mine. When the next shot from that buffalo gun hits the cabin, throw open the door and get out of the way. I'll reach the stable and finish him off if it's the last thing I do.'

Billowing smoke from burning hay was filling the stable now and, unable to walk, Wes could only drag himself to a corner. Here he drew his revolver and waited. He was in pain but could think clearly enough. He realized that when Gideon Denton sprinted from the cabin to the stable he would be fired at by members of the posse. Wes would hear the firing and realize what was happening.

His hope was that if the outlaw made it to the smoke-filled stable, when he entered from the bright sunshine outside it would take a moment or two for his eyes to adjust to the gloomy interior.

It happened exactly as Wes had believed it would. He was warned of Denton's imminent arrival by the crack of a half-dozen rifles, the last of the bullets hitting the stable wall.

A moment later the door was thrown open and the outlaw, gun in hand, leapt inside, looking around him for his quarry.

Wes had his revolver trained upon Denton, but the outlaw was standing sideways on to him and Wes wanted to be certain of his target when he fired.

'Looking for me, Denton?' he called.

His words had the exact effect Wes wanted. Denton swung around and Wes fired . . . then fired again.

Two red patches blossomed on Denton's shirt a hand's breadth above his belt buckle and he jack-knifed to the floor.

By the time Wes dragged himself across the stable floor to the outlaw, Denton had succeeded in turning onto his back. He was mortally wounded, but still attempted to raise his revolver and point it at Wes, his expression one of desperate malevolence.

Reaching out, Wes used his own weapon to knock Denton's gun from his hand. Looking down at the dying man, Wes said, 'How does it feel to be shot and left to die in a fire, woman killer?'

'You killed two Denton brothers,' Gideon gasped.

'Wrong!' Said Wes, 'By the time this day is over I'll have killed three.'

The flames had reached the stable roof now and small pieces of flaming bark were sashaying gently to the ground around the two wounded men.

'Then do it properly and put a final bullet in me,' gasped the dying man.

Looking contemptuously at the stricken man, Wes said, 'You aren't worth the expense of a bullet, Denton and you might as well burn here as in hell.'

Picking up the outlaw's gun, Wes threw it to the far end of the stable before crawling to the open door. Once out in the clean mountain air he continued his crawl to a wooden water trough at the end of the corral. Here, with the trough between him and the blazing cabin, he ripped open his trouser leg, bound his neckerchief around the wound and waited for the posse-men to come to his aid.

25

❧

The siege of the Rocky Mountain cabin by the Denver posse came to a bloody and one-sided conclusion when the cabin had been half-consumed by flames. The door was suddenly flung open and outlaws spilled out through the doorway.

Emerging from the smoke they fired at anyone their reddened, smoke-sore eyes could see — or thought they could see.

Of the outlaws of the Denton gang, two had been killed at the defile during the night and thirteen died at the cabin. Only eight were taken prisoner and of these five were wounded, three of them seriously. Ira Gottland was one of this number, but it was believed he would make a full recovery.

It was a great triumph for the posse, for Marshal Aaron Berryman — and for his deputy.

Left homeless by the fire at the house behind the Thespian Club, Aaron, Wes and Pat were accommodated in the self-contained wing of the Denver mansion owned by a very rich Denver councillor who had been a member of the posse. The accommodation came complete with servants and a doctor called daily to tend Wes's wounded leg.

During his convalescence here, Wes received a

number of messages from well-wishers in the town and letters from Governor Schuster of Kentucky — and his daughter Emma. It seemed the battle with the Dentons in the Rocky Mountain foothills and its successful outcome had made headlines in newspapers throughout the United States and the two lawmen become national heroes.

Aaron also received a congratulatory letter from President Ulysses Grant, in which he asked that his congratulations be passed on to 'Deputy US Marshal Wesley Curnow' and the upstanding citizens of Denver who had formed the posse to assist the two lawmen. He added that he hoped very soon to welcome Colorado into the United States of America as its thirty-eighth State.

The letter was printed in bold headlines on the front page of Colorado's newspapers and sparked off a wave of noisy celebration in the saloons of Denver.

Despite the acclaim received by Aaron and Wes, they did not feel like celebrating. The body of Lola had been recovered from the burned-out house and a bullet hole in her forehead told its own tale of the manner of her ending.

The funeral of the two women attracted mourners from all sections of the town and Wes was helped to the church and cemetery by Aaron for the sad occasion.

Both men felt very deep sorrow about the loss of the two women, but, following Aaron's example, Wes succeeded in keeping his feelings contained, and neither men spoke of their joint loss to anyone but, as the excitement of the action receded into memory and the acclamation of the citizens of Denver subsided, Wes thought more and more of all he had lost and of what might have been.

He missed Anabelita, of course, but he also found himself thinking of the baby who had never known life outside its mother's womb.

In the days preceding Anabelita's tragic death he had begun imagining what it would be like to have a son to whom he could teach the lessons needed to grow up into a man of whom his parents would be proud. To share with Wes the everyday things he himself had once known.

Or perhaps the child would have been a girl, someone to take his hand in absolute trust when the world seemed too large and beyond her understanding. A daughter for him to watch over as she learned lessons of life from her mother.

Wes had tried to tell something of his thoughts to Aaron, but the US Marshal had his own grief to cope with and, besides, he had witnessed too many deaths of those close to him.

Aaron's reply had been to say, 'America has not surrendered easily to civilised settlement, Wes, it has needed to be won and the price paid by men, women, children and even unborn babies has been high. By the time this country is secure the numbers of those sacrificed will be as uncountable as blades of grass in a Kentucky paddock.'

His words had made a great impression upon Wes until one rainy day when it was not possible for him to go out of the mansion, he had limped his way to the Denver Councillor's library and there found a book of Walt Whitman's poems on a shelf.

Remembering his time in Lauraville and the poetry that Tessa had been reading there, Wes took the book down. Leafing through it, he came upon a line in one of the poems that made him think of what Aaron had said to him, and of his own thoughts about the loss of Anabelita's unborn baby.

In words that Wes could never have emulated, the poet implied that in the scheme of things a blade of grass is no less important in its way than the stars in the heavens.

Somehow, for reasons that Wes did not even attempt to understand, the words gave him comfort and a feeling that, in spite of Aaron's implied explanation that such sacrifices were acceptable in a new country like America, he was right to grieve for the loss of his and Anabelita's unborn child.

While Wes was still confined to the house with his wounded leg he received a delegation from the mayor and councillors. They offered him the vacant post of Chief of Police, to succeed the late and little lamented Chief Kelly.

Astounded, he at first declined their offer outright, but when they persisted he agreed he would think about it, more with the intention of getting rid of the unwanted delegation than of giving their offer serious consideration.

He wished Aaron had been able to advise him how best to turn down the offer without offending the Denver dignitaries, but Aaron was in Kansas, giving evidence against Vic Walsh.

Ira Gottland had recovered sufficiently to be questioned by Aaron and, aware that he faced being hanged for past activities, he had been eager to broker a deal with the United States Marshal.

Aaron refused to offer Gottland any sort of deal. The most he would promise the outlaw was that when he came to trial, the judge would be informed that Gottland had 'co-operated' with the Federal authorities — but only if the outlaw leader disclosed all he knew of Vic Walsh's criminal activities and associations.

Aaron knew that such co-operation was unlikely to save the outlaw from the hangman's rope but, desperate to save his skin, Gottland agreed.

Armed with Gottland's statement, Aaron had gone to Trego, where Walsh was being held by Sheriff Murray and taken the dishonest Cornishman to Kansas City where he handed him over to the US Marshal stationed there.

Walsh would be taken on to Washington to await a decision on where, and under which name he was to be tried.

Returning to Denver, Aaron found Wes in the garden of the councillor's house using a stick to support himself as he exercised along the well-kept paths of the impressive Denver mansion.

Exaggerating his own war wound limp, Aaron greeted him with, 'You know, Wes, you get more like me every time I meet you, but it's good to see you up and about again.'

'I'm not sure that any similarity between us is

a good thing, Aaron — certainly not for me. Folk are beginning to see me as a possible substitute for you. To be honest, I'm flattered, but I couldn't fill your shoes and have no intention of trying.'

When Wes disclosed the offer made to him by the Denver mayor, Aaron said, 'Don't underestimate yourself, Wes, you've done a great deal more than many of the State Marshals I know . . . but you could do a whole lot better than being Chief of Police of Denver, so I hope you turned it down?'

'I told them I'd think about it,' Wes explained, 'but I was just being polite. I don't want the job.'

'What do you want, Wes? Have you finally decided that mining isn't for you?'

'Yes. To be perfectly honest with you, Aaron — and I hate to say this — you've given me a taste for upholding the law. I believe it's really worthwhile work, especially here in America, where the foundation is being laid for a new and potentially great country. At the end of his working life as a United States Marshal, a man could look back on what he's achieved and say, 'I've done something that's made a difference to people's lives, both now and in the future'.'

Giving Aaron a wry smile, he added, 'Trouble is, I'm not at all sure I'm happy with the thought of being a target for every man who carries both a gun and a grudge against the law.'

Looking decidedly smug, Aaron said, 'I find what you've said very interesting, Wes . . . very interesting indeed. If I understand you correctly, you're saying you'd like to take a major part in

427

seeing that the laws of the land are upheld, without putting yourself up as a target for every two-bit Western gunslinger out to make a name for himself.'

'That's about the strength of it, Aaron, but such work doesn't exist.'

'I'm not so sure about that, Wes, all parts of America aren't like the Territories — and you've already done more than most to clean up this part of the country. I'd like you to speak to someone you've met before. He heard I was in Kansas City and came along to see me. I think you might find what he has to say of some interest. He's in the house talking to the councillor right now. I'll go and fetch him.'

While he was waiting for Aaron's return, Wes sat on a garden seat thinking about the conversation he and Aaron had just had. Until now he had never seriously thought about what he really wanted to do with his life, but he *did* believe that ridding the world of the Denton gang and others like them was really worthwhile — and he greatly admired Aaron for what he was doing.

While he was thinking he was looking down into a garden pool in which a number of fish were swimming. Hearing a sound, he looked up and was surprised to see David Connolly, the young man he had last seen at the house of Senator — now Governor Schuster, of Kentucky.

'No, don't get up,' the young visitor said, as Wes struggled to rise to his feet, 'How is the leg?'

'It's coming along fine,' Wes replied, 'The doctor says that when it's fully healed the limp should hardly be noticeable.'

'That's good,' said David Connolly, 'You did a wonderful job up there in the Rockies . . . you and Aaron.'

'It was highly satisfying,' Wes conceded, 'but you haven't come here to talk about that. Aaron said you had something to say that might interest me.'

'I sincerely hope it will,' David Connolly said, 'but it is partly to do with what happened in the Rockies. Do you know that I'm married to Sophie Schuster now?'

'I didn't, but it comes as no surprise, you two make an ideal couple. Congratulations.'

'Thank you, Wes. I am living at the Schuster mansion helping to manage the Governor's estate — you've been told he's Governor of Kentucky now?'

'Yes, Aaron told me. He's well pleased about it.'

'So is everyone in Kentucky, my father-in-law is a popular man who has the welfare of Kentucky very much at heart. He is trying to gather men around him he believes will be able to help him do his best for the State — and that's why I am here, Wes.'

Puzzled, Wes could not think what he could possibly do for Kentucky, but David Connolly was still talking, 'Governor Schuster met with Marshal Berryman in Kansas some little while ago and sounded him out about becoming the US Marshal in Kentucky. Marshal Berryman declined because he's been sent out here to the Territories at the special request of President

Grant, but he and my father-in-law had a long talk about what the position entailed and Marshal Berryman left him mulling over a suggestion he made. When news of the annihilation of the Denton gang broke and he learned of the part you played in it, he made up his mind. Governor Schuster has sent me here to ask you to come to Kentucky as United States Marshal for the State.'

For a few moments Wes was absolutely speechless. When he eventually had his voice back, he said, 'I know next to nothing about the law. I couldn't take on something like that!'

'The last marshal knew nothing at *all* about the law. Not only that, he was so politically biased that *his* law protected less than half the residents of Kentucky. Governor Schuster knows you have no political affiliations and you've proved your courage and respect for the law. Besides, Marshal Berryman has promised to teach you all you need to know — and says it will be far more than he knew when he was appointed a United States Marshal. You have created a very favourable impression in Kentucky for the manner in which you and the Marshal dealt with the Denton gang, Wes, and Governor Schuster has already broached the subject of your appointment with the President. I might add that a number of Kentucky's leading families were present at Harrison's funeral and they are proud to boast of their meeting with you. It would be a very popular appointment, Wes.'

Still recovering from the astounding offer, Wes

said, 'I think I ought to tell you that the main reason I was so determined to bring the Denton gang to justice was because they killed someone I was very, very fond of . . . '

'You mean the croupier from the *Missouri Belle*?'

When Wes nodded, David Connolly said, 'I remember her too — as you well know. She was a fine girl, Wes, the way she died would have roused me to doing something about it — but smashing the Denton gang is not the only feat you've performed on behalf of law and order since coming to America. Let me go back to Kentucky and tell Governor Schuster you accept his offer, Wes. You will never regret it — and I don't think he will, either. He is a good and honest man who will return all the support I know you would give him.'

Wes and David Connolly were still talking together when Aaron returned some time later. Greeting Wes, he said, 'Well, have you thought over what David has had to say to you Wes?'

'I'm still thinking good and hard, Aaron — but you'll remember I was never keen on taking a deputy marshal's badge.'

Aaron's expression showed disbelief, 'You're turning down Governor Schuster's offer?'

Aware of Aaron's very real dismay, Wes said, 'Well I must admit a full marshal's badge is more tempting than that of a deputy — and this leg of mine is never going to be well enough to let me climb up and down a mine shaft ladder . . . so I reckon I might give it a try . . . '

During the celebrations that followed his

431

announcement Wes let it be known that he had no intention of forgetting his mining roots, nor the memory of the uncle who had brought him to America from England. He would ensure that the man who had taught him his skill with a handgun would be remembered too. The United States Marshal's badge that he would wear was to be specially made for him from silver ore he himself took from the Rocky Mountain mining claim that had once belonged to Peter Rowse, and was now owned by Old Charlie.

It was an item he would wear close to his heart in the years that lay ahead.

Books by E. V. Thompson
Published by The House of Ulverscroft:

THE DREAM TRADERS
CRY ONCE ALONE
BECKY
GOD'S HIGHLANDER
THE MUSIC MAKERS
CASSIE
WYCHWOOD
BLUE DRESS GIRL
THE TOLPUDDLE WOMAN
LEWIN'S MEAD
MOONTIDE
CAST NO SHADOWS
MUD HUTS AND MISSIONARIES
SOMEWHERE A BIRD IS SINGING
SEEK A NEW DAWN
WINDS OF FORTUNE
THE LOST YEARS
HERE, THERE AND YESTERDAY
PATHS OF DESTINY
TOMORROW IS FOR EVER
THE VAGRANT KING
THOUGH THE HEAVENS MAY FALL

THE RETALLICK SAGA:
BEN RETALLICK
CHASE THE WIND
HARVEST OF THE SUN
SINGING SPEARS
THE STRICKEN LAND

Other titles published by
The House of Ulverscroft:

THOUGH THE HEAVENS MAY FALL

E. V. Thompson

It is 1856. Cornish schoolteacher Talwyn is grief-stricken when her father's body is discovered on the rocks at the foot of cliffs near their home. But his death was no accident. He was murdered. And Talwyn's father is not the only murder victim — there have been two other unsolved killings in recent months. Local magistrate Sir Joseph Sawle is convinced that the killings are connected. When Sir Joseph asks for assistance from London's Scotland Yard, Cornish-born detective Amos Hawke is sent to investigate. Amos's relationship with Tawlyn gets off to a disastrous start but as he works hard to break through the veil of fear and silence in order to bring her father's killer to justice, Talwyn's help becomes indispensable.

BROTHERS IN WAR

E. V. Thompson

1915: Ben Retallick, owner of Ruddlemoor, the largest clay workings in Cornwall, is asked by a War Office friend to provide two traction engines for a secret expedition. The plan is to take two gunboats overland from Cape Town to Lake Tanganyika — a journey of almost 3,000 miles — to wrest control of the lake from the Germans. Ben sends the engines with Sam Hooper, a young engineer. When Sam meets Maria, a Portuguese East African nurse, he sides with her in a confrontation against a group of racist white South Africans. Meanwhile, accused of being pro-German, Ben is arrested on circumstantial evidence provided by a business rival. However, Ben's release is secured by the influence of the beautiful Dr. Antonia St Anna . . .

THE VAGRANT KING

E. V. Thompson

In Cornwall, farmer Joseph Moyle's stepson Ralf becomes page to the future Charles II. Britain is at war between the Royalists and the Parliamentarians. Ralf follows the heir to the throne through the western counties as he learns of court intrigue. When Charles begins the first of many affairs, Ralf also falls in love. But Brighid, an Irish Catholic, is also complicit in an attempt to kidnap Charles — a fact that Ralf discovers when he foils the plot . . . In 1645, when the conclusive Battle of Naseby marks ultimate defeat for the Royalists, Ralf follows Charles into exile. Desperate to return to Cornwall after years of loyal service to Charles, Ralf's dreams of the homecoming to his beloved Trecarne are shattered . . .

TOMORROW IS FOR EVER

E. V. Thompson

For Alan Carter the greatest personal sacrifice of the Great War of 1914-18 is being called up after only one week of marriage. Leaving his new bride is even more painful than the wound that, months later, sends him to Cornwall to convalesce. For, there, he has time to think about Dora and about the career as a writer that he secretly nurtures. A career that seems possible when he finds himself accepted by the established colony of Newlyn artists. There is one artist in particular — Vicky Hazelton — who encourages Alan's leanings towards the arts. And she stirs other feelings: inappropriate and impossible ones. For Vicky and her set inhabit a different world from Alan's. He belongs to London's East End _ and to Dora.

PATHS OF DESTINY

E. V. Thompson

Cornwall, 1854: Alice Rowe was rescued from the workhouse by the Reverend Arnold Markham, the parson of the tiny village church in Treleggan. He employed her in his parsonage as a housemaid, so when he dies of a sudden heart attack, Alice faces a fearful and uncertain future. But as one chapter in her life ends, another begins. For as she discovers the Reverend's body in the woods, she meets Gideon Davey, a 'ganger' who is laying a nearby stretch of railway line. Gideon helps her to recover the body and returns to Treleggan for the funeral — and also to see Alice again. Then, just as their friendship hints at something more serious, Gideon is given an offer he can't refuse: to travel to the Crimea, to build a railway to help the British troops . . .